FAMILY AFFAIR

FAMILY AFFAIR

Bill Dring

Acknowledgements

Special thanks to the following people, in no particular order, whose friendship, help, support and encouragement played a big part in the writing of this novel:

Jan Deberitz
Vikki Browne
Steve Fisher
Robert Ross
Bron Musgrove
Chris Whitehead
Marianne Rabanal
Mick Quinn
Ruth Craven
Murphy

[Author Photo: David Constantine]

For my family, may they rest in peace.

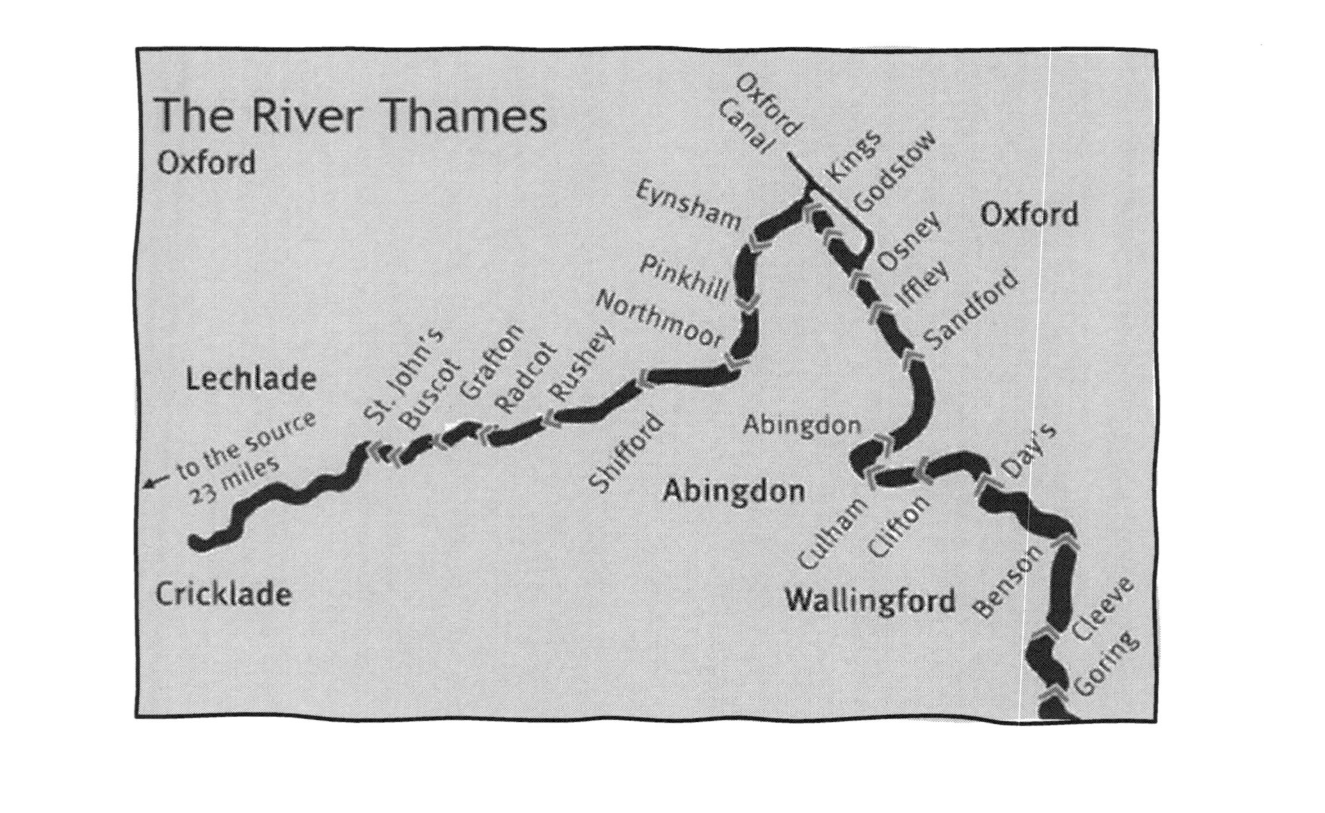
The River Thames
Oxford
Oxford Canal
Kings
Godstow
Eynsham
Oxford
Osney
Pinkhill
Iffley
Northmoor
Sandford
Lechlade
St. John's
Buscot
Grafton
Radcot
Rushey
Abingdon
to the source 23 miles
Shifford
Abingdon
Day's
Culham
Clifton
Cricklade
Wallingford
Benson
Cleeve
Goring

Chapters

PREFACE

A few words you will need to understand:

FAMILY
A group consisting of two parents and their children living together as a unit; a group of people related by blood or marriage.

KILLER
A person, animal, or thing that kills.

MURDER
Unlawful, premeditated killing of one human being by another.

SERIAL KILLER
A person who repeatedly murders and, when doing so, typically follows a characteristic, predictable behaviour pattern.

SPREE KILLING
Two or more murders committed by a person without a cooling-off period.

THRILL KILLING
Premeditated murder is committed by a person who is not necessarily suffering from mental instability, does not derive sexual satisfaction from killing victims, nor has any personal

vendetta against them; often they do not even know their victims; they are instead motivated by the sheer excitement of the act.

ANNIHILATION
The act or process of annihilating.

And one more:

<u>FAMILY ANNIHILATION</u>
The killing of wives, girlfriends, children and their family members, following which the killer usually kills themselves, but not always.

The area around Day's Lock is known as one of the most historic riverside locations in Oxfordshire. The World Poohsticks Championships are held each year on the Little Wittenham and Dorchester footbridges next to Day's Lock. The game is described in A. A. Milne's book, "The House at Pooh Corner", written in 1928.

Chapter 1

DAY'S LOCK

The pale yellow of an early morning sun had started slowly burning off a fine mist that hung over the silent river. Only the boat seemed to be moving, causing a gentle wash on the riverbank as it approached Day's Lock. The old Lister diesel engine was the only sound. A sharp chill was in the air, but Tom Hunter could tell it was going to be a fine, warm day, perfect for boating. It was good to get an early start; it was too early for the lockkeepers to be manning the locks. He dropped the engine into neutral and skilfully let the boat glide into the mooring area before the lock, gently bumping the nose against the wooden wall on the bank, helping to pull the stern in, then gave a short burst of reverse to bring her to a halt. He grabbed hold of the centre rope and jumped onto the mooring jetty. The rope was cold and wet with the morning dew; it stung his hands as he pulled the boat tightly in and tied her up.

Tom had performed this procedure several times, almost every day over the six years he had been living on the boat: open the sluices; empty the lock; open the gates; secure the boat in the lock; close the gates; close the sluices; open the other sluices to empty or fill the lock, depending on which direction he was heading; open the gates; leave the lock; moor up again; then return to close the gates and the sluices before continuing along the river. This time it was no different except that the lock was empty, so there was no need to drain it; just open the gates and cruise slowly in. The lock was deserted; peace and quietness were the only company Tom had. He assumed the lockkeeper and his wife were still sleeping; the curtains in the windows of their cottage, which sat just feet from where the river passed through the lock, were drawn closed, and Tom could see no movements coming from inside. This was of little surprise to him: lockkeepers did not start work until 7:30 am at that time of year, and it was still only 6:00 am, still early. Controlling his boat as the cold Thames powerfully forced its way through the open sluices, erupting upon the surface of the water as it filled the lock, Tom breathed deeply, smelling the freshness of the morning, and absorbing the tranquil surroundings. The surging water subsided, and eddies swirled, making ringed patterns that became smaller and stiller as their strength slowly faded. All the time, Tom paid careful attention to the boat; with no other crew to help, he had learned from experience that he had to take special care not to let her get pulled out across the lock by the current and not to let the ropes pinch, especially when they were wet. He secured her again and walked up to open the gates. It seemed not to matter how many times he had gone through this routine, passing through countless locks; it still felt good to be travelling, to be on the move; the journey. It always felt good. As he left the lock, something made him glance back, and he caught a brief glimpse of someone, possibly a man, sitting on the lock bench next to the flower beds opposite the lockkeeper's cottage. The figure seemed to be reading a book. Tom's sighting was only momentary, just a glance; he had to concentrate on getting out of the lock and mooring up again. It passed through his mind to say good morning when he went back to close the gates, but that was not to be. It took only a few moments to pull in and tie up, but when he got back to the lock gates, the bench was empty. There was no one to be seen, only a small dog, probably belonging to the lockkeeper (although he couldn't remember seeing it before that morning), scratching the flower bed beside the bench.

This was Easter weekend, which was why Tom had set off so early. He was heading upriver to the boatyard at Abingdon and wanted to avoid all the hire boats that were likely to be struggling through the locks later in the day. He hadn't passed another moving boat since leaving Goring and had made good progress, leaving him with only two more locks to go. The sun was doing its best at burning off the mist and taking the chill out of the air. The almost untouched banks of the river, with their trees, bushes, and grasses, looked at one with the Thames' flowing water. There wasn't much point in getting to the boatyard before it opened; he could afford to take a break, pull over for a while, and have some breakfast: bacon, eggs, tomatoes, beans, mushrooms, and toast, all purchased in Goring the day before in preparation for the journey. Tom knew that there are about a thousand calories in a full English breakfast, but since this wasn't something he ate every day and knowing he would be up early and on the move, he had decided to treat himself to the unhealthy fry-up. *'Plenty of day left to burn off those cals'*, he thought to himself.

The term "Golden Hour" refers to the principle that effective early action can result in securing significant material that would otherwise be lost.

[The "Golden Hour" principle]

Chapter 2

DAY'S LOCK ONE AND A HALF HOURS LATER

Ali Smith had seen plenty of grim sights during her time on the murder squad, but *'this one, albeit a cliché,'* she thought to herself, was definitely *'the worst.'* The call had come in from a postman who had made an early start with his deliveries, hoping to get away as soon as possible for the Easter break. He had knocked on the door of the lockkeeper's cottage at about 7:30 am to deliver a bulky parcel – something purchased from Amazon, he thought, judging by the packaging. When he didn't get a reply, he became a little suspicious; the lockkeeper and his wife were usually up and starting work at that time. He walked over to the front window, which looked into the living room, and peered through a small gap in the drawn curtains. Somehow, as shaky as he was after realising what he had seen, he managed to make the 999 call. He was now at the John Radcliffe Hospital, being treated for severe shock. A plain-clothed officer was waiting to interview him as soon as the doctors gave permission.

Outside the cottage, uniformed police were marking out and sealing off the area with police tape. Like many of the locks on that stretch of the river, Day's was quite isolated; the cottage stood alone with no neighbouring houses. The lock itself was close to the front of the cottage, and behind it lay a garden with flower beds and vegetable patches. Along the back of the garden ran the weir, which was used to control the flow of the river and make navigation safer. In many ways, it was similar to all the other locks and lockkeepers' cottages along the river, most having been built around the same time.

The Crime Scene Investigation team was busy getting their equipment together, climbing into their white incident suits and white overshoes, and pulling on surgical gloves; the CSI didn't want any complaints about their DNA evidence being contaminated when it arrived back at the lab. Two squad cars and two unmarked cars were parked just inside the taped-off area, and two more (thought to belong to the occupants) were parked nearer the cottage. Ali had been at the station at 6:30 am that morning with the hope that nothing eventful would happen and that she too could get away early enough to enjoy some of the remaining Easter break. It no longer looked like that would happen.

'There's another one up here,' Spencer, Ali's second-in-command, shouted down from one of the bedrooms. Ali, the Senior Investigating Officer – at least until someone more senior turned up and took over – was still staring at the late-middle-aged man and woman sitting as if watching television on a blood-soaked sofa; both their throats were deeply slashed. Ali and Spencer had been the first two in the house, having issued instructions before entering for the uniformed officers to protect the crime scene. Ali didn't reply to Spencer; she was taking everything in, visually examining the scene in a way that her experience and training had made automatic; scanning all the details, what was there, and where it was. She had already detached herself from the horror in front of her. You had to; she knew that.

The couple looked as if they had been propped up after being killed and judging by the amount of blood on the sofa, it had been very soon after death. Their arms had been positioned to look as if they were tenderly holding hands. Off to the right of the sofa, an open door led into the kitchen; there was a thick trail of blood smeared across the floor tiles, then over the carpet to the sofa. *'The kitchen is where it happened,'* Ali thought, *'then the bodies were dragged through one at a time and arranged on the sofa in the living room, like a window dressing with shop dummies.'* From where she was standing, she could see a kitchen table under a window that looked out to the back of the cottage. At least two mugs and a few broken breakfast bowls were lying on the floor tiles near the table legs, and another four mugs and bowls were still laid out on top.

'I think there may be more,' Ali eventually shouted back. 'I'm coming up.'

At the top of the stairs, she was met with the sight of Spencer, his back steadying him against the corridor wall; he was looking as white as his incident suit and noticeably shaken.

'What have we got, Spence?' she asked. She could tell that it was not good. Spencer, like Ali, had experienced many distressing sights on the job, but this one was his worst too.

'There's a white male body on the floor in that room,' he pointed across the corridor, 'and…' He paused, not for effect but because he was still trying to compose himself, trying hard to be professional, 'and in this one behind me, in the bed, the bodies of two small children, a boy and a girl.'

'What about that one?' Ali asked, nodding towards the only other door.

'I didn't get that far,' he said taking a deep breath. 'I only got as far as this.'

Ali could see the feet of the body on the floor of the bedroom behind her and glimpsed at the children in the bed as she stepped past Spencer to check the last room. She pushed the door open. There was a neatly made double bed, a bedside table, a small window with checked curtains drawn open, letting in the sunlight, and a bathrobe draped over the foot of the bed. To the left of the room lay another door, closed. Spencer had pulled himself together and was now standing next to her.

'I'll check inside that one, ma'am,' he said, moving over to the door. It was an en suite shower room, surprising in such an old and small cottage; it was probably a large storage cupboard at one time that had been converted. He could hear the shower running even before he carefully opened the frosted glass door. She was slumped in the base, naked, and bent forward with her head hanging low and her wet hair covering her face. Unlike all the other bodies, there was no sign of blood and no noticeable marks on her. Spencer turned off the taps that were now running cold, then instinctively checked for a pulse in her neck, being careful not to disturb anything in the process. He already knew he would find no sign of life.

'That makes six, ma'am,' he said, looking back at Ali.

'OK, Spence, go and get some air and make sure everything is under control out there. I'm going to look at the children and the other body, and then I'll join you. The camera boys and forensics can come in and do their bit then and see if that pathologist has arrived while you're out there.'

Spencer didn't need to be told twice; he badly wanted some fresh air, even if it was tainted with cigarette smoke. He had one out of the packet as soon as he stepped out of the cottage. First, he quickly checked on the progress of the rest of the team and then went over to his car to smoke a Marlboro Full Strength, away from anywhere it could contaminate. The forensic team and their van would be along any minute, and the pathologist was on the way. One of the uniforms was holding onto a small black and white dog that was yapping constantly. Everything else looked under control, and officers were searching the grounds.

Ali stared at the woman in the base of the shower. *'No blood,'* she thought, *'this one is different.'* She looked back towards the bed, and from where she was standing, she could see a large holdall and a small suitcase, both closed. *'Maybe guests, down for Easter?'* she was analysing all the information her eyes could take in. *'Probably the children's mother.'* Ali had already figured that the couple on the sofa were too old to have young children and were more likely to be the grandparents. The room looked neat and tidy – no sign of a struggle, in fact, no sign of anything untoward other than the body of the woman in the shower.

She left the bedroom and walked back down the corridor, glancing again into the room with the children. She would leave that until last. She was not looking forward to seeing them, but then again, there had not been many occasions when she had been looking forward to seeing a dead body of any age, gender, shape, or size. The man lay face down in a pool of blood, his legs and arms positioned in an uncomfortable way that only seems to occur with dead bodies. There was a lot of blood, but it was confined to the area of the body. Again, the room looked undisturbed – a neatly made double bed with small bedside cabinets on either side. On one cabinet lay a man's wallet and watch beside an alarm clock and a bedside lamp; on the other rested an opened crossword book and another lamp. In Ali's mind, this was the master bedroom, the one where the lockkeeper and his wife slept – the two downstairs on the sofa. Her eyes' attention returned to focus on the body: white, male, early thirties, clothed. His right arm was twisted around, with the hand under the trunk of his body. What Ali didn't see at first, as it was mostly covered by the body and the bit still protruding was covered, camouflaged, with dark blood, was the handle of a knife, a kitchen knife. She registered everything, and already her mind was running through possible scenarios. Ali was wise enough not to jump to any conclusion, to be open and explore all possibilities, but it looked likely to her that the same knife was the murder weapon used on the couple downstairs – and the children.

The children were lying side by side in the bed with the covers carefully tucked around them, their heads laid upon clean white pillows. Ali was taking it all in, the tucking in neatly: *'Why would anyone go to that trouble after killing? Whoever it was must have felt comfortable, not rushed for time.'* Blood had soaked through the white duvet, and both the children had their eyes open, looking up towards the ceiling. If only it were true that the image of the last thing looked at is stored on the back of the eye, it would make Ali's work easy. She stared at the children's young, innocent faces; their dead eyes stared back, still bright.

In the living room, Ali stopped at the bottom of the stairs to look at the two bodies on the sofa. The same questions: *'Why would the killer drag the bodies in from the kitchen – if that's where they were killed – and sit them propped up next to each other? Placing their hands together, why?'* She looked at the two clasped hands again. At first she hadn't noticed it – again, there was too much blood hiding things, covering them in sticky red – but now she could see something else – or, to be more exact, there was something else she couldn't see that should have been there. Something was missing.

The construction of Clifton Lock (also known as Clifton Hampden Lock) was first talked about back in 1793. Discussions continued in 1811, but it wasn't until 1822 that this lock was finally constructed.

Chapter 3

NEAR CLIFTON LOCK

Tom opened the side hatch in the kitchen area of his boat and let the smells of his "full-English" drift over the towpath. He had fitted this boat out from scratch. From the floor to the insulation on the walls and ceiling, every screw, every wire, and every water pipe had been put there by him. He knew her intimately. He vividly remembered the first time he lit the wood stove. That first night, he had slept on board, surrounded by saws, screwdrivers, hammers, bits of wood, lengths of pipe, and sheets of newspaper taped over the porthole windows as improvised curtains. That night, he had sat there for hours watching the logs smoke, burst into flame, and burn fiercely, sparkling behind the glass door of the Morsø Squirrel stove, as the water in the canal around him froze in one of the coldest Decembers there had been for years. That was over six years ago now; his life had changed so much since then, and he had changed with it. Tom and Josie had been married for six years, the same length of time they had been divorced. At first, he had thought about the disintegration of their marriage often. They had initially got along well but were having a few difficulties in that fifth year, as many relationships do.

Often, with a bit of work on both sides, problems can be resolved, and partnerships kept alive. Unfortunately, in Tom's case, it was during that shaky bit of their marriage that he got shot. The effect this had on him, both physically and mentally, and all those around him, cost him dearly. Josie, Josephine, on the legal papers, filed for divorce on the grounds of "irreconcilable differences," and at that time, "irreconcilable" was what the differences were. Neither of them had set eyes on or spoken to each other since then, and Tom's "boat years," as he referred to them, had changed him so much that Josie probably would not even know him now.

The shooting itself, as far as shootings go, could have been a lot worse. Tom was on a normal career path in the Met and did not really stand out from anyone else he worked with; the Head of the Armed Response Unit wrote in one of Tom's annual performance reviews: "Tom shows potential in his work but needs to show greater commitment." Tom had opted for a year working with firearms in the Armed Response Unit, hoping he could learn from the experience and that he would be doing "real" police work, saving lives, protecting the public, and bringing violent criminals to justice – something a bit more interesting than dealing with town centre drunks on Saturday nights. He took well to firearms and was one of the better marksmen on his team. He had managed to cover up his (understandable) fears of being exposed to potentially life-threatening situations and somehow managed to summon up the courage to do what was asked of him, at least on the surface as far as his team could see. In truth, no matter how many active missions he took part in or how many confrontations he had, he never lost the fear; he just "managed" it so that it was not noticeable. There was always the adrenaline buzz that got him through, but that was only part of it; mostly it was the fear that he felt, every time. Tom was not alone in that respect; "'the fear" came with the job. Like the rest of the team, he never spoke about it. Josie had not liked him working in firearms; she worried every time he was called out, but he had reassured her that "bobbies on the beat" face greater dangers than he did. This was not a complete lie, but it was an exaggeration of the truth – a big exaggeration.

It was a dawn drug raid on a known gang of dealers in a studio flat situated on the 11th floor of a tower block in Hounslow. The intelligence passed on to the Armed Response was that there were four men and a woman in the flat on that particular morning, at least one of them armed. Tom and two others in the team had been given the order to go in first. The instant the front door was rammed open, they ran in, visors down and SLR (self-loading rifles) in hand. Inside, there they were – the four men and the woman – kids, really – taken by surprise before they could do anything but stare at the armed police officers. There was a handgun lying on a table in the centre of the room. The table was covered with packets of white powder, weighing scales, and a box full of used bank notes. Tom and his team quickly secured the five suspects and carried out a sweep of the apartment, looking for other weapons or anything else of interest. The apartment was clear; they could relax. However, on that morning, intelligence got it wrong; there were in fact five men in the flat as well as the woman, not four, as Tom Hunter was about to find out.

Tom had been the first officer in the room, and he was also the last out, giving a final look around. Believing the flat was now empty, he dropped his guard and felt the tension slowly leaving his body. The studio flat had an open-plan kitchen along a windowless wall. The only other room was a small toilet with a shower. There was an empty cupboard opposite the bathroom that had been checked during the sweep. What they did miss, however, was that the cupboard had a false back, behind which there was a space big enough to safely hide not only drugs and many bundles of notes but, on this occasion, a sixth person. Just as Tom was leaving the room, he heard a noise coming from the cupboard. He pulled his visor down, took the safety off his weapon, and approached the door with the fear returning. He was only halfway there when the door was flung open and a young, deranged-looking man, screaming and waving his arms around, flew out faster than Tom could blink. There was no chance for Tom to shout any warnings or to do anything at all, for that matter. Before he knew it, the man had run straight into him. It all happened so fast that exactly *how* it happened would never be known for sure, but somehow in that instant, when the two men's bodies collided, the rifle was knocked downwards, and the trigger pulled. The bullet went through the top of Tom's left boot, through the right side of his foot, through the sole of the boot, through the thin lino floor tile, and flattened itself into a squashed lead circle on the concrete underneath.

PC Tom Hunter was rushed to the hospital in the back of a patrol car, alongside one of the firearms team members who was doing what he could to stop the bleeding. The shooting incident had been called through to the hospital's A&E in advance by the team commander; doctors and nurses were standing by when they arrived. Tom had not felt any pain during that drive; in fact, he had not felt anything. For him, it was like being in a strange black-and-white cartoon like Mickey Mouse in Steamboat Willie, flickering and unreal. After the shot, the first thing that he remembered with any clarity was waking up in the hospital several hours later, with Josie sitting beside the bed. He had lost two toes, the big one and the one next to it, and the nerve endings in his foot had been badly damaged. He didn't know it yet, but very soon he would start to feel pain – pain that he would have to learn to live with from then on. This accident and being forced into taking a disability pension and a very early retirement from the Metropolitan Police, coupled with his soon-to-happen divorce, would take him a considerable amount of time to accept.

Sitting on a stool at the breakfast bar in the boat's kitchen, Tom broke the yolk of his egg with the corner of a slice of warm toast. It was, in fact, his breakfast bar, lunch, dinner, supper, and everything else bar – the only table on the boat. A few ducks, or river fowl, as Tom now correctly referred to them, gathered under the open hatch. They were prepared to risk such close contact with humans for the chance of a few scraps of food. Tom admired them for their courage, and, especially during the winter, he would toss any scraps and left-over bread out for them to gorge on. Today, though they were out of luck, Tom's appetite that morning was greater than his charitable instincts towards waterfowl. There would be no scraps left over for them today.

Watching the river flow...
The Thames is the longest river in England, at 215 miles with 45 locks.
Thames Valley Police takes its name from the river, covering three counties: Berkshire, Buckinghamshire, and Oxfordshire.

Chapter 4

AN INCIDENT

'OK, LISTEN UP, EVERYONE!' Ali spoke loudly so that the uniforms and the rest of the teams could all hear.

'I WANT THIS ENTIRE ISLAND SEARCHED THOROUGHLY.' The grounds of the lock where the cottage stood were surrounded by water: the lock channel on one side and the river flowing down to the weir on the other, making it a small island surrounded by water. She had the team's full attention and continued.

'We are looking for a finger, a wedding ring finger.' She looked around the assembled officers, checking that they were taking in all she was saying.

'I don't want to see any members of the public stepping foot on this land, and no boats are going through here today. This whole lock is now a crime scene, until I say otherwise. Remember that, and make sure you all treat it like one.' As the team were about to recommence the search, she added, 'And one other thing: when the press gets here, I want you all to make sure they hear and are told absolutely nothing – and don't let them anywhere near this crime scene.'

Spencer walked over to ask her if she was OK. He was still shaken by what he had seen and assumed that she must be as well, but before he could ask, she turned to him and spoke.

'Spencer, get a dog on the scene ASAP, and seeing as that's what they do best, when they arrive, get the handlers to take that bloody, yapping dog somewhere away from here.' She shot a glance over towards the uniformed officer, still struggling to calm the dog down.

'And get a couple of divers down here to see if there's anything in the bottom of this lock that we should know about.'

'I'm on it, ma'am,' Spencer replied, pulling his mobile out of his pocket and moving off to leave and start directing events. Her words struck an odd chord with him: "bloody yapping dog." "Bloody" seemed like the word to describe everything he had seen in that "bloody" cottage.

Everyone was there now. The pathologist had arrived, as had the CSI forensics team in their van. They followed the crime scene photographers into the cottage. Spencer had briefed them on what to expect in there. A couple of early morning walkers and a cyclist had stopped to see what was going on. Spencer had instructed one of the uniforms to question them and find out if they had seen anything or anyone. He didn't need to tell any of the officers to keep this confidential; they already knew the sensitivity of crime scenes like this, and Chief Inspector Ali Smith had also made that very clear to them all. For now, this was all staying "in-house."

The CSI cameras would take 360-degree shots of each of the rooms, as well as body close ups and other shots. Also, like Ali and Spencer, they were fitted with body-worn video cameras. They would measure, take prints, bag evidence items, and take blood samples. There was enough blood in that cottage to fill a bathtub; there would be no difficulty with getting sample smears. The pathologist would examine each of the victims and record his initial findings; a full postmortem would follow. Six dead bodies – more than average for the week! Ali was busy making sure everyone knew what they had to do; a uniform was posted on the door keeping a scene attendance log, and other uniforms were assigned to logging each room. She was too busy to make any of her own notes, but she had studied and memorised all the things she'd observed. Later, there would be time to go through the logs and her and Spencer's body-worn camera footage – never as good as looking at holiday videos. There would also be the CSI photographs and video to look through when they became available. Arrangements had been made for a mobile incident room to be set up just inside the lock grounds. The investigating team was likely to be there for a few days, maybe longer, sifting through, measuring, cataloguing, and examining every little thing that might be of importance. Ali would also need to brief the Chief Superintendent, who would probably step in to supervise the investigation at some point, but that could wait until the time came. There were going to be no Easter holidays for Ali Smith and Spencer Davis this year.

The yapping dog had been moved into a police van, where its muffled yaps and whelps could still be heard but were now bearable. It could stay there until the dog handlers dealt with it. They could *handle* that one as well. Ali wandered over to her second-in-command.

'What have we got here then, Spencer?' She asked, not waiting for an answer or expecting one.

'Six bodies, all white, two adult males, two adult females, and two children, one boy and one girl.' She was summarising the facts and theorising.

'Five of them had knife wounds, probably causing their deaths. And one naked in the bottom of the shower with no immediate signs of injury – that is to say, no noticeable knife wounds.'

Spencer listened carefully. He knew not to interrupt her when she was speaking like this; he could tell she was thinking out loud as much as she was telling him what she had seen.

'The poor children still had their pyjamas on. They must have just been getting up for breakfast. Give me one of those cigarettes, please, Spencer.'

Spencer held out his packet of Marlboros for Ali to take one. As he did so, he noticed a smudge of dry blood on the white sleeve of her incident suit, the contrast of red on white leaping out at him. He also noticed her hand was shaking a little as she placed the cigarette between her lips. He flipped open his Zippo, and Ali heard the sharp metallic click of the lid and smelled the fumes of lighter fluid as he spun the flint wheel and held it up for her to take a light. All of her senses seemed heightened, sharpened, and honed. She had noticed this before when she had been around murder scenes. Not a bad thing, really, as it helps you observe and take in the vast amounts of information that are sometimes only briefly available, like smells, sounds, and movements, the nuances of the crime scene, and the subliminal references. There was a smell in that cottage. The normal smells of a house were there: the smell of breakfast in the kitchen, a faint smell of perfume in the bedrooms, and the smell of soap in the shower. Predominantly, though, there was one single smell that seemed to fill the cottage: the smell of blood – wet, sticky, drying blood – and there was one predominant sound – silence. Ali's were not the only hands that were shaking as Spencer held out the lighter. She took a long, hard pull on the Marlboro and held the smoke deeply in her lungs for what seemed to Spencer like a serious amount of time.

'What do you make of it then, Spencer?' This time, she was expecting an answer. Spencer had been mulling it all over and replied quickly; he already had his own theory. For him, it was clear.

'Family: grandparents, son and wife, or daughter and husband, and their children, probably staying for the Easter weekend. I've got someone checking on all the family connections. It's early to say, ma'am, but my guess is that it was the husband, the son. Something triggered him off, and he killed the wife first, the one in the shower, then the kids, which would have been silently, then downstairs to slaughter the grandparents in the kitchen while they were getting breakfast ready for the family. The killer was not bothered about noise by then: the grandparents could scream as much as they liked; there was no one left alive to hear, except him.'

Ali looked at Spencer expressionlessly and then finished his theory for him.

'Then he topped himself in the grandparents' bedroom. I think if the killer is one of them, it will be him, the son. I can't see a woman doing this, not in that way, not as savagely as that.' She paused and took another pull on her cigarette.

'So, do you think what we have here is a family annihilation, Spence? He kills the wife and kids, followed by the grandparents, and then himself. A textbook definition.' She paused and took another long pull on her cigarette. 'But why the finger? And where the bloody hell is it?!' Stamping on her cigarette butt, she turned and shouted out to the rest of the team as she moved away from Spencer and back into the throng of activity: 'I WANT THAT FINGER FOUND!'

Spencer stayed by his car, having another smoke, silently running through his own construction of events. As a detective, he knew it would be wrong to jump to conclusions too early, but what else could it have been? He was still leaning against the car smoking when the young officer who had been speaking with the public, the passersby, came over.

'What have you found out for me then, Constable?' Spencer asked, unintentionally mimicking Ali Smith as he exhaled his own lungful of tobacco smoke.

'Well, sir, the walker and his wife, a Mr and Mrs Wilson, live in Didcot and were out here for an early morning walk along the river. In fact, they had only just started out when they saw us. Well, the patrol cars. Their car, a silver Yaris, is parked up on the road, and according to them, they didn't see anyone or anything that they could remember. They are retired and come here two or three times a week to walk along the river in the early mornings when the weather is…'

'What about the other one, the cyclist?' Spencer interrupted, having heard more than enough about the Wilsons already.

'Ah, yes…' The constable smiled eagerly and looked at his notepad.

'He lives in Clifton Hampden and cycled down from Clifton Lock; that's the next one up. He told me he saw a boat heading upstream, that is, towards Clifton from here, sir.'

'I know which direction the Thames flows in, Constable, thank you.' Spencer was getting impatient. He could not see much use in what the young officer was telling him, but he knew it was ground that needed to be covered.

'Yes, of course. Sorry, sir. Well, he said he passed a narrowboat about half a mile upstream, half a mile from here. It looked like it was pulling over to moor up and must have come through this lock shortly before, unless it had been moored up nearer here overnight, but then why would you pull away and moor up again so soon?'

'OK, Constable, good work. I'll take it from here. Did the cyclist happen to notice the name of the boat by any chance?' Spencer asked.

'Yes, he did, sir.' The constable was flicking through his notebook again. Spencer liked to see this: good old-fashioned policing, notebook, and pencil.

'It was dark blue, and… here it is, *Wandering Aengus*.' He said he remembered the name because he thought that "Aengus" was an odd way to spell Angus.'

'It's the title of a W. B. Yeats poem, Constable. The Song of *Wandering Aengus*.' Spencer responded, feeling pleased that his 2:1 in literature all those years ago had come into use after all.

I went out to the hazel wood,
Because a fire was in my head,
And cut and peeled a hazel wand,
And hooked a berry to a thread

[W B YEATS – "The Song of Wandering Aengus"]

Chapter 5

CHARLES STREET, EAST OXFORD

Tom had bought his boat from someone he had met during his first year back in Oxford, what he now thought of as his "lost year," the year during which he lost everything. His marriage irretrievably broke down, and there was a pending court case about who got what seemed to be the only thing left of it. Everything seemed to come down to money in the end where the solicitors were concerned, especially as there were no children involved – he and Josie had never managed to have children. It was during the "lost year" that he last set eyes on Josie across a big austere table in the civil court where the divorce settlement was finally agreed. They had not seen or spoken to each other since that day. Tom Hunter wanted his freedom; he wanted his life back. He wanted a fresh start, so he agreed with all the barrister's demands and settled it for good. He had received the decree nisi, and a few months later, after paying even more money to solicitors, the decree absolute – it really was over.

As well as his marriage, his home, and his money, the lost year saw other losses and disappearances for Tom. His job – his career – was one of them, causing him to lose even more. Next came the loss of his self-esteem, his confidence, and his sense of direction in life. This was followed by the loss of his friends. Many of his colleagues turned out to be just that, "colleagues," and not "friends," as he had always considered them to be, and his other friends were really friends of Josie's and quickly drifted away from him. To Tom, it really did feel as if he had lost "everything," and in some ways he had. Not least of all, he had lost two of his toes! Unlike the pain of the divorce and all the other losses, the pain from the toes would stay with him as a constant reminder for the rest of his life. Without that pain, he thought he would probably have been able to let go of the past far quicker and really leave it all behind, but with the pain as a reminder, the forgetting would take him a long time. There was, however, one thing that he gained during that time, one thing that was not a loss: his freedom.

Tom wanted distance put between himself and everything that had happened, distance between him and Josie and everyone they ever knew, distance between him and the Met, distance from who he used to be, the old Tom Hunter. He had spent his years in the Met struggling with his own rebellious nature, which made it hard for him to take orders, to do what he was told, and to give in to institutionalisation. The police service is institutionalised and most definitely has a strongly defined hierarchy of command that must be obeyed; this is in many ways what makes the police service work, but it grated on Tom. Then there was the fear he always felt in confrontational situations – the fear that he hid carefully from all those around him, the fear that drove him deeper inside himself. Tom was never sure if he should be a police officer. The sacrifices and compromises had cost him many things: the long, unsociable hours, working when everyone else was on holidays, the demanding and often stressful work, the things he was sworn not to talk about and the things he didn't want to talk about, the things he had seen and the things he wished he had not seen. This abundance of negatives seeping into his life probably cost him his marriage and may have also been the reason he had no real friends. He admitted to himself that he stopped even trying to make friends, leaving him with no one to turn to when he needed company most. There was no one he could rely on to share his troubles with – his happiness, his sadness – no one he could trust.

To say there was "no one" was not quite true. There was one person, Simon. Simon was an old friend from Tom's college days at Oxford Polytechnic, as it was called before it changed to Oxford Brookes University. Tom could have had his degree certificate changed to reflect the new, more posh, more academic-sounding name, but he had never bothered. Straight after graduating, he joined the Met and never really gave his degree another thought. On the other hand, Simon had fallen in love with Oxford and had never left the city, staying there after he had graduated, never to move away. Simon and Tom had been almost inseparable buddies during their college years but had gone their different ways after their graduation, and with time, they had grown apart the way people often do. They had not seen much of each other over the decade or so since, but they had kept in contact with the odd Christmas card and met up on the odd occasion. However, the year prior to everything falling apart, Tom's "lost year," he and Josie had driven up to Oxford several times to visit Simon, now living with his long-term partner Jacky in a small, terraced house in East Oxford. Strangely enough, it was on Charles Street, the same street where Tom had lived as a student. Simon had followed his passion for photography and had been an established freelancer for a considerable number of years now. Jacky worked for a computer company in one of the business parks. Tom had liked his visits to Oxford as it gave him some space from the demands of his job. He liked renewing his friendship with Simon, and the weekends that he and Josie spent there seemed to put their marital problems on hold for a day or two. It gave them brief periods of respite.

The night that the marital problems went beyond boiling point was the night the marriage ended. Tom left the house, the "former matrimonial home," as the solicitors had called it, with just the clothes he was wearing, getting into his car, and driving off, not thinking anything through. In fact, he had not "thought" at all. He had no idea exactly what he was doing or where he was going, and worryingly, he didn't even care. Just as long as he was going away. Away from the madness, away from the shouting and fighting, away from the sadness and the crying, over the hills, and far away *because a fire was in his head.*

That same night, it was raining heavily, and Tom stared at the world through his windscreen, the wiper blades and cat's eyes mesmerising him as he drove through the darkness. The further he went, the gentler the fire in his head burned, and numbness took over. He stared at the road ahead, not knowing where the headlights in front of him were coming from or where the ones in his rear-view mirror were going. He slowly began to realise that he too didn't know where he was going; he didn't even understand where or what he was coming from. Time passed and the miles clicked by, how long? An hour? Two hours? However long it was, it was enough to make the needle on his fuel gauge enter the red, enough to force him into action and start looking for a petrol station. It was only then that he realised he was driving west on the M40, in fact, he was nearly at the A40 junction, the turn-off for Oxford. From the trips he and Josie had made along that road, he knew that there was a service station just off the junction, and so that was where he headed. It was only after he had filled up, replaced the pump, and paid for the fuel that he realised how exhausted he was, and how completely drained of everything he had become. It was only then that it started to dawn on him what a predicament he was in.

Sitting in the Café Costa area of the services with a hot white coffee in front of him, far too hot to drink, Tom checked his mobile phone. No messages, no one had tried to call. It didn't surprise him – he got very few calls or messages since being relieved of his job. Work calls had been the only ones he ever seemed to get. As he stared at his coffee, Simon's face jumped into his mind; Oxford had drawn him from London like a magnet. He dialled Simon's number while he waited for the coffee to cool down.

'Hi Simon, it's me, Tom,' Tom said, trying to sound as normal as possible.

'Hello Tom. Are you okay? Is everything alright?' Simon replied, puzzling Tom slightly.

'What makes you ask that, Si?' Tom asked.

'Well, it's quarter to one on a Thursday night, or should I say Friday morning, for one thing.'

Simon's answer jerked Tom back into reality. He had not even been aware of the time of day.

'Oh shit! I'm sorry, Simon; I didn't realise it was so late; I didn't mean to disturb you.'

'You're OK, mate, Jacky and I are watching a DVD and polishing off a bottle of red; the joys of being freelance – you don't have to get up early – well, I don't, that is, at least.'

Tom could hear Jacky declaring a pretend annoyance in the background.

'So, what can we do for you, Tom?'

He hesitated before answering; it felt like a big favour he was calling in, and he was not used to asking for favours from anyone.

'Would there be any chance of you putting me up for the night? Tonight, I mean, it's just that… Well, look, it doesn't matter. I'm sorry I called so late. Say hello to Jacky for…'

'Whoa! Tom! We are up for a while yet,' Simon interrupted. 'Just get yourself here; you're very welcome. If we're in bed, I'll leave a key under the plant pot next to the front door. You know where your bed is.'

'I don't know what to say, Si. Thank you. Thank you both. I should be there in about 20 minutes, but don't wait up for me.'

Tom ended the call; his coffee was now ready to drink, and he did. At the other end of the line in East Oxford, Simon had realised that something significant was wrong and started discussing it with Jacky. They guessed it was something to do with Josie – some kind of domestic, probably.

When I had laid it on the floor
I went to blow the fire a-flame,
But something rustled on the floor,
And someone called me by my name:
It had become a glimmering girl
With apple blossom in her hair
Who called me by my name and ran
And faded through the brightening air.

[W B YEATS – "The Song of Wandering Aengus"]

Chapter 6

THE SONG OF WANDERING AENGUS

It was nearly a year later that Tom finally moved out of Simon and Jacky's spare room; most of his lost year was spent living there. On reflection, he could see that he probably overstayed his welcome by several months. But Simon and Jacky had never even hinted that he should go, and they always made him feel welcome. They had helped to mend him, nursed him back to good mental health, and seemed very happy to have him around. On the afternoons when Simon was around, the two of them would sit in the little back garden, drinking cold bottles of beer and chatting about everything, past and present. They touched on the future occasionally, but this was not a place where Tom felt comfortable; Simon was sensitive enough to see this and to leave the future where it was until Tom was ready to talk about it. Tom grew to really appreciate Simon's life and many of the choices he had made – his career. staying in Oxford, not getting married. The house in East Oxford was small but very much a home, full of music, pictures, and books. Then there was Oxford itself: Tom had fallen in love with it again; this time around, however, it was not through the eyes of a student. It was through eyes that had grown to see many things, through eyes of experience, that had shaped values and understanding. Along with the good things that those eyes had seen, there were many others – things that most people would be grateful not to have seen, things never to be spoken of.

Compared to London, Oxford was a paradise – small enough to get around but big enough to remain anonymous – with beautiful architecture, friendly pubs, and some good live music. Tom only went back to London twice during that year at Simon's, once for the divorce hearing at the civil court and once when he took the bus to Notting Hill Gate with Simon and spent the day trawling Portobello Road. Tom realised on that day that he had left London, in his head and his heart. He now felt like all the other visitors around him: this was no longer his home; he too was now a tourist.

It was at a dinner party at Simon's that Tom met Jamie. Jamie was a teacher, or at least had been one for several years before taking time off and vowing that he would never go back to teaching again.

'About ten percent of them want to learn, and that is rewarding. The rest of them you just feel like thumping, belting some education into them,' Jamie told everyone over glasses of wine and mouthfuls of Tom's fish pie.

'That's why I had to quit teaching. It would have reached a point where I actually did thump one of the little buggers, and then I really would have been in trouble.'

Jamie was living on an old narrowboat on the Oxford Canal during his teaching years. He had also worked as a supply teacher and had taken a term's teaching at a school in Hungerford. He moved his boat there for the few months he worked at the school, as a home from home.

'The same school where Michael Ryan's life ended,' Jamie had told them: 'the man that shot and killed sixteen people, including his mother, sometime in 1987, when the pressure got too much, poor bastard. They still talk about him in Hungerford, even after all these years.'

Jamie had not worked for over a year since his term in Hungerford. Not working was something Tom was starting to be able to empathise with. An opportunity had arisen for Jamie to take over the ownership of a pub in Oxford. He was looking to sell the boat to raise some money for the new venture. He would be able to live over the pub. Sitting around the dinner table, they all discussed the pros and cons of living on a narrowboat.

'Narrowboat, not a barge,' Jamie had stressed when the word barge was used. The usual questions were asked by everyone:

'Isn't it damp?'

'Doesn't it get cold in the winter?'

'Is it safe?'

'What do you have for a toilet?'

'How do you wash?'

All of these questions were laughed at by Jamie, who had heard them many times before; he found them easy to answer and to dispel the myths and misconceptions. However, the question Jacky asked caused Jamie to stop and think before replying.

'Doesn't it get lonely, Jamie?' She had asked.

Jamie filled his wine glass up as he considered his reply.

'Well, you have to like your own company,' he said as he took a sip of his Rioja, 'and when you think about it, you can be lonely in a house in a street full of people.'

'And in a marriage!' Tom thought to himself.

A few days later, Tom went over to visit Jamie on his boat moored near Thrupp on the Oxford Canal. The boat was not in the best state and was in need of a considerable amount of work. In reality, it could do with a complete makeover and a full refit. Jamie made a couple of mugs of tea, and they sat on the back deck, chatting as they drank. Jamie told Tom how it was his love of poetry that had led him to become an English teacher, and how his love of poetry was also how the boat came to be named *Wandering*

Aengus. He explained he had chosen the name from that particular poem, "The Song of *Wandering Aengus,"* because the boat was badly ballasted with too much weight on one side, making it difficult to steer in a straight line; instead, it tended to "wander" all over the canal.

Tom liked Jamie. He was a straight talker and a good talker. Jamie could really tell a story and had the ability to make anything he talked about sound interesting. He was also a people person who could make almost anyone feel that he empathised with them and understood them. Tom was not sure if Jamie really did empathise with and understand everyone or if he was just able to make them think he did; either way, it was a good trait to have. Tom also admired Jamie's independence, or the independence that living on a boat had given him. No mortgage, gas bills, water rates, council taxes, or electricity bills; just a boat license, insurance, and some diesel. Tom also liked the idea of being surrounded by everything you owned and being able to see it all. Most of what Tom had ever owned had been lost, and it appealed to him to be able to keep a watchful eye over the little he had left.

Tom had never considered living on a boat, and when he offered to buy it from Jamie, he was really only thinking of it as a building project, something he could keep himself busy with and maybe make a little bit of a profit on when it was finished. Jamie was asking a very fair price, so a deal was swiftly done. *Wandering Aengus* had a new owner; it was now in the hands of Tom Hunter.

Someone came knocking
At my wee, small door;
Someone came knocking;
I'm sure-sure-sure;

[WALTER DE LA MARE – "Some One"]

Chapter 7

DON'T COME KNOCKING

It had been a very long few hours, and it was still a long way from being over yet; in fact, it had hardly begun. The search for the finger and whatever could be found was underway, with nothing of interest being found as yet. The arrival of the sniffer dog would hopefully speed things up. Detective Chief Inspector Ali Smith and Detective Inspector Spencer Davis would need to go back into the cottage at some point, but for now they were giving space to the pathologist and the forensic team – room for them to manoeuvre. Besides, neither Ali nor Spencer were in a hurry to go back into the scenes of carnage that they knew awaited them there. Spencer handed Ali a couple of his cigarettes.

'For Ron, later on,' he said with an attempt at a smile.

Ali tried her best to smile back as she took them from him.

'I'm going to get out of this suit and walk up the river a bit, see if I can find that boat that came through here this morning,' Spencer said to Ali as he started climbing out of his forensic whites. 'I need to stretch my legs and clear my head; would you like to come with me, ma'am?'

'No, you're all right, Spence; I'll hang on here and keep an eye on things just in case anything else comes up.'

It was a good fifteen minutes of brisk walking along the grassy, tree-lined towpath before Spencer could see a boat moored up. Luckily, it was on the same side of the river that he was on. A plume of white smoke coming out of the small chimney in the middle of the roof was the first thing that caught Spencer's eye. As he got nearer to the boat, he could smell not only the smoke but also the distinct aroma of bacon and eggs. Spencer had not visited many narrowboats in his career – none, actually – and he was not sure of the protocol. Do you step on the back deck and knock on the door, or should you just tap on the roof or a window? He debated with himself. As it turned out, he didn't need to do anything. Just as he was about to make a decision, Tom Hunter's head and shoulders appeared out of the open side hatch, making Spencer visibly jump.

''Morning,' Tom said, scraping a few fragments of bacon rind from the plate he was holding.

'Good morning, sir.' Spencer held his warrant card so that Tom could see it: 'Detective Inspector Spencer Davis, Thames Valley Police.'

'How can I help you, Detective Inspector?' Tom asked.

'Would you mind telling me if you went through Day's Lock earlier this morning?' Spencer asked. He was now standing in front of the hatch, looking down at Tom.

'I don't mind you asking at all. Yes, I did – about a couple of hours ago. Do you mind me asking you? *Why* are you are asking *me*?' Tom said, looking up and seeing only a silhouette of Spencer's body against the blue sky.

Sensing that Tom did not appreciate this invasion of his privacy, Spencer trod carefully.

'That would make it about six, six thirty. Would you say that's about right?' Spencer moved slightly to one side as he spoke so that Tom's face was in full morning sunlight; he could read him better that way. Tom didn't speak. Spencer could not see any telltale signs of annoyance in Tom's face, and maybe he had read him wrong. After all, Spencer had been through a pretty distressing morning so far, so it was highly possible that his judgements were a bit askew at the moment, a bit on edge.

'I'm sorry for disturbing you, sir, but there has been an incident at the lock, Day's Lock – a serious incident. It is important that we establish if you saw or heard anything that may be helpful to us.' Even to Spencer, this sounded like police speak. 'So would you say it was about six thirty this morning that you took your boat through?'

'It must have been about that, though I'd say nearer six judging by the position of the sun and the smell in the air. I don't have a watch, and I didn't have my phone with me or the radio on, so I can't be certain, but it would have been close to that, give or take.' Spencer could see Tom's brain working, but that was to be expected after being told that there had been a serious incident close by.

'Would you like to come inside, Detective Inspector? We can talk better in here, and I've just made some coffee if you would like a mug?'

Spencer was beginning to think he had misjudged Tom; he was more helpful than Spencer had first thought he was going to be. He didn't fit with Spencer's preconceptions about what boaters were like. Then again, Spencer didn't really have any actual preconceptions; he just didn't expect boaters to be like Tom.

'Thank you, sir. That would be very welcome.' After everything that had happened at the cottage, he was dying for a cup of coffee. The canteen at the station didn't open until 7:45 am, so all he had managed to get before leaving with Ali, when the call came in that morning, was a weak cup of tea from the vending machine.

'Jump on the back deck; I'll get the door.' Tom disappeared. Spencer stepped off the bank onto the back deck of *Wandering Aengus* and felt her rock in the water underneath. It was a strange sensation, one that he had not experienced before, having never set foot on a boat. Tom opened the metal door, and Spencer could see that there were a couple of steep steps that dropped down about two feet to the floor of the boat.

'Mind your head on the roof hatch as you climb in, Bud.' Tom had taken to calling everyone "Bud" over the years; it made it easier on the river when it could be many months after meeting someone that you would bump into them again. Remembering names could be difficult, and "Bud" didn't seem to upset anyone; he even used it for women these days.

Spencer stepped down carefully, as advised. The back of the boat was open, with porthole windows on both sides. To his left was a canvas wardrobe, and next to that were some painted metal shelves that held an assortment of neatly stashed tools, cans of paint, brushes, ropes, and other bits and pieces. Spencer noticed how tidy it all was, how orderly. It put his shed at home to shame. Then again, he didn't really have much time for DIY, nor was he any good at it, or so he thought. He was a police detective; he had time for that, and he was good at it. Straight ahead to the left was a wooden wall, a bulkhead, with a narrow corridor to the right.

Tom noticed Spencer looking around and asked, 'Have you not been on a narrowboat before, Detective?'

'No, sir, not that I can recall,' Spence replied, feeling that he had been caught out.

'I'll give you a guided tour as we go through; it should only take a few seconds,' Tom said, smiling, to himself as well as to Spencer. They squeezed through the narrow corridor, past what Tom pointed out as the bathroom, with a shower and a toilet. Spencer had to take his word for it as the door was closed. At the other end of the corridor, the boat opened out. To the left ran a small galley kitchen under a square window. The window looked out over the river and was opposite the side hatch where Tom had popped his head out. The floor of the boat was about eighteen inches below the water level, giving a different perspective of the river and one that Spencer found slightly disconcerting. Beyond the open-plan kitchen was a living area with two brown armchairs, a wooden trunk, a bookshelf, and a cast-iron solid-fuel burner. Spencer now knew why the boat had felt so warm in comparison to the chill of the morning that was still in the air outside.

'Sugar?' asked Tom as he went over to the coffee pot sitting on the hob.

The two of them sat in the armchairs and sipped their coffees as Spencer carefully asked Tom about what he had seen and anything he might have noticed. Tom told him that it was early, there were no other boats around, and it was too early for the lockkeeper to have started work. *'Nor will he ever again,'* Spencer thought to himself. Tom wanted to know what had happened at the lock and what the "incident" was, but Spencer apologised, explaining that it was a police matter and that he was not able to give any details at this point. Tom asked if anything had happened to the lockkeeper; he knew him – that is, he knew him well enough to chat with him as he passed through the lock. *Wandering Aengus* had been through there many times before. Spencer gave him the same answer, apologising again. The image of the man and woman on the sofa sprang back into his head, along with all the blood.

'You saw nothing unusual then; no one around?'

'Wait a second; I nearly forgot.' Tom had remembered the man on the bench.

'I only saw him for a second – not even that – just a glance, really. All I can say is that it looked like a man, not a woman, but even that I can't be sure of.'

Tom explained that he had intended to say hello when he went back to close the lock gates, but by then he had already gone. He remembered the dog near the bench, scrabbling around. He didn't think the lockkeeper had a dog, but that was about it. There was nothing else he could say. There was nothing else.

'The only other person I saw was a bloke on a bicycle who cycled past towards the lock, which was about an hour ago,' Tom said with a shrug, not knowing if that would be useful or not.

Spencer felt the boat rock again as they both got up.

'By the way,' Spencer asked as he climbed the stairs onto the deck, 'what's the protocol for knocking on a boat: do you climb on and knock on the door, or do you bang on the side or the roof?'

'The way us boaters do it, Inspector, is to tap on the roof. Boats are very personal things, very private, especially to those of us who live on them,' Tom replied, and with a smile, he added for

Spencer's benefit, 'and the golden rule to remember, Detective, is, if the boats a rocking don't come a knocking.'

Spencer smiled too, for the second time only that morning; this time it was not quite so forced. He stepped off the boat onto the bank, good old terra firma again.

He thanked Tom for the coffee and for being so helpful, and he asked him not to go too far for a few days as they might need to speak with him again. Tom had already explained that he was going to Abingdon to get fuel and to do some work on his engine, meaning he would be there for a good few days, probably a week. Spencer was aware that Tom might be their only witness, and if they found the guy he had seen on the bench, they might need Tom to try and ID him if nothing else. In the meantime, he had got all he could from Tom for now. In fact, Tom had been very helpful and passed on a lot of incidental information in their brief chat. Spencer now knew that Tom didn't work because he had some kind of disability, though Spencer didn't actually find out exactly what that was. Another snippet of information he gleaned was that Tom had built the boat, at least fitted it out himself, and had been living on it for just over six years. The first year he spent on the Oxford Canal and the other five or so years travelling up and down the stretch of river between Henley and Lechlade, the source of the Thames. Much of the winter months he spent on the Isis, the part of the River Thames Iffley Lock that flows through the city of Oxford. Spencer knew from his literature days that the name "Isis" is nothing more than part of the word "Tamesis," the Latin name for the Thames. He also had Tom's mobile phone number and a note of the boat's registration number; he would get one of the team to check with the Environment Agency boat licensing department and see if they could shed any more light on Mr Tom Hunter. For now, though aware of the time and that Ali would be needing his help, Spencer headed briskly back towards the lock.

The Barley Mow inn is described as a "capital little inn" and "one of the thatched, old-fashioned resting places that have been almost improved out of existence by the modern system of hotels."

[CHARLES DICKENS Jr. – "Dickens's Dictionary of the Thames, 1879"]

Chapter 8

THE BARLEY MOW

The divers had been in the water for about half an hour. They had found nothing of interest, just a few old boat fenders and an assortment of bottles, probably dropped over the years by stag-weekenders on hire boats. The lock was not very big, so they would only spend another hour or so down there before calling it a day. It was not looking as if they would find anything useful. Ali had smoked the last of the cigarettes that Spencer had left with her and was busy taking and making calls on her mobile. She had got one of the team to stop any boats coming through either Clifton Lock upstream or Day's and Benson downstream. That should help prevent a build-up of inquisitive boaters to deal with on top of everything else. All the other lockkeepers had been busy phoning and asking the police questions, but they were told the same as the rest of the public. It was a police matter, and it was not possible to release any details at that time. This didn't stop the lockkeepers from speculating, though; they knew that something bad had happened. They also knew that none of them could make contact with George, the lockkeeper at Day's, and his wife Brenda. Lockkeepers seem to spend at least half of their working day on the telephone with each other; even when they are opening and closing the gates, they have a mobile propped up to their ear. The conversations are generally about water levels, what boats are heading their way, and general moans about the sweeping changes the Environment Agency has in store for them. It was no longer the job it once was. That morning, all their phones were even more alive with the buzz of gossip over the police activity at Day's Lock. However, none of their speculations came even close to the true horror of what had taken place in that small cottage.

Ali, still on the phone, beckoned for Spencer to come over to her. She was no longer wearing her white incident suit; somehow she looked a little out of place now wearing her day clothes; it was as if she were at the office, the place where both she and Spencer thought they would be today. She ended her call with, 'Yes, ma'am, I will.' Spencer guessed it was the chief she had been speaking to.

'The divers are getting ready to call it a day,' she updated Spencer. 'They haven't found anything out of the ordinary. I didn't think they would really, but it would be better to leave no stone unturned with an incident like this.' Spencer nodded in agreement, and Ali continued. 'The search team hasn't come up with anything either, but the dogs have arrived and have made a start at the back of the house. The pathologist is still in there with the forensics; I think they could be there for a few hours. Did you get anything from the boater?'

Spencer was about to pull out his notepad when Ali said, 'I could really do with a coffee and something to eat, something to settle my stomach. Everything is under control here. Shall we go and grab a sandwich somewhere? I need to get away to help me think clearly. Come on, Spence, a change of scenery, my shout. You can tell me what you know in the car.'

Spencer went through his notes and filled her in on all he had on Tom Hunter. As Spencer had anticipated, she was particularly interested in Tom's report of seeing someone at the lock. Spencer had a lot of time for Ali: she was like him in some ways, she liked her job, it was important to her, and she was smart. Like him, she also had two children: a married daughter who now lived in the Norwegian capital Oslo, and a 19-year-old son who still lived at home with her and showed no signs of ever moving out. However, unlike her, Spencer had been happy to reach the level of detective inspector and stay there. Ali, although younger than him, had already risen to Detective Chief Inspector. Another difference between them was that Spencer was still happily married, whereas Ali's ex-husband had left her years ago when her son was only five years old. Spencer knew that he had run off with another woman, but Ali had never told him about that; it was something he had heard around the station, and like everyone else other than Ali, Spencer only knew half of it. Luckily, her son Andrew was an independent and resourceful teenager; the situation he grew up in had made it almost impossible for him not to be. Andrew took care of himself as well as making sure his mum was OK. Andrew also seemed to keep himself to himself, a loner in some ways. Ali often worked long hours, especially when things like the Day's Lock incident cropped up. Many nights she would return home, and Andrew would have cooked a meal for the two of them. Andrew, like many other young people of his generation, was finding it hard to get a job; he had almost given up looking. This meant he had plenty of time to help out. Even so, Ali knew she was lucky that he actually did help; most sons of his age would not have. She also hoped and believed he would find a job that he liked one day and that he would be successful, the way most mothers feel about their children. But by successful, she didn't mean rich; she simply meant "happy." Money was not the most important thing in Ali's life; she would never have joined the police otherwise. Nevertheless, she did have some concerns about how little effort Andrew seemed to put into looking for work.

They pulled into the pub car park; it was early still, but the weather was good. The local pubs relied on all the trade they could get during the warmer months before winter set in again and business went quiet. Spencer ducked under the wooden beam over the door of the thatched pub, and Ali followed him to the bar. Soon they were seated by an old window with steaming cups of coffee in front of them, waiting for their cheese and pickle sandwiches to be brought over.

'They would've gone through Day's Lock,' Spencer said to Ali, nodding to a framed picture on the wall. The inscription underneath read:

'The Barley Mow, Clifton Hampden, is a thatched pub of great antiquity that has been on this site since 1352. The Barley Mow is featured in Jerome K. Jerome's famous book Three Men in a Boat (1889), in which J (believed to be Jerome), Wingrave, Harris, and their dog Montmorency stopped before heading to Oxford.'

Spencer had read the book as part of his degree and remembered it well. He was particularly pleased that he had remembered the dog's name before he read it in the inscription; this confirmed to him that he had the traits of a reasonable detective.

Ali looked up at the picture and silently read the inscription. When she had finished, she turned back to Spencer and said, without any trace of humour, 'I bet they don't let dogs in here now!'

Spencer could not help smiling. When confronted by scenes like the one up at the lock and others, maybe not quite so gruesome but nevertheless disturbing, humour was always the way through it. Both Spencer and Ali and most officers in the force knew this. Without a sense of humour, it would not be possible to survive the demands of their jobs and the dark places it took them to. Yes, he and Ali were very similar, both "old school" in a way. Not old school like you see in "The Sweeney," where they knock "*scrotes*" around, but old school in the way they both clearly saw the value and importance of their jobs and the work they did. Not like some of the younger, "climb-the-ladder"-oriented university graduates that applied to join these days, only interested in a quick career path and looking important. Ali and Spencer were far wiser than this; they had been in the job too long to care about trivialities like looks and self-importance.

The sandwiches arrived, and the two detectives sat in silence, slowly eating and gazing around the low-ceilinged bar with its oak beams and slab stone floors. Spencer noticed a middle-aged couple across the bar, deep in conversation; they looked as if they were quietly arguing. There was something familiar about the pair, and he continued to study them until it clicked – the walkers that arrived on the scene at the lock. What did the PC say their names were? Oh yes! Spencer once again felt pleased with his memory: Mr and Mrs Wilson, the walkers from Didcot!

Ali's phone rang, jolting both of them out of their gazing. She answered it as Spencer stared at her intently, listening to every word. He knew this was not a private call; it was about Day's Lock.

'They've found the finger,' she exclaimed to Spencer as she stood up and started putting her suit jacket back on.

Back at the lock, Ali and Spencer were greeted by one of the dog handlers, who seemed proud to give her details of how "Murphy," one of their best sniffer dogs, had found the severed finger buried, not very deep, under the wood chipping on the flower bed next to the bench opposite the cottage. It had been put into an evidence jar and catalogued by the forensics team, who would investigate it further back at the lab, along with everything else they had bagged and bottled.

'Good work, Officer,' Ali said to the dog handler, 'and thanks for getting that yapping dog out of the way. Did you find an owner?'

'Not for definite yet, ma'am, but it looks like it belonged to one of them in there.' The dog handler nodded over towards the cottage. 'I'll get it checked back at the base; see if it's been chipped.'

From what Spencer had said and what he had gleaned from his interview with the boater, the yappy little dog did not belong to the lockkeeper. Ali was already guessing it belonged to the bodies upstairs – the couple and the children. A mobile incident room had been set up in the car parking area. A blue tarpaulin canopy had been erected next to the cottage so that it sealed the front door area from view and from the telephoto lenses of the press photographers. A few journalists and other members of the inquisitive public had started to gather as close as they could to the lock. Uniformed officers were doing their best to get them to leave. The press photographers had guessed they were onto something big: something serious had happened in there, and they were not intending to go anywhere. They stood chatting with each other, smoking and joking, cameras always at hand. They were in it for the long haul and knew from experience that this was already looking as if it would be very long. The blue tarpaulin was a familiar sight to them, and they knew it meant there were fatalities. It would be several hours before the body bags were ready to be stretchered out.

What I love most about rivers is:
You can't step in the same river twice
The water's always changing, always flowing
But people, I guess, can't live like that
We all must pay a price
To be safe, we lose our chance of ever knowing
What's around the river bend
Waiting just around the river bend

[POCHONTAS – "Just Around The River Bend"]

Chapter 9

THE ROCK OF GIBRALTAR

It was not long before Tom heard about the fate of George and Brenda. News travels faster than narrowboats on the river! Exactly what had happened was still not known, but the other lockkeepers had passed on the news that George and Brenda were dead – dead in their cottage at Day's Lock. There was no mention of the children or the other two adults, but the word was certainly that the lockkeeper and his wife were dead, and the number of police involved was making it look as if the circumstances were suspicious. Tom locked up *Wandering Aengus* and walked back towards the lock. The day was turning warmer and looking better by the hour; it could be a good Easter after all. Tom knew George to say hello to, and he remembered him as being a nice guy, a friendly lockkeeper. George had once told Tom that he had been in the RAF but retired early and drifted into lockkeeping. He also told Tom one of the times *Wandering Aengus* passed through Day's that it had been the best move he and Brenda had ever made: he loved the job, and they both loved living at Day's. Tom did not really know Brenda; he had seen her around and about at the lock but had not really spoken with her. She kept herself to herself, but she seemed nice enough.

As Tom walked, the lock started to come into view. He could just make out the white incident suits and the uniforms moving around behind the blue and white "POLICE LINE. DO NOT CROSS" tape. Tom had been a police officer long enough to know that he was looking at the scene of something big, something serious. He stood on the bank for a while, keeping his distance from the lock. He didn't want to get questioned again, and he knew too well that there would be no information coming out from inside the sealed-off area. He turned and walked slowly back to the boat. The locks on either side of Day's were still closed to all boats, and the empty river flickered calmly and silently in the morning sun, as it had done for centuries.

During the time Tom had been refitting *Wandering Aengus* up on the Oxford Canal, he had found the canals "charming." They cut through pretty countryside and had ancient, manually operated locks and bridges that were there, keeping the water traffic moving and the past alive. Many of the tunnels under bridges on the canal bore deep grooves in the corners of the brickwork where they had been scarred by the ropes of old horse-drawn narrowboats, laden with cargo, being pulled through by hand, often by children. Tom had read much about this way of life and had many conversations with other boaters about the canals and their history. Every time he ever went under one of the bridges, the image came into his mind of children lying on the top of wooden narrowboats to help "walk them through" using their feet on the underside of the tunnel roof while others dragged and pulled on the ropes, often moving fifty or more tonnes of cargo-laden boat. However, as attractive as the canals could be when Tom first took the newly refitted *Wandering Aengus* through Duke's Cut (the short, narrow strip of canal that joins the main canal to the River Thames), when he saw the river stretching out in front of him, he knew that was where he belonged. The canals were charming, but the river was majestic. The canals were man-made, cut out of the open countryside, and where they did pass through towns and cities, they were usually routed through the grey industrial areas. The river was a different story: it was natural and had its own power; it was alive. Rivers did not pass through towns and cities; towns and cities came to them and were built around them, built because of them. They were at the heartbeat of life wherever they flowed.

The excitement Tom felt when he first saw that wide expanse of deep flowing river, in contrast to the narrow, shallow, still-water canals, was something he had not felt since he was a schoolboy – on the last day of summer term with the seemingly endless holidays stretching before him. It was magnificent! You could turn a long narrowboat around almost anywhere on this big, wide river, something that was always a problem on the Oxford Canal, where turning points are few and far between, and there was room to manoeuvre and room to breathe. Freedom! It was then that Tom realised how overgrown and shaded by trees the canal had been, how dark, almost claustrophobic in places, and how still the water was. But the river was open, light, wide, deep, flowing, and alive – beautiful, enchanting, and magical! That was where he wanted to be.

It had taken Tom six months of hard work to refit *Wandering Aengus*: new panels, new floor, new kitchen, new bathroom, new everything. The existing floor was just painted marine ply, still in good condition, but Tom wanted the best for his new home: he would cover the ply with solid oak boards. The wood for the floor, every other piece of building material, and all the equipment had to be carried or wheeled down the canal towpath and loaded by hand onto *Wandering Aengus*. The lack of space to work inside the boat meant that stacks of wood and heavy boxes containing fridges and cookers needed to be constantly moved around, especially when laying the solid oak floor. One area would be laid, then, as much stuff as possible, moved onto that while the next section was laid, and so on. He learned very quickly what it was going to be like to live in such a restricted space.

Fitting out the boat was slow, hard work, and thirsty work at that. In the evening, when the light had gone and working became too difficult, Tom would invariably wander up to the pub, The Rock of Gibraltar, and drink. Jamie had introduced him to some of the other boaters and the locals that frequented the pub. They had gradually come to accept Tom into their fold. It was the beginning of Tom's new world, different from everything he had known before – a new world with new people and new things to learn and understand. He had started to become part of it.

The Rock of Gibraltar was home to a real mixed crew. Not long ago, Tom would have been more likely to arrest some of the punters than have a drink with them, but it was different now. Tom was different, or at least he was getting to be; he was changing. The Rock of Gibraltar had an open fire, a pool table, food, company, and a quirky landlord. It was somewhere Tom could spend time away from Simon and Jacky's house in Charles Street, where he could keep out from under their feet. Tom was fully aware that he had overstayed his welcome, and the quicker he moved onto *Wandering Aengus*, the better it would be for everyone. Not that either Simon or Jacky would have said as much. They had helped him immensely, and he was mending. He was starting to see a future, one that he felt comfortable with. He was starting to be happy again. During that time, the Rock of Gibraltar was Tom's rock; the time he spent there and the company he spent it with opened his eyes to another way of life, one that would very soon be his own.

Craig was the misfit of the pub – the misfit in a pub of misfits – not liked by everyone, and certainly more than a little bit strange. Despite his oddities and being the most criminally suspect of them all, Tom was fond of him. Craig had a sense of humour; it was sharp, and he was intelligent. He was also self-sufficient, i.e., he had a job, which was something compared to most of them. He worked in a wood yard, worked hard, paid his way, and would often offer to buy a round of drinks (unlike most of the Rock of Gibraltar's clientele). Tom recognised these qualities and liked him for them. The two of them would play pool together, and on the days that Craig was not working, which were actually few and far between, he would turn up at the boat and help Tom carry materials down the towpath. They would sometimes have lunch together in the Rock of Gibraltar, usually a sandwich and coffee for Tom and three or four strong lagers for Craig. Some of the others also helped Tom out – quite a few of them, in fact – but Craig did more than most, something that Tom appreciated and respected him for. It was the boat by day and the Rock of Gibraltar by night, and drinking. There was a lot of drinking – a lot, sometimes too much. Tom took to the drinking with the same enthusiasm he had for all the other changes he was going through. Many of those nights would never be remembered, at least not by Tom Hunter.

On odd occasions, Jamie would turn up to see how *Wandering Aengus* was taking shape under its new ownership. Jamie was more of a talker than a worker, and he didn't really help out much; in fact, he didn't know one end of a screwdriver from the other, but Tom enjoyed his visits, his company, and his conversation. Jamie would make endless cups of coffee for them in *Wandering Aengus*' kitchen while Tom worked away. It was amazing for Jamie to see how much the boat had changed; he had not really thought that the amount of work Tom had done to the boat was possible. Even if he had thought it possible, he would never have had enough spare cash to make it happen, not to mention the skills, patience, and application it required. Tom gleaned from their conversations that the pub deal had been completed and Jamie had moved in. Jamie commented several times on how strange it was to have so much space after living on a boat for so many years. Tom was realising he would be experiencing the reverse, moving from big to small, but in fact, he was really moving from nothing to something. Tom was invited to visit Jamie's new pub as soon as it opened, which of course he did, and it became something he would do many times over the years ahead.

A splash, something on the edge of the water just next to where Tom was walking, made him turn and look – a fish or a water vole, maybe a water rat. It snapped him back to the present, George and Brenda. What could possibly have happened? It would come out soon enough, but in the meantime, waiting was all he could do;

with the locks still closed, he was going nowhere, at least not with *Wandering Aengus*. He reached the boat and stepped back on it. Inside, it was hot – too hot. The fire had been left burning too high. He closed the vents and damped it down, then opened the boat's side hatch and doors. It would quickly cool down. There was still a slight chill in the air outside, even with the sunshine, so it was comfortable to keep the burner ticking over. There was plenty of food in the fridge, a stack of books he had yet to read, and gigabytes of music to listen to on his laptop. Besides, he was in no hurry; the destination was not so important; it was all about the journey. It was about time to put the kettle on, relax, and enjoy the view, and what a spectacular view it was. The river Thames was now Tom's home; it had been six years since that first trip through Duke's Cut from the canal. In particular, home to Tom was the stretch of river from Henley to Lechlade, the stretch of river that has seen the least development and is bordered by fields and trees. That Duke's Cut moment changed everything.

1 small potato, chopped
2 tablespoons of butter
1 small leek, chopped
2 large carrots, finely chopped
1/2 teaspoon grated fresh ginger
1/2 stalk celery, chopped
1/4 teaspoon thyme
1/8 teaspoon nutmeg
1/4 teaspoon salt
1/2 teaspoon pepper
2 cups of milk

[Sweet Dream Soup]

Chapter 10

DREAM SOUP

'Evening, Mum, late again, I see.' Andrew said jokingly as Ali walked through the front door. 'Well, in case you're interested, tonight we have chilli con carne, rice, and a mixed leaf salad, served with fresh warm pitta bread, all prepared by the chef supreme, Andrew Smith.' Andrew had changed his surname to his mother's maiden name as soon as he turned eighteen. He never forgave his dad for walking out on them and wanted to sever all connections, including his name. He was no longer Andrew McGillivray; he was a Smith now.

'And there is a bottle of Chenin Blanc with "Ali Smith" written on it chilling in the fridge.'

Andrew was smiling proudly, blissfully unaware of what his mother had endured that day. It was now 10.30 pm, and she had been working since 6 am. Sixteen hours, sixteen long gruelling hours, sixteen grim, sad, disturbing, and distressing hours, sixteen long sickening hours.

'Thank you, Andrew,' was all Ali could manage to say. At that moment, she wanted to burst into tears and tell Andrew everything that had happened, unload the horrors she had seen, but she knew better than to do that, and she was stronger and more professional than that: she was a mother. Work was work; the horrors belonged there and could stay there; she was at home now; she could fight off those tears and put work behind her for a while. She could clear her head of the nightmare images and enjoy her own family. Could she not?

If anyone had asked her if she was hungry before she stepped through that front door, she would have said no. After what she had been through and what she had seen that day, she would have expected her appetite to have gone completely, but in fact, she had not eaten anything apart from nibbling at her sandwich in the Barley Mow with Spencer some twelve hours earlier, and the chilli did smell good.

Andrew was a good cook, which was lucky for both of them as Ali seldom had time for the domestic chores of cooking, shopping, and cleaning. She felt a bit guilty about it sometimes – most of the time, in fact – but then again, Andrew was trying to earn his keep and pay his way. He would not always be around to look after her, so why not let him get on with it? Besides, he really did seem to enjoy it. The events of the day would hit the press soon enough, and Andrew would no doubt have lots of questions, but until then, chilli con carne and Chenin Blanc sounded just what she needed.

Sitting in the kitchen, Andrew told Ali all he had been up to that day – at least the bits he wanted to tell her about. He knew her well enough not to ask her about her day; he just let her enjoy being at home and eating some of his tasty food. She tried as hard as she could, but Ali could not completely switch off; the images were etched into her mind. She had seen and experienced many traumatic things in her career, but none as bad as today; what she had witnessed at the lockkeeper's cottage was in a different league. She struggled to get the image of the children and their open eyes from her mind. Family annihilation – what drove anyone to do something like that? How could anyone destroy something so precious and so important? What was it that could have driven that man to kill his wife, children, and parents? Ali knew there would never be definitive answers; there had been textbooks written on the subject, but none of them were able to explain exactly why – only where, when, and how. In that sea of horror, that bloody landscape that the inside of the cottage had become, there was one thing – one small thing – that played on Ali's mind more than anything. The finger – why the finger?

When they had finished eating, Andrew loaded the dishwasher and put the kettle on for a hot water bottle for his mum. He knew how much she liked one of those to cuddle up with, and he could see how tired she was. He intuitively knew her day had been a tough one, having seen her like this before. Just how tough he could never have guessed, but he would find out soon enough. For now, it was important that she be warm, fed, loved, and wanted. However, Ali could not quite understand why her son was being so nice. Most boys his age didn't have the level of sensitivity he seemed to have.

Andrew had taken on being "the man of the house" since his dad walked out on them. From that moment on, it became his job to make them feel safe and happy, or so he thought. Even though he was just a young boy at the time, he had adopted the role with relish. Ali had considered counselling for him, but "being too nice" seemed like poor justification. In many ways, it had drawn Andrew and Ali even closer together; they looked out for each other. Andrew knew he was earning his keep, but he also knew it made life easier for him in return; it meant his mother was less likely to be on his case about him not having a job, or worse still, asking too many questions about what he did all day on his own. It was worth putting in some domestic effort to keep his privacy. Besides, he genuinely wanted her to be happy, he even wanted her to meet another man – someone to share her life with. Apart from the odd drink after work, Ali hadn't been involved with anyone since her husband left. Not that she wanted him back, that was something she would never even consider, but her work was demanding, Andrew had been young, and maybe she was just frightened to share her life and her world with someone else again.

She lay in bed and thought about Spencer and his family. He seemed to be a good father and husband. Ali could never see Spence doing something like Andrew's father had done to her. Spence loved his wife and his children – his suburban family. *There it was again, "family." How could anyone do such a thing? What drives someone to destroy?* Spencer, like Ali, was one of the good cops. Not in the job for ego, power, or self-importance, but to contribute to the society he lived in – the one his children were growing up in. Both he and Ali wanted to do something of value, something of worth. Pointless office jobs or careers in business would never have suited them. Despite that, they had been recognised for their work, and promotions had come to Detective Inspector and Detective Chief Inspector. Ali and Spencer liked being hands-on – doing real detective work. They didn't want to be promoted to what inevitably ended up as a desk job – a management role. This was why neither of them had applied for more senior posts that had arisen over the years. Ali knew that Spencer would be thinking about what they had both been through that day as much as she was; how could he not? He would also be hiding it from his family, trying to keep work and its nightmares well away from his loved ones. It would be as difficult for him as it was for her, but somehow they would cope.

Earlier that day, the forensics team had spent most of their time in the house; some of them were still there, working through the night. All six bodies were moved out at about 7 pm and taken to the city morgue in two unmarked police vans, the press clicking away the whole time. Ali was surprised that Andrew had not seen anything on TV, but then he was probably absorbed in his music, playing his guitar, cooking, or whatever it was he did all day. Andrew was not a news hound. The yappy dog from Day's Lock and suspected burier of the finger turned out to be micro-chipped; it was identified as belonging to Ian Gibson of Gloucester. The lockkeeper was George Gibson, and so it was assumed that Ian was his son and was also the male body upstairs in the cottage. None of the bodies had been formally identified yet, but it was expected that there would be no surprises. The dog itself was now in kennels at the local animal sanctuary; it might be re-homed with another family if it was lucky. Background checks had been completed for George and Brenda Gibson and their family. Their son Ian had married Fiona Salter, and between them they had two children, Peter and Elizabeth, five and seven years old, respectively. George and Brenda had no other relatives. Thanks to his son Ian, there would be no more "Gibsons." He had made sure of that. Ian Gibson had annihilated them.

The sofa, bedding, mattresses, and other items in due course were being wrapped, bagged, or boxed, run through forensics, and then sent to the police evidential property office for storage. The property office already had over 35 mattresses; as Ali and Spencer well knew, many murdered people seem to meet their end in their own bed or someone else's. There was no news of the man that the boater thought he had seen sitting on the bench at the lock, but there was some news about the boater. He had been checked routinely, along with all the others that were interviewed or spoken to that day. None of them had any criminal record, and the addresses they had given were all checked out, except for Thomas Hunter. Mr Hunter claimed he had been living on his boat for six years, did not have a permanent mooring as he was constantly cruising, and was, therefore, technically speaking, of no fixed abode. The Environment Agency had an address in East Oxford on file, Charles Street, where the boat license was registered. The occupation recorded for the owner was retired. Ali did not feel comfortable with the "no fixed abode" or the "retired" status and would be sending a PC round to the Charles Street address to make a few inquiries. The knife, prints, and DNA samples were all in the forensics lab being worked on by Graham Nash and his team, along with the finger.

In bed, Ali pulled the hot water bottle close to her. She could smell the freshness of the sheets. Her eyes were heavy. The many pictures still turning in her head blurred into one senseless image as sleep took control and her aching body started its shutdown for the night: sleep where she could escape and rest safely without pressure, without responsibility, without the evils of the woken world.

Alongside the entire river runs the Thames Path, a national route for walkers and cyclists.

Chapter 11

BRENDA'S FINGER

It seemed to Ali that she was back at Day's Lock before she knew it. Somehow it was as if she had never left the cottage, except that now the settee and the beds were empty, as was the shower. A chalked outline marked where Ian Gibson's lifeless body had lain. Andrew was already out when Ali left the house that morning. She had no idea where he could have gone so early, but he had made her some sandwiches that now sat, still wrapped in cling film, on her table in the makeshift office in the mobile incident room inside the lock grounds. Next to her sandwiches lay a Tupperware box containing more untouched food belonging to DI Spencer, made by his wife, Ali assumed. Spencer and Ali were on their feet in front of a white board covered in photographs, each with marker-pen writing underneath and lines drawn, mapping the pictures together. Four photographs were of white adults, all dead: George, Brenda, Ian, and Fiona Gibson. They had been formally identified by one of the other lockkeepers. Two further photographs were of the children: Peter Gibson, five years old, and Elizabeth Gibson, seven years old. Ali was drawing a line from a photograph of Brenda Gibson to one below showing a severed finger, marked "Brenda's finger."

The newspaper carried the story with black-and-white shots of stretchers being lifted into the back of an unmarked van, but the details in the "story" were scant. Ali's team had done a good job of keeping the crime scene and all of its contents very private. All the newspapers speculated on unconfirmed reports of two dead, believed to be the lockkeeper and his wife, but made no mention of any others. One of the local papers had an unflattering picture of Ali climbing out of her car with the caption, *"Detective Chief Inspector Ali Smith arrives at Day's Lock, where it is believed two bodies were found yesterday morning."* The local news journos knew Ali by name, along with many other senior detectives who at one time or another had delivered television addresses and made statements to the media. The journalists knew they were on to a big story, and like true "hacks," they would continue to hack away. It was a trait they shared with Ali and Spencer – letting go was not in their nature either, and they too would hack until they found the truth.

The Chief Superintendent had now taken control of the whole incident, which left Ali and Spencer free to do what they did best – investigate. There were no witnesses, save for the postman, who had first peered through the cottage window. He was still sedated in the hospital, but from what he had managed to say when he made the 999 call, it sounded unlikely that he saw anything more than George and Brenda holding hands on the settee, dead. Ali and Spencer would have to rely on the crime scene and whatever that could reveal, along with the photographs, forensic reports, and pathology autopsy findings from the post-mortems when they were available. The Chief Superintendent agreed with the family annihilation theory, and he was preparing a press release. A statement had to be made soon to stop the speculation. This was not a good thing to happen on his watch. He wanted matters cleared up as soon as possible, and now that they had received formal confirmation of the victims' identities, he felt comfortable calling the press conference. By midday, he was standing in front of flashing cameras and microphones. He announced that the bodies of six members of the Gibson family had been found in the cottage at Day's Lock. From the evidence available so far, they believed that Ian Gibson had killed each family member and then taken his own life. There were no known motives for the killings, but it was unlikely that anyone else would be sought in connection with the same. Furthermore, although they were awaiting post-mortem results, it was unlikely that these would reveal anything that would change the current assessment of the events leading up to the deaths.

That was the official line for the press, but behind the scenes, the investigation would continue. Even if Spencer and Ali were also convinced by the family annihilation theory, they still needed to investigate, to dig deep and try to piece together what had happened in that house, and most importantly, to try and find a motive or at least a reason. They knew there would be little chance of ever knowing precisely what happened, but with six bodies to account for, no stone would be left unturned. For Ali, the "unturned stone" that continued to niggle her was Brenda's finger. Ali left Spencer going through a stack of photographs and some of the video footage shot by the body-worn cameras.

The forensic team in the labs at police headquarters knew Ali Smith well. She respected the hard and unpleasant work they did, and in return, they too respected her. Ali had sought favours from them many times over the years, mainly asking to get results back quickly, which meant working long, unpaid hours. This time, though, it was not difficult to ask a favour: with six bodies, they knew how important their work was and would be going all out to provide answers. The forensic team was not surprised when she turned up at the lab; they had been expecting her.

'How are you getting along with the Day's Lock investigation?' she asked, after saying her hellos to everyone and being handed a mug of coffee. Graham Nash, head of forensics, answered her. Nash was in his early thirties and younger than many of the team, but he was a highly qualified expert, looked up to by everyone in the team, including the more senior members.

'Everyone has been working flat out on this one, Ali. Some of us were here half the night.' He flipped open a spiral-bound notepad full of scribbles. 'This is still a work in progress; it hasn't been written up yet and may change, so please don't quote me.' He knew that Ali would treat the information he gave accordingly and didn't need to wait for a reply. 'There's a lot, so it's difficult to know where to start.'

He picked up a transparent plastic bag containing a soiled knife. 'It has blood traces from at least three of the victims, and the pathologists think the wounds on all the bodies were consistent with a weapon similar to this. The children's bedroom only had traces of their own blood, so the knife and the killer must have been clean when those two attacks happened. The children could have been the first victims, but there is also the woman in the shower to consider. We don't know how she died yet, but we assume it was strangulation. There were not any traces for us to examine because the shower had been running for some time. However, a considerable amount of her hair was found in the bedroom where the knife was located. Presumably she struggled with her killer, but we can't say which room she was killed in – well, not yet anyway.'

Ali was taking this all in and didn't write anything down; she would remember. The head of forensics continued,

'There was a mixture of blood on the kitchen floor – an awful lot of it, as you know – and a partial footprint – a bare adult foot that had slipped in some of the blood. We were slightly puzzled by this because all the adult victims had shoes on apart from the woman in the shower, but as I said, all traces were washed from her body. The footprint could also have been made by the killer, but if that was the case, why did he then put his shoes back on before going up stairs to take his own life?'

'What about the finger?' Ali interrupted; the question was burning away at her.

'I thought you'd be interested in that particular item. I did the finger work myself,' Nash replied. He flipped over a couple of pages in his notebook. 'Here we are – third finger on the left hand. It most certainly came from the woman found downstairs and may have been hacked off while she was still alive, but I can't be certain. There was nothing under the fingernail other than what we would expect to find. However, there was one thing of note.'

The interest roused in Ali by these words was physically noticeable.

'There was a callus, some hard skin at the base of the finger, in keeping with wearing a ring for many years.'

'A wedding ring?' said Ali. The niggling in her head now at peace gave way to frustration for not making the link before.

'You are the detective, DCI Smith,' Graham Nash said, slightly cheekily. 'You tell me.'

Ali was on the phone to Spencer as soon as she left the lab.

'Spence, we need to search that house from top to bottom, down the back of every chair, every floor, and every drawer.'

'What will you be looking for, ma'am?' Spence replied.

'A ring, Spence; a wedding ring!'

History tells us that barges travelled daily from Oxford to London carrying timber, wool, foodstuffs, and livestock.

Chapter 12

CH-CH-CHANGES

They searched every crack in the house for the ring and found nothing. It could have been that she didn't wear a wedding ring. But Ali knew better than that: married for 20 years, Brenda would have definitely worn one. The bloody footprint was also added to the list of matters eating away at Ali's mind; the print turned out to be too smudged to identify who it belonged to. That was not all that bugged Ali; in addition, no other traces of blood (other than his own) were found on Ian Gibson or in the room he killed himself in. With the amount of carnage in the kitchen and multiple traces of blood found on the knife, the killer should have been soaked in blood from all the victims.

Delving into the family history and relationships had not revealed any problems or concerns. A normal, happy, loving family – kids that were getting along well at school, neighbours that all liked them, never known to have big arguments, no financial difficulties, no family history of mental illness, loving parents and grandparents – so why would Ian suddenly decide to savagely murder them? It made no sense, and Ali didn't like things that didn't make sense.

Four days after the postman made the 999 call, the locks were finally re-opened, and boats were once again moving up and down the river. Meanwhile, the lockkeeper's cottage would remain sealed off for some months to come. The other lockkeepers and boaters, including Tom, were all shocked by the news of what had happened to the Gibsons at the hands of their son. No one could understand it. Brenda and George were a lovely couple, and, liked by everyone, they would be sadly missed on the river. The other lockkeepers placed wreaths of flowers on their locks with words of remembrance for the couple and their extended family.

Tom had continued upriver to the Abingdon boatyard as planned. While his boat was being serviced, he was getting on with sprucing up some of the exterior paintwork in need of attention following another hard winter. Simon told him that the police had visited the house on Charles Street and asked lots of questions, but nothing had come of it. Tom was not bothered; he didn't have any secrets, and there was nothing they could find out that would upset Tom. It was probably known by now that he had served in the Metropolitan Police Service, and his police records would have been checked. No doubt his private annual personal development reviews would have been studied as well. There would not have been anything of interest in those documents, or would there? Tom thought DI Spencer would have drawn the conclusion that Tom's policing career was "average." Even Tom could see that now. He had been averaging in everything – his work, his marriage, his social life, even the books he read and the music he listened to. But that had finally changed. Six years of living alone on *Wandering Aengus* had changed him for the better. He was no longer "average"; he was Tom Hunter, a journeyman, traveller, and boater. Over the years on the boat, especially in the early months, he had spent lengthy periods of time, sometimes weeks alone, moored up at isolated spots along the river. There was no shortage of space, with places offering solitude. He had soon realised that throughout his life he had very rarely been alone – not completely alone, but on the river it was easy to disappear; you could withdraw from the world almost completely. During those reclusive times, Tom got to know himself – his real self. All alone, there was no need to adapt his behaviour for other people, no one to question or be questioned by, and no one to lie to or be lied to, except himself. Eventually, all the pretences and self-delusions and all the artificial appeasements to others disappeared. What happens when you are alone for so long, Tom realised, that you become your true self; there is no one else to be or any reason not to be anyone but yourself. The real Tom Hunter was beginning to emerge.

It was not just the self-imposed "isolation therapy" that had changed Tom. It was the river as well – the river and everything about it. He had become closer and far more knowledgeable about nature and the world around him than he had ever been. He had seen fields changing through the seasons – the small daily changes, nuances, and the dramatic ones – as crops would shoot, turn green, then yellow, be harvested, and then return to soil once again. He had seen stars and moons in a way that he had never known before. On the warm summer evenings, he would sometimes lie on the roof of *Wandering Aengus* for hours, staring at the endless size, depth, and wonder of the dark star-studded sky – the Big Dipper, Betelgeuse in Orion's constellation, the vastness of the Milky Way, and the endless stars and planets that make up the solar system. The thoughts those skies and planets had provoked. He had seen shooting stars by the dozen; before his boat days, he had never seen even one. He had seen wildlife that he didn't even know existed: red deer, roe deer, muntjacs, foxes, badgers, voles, moles, squirrels, mice, and rats, all living on the same land and the same river as him, living as they had done for hundreds, if not thousands, of years. Birds that he had never seen in London: cormorants, herons, vultures, falcons, hawks, owls, magnificent red kites, and the beautiful, magical kingfishers. On more than one occasion, he had sat looking through the side hatch, watching kingfishers dive for fish, catch them, eat them, and then dive again. Not many people could say they had seen that. Kingfishers, to most, are just a glint of turquoise blue that disappears from the corner of the eye, never motionless long enough to be properly seen. Then there were the ducks that would sometimes wake him up as they pecked at the algae from the hull of *Wandering Aengus*. The river was also teeming with fish. On stretches of really clear water, they could be seen swimming and glinting in the sun: barbel, chub, carp, flounder, grayling, mullet, gudgeon, minnow, perch, pike, roach, rudd, eel, tench, stickleback, the big and the small, the fat and the thin, all of them. He just had to relax, sit still for a long time, and watch. One of the things Tom had been most impressed with was seeing grass snakes swim across the river, zigzagging their way with their green bodies, black spots, and black bars, dull on the land but sparkling and vibrant when wet, their pointed faces held up above the surface. Tom didn't know that grass snakes could swim or what one even looked like until the boat showed him.

The Thames had always been a feature in Tom's life. He was born close to the stretch that runs through Brentford and Chiswick, not far from his first posting at Hammersmith police station. Now it flowed all around him and underneath him. It flowed fast; it flowed slowly. It was high and it was low, but always it flowed; it never stopped, not for anything – even murder. Within a few weeks, life slowly returned to normal on the river. For many things, it had never changed and never would. All the members of the Gibson family were buried on the same day, in the same graveyard at a small church to the north of Oxford, not far from the canal. Pictures of the funeral were published in all the newspapers. Hundreds of mourners, including all the lockkeepers and boaters, went along to pay their respects. Tom decided not to go; he had not known George and Brenda that well and thought it should be a private matter. He didn't like funerals much anyway, and he had always avoided them. Private? That's what he thought until he read the paper – it was one of the most public funerals Oxford had ever seen, thanks to Ian Gibson's decision to slaughter his whole family.

The Oxford Mail had covered the Day's Lock story from day one and had their photographers and reporters continually on the case. One hack had even tried to interview Tom on the day of the murders, but he had let them know very clearly that he didn't want to be bothered. The funeral was now the lead story, with a large photo taking up most of the front page. Some of the mourners looked familiar to Tom, and he recognised boaters from the canal. He was not sure, but it also looked like Jamie in the background with a couple of regulars from the Rock of Gibraltar. He definitely recognised the detective inspector that had been to his boat on the day of the murders, in the front right of the photo, standing next to a woman whom Tom didn't know but could guess was another police officer. Unlike everyone else, the two were not looking towards the coffins but were instead scanning the crowd. For DI Spencer Davis and DCI Ali Smith, this was not just a funeral, it was part of their investigation. For them, this was far from over.

Deep into that darkness peering, long I stood there, wondering, fearing, doubting, dreaming dreams no mortal ever dared to dream before.

[EDGAR ALLAN POE – "The Reven"]

Chapter 13

NECKLACE OF RINGS

That night, he was drunk – very drunk. He laughed loudly, very loudly. The few people there who knew him thought he was behaving strangely, even for him. He stumbled out of the door of the Rock of Gibraltar and into a black night. A fat yellow moon was hanging low in the sky, and a few stars were the only lights. Somewhere in the distant woods, an owl hooted. He looked up at the expanse of dark sky and stared into the moon. Putting his hand inside his shirt, he touched the three gold rings hung around his neck on a golden chain. He stopped laughing and stood up straight; his head cleared, his fingers tingled, and his mind became pure clarity. He was sober again. He could smell the soil in the distant fields. He could hear the movement of the trees and the rustling of their leaves. He could taste the river, the darkness, and feel the night. What was left of the night? What would it bring? What fun was there to be had out there? What could we do?

Retail therapy: shopping with the primary purpose of improving one's mood or disposition.

Chapter 14

SHOPPING SPREE

It was early morning. Ali had left home for work, taking Andrew along with her. He wanted to be dropped off in the city centre to do some shopping in the covered market. In the back of his notebook was a shopping list, one of many. There were, according to Andrew, two types of people: those that make lists and those that don't. Andrew was a list maker: menus, things to do, things to buy, and things to sell. Another chilly morning enticed him to turn the collar of his coat up and pull a woollen hat out of his shoulder bag. A long day stretched out before him, meaning that there was plenty of time to do other things he had in mind before he visited the covered market – things he did almost habitually but told no one about.

There was a blast of hot air from above as he stepped through the entrance of Debenhams, the department store on George St. He took off his hat and placed it back in the bag, turned his collar down, and ran his fingers through his hair to make himself appear more presentable. Surprisingly, for the time of day, there were already several customers milling around the store. Andrew knew the layout of each department like the back of his hand, as he did many of the other large and small shops in Oxford. Over a series of visits to each, he carefully mapped where every entrance and exit was situated, the placement of cameras, security staff, and the goods that were available. Each of these details he wrote up in his notebook, along with neatly drawn plans showing items of interest. First up this morning was the department store, and today, he felt, was his lucky day. In the cosmetics section, girls with white jackets and smart outfits were busy arranging goods on shelves, refilling display cabinets, and checking paperwork. Yes, today was the day; he could feel it in his bones. He stopped by a cabinet full of men's aftershave and eau de cologne, acting as if he were browsing the products as he carefully looked from side to side and in the mirror above the display. A few yards from where he was standing, he could see the door of the cabinet he was interested in. Its door was slightly ajar while restocking was in progress. Yes, this was the one he was interested in, alright! His heart started to beat faster, and he felt the adrenaline surging through his body. His hands tingled with expectation. There was no one looking, and he knew where the store cameras were. Moving quickly, brushing past the open cabinet marked "Chanel," he skillfully and almost unnoticeably scooped three small boxes into his bag. Each box contained a 15-ml bottle of Chanel No. 5 perfume. The rush of excitement he felt as he headed for the exit was one he had felt many times before. As he became more skilled in his craft and more confident, the items he chose became more expensive, and the buzz became greater. Andrew calculated that the three bottles retailed at £138 each, which meant he could definitely get at least £200-250 for them on eBay; maybe he would keep one as a present for someone. On his way out of the store, he passed through the stationery section, where a Montblanc Meisterstuck Classique ballpoint pen priced at £265 caught his eye. He smiled, made a mental note, and continued to the exit.

Directly opposite the department store was Waterstones, the large bookshop sitting on the corner of Cornmarket Street and the end of Broad Street. Andrew didn't bother to put his hat back on as he crossed the road and entered the bookshop. He made his way up to the coffee shop on the first floor, picked up a newspaper that was lying on one of the tables, and treated himself to a medium latte. The front page of the newspaper carried the headline,

"FUNERAL FOR THE DAY'S LOCK FAMILY DRAWS CROWDS." It sent a shiver down Andrew's spine. He knew this was the case his mother was working on – the reason why she was home so late every night, the reason why she was at work most weekends, the reason why he could hear her walking up and down across her bedroom floor long after she had gone upstairs to sleep. Two victims were named George and Brenda Gibson, the lockkeeper, and his wife. They had been buried along with members of their extended family, including two grandchildren.

Andrew stared blankly at the newspaper, realising clearly for the first time that whatever had occurred at Day's Lock, his mother would have seen the aftermath. She would have seen the dead bodies and what had been done to them. She must have been working with and living with those images since it happened. He drank the last of his latte and sat, feeling helpless. There was nothing he could do to ease the burden his mother was now carrying, except maybe help out at home as much as possible and make sure she ate well and kept her strength up. Whenever he managed to get her to sit down for a meal, he would make sure it was a good one – always special. Good food costs money, but fortunately for Andrew, he knew exactly how to get plenty of it. There was ample room in his bag for a few books as well as food shopping, and besides, books always sold well on eBay. £10 here and £5 there – it all added up. The bookshop was a doddle, like taking candy from a baby, easier than scrumping apples from an orchard. Books practically jumped off the shelves into his bag.

Andrew decided there was time for one more shop before he headed to the covered market. Robert Dyas, the hardware store, was always good for a bit of lifting, and he needed some bin liners anyway. Once inside, he spotted Wi-Fi signal boosters, two at £33.50 each. They would also sell well and fit comfortably in the bag next to the two books. He paid for the bin bags, thanked the shop assistant, and left.

In the covered market, a revolving display of Zippo cigarette lighters in the shoe repairers caught his eye – £38 each. Normally the revolving glass display would have been locked, but he noticed that today, for some reason, it was slightly open. This really was his lucky day. Removing the house key from his key ring, he entered the shop. This was getting his excitement going again – the thrill. He had never been in this shop before, so it was new ground, fresh territory. It was not even on the list of shops he had mapped out, but it was small. He could handle it, and the not knowing made the buzz greater and more intense. A man in a brown work coat and grubby hands took the key and looked at it, holding it up above him like a jeweller would do a diamond, then said it would be £5 to cut one, or two for £8. Andrew asked for two and watched the man slide his protective goggles over his eyes, then start to cut the first key. By the time he had started the second, Andrew's heartbeat had doubled, and he had three Zippos in his bag.

The back end of the covered market was the part he loved best. Full of butchers, greengrocers, fishmongers, shops selling cheeses, and other specialist food stores with homemade pastas and pies. This is what he called "shopping," buying good, fresh food and good ingredients to cook with. He never stole from the food shops; he respected them too much. There was plenty of room in his bag for a couple of pieces of fresh line-caught tuna and an assortment of fresh vegetables. All he needed now was a bottle of white wine, and Ali would be having a quality fish supper.

Early afternoon, on the bus on his way home, Andrew took his notebook out of his shoulder bag and turned to a section marked "Duke's Shopping Sprees." This section of the notebook contained about thirty lists, similar to the one he was about to pencil in.

<u>Debenhams</u>
Chanel No 5, 15-ml bottle - 3 @ £138.00

<u>Waterstones</u>
Where the Wild Things Are, Maurice Sendak (Hardback) - £12.99
Oxford English Dictionary (Hardback) - £27.00

```
Robert Dyas:
Wi-Fi boosters - 4 @ £33.50

Timpson's
Zippo lighters - 3 @ £38.00
```

That gave him a grand total of £701.99, less the £8.00 for the key cutting, a necessary expense. That would be at least a £300 to £400 return when sold on eBay. Not bad for a morning's work – not bad at all.

In hat of antique shape and cloak of grey
Crossing the stripling Thames at Bab-lock-hithe
Trailing in the cool stream their fingers wet
As the slow punt swings round.

[MATTHEW ARNOLD – "The Scholar Gipsy"]

Chapter 15

BABLOCK HYTHE

Mid-June, and the weathermen had it right for once: the elusive summer was finally arriving. The caravan park next to the Ferryman Pub at Bablock Hythe, home to a small contingent of full-time residents, was primarily comprised of holiday homes. Hundreds of caravans stretched downstream from the pub along the riverbank. Until sometime in the 1970s, the pub had been accessible by a chain ferry from the village of Eaton on the other side of the river; now out of use, the pub relied on the trade from the caravan park. *Wandering Aengus* had passed by the caravans and moored at the pub many times, with Tom at the rudder, before that, under Jamie's captainship. Business had been tough in recent years for the park and pub, but this summer, the promise of sunshine had brought the visitors back in their droves. Most of the caravans were privately owned and let out to friends and family to help subsidise the costs. It was in the large, light-green, double-width caravan at the furthest point from the pub along the riverbank that the Daltrey family were holidaying for two weeks that June. They had paid more than they intended to, but the caravan came with the use of a small, two-berth cabin cruiser moored just outside.

Boating, countryside, peace, good weather, privacy, and a pub within five minutes' walk. All of that, coupled with the fact that the fishing season had just started, made it feel like heaven for Roger Daltrey and his wife Shirley. Their family of four children loved it too. There was something for each of them, and with fields or woods on three sides of the site and the river on the other, it meant there were no busy roads that Roger and Shirley needed to worry about. The three young boys could happily and safely ride around on bicycles, and Jenny, the daughter and youngest child at just three and a half, was content with feeding the ducks, helping her mum in the caravan, and playing with her toys. The children all knew that they had to be careful not to go too near the river edge.

'Shangri-La' was the name of their caravan. It may have been a cliché, but for Roger and Shirley, it would be their Shangri-La for two weeks. Besides, it also happened to be the title of Roger's favourite song by the Kinks, and, much to Shirley's annoyance, he had been singing it non-stop since they arrived three days ago. The Ray Davis song painted a picture of English suburbia and a way of life that had now long since gone, but for two weeks, "Shangri-La" at Bablock Hythe would bring that simple past alive again. Two self-catering, carefree weeks in a place that time had forgotten. Even the pub seemed like something from another era. When the chain ferry broke, Bablock Hythe had not just been cut off from Oxford; it was cut off from the rest of the world. Time seemed to have stopped there and then, somewhere in the 1970s.

Roger sat on the back of the boat, also named Shangri-La after the caravan. He opened a cold bottle of beer and cast his fishing line into the Thames. The experts said that the river was the cleanest it had been for two hundred years, and it was clearly teeming with fish. Shirley and her daughter were preparing a salad with hard-boiled eggs, cold meats, and pickles for the evening tea – a 1970s salad. It was a balmy evening, and Shirley didn't want to have the oven on, making the caravan uncomfortably hot. They would eat in the open on Shangri-La's decked veranda, as it was certainly warm enough. The three boys were off cycling around the site and playing in the small strip of woodland, which to them was a forest. They were under strict orders to be back by 5:30 pm at the latest.

Suddenly, Roger's float disappeared under the water, and the line became taught. He let out a yelp of excitement, knocking his beer over in the process. It took him about five minutes to bring in the large perch without breaking his line. It was the biggest fish he had ever caught. He reached into his pocket for his mobile phone to take a photograph. Without that as evidence, he would be accused of exaggerating, as most fishermen are. What a beautiful specimen! Its wet silver scales glinted in the afternoon sun as it writhed around on the deck of the boat; after a while, it seemed to give up and lay there with its gills open and pink on the inside, as if it were panting, gasping for air, gasping for water. Roger carefully removed the hook from the fish's bottom lip and gently placed it in the keepnet hanging over the side of the boat. The boys could have a look when they got back from playing, and then he would release it again into the river where it belonged. In the water, it was a proud, strong creature and, in control, the master of its environment. On the back of the boat in the sunshine. It was like… well, a fish out of water.

Oxfordshire, the river, the sunshine – what more could anyone want? Roger and Shirley had never been ones for airports and foreign holidays. It was too expensive, and with the four kids, the logistics of foreign travel were far too complicated to make it an enjoyable option for a holiday. To the Daltreys, travelling abroad was just a lot of hard work and money. They hadn't been abroad since their first son was born and didn't miss it. When they were dating, they went for a week of self-catering in Crete. Shirley's mum hadn't liked them going there alone and asked Shirley what the sleeping arrangements were. Shirley did what all young people in those circumstances do: she lied. Shirley's mum, like all mums in that situation, knew she was lying, but at least she felt she had gone through her parental motions. Years before, Shirley's mum had lied to her own mother when she went camping in the Lake

District for a week with the young builder, who would later become her husband and Shirley's father.

Catching that perch was a moment much appreciated and enjoyed by Roger. However, it would have been even more special to him had he known that it was to be the last fish he would ever catch. It would also be the last sunshine to be seen all week, as dark, ominous-looking rainclouds were gathering on the horizon when he packed up his fishing gear. The weathermen had not got it right after all. The three young brothers would finish their last ever bicycle ride and be back at the caravan by 5.30 pm, as promised. They would see the last fish their dad had caught. Shirley and Jenny would prepare the last supper the Daltrey family would ever eat on the last evening they would ever spend together. For that night, they would all be killed – slaughtered in Shangri-La.

And when white moths were on the wing,
And moth-like stars were flickering out,
I dropped the berry in a stream
And caught a little silver trout.

[W B YEATS – "The Song of Wandering Aengus"]

Chapter 16

TOO MUCH BLOOD

By the time DCI Ali Smith and DI Spencer Davis arrived at the Bablock Hythe Caravan Park, both of the Shangri-Las, the caravan and boat had been sealed off with police incident tape. Crime Scene Investigation officers were milling around, wearing their white protective CSI suits. The chief superintendent was also there in full uniform, standing perfectly still with a look on his face that neither Ali nor Spencer had seen on him before. It was a look of deep shock – shock and horror.

'We just got the call, sir,' Ali said as she and Spencer approached the superintendent. He didn't respond.

'We came straight here,' Spencer added.

'In case you don't know, detectives, we have another murdered family on our hands – two adults and four children.' The superintendent's voice was tinged with anger. Two families had now been annihilated on his watch, and this was not looking good for him or the force.

'I spoke to CSI on the way here with DI Spencer, sir,' said Ali carefully.

'They filled us in on some of the details. They told us about the...'

Before she could finish, the chief superintendent interrupted with the same anger in his voice and completed the sentence for her.' ...The finger! The bloody finger! And don't tell me you were right about Day's Lock, Detective Chief Inspector Smith.' The Chief Super managed to bring his voice under control. 'There is no need to tell me – it's now blatantly obvious, don't you think?' Still not happy, he continued, 'I have told everyone here this morning that not one single sniff of this or any other connection to the Day's Lock family deaths is to get out. I will personally make sure that, if it does, the person responsible will never work for any force ever again! I don't need to tell you that if the public gets wind of this, there will be panic, not to mention what would happen if it got into the hands of the press. We can't afford for any of that noise to clutter up the investigation at this stage. I want whoever is responsible for this identified, caught, and locked up.' He looked at the two detectives, who were not moving. 'Well? What are you standing around talking to me for? Start doing what you are paid to do. Detect!' Adding as they went to move away, 'And when you find anything that moves this investigation forward, I want to know immediately, and I mean immediately. Understood?'

Spencer and Ali said, 'Yes, sir!' in unison as they headed towards the CSI van to get suited up.

As bloody as it was at Day's Lock, the various murders had taken place in separate rooms, helping to thin out the horror. In the confined space of the caravan at Bablock Hythe, the blood was everywhere – walls, ceilings, furniture, windows, doors, and floors – gallons of it. Shangri-La was wet and sticky wherever they trod; its carpet was sodden with the blood of six family members. The horror was condensed.

Inside the caravan, the smell of festering blood and death was overwhelming. This time no effort had been made by the killer to make it seem as if one of the victims had been responsible, to appear like a classic family annihilation as they had at Day's Lock. This was the work of a cold, calculated killer who wanted everyone to know what he was doing: taunting the police to work out how he had been able to commit these grotesque murders without being seen or heard.

Each member of the Daltrey family had suffered multiple knife wounds – stabs, cuts, and slashes – far more than were needed to kill them, far more frenzied than those at Day's Lock. The killer had escalated his level of violence to a new high, or a new disgusting low. According to the pathologist's first guess, each of the Daltreys' lives ended sometime between 3 am and 4 am. *"The dead of night,"* Ali thought to herself.

The victims had been initially stabbed in their respective bedrooms, then dragged, still alive, into the living room area; he had sat them in the armchairs facing the television before he repeatedly stabbed, slashed, cut, and hacked away at them. The little girl's body, the daughter, lay face down with her head propped up on a cushion, now soaked with her blood, as if she too were engrossed in the TV. The two adults had been placed to look as if they were holding hands in the same way that George and Brenda's bodies were at Day's Lock. Like Brenda, Shirley, the dead woman now in front of Ali, also had her wedding ring finger missing.

'Any sign of the ring or the finger?' Ali asked one of the CSIs.

'Not yet, ma'am; we are still looking for them.' It was the reply she was expecting.

'He's collecting them, Spence; he's collecting wedding rings,' Ali's voice showed her contempt, 'like bloody souvenirs! What is it to him? Does it represent the mother? Is it about his mother? Is it something that relates to his own family life? Or is it for some other reason, or is it for no reason at all? He just likes them.'

'We don't know that it is a 'he' yet, ma'am,' Spencer replied.

'Yes, we do, Spencer,' she said. 'No woman would do this, not to a family.'

The wooden steps outside the front door to Shangri-La were now a deep, dark red. A mixture of Daltrey family blood had unavoidably been picked up on the CSI team's overshoes and trodden into the wood. The soles of Ali's and Spencer's overshoes were also red when they stepped out of Shangri-La. Ali's senses were once again heightened by the murder scene. Everything was sharper, clearer, and more vibrant. She could smell bacon frying in the distance – another family having breakfast somewhere on the site, unaware of the slaughter that had taken place so near to them in a caravan just like theirs. She could hear the river flowing past Bablock Hythe, on its way down to Eynsham Lock, to Oxford and beyond, through Day's and all the other locks, on its way to the sea. She could hear the rain dripping from the leaves of the surrounding trees. Standing outside the caravan in silence, breathing deeply, she felt all of her senses peak. Without asking, Spencer took two cigarettes out of his packet of Marlboros and handed one to Ali. She smelt the lighter fluid and heard the flint wheel strike as Spencer flipped open his Zippo and lit the cigarettes, then the burning smell of the tobacco and the taste of the smoke and nicotine. The senses heightened, but no sense could be made of any of it. No sense at all.

The early promise of a good summer had disappeared. It had rained almost constantly overnight. The pounding, relentless sound of the heavy rain that fell on the thin roofs of the caravans during that dark, moonless night explained why none of the other residents had heard or seen anything. The young head of forensics, Graham Nash, who had also arrived at the scene, had a theory. From what he could see, there was nothing to indicate that a struggle had taken place inside the caravan, and none of the victims showed signs of any injury that could have been caused when trying to defend themselves. None of them had put up a fight. Clearly, they hadn't been in a position to do so – either unconscious or conscious – and were unable to move.

As a medical student, Nash had travelled around Thailand. He remembered hearing about several incidents where tourists, travelling in first-class compartments on trains in the north of the country, had been robbed. The perpetrators had gained entry to the compartments at night by pumping an anaesthetic gas under the door, paralysing the occupants. The door to the compartment was then kicked in, and the thieves took their time to find and steal everything of value. The tourists had reported that, although they were acutely aware of what was going on, they were unable to move or make a sound to raise the alarm. They were completely frozen, completely helpless. If the killer had done that at Bablock Hythe, he would have been able to break into Shangri-La and take his time to do whatever he wanted. The Daltrey family may well have been watching the whole thing, unable to resist and helpless to do anything about it as the horror unfolded, screaming in silence.

Graham continued talking, as was his way, and added that coincidentally, Mae Sariang, a small town in northern Thailand near the Burmese border, was thought to be British author James Hilton's inspiration for the fictional location in his 1933 novel Lost Horizon; it was the real "Shangri-La." Graham had often tried to impress Ali with his broad general knowledge, trying to show how intelligent he was. It was his way of flirting with her, and it seemed to him to have worked on some occasions. This time, however, with six dead bodies lying in a blood-soaked caravan just a few feet away from where they stood, his comments were ill-timed, poorly judged, and in very bad taste. This time, he had not impressed her.

'Can the lab find out if your gas theory is right, Mr Nash?' Ali quickly asked before Graham could say anything else out of place.

'Not sure. really, but we can try. There may be some traces absorbed by the blood, and we've got plenty…' He stopped short, realising he was about to make another inappropriate remark. Ali realised that as the forensic investigators and pathologists spent a considerable amount of their working lives dissecting and examining human remains, Graham Nash had become immune to the sight of slaughter, of blood, and of bodies. Maybe this was how she needed to become: immune, desensitised, not to let the horror cloud the facts and hinder the investigation. She knew she would never be able to be as removed and unaffected as Graham seemed to be; she would never stop feeling.

An unmarked police van pulled up close to the caravan, and from the back doors jumped Murphy, the sniffer dog. He had another finger to sniff out, with a biscuit as a treat if he did well. He was ready for the challenge. With his nose twitching, head up, head down, up and down, Murphy sniffed around the van and then seemed to find something of interest and almost buried his nose in the ground. Slowly, he sniffed his way through the wet grass and down to the boat moored up on the bank. Ali and Spencer followed and climbed on board. Spencer felt a familiar movement under his feet, the same balance sensation he had when he stepped onto Tom's boat after the Day's Lock killings, but this time, the small fibreglass cabin cruiser moved much more under his and Ali's weight than the steel-hulled *Wandering Aengus* had. In his teens, Spencer had done a bit of fishing. Occasionally, when on holiday, he still did if the opportunity arose. It didn't take long for him to spot the keepnet hanging over the back of the boat and the small traces of bait and fish scales stuck to the deck – even the overnight downpour had not managed to wash them away completely. Then he noticed the staining on the thin rope tying the keepnet onto the cleat, a brownish colour.

Spencer shouted over to the CSIs. 'Can someone get a couple of uniforms to go along the banks, speak to the fishermen, and ask them if they saw anything? There may have been a few of them night fishing.'

'Do you really think there would have been people out night fishing in all that rain?' Ali asked, believing it would be very unlikely.

'Anglers are a rare breed, ma'am; fanatics many of them. On the first night of the fishing season, they would have been out there for sure, come rain or shine. It wouldn't surprise me if one of them did this.' He nodded towards the caravan, half smiling to himself; he obviously found it amusing that a fanatical fisherman could have turned killer. 'And can one of you get a sample of this?' He pointed at where the keepnet was tied as he shouted to the forensics team.

'What have you seen, Spencer? What is it?' asked Ali.

'It looks like the keepnet rope has been soaked with something, maybe blood.' He nodded towards the back of the boat in case Ali didn't know what a keepnet was. 'The cleat and its cover may have stopped the rain from washing it all away. It could just be fish blood, but it's worth getting forensics to have a look.'

'If it's human and not fish blood, what would it be doing here?' Ali asked. Spencer knew she was thinking aloud and didn't try to answer. Ali continued, 'The killer had to get here, and like at Day's Lock, no one seemed to have seen or heard anything. No one unusual was seen coming or going, no witnesses.' She stopped speaking and locked herself in her thoughts. A narrowboat went past them heading upriver, creating a strong wake and rocking the boat under Ali's and Spencer's feet so much that they had to cling on to each other for balance.

'This is no time for romance,' Spencer remarked, smiling. Ali smiled back and appreciated what Spencer was trying to do – trying to help her cope with it all better than she thought she was.

'Shall we get back on dry land, ma'am?' He asked, taking Ali's hand and helping her back onto the bank, secretly as keen to get off as she was.

'Spence, what connects these two sets of murders?' She asked once they were both safely off the boat and back on their land-legs.

'Well, plenty of things, as far as I can see: the victims were families; a knife or sharp blade was used on each occasion; they both occurred during the early hours of the morning and both were extremely bloody; oh, and the missing fingers.' He ran through the connections he could see.

'They are all similarities, Spence, but what "physically" connects them is in front of us – the river Thames.'

Spencer nodded in thoughtful silence before responding. If the river connected the murder sites, so too did a person with a boat who knew the river well enough to travel at night. He knew one person who fit the bill.

'I think we should get that boater from Day's in for some further questioning, ma'am, Tom Hunter.'

Ali straightened up and breathed deeply; there was an intense look in her eye. 'Let's do it, Spence. While we're at it, let's get in touch with all the others we spoke to at Day's Lock. Let's start again at the beginning.'

Preserve life
Preserve scene
Secure evidence
Identify victims
Identify suspects

[From the "Murder Investigations Manual"]

Chapter 17

NECESSITY

The warm smell of something slow roasting was the first thing Ali noticed when she finally arrived home at about 10 pm. The Shangri-La killings had consumed her whole day and would consume the days ahead; but right here, right now, she needed some down time. Andrew could tell the kind of day his mum had been through, and, not for the first time, he knew not to ask about it. He had been busy cooking the evening meal and preparing everything, so the only thing Ali had to do when she eventually got home from whatever hard day she'd had was relax. Andrew knew she would need to rest, eat, and take her mind off any unpleasantness she had endured during her day at work. It was nearly always the same when she got back so late; it invariably signified that her day had been grim.
'Leg of lamb, slow-roasted, with all the trimmings. I even made my own mint sauce, Mum.'

It was comforting for Ali to hear Andrew's cheerful voice; he sounded happy, and he sounded like family. Despite all the horrors of the day, she was actually starving.

The two of them sat at a small dinner table at one end of the living room with the Gotan Project playing quietly on the stereo. Andrew had a very eclectic taste in music, especially for someone so young, liking everything from jazz to classical and all flavours in between. A lot of his musical tastes had been influenced by his sister Pattie when she was still living at home. He considered the Gotan Project, with its mixture of French, Argentinean, and Swiss musicians, to go well with a classic English roast. The lamb was cooked perfectly and fell from the bone. Andrew had done a good job.

'Thank you for this, Andrew; what would I do without you?' Ali asked before tasting her first mouthful of food. As good as it tasted and as nice as it was to arrive home to such a welcome, she could not help wondering how Andrew could make the few pounds a week she gave him for shopping go so far. She wanted to question him about it, but tonight was not the time. She had been through too much already and asked more than enough questions for one day.

'It's nothing, Mum,' he replied. 'It's just a classic English dish, a bit of roast lamb.' He cut himself a large slice of meat, filled two wine glasses with Rioja, and they both started to eat. Andrew was the first to break the initial silence that can sometimes accompany the eating of good food.

'We've got a postcard from Pattie today, Mum; I'll get it for you when we've finished eating.' Now was the time to relax and talk about happy things. Now was family time, and a card from Pattie made it feel a little like it did when all three of them lived in the house, a little as if Pattie was back home with them.

'She says the summer has finally arrived in Oslo, and she has been to the beach a couple of times, but the water is still too cold to swim.' Pattie lived near the centre of Oslo but not far from the beach. Nowhere in Oslo is far from the beach. Andrew laughed at his sister's comment about the cold water. 'She was always a wimp! She says that she is really looking forward to us going over there in August.'

Ali was also looking forward to visiting her daughter. In fact, she was looking forward to going anywhere, just getting as far away from work, murders, and dead bodies as she could. She didn't say anything to Andrew, but she was already wondering if she would get any free time this year – unless their killer had been caught. Two weeks' holiday in Norway was looking unlikelier by the day.

'Yes, it would be great to see Pattie,' she said. 'I hope you'll still be able to go. You may have a job by then, and they might not let you have the time off.' She smiled as she spoke, knowing that mentioning "work" could touch a nerve with Andrew, and she didn't want the evening to be spoiled.

'Mum, even if I do get a job, I'm sure I can tell them I've already arranged a holiday. I don't want to miss the trip. It will be really nice to see Pattie, and besides, I'm interested in finding out what Norway is really like. Do you think it's just elk and reindeer?'

They both laughed. It was Ali's first genuine bit of laughter, the first bit of happiness, and the first bit of normality that she had felt all day.

After the meal, Andrew went and got the postcard from the kitchen, where he had pinned it to a small, framed corkboard on the wall, next to some recipes he had cut from magazines. Pattie's card had a Norwegian flag in the top left corner and a drawing of a ferocious Viking helmet. Underneath, in an old, supposedly Viking, typeface, it read "Oslo, Norway." Ali looked at Patricia's neat handwriting and read the card silently. As she read, she could not stop herself from remembering how worried both she and Andrew had been the year before when they first got the news of the car bomb explosion in Oslo. It was Saturday, 22nd July, and Ali and Andrew were on their way to the Truck Music Festival, just outside Oxford. It was not something they usually did together as mother and son, but Andrew desperately wanted to see the DB Band play – a band formed by one of the members of his favourite band, Supergrass – after they split up. Patricia had got him into Supergrass, and he had been a fan ever since. He was devastated when the "Grass" announced their split, but over the moon when he heard that the DB Band had risen from their ashes. Ali had agreed to go to the festival with him and was actually really looking forward to it. That was until they pulled into the festival site car park and the car radio announced the Oslo bombing. Ali and Andrew spent the next couple of hours desperately trying to contact Patricia to check that she was OK. More news trickled in; at first, it said there were about eight dead and over two hundred injured. The bomb was in Regjeringskvartalet, the executive government quarter, which Ali knew, from a previous visit to Patricia in Oslo, was just a street or two away from Pattie's apartment.

Ali and Andrew still hadn't managed to contact Patricia when news of a second attack at a summer camp on the island of Utøya came in over the radio. Eventually Ali's phone rang, and it was Patricia calling from Norway. She was at the beach and had been oblivious to everything that had happened in the city. News of the bombing and the shootings on Utøya had spread fast in Oslo, and it didn't take too long to reach the beach. When Pattie did hear the news, she knew that if her mother had heard about it, she would be worried sick. Pattie had dug her phone out of the bottom of her beach bag and turned it on. Seeing all of her mother's missed calls, she rang her right away. Ali could clearly remember the relief she had felt upon receiving that call. Andrew and his mum never did get to see the DB Band; by then it was too late.

Sixty-nine were killed at Utøya, most of them between seventeen and twenty years old, Andrew's age. Some shot in the back as they ran trying to escape, others picked off in the freezing water as they desperately tried to swim for safety. One survivor had described the shootings he witnessed on the island by saying they had not been like the movies or on TV where you hear screaming and see blood – what he remembered was three people running, the cracks of shots being fired, but no blood, no screams, only silence as their lifeless bodies fell to the ground. A gunman dressed in a home-made police uniform and showing false identification had gained access to the island where a Labour Party summer camp was being held. He then opened fire with automatic weapons. It was the deadliest attack in Norway since World War II. The Norwegian police arrested Anders Behring Breivik, who was still on Utøya. Breivik, a 32-year-old Norwegian right-wing extremist, was charged with both of the attacks – the bombing in Oslo and the shootings on the island. Nine months later, when the main court trial began, as at all his remand hearings, Breivik admitted to having carried out both attacks but denied criminal guilt. He claimed the defence of "necessity." Ali wondered if that would be the plea of the Day's and Shangri-La killers. Would he too plead necessity, "jus necessitatis," the right to do what was required?

A year had passed, summer had arrived in Oslo, and Patricia was at the beach again. Ali turned the postcard over and studied the metal helmet with its full, scary face mask, then put it down on the table and took a large sip of her Rioja.

'Do you know what, Andrew?' She asked rhetorically. 'I'd really love a cigarette!'

The word caravan does not come from Romany, where they are a relatively recent addition, but from the Persian word "karwan." It is the origin of the word "van."

Chapter 18

SMELL THE PHEROMONE

Spencer spun the flint wheel of his Zippo, lit a Marlboro, and drew the smoke deeply into his lungs. His wife and kids didn't approve of him smoking in the house, but they were in bed asleep, so none were wiser. As for Spencer, he was wide awake, systematically going through all the notes from the two-family murders, paying attention to every detail. One of the uniformed police officers had located Tom Hunter earlier that day, moored up on *Wandering Aengus* just outside Eynsham Lock. The officer had arranged for Hunter to come to the station the next morning, where Ali and Spencer were going to interview him. Tom had told the officer that he was on his way to the Eynsham boatyard to fill up with diesel. Spencer took an Ordnance Survey map of Oxford and the surrounding area from his neat and organised bookshelves and spread it out on the coffee table in front of him. Eynsham Lock, as he thought, was very near Bablock Hythe. That put Tom Hunter at or near the scene of the second family murder location. Was this a coincidence? Was the man who had called Spencer "Bud" and made him coffee capable of such bloody, vicious multiple murders? Maybe they would find out at the interview. Spencer was also wondering what else they would uncover and what, if anything, that boater had to hide. Mr and Mrs Wilson, the retired couple from Didcot, and David Clarke, the cyclist, all at Day's Lock on the morning of the Gibson family annihilation, were coming in to be interviewed again. They were all present and inquisitive about what was going on at Day's Lock that day. There was nothing that Spencer could see that implicated them or was suspicious, but "leave no stone unturned" was his golden rule of "*detectiveness.*" There was always the chance that on a second questioning, they would remember something else, something that could give him a lead. He placed the map back on the bookshelf and noticed that it was wedged next to his old cloth-bound copy of Three Men in a Boat – another coincidence?

The police sniffer dog had uncovered nothing in the way of severed fingers at Bablock Hythe. What Murphy had done, though, was draw Spencer's attention to the possible blood residue on the rope of the boat. The lab was analysing it and had promised to let him have the results first thing in the morning. If it was human blood, then whose was it and what was it doing on the back of the boat? Why would the killer want to tie up or untie the keepnet? Spencer's family had long since drifted off into deep sleep up in their beds, but he was still mulling over all possibilities, in spite of it being nearly midnight and needing to be at the station for 7 am. He had a glass of whisky beside him, but he was still working, still on the job.

The killer would have been covered in the blood of the victims, but the rain would have washed away any trace outside the caravan. Murphy had still picked up a scent – maybe not much of one, but enough to lead him to the boat. Spencer remembered reading that dogs use smells to communicate, and a dog's sense of smell is between 1,000 and 10,000 times stronger than that of a human. When dogs smell something, they are not just registering a smell; they get an entire story. They can smell pheromones, not only found in urine and faecal matter but also on skin and fur. From this, they can tell a lot about another dog or human, including if they are male or female, what they have eaten, where they have been, what they have touched, if they are ready to mate, if they have recently given birth or had a false pregnancy, what mood they are in, and if they are dead or alive. Dogs also have a "universal sense" that humans do not have. They can feel the energy and emotions of other beings around them. If only they could talk as well, Spencer considered what Murphy would tell them about the killer at Shangri-La. What kind of mood was that killer in after slaughtering the Daltrey family? What energy and emotions could Murphy have possibly smelled? What does someone who has just stabbed and slashed to death six people – men, women, and children – smell like? What emotions would they have shown after cutting off the woman's finger? What was that story?

If it was blood on the keepnet, then more questions presented themselves. What was the killer doing on the boat? Why was there blood on the rope? Spencer was thinking more clearly than he had done all day; this is what made him a detective. What about the blood on the boat? There would have undoubtedly been some on the deck if the killer had been on it, but then the rain would have washed it away. The rope was slightly more protected and absorbent, which is why traces of blood could possibly survive overnight. 'Spencer, what connects these two sets of murders?' Ali had asked earlier that day when they stood on the boat's small deck. "The river," was the answer she was looking for. They were standing on the boat on the river; the blood-stained rope was on the boat, so that was also on the river. Spencer was forming a picture of the scene in his mind, then he rolled it back to nighttime, the time of the killings. How did the killer get there? How did he get through over two hundred caravans without being seen or heard, without a dog barking and alerting a resident? The river connected the two murder sites, and it must have been the "road" used by the killer to reach them. In the dead of night, under the cover of darkness, who would notice a small boat as it made its way silently up and down the river, cutting through the night as if invisible? Tying up somewhere, like the cleat on the back of the boat that the keepnet was tied to, then later, after the slaughter, the killer, while untying his boat, hands covered with the blood of the Daltrey family, left their blood on the rope.

As Spencer sat in an armchair next to his bookshelf, cradling the whisky in his hands, somewhere in the Dog Unit kennels, Murphy lay dreaming. He was dreaming of the smells he had tasted that day, the feelings he had felt flying around him, the dead flesh of the human bodies, and the river. But most of all, he was dreaming of food and running wild through open countryside, chasing rabbits; these were things to dream of. Dogs choose their battles well and never kill unless they need to survive, only out of "necessity." Dogs could never understand human behaviour, what would drive a man to murder, or why we kill each other.

The muffled sound of the cuckoo clock in Spencer's kitchen interrupted the silence of the living room where he was sitting. It was 12.30 am. Spencer had purchased the clock many years ago while on a school trip to Switzerland. It was a present for his mother and father, and when they had died, it found its way back to his hands again, mainly because none of the rest of his family wanted it. Spencer's wife hated it. She hated the way it looked, the noise it made, and she especially hated the little cuckoo that popped out every fifteen minutes, but she knew how much it meant to her husband, and because of that, she had never said anything to make him aware of her feelings towards it. Ever the detective, it had not taken Spencer long to work out that his wife hated the clock, but just like her, he had never said anything to make her aware that he knew. He refilled his glass with one more shot of single malt and took a small book of poems from the shelf, The Wind in the Reeds by W. B. Yeats. He opened the book, found the poem he was looking for, and read it silently as he slowly sipped his whisky.

The Song of Wandering Aengus
by William Butler Yeats

I went out to the hazel wood
Because a fire was in my head,
And cut and peeled a hazel wand,
And hooked a berry to a thread;
And when white moths were on the wing,

And moth-like stars were flickering out,
I dropped the berry in a stream
And caught a little silver trout.

When I had laid it on the floor
I went to blow the fire a-flame,
But something rustled on the floor,
And someone called me by my name:
It had become a glimmering girl
With apple blossom in her hair
Who called me by my name and ran
And faded through the brightening air.

Though I am old with wandering
Through hollow lands and hilly lands,
I will find out where she has gone,
And kiss her lips and take her hands;
And walk among long dappled grass,
And pluck till time and times are done
The silver apples of the moon,
The golden apples of the sun.

I keep six honest serving men
They taught me all I know
Their names are
What and Why and When
And How and Where and Who

[RUDYARD KIPLING – "The Elephant's Child"]

Chapter 19

A ROOM WITH AN INTERVIEW

INVESTIGATIVE INTERVIEWING

The aim of investigative interviewing is to obtain accurate and reliable accounts from victims, witnesses, or suspects about matters under police investigation.

1: Investigators must act fairly when questioning victims, witnesses, or suspects. Vulnerable people must be treated with particular consideration at all times.

2: Investigative interviewing should be approached with an investigative mindset. Accounts obtained from the person who is being interviewed should always be tested against what the interviewer already knows or what can reasonably be established.

3: When conducting an interview, investigators are free to ask a wide range of questions in order to obtain material that may assist an investigation.

4: Investigators should recognise the positive impact of an early admission in the context of the criminal justice system.

5: Investigators are not bound to accept the first answer given. Questioning is not unfair merely because it is persistent.

6: Even when the right of silence is exercised by a suspect, investigators have a responsibility to ask them questions.

By 7.45 am, Ali and Spencer were back in their office, eating bacon rolls and drinking from mugs full of strong, hot coffee as they prepared for the interviews. They had no real witnesses; the victims were all dead, and as for suspects, all they had so far was Tom Hunter. First in were Mr and Mrs Wilson, the retired walkers from the Day's Lock incident. There was nothing new to gain from their second interview. The story was the same as they had given on the day. They had got there early to go for their usual walk along the river and had not seen anyone or noticed anything unusual other than the police presence at the lock. Ali and Spencer were not really expecting much more, but every possible avenue had to be explored. This was work that had to be done. Twelve murder victims were in their hands, so they needed to explore every new possibility they could uncover. The Wilsons were thanked for coming and given a contact number in case they did happen to remember anything.

Next up was David Clarke, the cyclist who had passed *Wandering Aengus* on the towpath just before Day's Lock. His story too was much the same as on the day, except he was able to add that he had since seen *Wandering Aengus* and the man whose boat it was several times: a couple of times near Day's and a while back on the river in Abingdon, near the bridge. He had not spoken to the man on *Wandering Aengus* or noticed anything unusual; he just remembered seeing him. He probably would not have even noticed him if it had not been for the connection with Day's Lock. Again, Ali and Spencer thanked him for coming in and gave him a contact number.

It was mid-morning now, and Tom Hunter had been sitting in a room at the station waiting to be interviewed for over an hour.

'Let him stew for a bit longer,' Spencer said to Ali, who nodded in agreement. 'Another coffee, ma'am?'

The chief superintendent arrived as they were drinking their second cup and discussing how to handle the questioning of Tom Hunter. Ali got the chief super up to speed and gave him a coffee. Spencer joined in to help her as they described the scene at Bablock Hythe. Neither of them accentuated the horror of it; there was no need; the super had been around long enough to have experienced his share of harrowing scenes to get the picture without graphic details.

'And this man, Tom Hunter, he's an ex-police officer – is that right?' asked the chief superintendent.

'Yes, sir,' Ali replied, 'five years in the Met. He somehow managed to shoot a couple of his own toes off and got retired early with a disability pension – early, very early.'

'Is he married? Children? Parents?' the chief asked. These were all questions that Ali and Spencer had asked themselves and had the answers to. Ali gave them to the chief in a full dossier that detailed almost every known aspect of Tom Hunter's life, especially the time he spent at the Met. The researchers had done a good job, called in lots of favours, and rattled many cages. The dossier contained Tom Hunter, in a nutshell.

'There's a couple of blots on his copybook, but other than that, and shooting a couple of his own toes off, he seems to have had a pretty uninspiring career as a police officer. He was married to…' she checked her notes, 'a Josephine Harris. No kids. It seems things went a bit wrong for them after the shooting incident – we don't know if it's related – and they split up and divorced about six years ago. Both parents died from natural causes. All of this is in the report you have.'

'So, our Mr Hunter is an orphan, is he?' said the chief as if he read something into that, something that neither of the two detectives could fathom.

'From what we can tell, he doesn't seem to have kept in contact with anyone from his Met days. He seems to have moved his life away from London and left his old life in the past. He does have a friend.' She checked her notes again. 'Simon John Ritchie, who lives in East Oxford, Hunter stayed with him for about a year when he first moved to Oxford.'

'Sounds like a good friend, putting someone up for a year,' the chief muttered, not intending anyone to hear him. 'Well, I'll be watching that interview when you are ready. Let's see how the man from the Met reacts to a bit of Thames Valley Police questioning!'

There had always been a bit of rivalry between TVP and the Metropolitan Police. The Met viewed the TVP as "carrot crunchers" because of their largely rural patch of the country. Names like "Chad Valley," referring to the toy manufacturer, were mockingly banded around the Met when referring to TVP. Whether any of this was true or just rumour, TVP resented the Met's attitude towards them, or at least their perception of what the Met's attitude towards them was. TVP saw the Met as being a law unto themselves, not like the rest of the police services in the country. Next up for the interview room was the Met's ex-officer, Tom Hunter.

The chief superintendent silently watched through a one-way window that overlooked the sparse room where DCI Ali Smith and DI Spencer Davis sat at a plain laminated office table. Seated opposite them was a dark-haired man, early forties, wearing a checked shirt and washed-out jeans. *'Not so arrogant now, Mr Met, are you?'* the Chief Superintendent thought to himself. Ali started the questioning, and the chief super followed every word over the speakers.

'Thank you for coming in, Mr Hunter. I would like to clarify that this is not a formal interview; nothing is being recorded, and while you are here at our request, you are also here out of your own free will.' From Ali's tone of voice, it was clear that this was a sentence she had reeled off many times before, probably in this same room. Tom was fed up after sitting around for over an hour waiting for them to speak to him; he had not even been offered a cup of coffee. He nodded his agreement to Ali and looked around the room. It was not dissimilar to the interview rooms he had used many times while at the Met. These rooms are places where people are broken and confessions are gained; rooms where justice and injustice are determined; and rooms where murderers are interrogated. Stark, drab, and no outside windows, the only window being one-way glass looking in. Tom wondered who would be on the other side of that; there was always someone. The only difference was that this time he was on the other side of the table; this time he was being asked questions, not asking them.

'I am Detective Chief Inspector Smith, and I think you have already met Detective Inspector Davis.'

Tom nodded again.

'We would like to go over everything from the morning of the deaths at Day's Lock when you passed through on your boat. Could you talk us through what you did again, please, Mr Hunter, and try to remember as much as you possibly can?'

Like the others that Ali and Spencer had interviewed that morning, Tom's recollection more or less matched what he had said on the day, even down to the glimpse of the mystery man on the bench, but nothing more.

'Did you go to the funeral, Mr Hunter, the one for the Gibson family? The lockkeeper from Day's who was…' Before Ali could finish, Tom interrupted.

'I know who he is or was, and I think you know I didn't go to the funeral.'

'And why would we know that, Mr Hunter?' Ali asked.

'Because you were there, I saw your picture and his.' Tom nodded at Spencer. 'It was on the front page of the Oxford Mail.'

'Would you mind telling us why you didn't go? There were a lot of other boat owners there, and he was a well-liked lockkeeper, I am told.' Ali could see Tom didn't like this question and was getting noticeably irritated.

'I didn't go because I don't like funerals. Besides, I didn't really know George very well, just enough to have a quick chat with him as I passed through the lock. It wasn't like we were best buddies or anything.' Tom had realised he may have started to sound impatient and concentrated on speaking calmly and clearly. After all, they were only doing their job.

'And you have no idea who the man you think you saw on the bench was?' Ali asked again, already knowing what Tom's answer would be.

'Absolutely none,' came the sharp answer from Tom.

Spencer had been sitting there in silence throughout Ali's questioning. He was watching Tom closely, analysing his voice, his posture, and his facial expressions. Now it was his turn to ask a few questions.

'Would you mind telling us what you and your boat were doing at Eynsham Lock last night, Mr Hunter, and how long you'd been there?'

'What's that got to do with Day's Lock, Inspector?' Tom asked, already beginning to be suspicious that this interview might be about more than just the Day's Lock affair.

'Just answer the question, Mr Hunter, if you don't mind,' said Spencer a little more firmly than he had meant it; he was aware that the chief was watching through the one-way glass and would want them to give the "Met boy" a bit of a grilling.

'Well, you should know already,' Tom said, looking at both of them. 'I told one of your uniformed officers that you sent looking for me why I was there; he asked me the same question yesterday. As you seem to have had a slight communications breakdown, Inspector, I will bring you up to speed.'

The chief superintendent sneered at this from the other side of the glass. *'Typical Metropolitan Police smug attitude,'* he thought.

Tom continued, 'It's a simple explanation, actually, detectives. There are only two places on the Oxford stretch of the Thames where you can get diesel; one of them is Eynsham Boatyard. I was on my way there to get diesel.'

'The other, I believe, is Abingdon Boatyard, Mr Hunter: why didn't you fill up when you were there?' Spencer asked.

'Yes, Bud, the other is Abingdon, but Eynsham is cheaper, and I like the trip upriver; I like the countryside,' came Tom's slightly less tempered reply.

Spencer noticed that Tom had called him "Bud" again, but this time he was not flattered by it. It felt far more contemptuous in the interview room than it did when sitting on Tom's boat; it was not so friendly. It was meant to be contemptuous; Tom was losing his patience.

'You like that part of the river then, do you? What about Bablock Hythe, the Ferryman Pub – do you ever go there?' Spencer asked.

'I've been there a few times over the years.'

'What about in the last few days?'

'No, I didn't get as far as the boatyard at Eynsham. I'm in no hurry, Inspector. If I like a spot, I moor up and stay there for a while, and there is a good pub near the Swinford Toll Bridge, by the lock. That's how it is: life on the river; you go with the flow, not tied to a pile of orders and paperwork or stuck in a room like this.'

For a second, Spencer could see how nice it might be to be free from all the drudgery, but no, that way of life was not for him.

'That would be the Talbot, if I am correct, Mr Hunter?' Spencer was showing off his local knowledge, and Hunter nodded. Spencer asked another question.

'Do you know the mobile home site next to the pub at Bablock Hythe?'

'Well, given that the caravans dominate the bank for about half a mile, it would be hard to miss it, Inspector, and the Ferryman is a popular place for boaters to pull up and have a pint or two,' Tom replied.

'Have you ever been on the site?' asked Spencer.

'No, never,' was Tom's reply.

'Do you know anyone who lives there or uses it?'

'No, no one,' Tom repeated.

Ali switched the line of questioning out of the blue, leaving Tom looking puzzled.

'You were married to a Josephine Harris, Mr Hunter, is that correct?' asked Ali.

'Yes, I was, but what the hell it's got to do with you, I don't know.' Tom didn't like this. He wanted to forget all about Josie. He had forgotten all about her. She was in his past – the past he had moved on from, the past he had left behind. So, what was this about?

'You are divorced now, aren't you, Mr Hunter?' Ali continued.

'Yes. Six years ago, if you really want to know, nearly seven.'

'Did your wife wear a wedding ring?' Ali's question puzzled Tom even more.

'Of course she did. We were married; that's what you do when you are married, Detective; you wear bloody wedding rings!'

"Bloody wedding rings." Those three words in Tom's reply threw an image into Ali's mind that she would rather not have seen again.

'Does your wife still have her wedding ring?' she asked.

'I have no idea! Look, what is all this about? What are you after?'

'Do you still have your wedding ring, Mr Hunter?' Ali continued.

'Somewhere, I can't remember where.' Tom's voice reflected the mixture of anger and puzzlement he was feeling, and then it occurred to him: 'Am I a suspect? Do you suspect me of killing those people at Day's Lock? Do you think I murdered that family?'

'Did you, Mr Hunter?' asked Spencer.

'No, I fucking did not!'

A few more questions were asked by Ali and Spencer before the interview was drawn to a close. Tom was given a contact number, which he begrudgingly took and tucked into his wallet.

'Is that it?' Tom asked. 'Can I go now?'

'Just one other thing, Mr Hunter.' Spencer said as Tom started to stand up, 'Do you own a canoe?'

1/2 a pear – sliced
2 big handfuls of watercress and
2 big handfuls of rocket
1 handful of halved walnuts
Drizzle with extra-virgin olive oil and a small squeeze of lemon juice
Season well with salt and freshly ground black pepper.
Toss all this together and serve with shaved Parmesan.

[Pear and Watercress Salad]

Chapter 20

GONE FISHING

The lab reports were waiting on Spencer's desk when he arrived back at his office after the interviews. Much of what they said, he and Ali already knew. All the Bablock Hythe deaths occurred in the small hours, somewhere between 2 am and 5 am. Each of the bodies had multiple cuts and stab wounds. The wounds were not frenzied but appeared to be more considered, deliberate, and arranged. The bodies were likely to have been moved into the positions they were found in after the deaths occurred. The stomach contents of each of the victims contained white bread, lettuce, tomato, cucumber, ham and cheese, and their last summer salad – their last ever salad. Blood samples taken from each of the victims all contained traces of an unidentified substance believed to have been caused by exposure to a toxic gas, possibly a nerve gas, but this was not conclusive. No defence wounds or any indications of struggle were present at the scene or on any of the bodies. Forensics agreed that it was likely that the victims were conscious at the time of the killings but paralysed by a noxious substance or gas. The Daltreys would have been aware of what was being done to them – and to each of the members of their family – but unable to resist or raise the alarm, unable to fight back. Coldness came over Spencer as he read the reports and tried to imagine what it must have been like for the Daltreys to be frozen and watch each other being systematically cut and knifed, bleeding to death, not knowing which of them would be next. It was a disturbing image that reminded Spence of a chilling horror story he studied at university, "The Premature Burial" by Edgar Allan Poe. It was a short story about being buried alive and not being able to resist, not being able to stop the earth being shovelled on the coffin, not being able to move. Is that what it was like for the Daltrey family? For them, it was not just an Edgar Allen Poe story; for them, it was real.

The stain spotted on the keepnet rope proved to be blood. Spencer had been right, and Murphy's discovery had been invaluable. Even though the rain had got to the rope, diluted the blood, and washed much of it away, the lab was still able to determine that it was a mixture of at least two types, each matching one of the victims; the other blood types were too unclear for the lab to identify.

Reports from the uniformed officers that had patrolled the banks near Bablock Hythe had also arrived. No suspicious objects had been found, and there was no murder weapon. Spencer was not surprised by this; he had not really expected them to find anything. There had been a few fishermen out doing some early-season night fishing; three of them claimed to have seen or heard nothing, but one said he saw something across the bank from him. It was just before daylight but still very dark, and he could not be sure, but he thought it was a small boat, possibly a kayak or a canoe, heading towards Eynsham Lock. He had assumed it was someone out emptying crayfish nets or another fisherman, but really it was too dark to see, and it could have been just a trick of the light. On the river, the darkness of night can play strange tricks on the eye. *'Just before dawn comes "the darkest hour,"'* Spencer thought to himself as he read the report. If it had been a canoe or a small boat, then he could be right about his theory: the blood on the keepnet could have come from the killer untying his canoe or boat with hands wet with blood. That would answer the question of how he was able to get to the murder sites without being seen. It would have to be someone who knew the river well enough to navigate it in the dark. Maybe someone who even lived on the river? Someone like Tom Hunter.

'Spencer,' Ali said as she entered the office, 'I've just received a lecture from the Chief Superintendent.'

This jerked Spencer out of his thoughts, and, still holding the stack of reports, he looked up at Ali as she spoke.

'This is now the force's number one focus. We are to be given all the resources we require – boats, divers, helicopters, dogs, firearms, the lot! Not surprisingly, the Super wants this killer caught and safely behind bars before he can kill any more of, and I quote, *"the public we serve."* He wants the lid to stay on things for as long as possible, but pretty soon the media will hear something and be on us like a tonne of bricks. We need to be ready for that and know what we are and are not prepared to release to them. There could be a panicked public to deal with, and at some point we need to issue guidelines to the inquiry centres so they can try to deal with callers without scaring them off or revealing anything that we need to keep covert at the moment. But for now, everything stays in-house.'

Spencer found none of what Ali was saying surprising; it was exactly what he would have expected any chief superintendent to say given the situation. He was about to ask if there was anything else he should know when Ali started speaking again.

'He also made it very clear that he didn't like Tom Hunter, which may have something to do with the fact that Hunter is ex-Met; he also seemed to think his reactions when being interviewed showed all the signs that we should pay special attention to him. We need to get some of the team looking into Hunter's background in detail: what he did in London – more than just his Met records – who his friends were and are, and especially what he has been doing living on that boat for the last six years.' She moved towards her desk, sat down, and grabbed a pile of papers from the in-tray on her desk.

'I've already got someone on that, ma'am, but I will brief them again and get them some more help. I'm with the Super on this one,' Spencer said, feeling pleased that he was ahead of the game – on the ball.

'My gut feeling too, Spence – Hunter isn't playing as straight with us as he wants us to think,' Ali said. 'And Spencer, what was that question you stuck in at the end about a canoe? Even the Super was baffled by that.'

Spencer filled Ali in on his theory. He told her about the lab reports on the blood found on the keepnet rope and the night fisherman's possible sighting of a small boat. It would need to be someone who knew the river well enough to navigate their way at night, someone like Tom Hunter.

Ali talked about the missing fingers and wedding rings. This had been bugging her since the Day's Lock killings and was the single most important thing tying these two sets of murders together. The press had never been told about the severed finger and the ring at Day's Lock, so copycat killings could be ruled out. It had to be the same man. Ali knew the rings were key to the killings – something special to the killer: perhaps he hated his mother or there was something connected to his mother that was driving him to kill. The rings must be a trophy or a souvenir. Many known serial killers collected souvenirs. Harold Shipman, the British doctor who put to death over two hundred of his patients, was found to have various rings and other objects he had collected from his dead victims. It had also been theorised that, as a boy, Shipman's mother, Vera, had influenced him in a way that could have created what he was later to become. Maybe the same was true of the killer that Ali and Spencer were now looking for.

What did they know about their murderer? Not much, really. Twelve were stabbed, all very bloody. Two severed fingers and missing wedding rings. No witnesses, no motives, no suspects – except maybe Tom Hunter. What they did know was that this was not the end – far from it. They had a "serial family annihilator" on the loose and on their patch. This killer was wiping out whole families - men, women, and children - and this killer would undoubtedly strike again. They had to find him and stop that from happening. For now, all they could do was set up night patrols along the river and delve into the backgrounds of the victims and Mr Tom Hunter. Re-examine everything they had, then re-examine it again, as many times as it took. The killer was out there and was clever at covering his tracks, at moving around in the night, and at killing, but he would make a mistake. Ali and Spencer would find him if it was the last thing they ever did. Right now, though, this was their darkest hour, just like the one that comes before dawn.

From stardust everywhere
Floating through the air
I can see it even when I'm sleeping
That sun touching my face
Gives life to our place
I can feel it even when I'm dreaming
Are we children in this universe?
Perhaps the first to be made
Of rocks and dirt
Are we alone in this universe?
We could be all there is to see

[DANGEROUS DAVE – "Stardust"]

Chapter 21

ARE WE ALL JUST STARDUST?

Tom left the police station on St Aldate's feeling a mixture of things – confused, annoyed, angry, but most of all, puzzled by the questions that Spencer and Ali had thrown at him. Did they really think he was capable of murdering the lockkeeper and his family? Did they really have him down as a suspect, or were they just clutching at straws? He was trying to figure out why they had called him in for questioning – why at this time, and why their interest in Bablock Hythe? Every thought he had was punctuated with his own question. "Why?" What was it that interested them about Eynsham? Was it because he had moored *Wandering Aengus* near the lock? Did that make him a suspect? Suspected of what? The Day's Lock murders had been committed by the son; it had been revealed in the papers that it was a "family annihilation," as they termed it. No one else was being sought in connection with the deaths, so why the interest in Bablock Hythe and why the interest in him? And what was all that about a canoe?

Not far from the police station was the Head of the River pub. Tom got as far as their terrace and went in. He needed a beer. Outside was grey and windy, but for a change, it was no longer raining. Tom ordered a pint of Old Speckled Hen from the young South African barmaid and took it outside to drink. There were a few lunchtime stragglers drinking inside the pub, but the terrace was virtually empty. He zipped his jacket up and sat at a table against the pub wall and next to the river. To his left on the river were a couple of the large passenger boats owned by Salter's Steamers. Normally at this time of year, they would have been out taking scores of tourists down to Abingdon and back, but the continuous wet weather had deterred all but the hardiest visitors to Oxford. Those that did come chose not to sit on the back of an open boat for three hours in the rain. In front of him, cars, buses, cyclists, and pedestrians crossed back and forth over Folly Bridge, some heading towards Oxford and others heading out of town towards Abingdon. By road, Abingdon was only a few miles away, but the river twisted and turned, making it a good couple of hours by boat.

The Old Speckled Hen tasted good. Tom started to relax again and went back inside for another pint. There were no answers as to what was happening – at least none that he knew of – but he felt sure he would find out in due course. One thing he knew for certain was that it had nothing to do with him. Whatever the truth was, the police were sure to find that out soon enough, or so he believed. They had called him in for an interview, and it was over now. It was time for him to put that behind him, clear his head, and get on with his life. He drained his second glass and walked back towards the station to catch the Eynsham bus back to *Wandering Aengus*, back home. He had fuelled up early that morning and brought her back to beyond the lock. Now, after all the questions about Eynsham Lock, he considered it time to move on – time to cruise back upstream to Oxford and moor outside the Isis Tavern, near Donnington Bridge. That was the unique thing about living on a boat: if you grew tired of your immediate environment or your neighbours, you could just move your home nomadically to somewhere else. There were a few things he needed to do in town, and he needed a friend to catch up with. He had not seen Simon in Charles Street for quite a while, and he could do with saying hello. Maybe find out what the police had been asking and what they had been told.

The bus stopped outside the Talbot pub, and Tom made the short walk back to the mooring. There was no one around at Eynsham Lock when he arrived; it was probably the lockkeeper's tea break, so he went straight to *Wandering Aengus*. Having no reason to stay any longer, he started the engine and pulled away. Heavy rains had swollen the river, and the strength of the current cutting across from the weir tried to force the boat to one side, into the bank and the overhanging trees. Tom knew how to react to this and steered into the stream. *Wandering Aengus* now had full fuel and water tanks, and the additional weight always made her handle better. Tom loved it when she felt like that – straight and responsive cruising. Less than an hour and a half later, he arrived at the Isis Tavern. The river wall there had metal rings fixed to it, which meant there was no need to hammer mooring pins into the bank. The Isis Tavern had free Wi-Fi close enough for him to get a signal, which was another reason he liked to moor there. Having some time to kill, he booted up his small laptop and checked his emails – nothing of interest. He checked the BBC news – nothing of interest. His thoughts returned to the interview and to Day's Lock, and he inadvertently found himself searching the Oxford Mail's website for articles about the deaths of the lockkeeper and his family. Soon a black-and-white photograph of the Gibson family funeral filled the screen; it was the picture he had seen on the front page at the time of the deaths. There was DI Spencer Davis to the left of the picture, and the woman with him Tom now knew to be Detective Chief Inspector Alison Smith. In the background, a group of boaters were gathered, some of them he knew, and a small distance behind them was the grainy but unmistakable image of Jamie. The first time Tom had looked at this photograph, when it was in the newspaper, he had seen Jamie but had not noticed the even grainier figure standing behind him. Using the mouse pad, he zoomed in closer, but the resolution of the image was so low that it just became even more unclear. He could not be sure but thought it might have been Craig from the Rock of Gibraltar.

Tom switched on the radio and tuned into Radio 4. A current affairs programme was in progress, discussing the forthcoming Olympic Games – the security, the costs, the benefits, and ticket availability. This seemed to be the topic of most programmes on the radio at the time. Everyone had gone Olympic-mad. Somehow the discussion brought in the Queen's recent Jubilee celebrations, and comparisons were made between the organising of the games and the jubilee. One of the panellists referred to the jubilee river pageant and the festival-type concert at Buckingham Palace as being *"the last gasps of breath from a dying society."* That sentence struck a chord with Tom, except it was not a dying society that came to mind, but the last breaths of the dying Gibson family at Day's Lock. He switched off the radio and laid down on his bed. The bit of walking he had done that day had made the pain in his foot worse. The pain was always there, but normally he could ignore it, put it out of his mind, and manage it. But too much exercise and stress could cause a flare-up of pain. Between that and the beers he'd drunk at the Head of the River, he now needed to rest for a while. Soon, he was sound asleep.

Gently, the boat rocked while outside the rain began to fall again, and a breeze bumped *Wandering Aengus* softly to and fro, making a dull thud on every contact with the wall. The garden of the Isis Tavern was empty when Tom awoke, and the pub looked closed. He had slept, unintentionally, for about three hours. It was now 6.30 pm, and he was hungry. The James Street Tavern was only about half an hour's walk away; he could eat there and maybe catch up with Jamie, plus the walk would help clear his head. The rain had stopped, the clouds had moved from above, and Tom's head was also starting to clear as he climbed the path at the side of Donnington Bridge and walked towards James Street.

It was still only seven o'clock, early for the James Street Tavern, but there were a couple of customers at the bar. Tom didn't recognise either of them. He ordered food and a pint before taking a seat at a table in the bay window at the front of the bar. The food did not take him long to demolish; it was the only thing he had eaten since a slice of toast for breakfast. He stared out of the pub window onto the street as people and cars passed by. Tom's mind was empty and relaxed for the first time that day. Suddenly, an affected pirate voice snapped him back to the room.

'Ahoy there, me old shipmate – Arrrggghhh!' Tom looked around to see Jamie beaming from ear to ear.

'Jamie!' Tom exclaimed. 'Really good to see you, mate.' Jamie grabbed another couple of pints from the bar and joined Tom at the table.

'So, what's new then, Captain?' Jamie asked jokingly. 'How is *Wandering Aengus* faring?'

'All's well with her, Jamie. I just had her serviced, and everything was OK. She only needed a new filter and an oil change. Sweet as a nut!' Answered Tom, not mentioning the police interview.

'Have you seen anything of Simon and Jacky lately?' Jamie asked.

'No. Not for some time now. No fault of theirs, all down to me. I was thinking about popping around there later this evening or maybe tomorrow. What about you? Have you seen them? Do they ever come to the pub?' Tom asked.

'You'd think they would, as it's only a few streets away, but I haven't seen them since before Christmas.' Jamie took a swig of his beer and carried on talking. 'When I got the place over six years ago, the same time you took over the boat, they came in regularly at first. That must have been about the time you moved out of their house; they probably missed your company.' Jamie smiled at his own comment. He knew how awkward Tom had felt about it at the time. 'I haven't really seen much of them since then, maybe once or twice a year, if that.'

Tom looked out the window in silence for a moment before replying, 'Well, I guess things change and people have different focuses in their lives. My life has changed completely since moving on to *Wandering Aengus*.'

Jamie smiled again and quickly replied, 'And mine has changed since I moved off her!'

A small television hung on the wall above one end of the bar. It was tuned to a news channel with ticker-tape updates at the bottom. Tom had not been paying much attention, but this changed when he saw the image of a caravan with police tape around it and the words "Murders at Bablock Hythe" scrolling across at the bottom of the screen. He froze and stared, open-mouthed, at the screen.

'What is it, Tom?' Jamie asked. 'You look like you've seen a ghost.'

'Can you turn the volume up on the TV, Jamie?' Tom asked, not taking his eyes off the set for a second.

'Yes, of course, mate, what is it?'

The news had hit the media. Two adults and four children were murdered in a mobile home park at Bablock Hythe. They had rented the holiday caravan where their mutilated bodies were found. Now Tom knew why DCI Smith and DI Davis had called him in for questioning. Bablock Hythe was not far upriver from Eynsham Lock, where he had been moored that night. Even more disturbing was that the news item went on to say that there were believed to be similarities with the death of a family at Days Lock earlier in the year.

'This has been on the news all afternoon, Tom,' Jamie said. 'I'm surprised you haven't seen it already.'

'I was sleeping this afternoon,' Tom explained, still looking shocked.

'Apparently the police now think that George and his family were not murdered by his son, and it could have been the same person who did the Bablock Hythe murders. Do you want another beer?' Jamie stood up and went to the bar. Tom sat there; now he knew why he was a suspect and, even worse, what it was they suspected him of. Tom looked away from the TV and caught

Jamie having a few harsh words with a guy on crutches at the end of the bar before picking up two pints and returning to the table.

'Just an arsehole I put up with sometimes. I feel sorry for him,' Jamie said, realising Tom had seen the altercation. 'You look shaken up, Tom,' he said as he put one of the beers on the table in front of Tom. 'It's a bit close to home, isn't it?'

'I was moored up at Eynsham Lock the night they say that family was murdered at Bablock Hythe.' Tom looked at Jamie, but Jamie didn't speak, so he continued, deciding to talk about the interview. 'The police called me in this morning and asked me a load of questions about what I was doing in Eynsham. I didn't know anything about these murders until just now. It all makes a bit more sense now.'

'They were probably checking everyone in the area, Tom, and you know how dodgy you boaters are,' Jamie joked.

'They think I may have done it!' Tom said sternly.

'Did you?' Jamie looked Tom in the eye as he asked.

'That's not even funny, Jamie! It's the second time today I've been asked that.'

'Sorry Tom, I couldn't resist. I wouldn't worry about it if I were you. They're probably telling everyone with the slightest connection that they're a suspect. It will all blow over. Whoever did these murders has to be a complete nutter; you don't strike me as being one of those.' They both smiled and chinked their glasses together.

'Are you staying for the evening, Tom?' Jamie asked. 'It's open mic and poetry night tonight; you'd enjoy it; there should be some good performers in.' Jamie was trying to encourage Tom to snap out of it and start enjoying the evening. Tom had been to a few of the open mic evenings at the James Street Tavern over the years, and he had to admit that some had been excellent. There were always a couple of good singers and guitarists turning up, as well as a surprising range of random poets. Tom liked the poets; many of them read deeply personal stuff about their lives – their failed relationships, their losses, and their happiness. The personal stuff he could relate to – things he had experienced but never really been able to articulate or express. Tom was a closed and private man, especially when it came to his emotions. Maybe it was from his time in the Armed Response Unit trying to cover up his fears, hiding his emotions from his colleagues, and trying to fit in with the team. His marriage to Josie was also a time when he had bottled up his feelings so much that, on reflection, he now realised he had shut her out. At some point in his life, Tom Hunter had become a very secretive, very private man. This probably contributed to why the police had him down as a suspect: an instinctive mistrust of the unknown, and Tom Hunter was the unknown.

A few more customers had filled up the pub, and Jamie was now behind the bar, pulling pints, chatting, and smiling. He was a well-liked publican, and Tom could see that all of the customers treated Jamie as a friend. Tom also saw how Jamie was behaving with the young barmaid who had served him his first drink. Every time she moved past Jamie, he would place his arm around her to "guide" her safely by, but in a way that seemed far too close and touchy-feely for it to be completely innocent. Tom guessed her to be less than half Jamie's age, but then that was none of his business, each to their own, different strokes. A guitar player started singing and playing, and Tom's attention moved from Jamie to the performers' area. An old American blues song filled the bar; it was being sung by a skinny young white English boy with scruffy hair and a torn T-shirt with the words "I never went to art school" printed across the front of it. He sang,

'Well if the river was whiskey
I'd be a diving duck
I would dive down to the bottom
I would never come up...'

The evening passed by as Tom drank a few more pints and a selection of poets and musicians did their thing. He sat, concentrating on a poem being read by a Welsh poet about a rugby team. A beer glass plonked onto the table next to him, and he looked around to see Jamie smiling above him with two pints in his hands.

'Mind if I join you, Tom?' he said as he sat down.

'Not a bad bunch again tonight, is it? You have to listen to Dave. He is here every week. I love his stuff, a bit like "John Martin."'

Tom smiled back at Jamie and picked up the fresh pint, his seventh of the day, saying, 'Cheers, Bud.'

Jamie nodded in acknowledgement. He could see that Tom had drunk a fair bit; he was not slurring, but he looked drunk, tired, and relaxed.

'What do you think of Emma?' Jamie asked Tom, nodding in the direction of the bar.

'Are you two together then?' Tom asked, 'Or just "good friends."'?'

'I would have to put it in the "Just good friends" bracket, mate, unfortunately. She is a lovely girl, though.'

'How old is she?' asked Tom. He probably wouldn't have asked if it hadn't been for all the beer he had drunk.

'She looks younger than she is, mate; she's nearly 26, and I know what you're thinking – far too young for me even at 26, but as I said, just good friends.'

'She looks sweet, and none of my business. Cheers.' Tom chinked glasses again.

'She is "a glimmering girl" indeed,' Jamie said as if to no one. 'I love this pub, Tom,' he added with enthusiasm. 'It has the best musicians and poets in Oxford, all that talent for us to enjoy, all in this pub, my pub. I know you like your music, and I do believe we've even got you into a bit of poetry now.' This sounded patronising, but it was true: Jamie had opened Tom's eyes up over the years, not just to poetry but to many different authors; he had introduced Tom to his eclectic tastes in all the arts.

They sat in silence for a while, supping beers and listening. It was Jamie who spoke first,

'I miss her, you know – the boat, *Aengus*.' He spoke as if he were thinking out loud. 'She was home to me for a good few years. We went through a lot together; she looked after me and treated me well. It's a pity I didn't treat her as well in return, eh mate, then you wouldn't have needed to do all that work!' They both laughed and drained their pints. It was dark outside, and the James Street Tavern would soon be closing its doors; the bar would become silent again. Jamie called over to Emma to bring two more beers, and Dave got back up to the microphone. Tom and Jamie sat in silence and listened to Dave sing his own song – a magical, mesmerising, poetic song – repeating the lyric, fading at the end.

'Stardust, we are all just stardust… stardust…'

* * *

The sky was clear and full of stardust as Tom, having drunk far too much, slowly made his way home – home to *Wandering Aengus*, home to his peace and solitude, home to his bed. Before he reached the back of the boat, he could see the door was open and started to sober up quickly. Had someone broken in? Were they still in there? Some of his old fears returned for a moment, but the beer had made him braver than he would have been, and he quickly entered the boat and turned on all the lights. There was no one there. Everything looked exactly as he had left it, and as far as he could see, nothing had been taken. There was a bowl on the kitchen table with a few pounds of loose change that was untouched, and two bottles of wine were still on the rack. Boat robbers usually go for cash and booze, so maybe he had not been robbed. He checked the lock on the door, and it looked OK; it had not been forced. In the end, even though he had never done so before, he assumed that he had left earlier without locking up. Maybe the beers he had at the Head of the River and the afternoon sleep had made him less attentive. Maybe… Nothing was stolen or damaged, and there was nothing he could do now but lie in his bed, where the flowing Isis gently rocked his beery head to sleep.

Darkness, darkness, be my pillow...
The polar opposite of brightness is understood to be the absence of visible light. It is also the appearance of black in a coloured space.

[Wikipediea]

Chapter 22

DARKNESS, DARKNESS

On the blackest of nights, on the darkest of rivers, through the quietest of silence, barely a ripple is made as the canoe silently glides close to the overgrown bank. Cutting through the cold river, mastering its way around unseen obstacles with awareness and knowledge gained over the many times it had passed this way. Disturbing only the water rats, reeds, rushes, and voles; seen only by the fish, owls, and deer. Steadily going home to hide away in the tall grasses, amidst the prickly hawthorns, under the cover of trees on the remotest bank of the river Evenlode, the most inaccessible bank where even dog walkers never go. Steadily, it makes its way. There is blood on the paddles, blood on the seats, blood on the sides, and blood on the ropes, but the river washes away everything; every trace dilutes until it is no longer there, no trace at all, as if it never existed or never happened. The clear water of the Cherwell flows close to the Rock of Gibraltar, close to the Oxford Canal, and joins its big brother, the Tamesis, taking all it engulfs and swallows with it. All that is not fastened, all that is not rooted, is carried away. The rivers flow, the rivers cleanse, the rivers consume, the rivers can be deep, and the rivers can be cold. The rivers hold secrets never to be told.

Row, row, row your boat,
Gently down the stream.
Merrily, merrily, merrily, merrily,
Life is but a dream.

[A traditional children's song – often sung as a round.]

Chapter 23

GYRODACTYLUS SALARIS

There were several thousand canoes registered in Oxfordshire, and there was a likelihood of hundreds more that were unregistered. Many of those registered were on the Thames, and many of them were in the Oxford city area. There were too many, even for the large number of officers that had been drafted into the investigation team to follow up. Spencer had told them to concentrate on canoes that were registered to addresses close to the river, within a mile either way of Bablock Hythe. An early find caused excitement when a report came in of a Canadian-style canoe registered at an address backing onto the Thames just past Eynsham boatyard. The report had identified the boat as very suspicious. There had been no answer at the front door of the house when the young officer who called it in arrived at the house. He had gone through a side entrance that led to the back of the building to double check if anyone was home when he saw something covered over with a tarpaulin at the foot of the garden, near the river. The officer had decided to take a look, and he had found a sparkling, clean canoe underneath. Not only had it been scrubbed clean, but it had a strong smell of bleach to it. Could it be a breakthrough?

Spencer got the call from the Command-and-Control centre giving the details of the find, the officer's Blackberry number, and the location. He quickly called the officer, telling him to wait at the house and not to touch or let anyone else touch the canoe. He then called forensics and told them to get one of the team with their kit in his car in five minutes, sharp! On his way to the car park, he called Command and Control back and requested that they send the nearest patrol car to the address as backup. Spencer was surprised to see Graham Nash, the head of forensics himself, waiting by his car with a large silver metallic case full of all the tricks of the forensic trade.

'DCI Smith isn't going to be there, you know, Graham.' Spencer quipped, knowing full well that Graham Nash had a crush on Ali Smith, as everyone at headquarters knew. The "older woman" syndrome, they all said it was. In fact, Ali did not look her age at all, and most people would have put her at least ten years younger than she was. As well as looking younger, Spencer had to admit that she was a very attractive woman. It was not really surprising at all that Graham Nash had his eye on her. Spencer had noticed that Ali also seemed at times to have had a soft spot for Graham Nash as well. Spencer didn't have Ali down as a toy-boy type, but he had been in the job long enough to realise that you can never really second-guess people. Besides, it was her business and not his; he had a great deal of respect for her professionally, and whatever she chose to do with her personal life was up to her and not for him to judge. Graham Nash's face showed signs of embarrassment as he climbed into the passenger seat of Spencer's car.

The back-up patrol car with two officers inside had already arrived and was parked outside the address. One of them rolled the window down when Spencer and Nash walked over and told them that the officer who had put the call in was around the back of the house. It wasn't like that when Spencer started out as a young police officer; they would have been out of the car and almost standing at attention with the arrival of a detective inspector. Was this the new face of policing? The garden at the back of the house was narrow and long, with neighbouring properties on either side. The river ran past the bottom, where Spencer Davis and Graham Nash could see the officer waiting to greet them and show them his find. Graham handed a pair of surgical gloves to Spencer, and together they carefully pulled back the rest of the tarpaulin. The canoe was about twelve feet long and in a bottom-up position. The hull had indeed been scrubbed clean, almost gleaming, and there was a smell of bleach. Graham Nash got Spencer to help him carefully turn the boat over, and they found the inside as clean and as bleached as the hull.

'I don't think you'll be finding anything in the way of DNA on this little baby,' Nash said slightly cockily, still feeling slightly uncomfortable at Spencer's earlier comment about Ali. 'Whoever cleaned this did a good, thorough job. It's exactly what you would expect a killer to do: destroy the evidence and remove all the incriminating traces. There is one thing though that you may wish to consider, Detective Inspector.' The slight cockiness was still in Nash's tone of voice.

'And what would that be, Mr Nash?' Spencer asked, batting back the smugness. He had seen Graham Nash show off his general knowledge to Ali, to try and impress her, and he sensed that he was about to get the same treatment, but for different reasons.

'Well, did you know that over the past few years, the UK's freshwater rivers have seen a rapid decline in the number of endangered, white-clawed crayfish – the only British native species of the crayfish?' Nash was off.

'No, I did not, Mr Nash, but I am sure you are going to tell me all about it,' Spencer replied slightly irritated.

'For the most part, their demise has been blamed on the spread of the crayfish plague.' Nash was loving this, showing off his intelligence and wealth of knowledge and making DI Davis feel just slightly inferior. That would teach him to mock Graham Nash.

'The demise of the British clawed crayfish followed the introduction of the North American signal crayfish, which carries the crayfish plague – it's a fungal disease fatal to white-clawed crayfish. Just one single crayfish can wipe out the entire population of native crayfish in a river. Can you imagine how much damage that is, Inspector?'

Spencer didn't answer, and Nash continued speaking, still enjoying this one-upmanship.

'Crayfish plague can survive up to fourteen days, and the salmon parasite can survive for five to six days. It can spread from river to river on wet material such as clothing, spray decks, and the hulls of kayaks and canoes.'

'Is this relevant, Nash?' Spencer interrupted impatiently.

'I believe it could be, Inspector. Our wild salmon are also facing a similar threat due to a European parasite, Gyrodactylus Salaris. That's its Latin name, Inspector. That could start a deadly epidemic if transferred to UK rivers on canoeing kits brought back from Europe.' Nash continued, undeterred by the inspector's irritation. 'The Environment Agency has asked all canoeists to help fight this blight and to give the clawed crayfish and the salmon a better chance of survival. They ask for boat owners to disinfect all equipment, including wetsuits, spray decks, footwear, and canoes.'

Spencer was starting to see the relevance of Nash's line of thought, but Nash was not quite finished.

'I suggest that you check if the owner of this canoe has been abroad with it recently or taken it on any other waters. The parasite is now widespread in Norway, Sweden, Finland, and Denmark and has also been reported in France, Germany, Spain, and Portugal, so you can see how serious it is, Inspector, can't you?'

Spencer knew that Nash was not expecting an answer but could not stop himself from reacting.

'Serious, Nash? I've got twelve violent murders to deal with; now that is what I call fucking serious!'

Spencer turned to the young officer who had been standing, watching, and listening throughout the "Nash Lecture" and, in the same disgruntled tone, instructed him, 'Find out where the owner of this canoe is, Constable, and where he's been with it. I want some answers quickly.'

"And that's why, thanks to Mickey, we all have cake in the morning."

[MAURICE SENDACK – "In The Night Kitchen"]

Chapter 24

THE NIGHT KITCHEN

'Mum. You will never guess what your favourite and only son has done?' Andrew said to Ali out of the blue over a cup of tea in their small conservatory one evening.

'I'm sure you are going to tell me, Andrew, and I am guessing from the tone of your voice that it's going to be something that you think I will like,' Ali said, humouring him.

'You're right, I think you will like it, but aren't you going to try and guess what it is?' Andrew persisted. Ali was doing her best to sound interested, but she really was not in the mood for this.

'You just said it was something I would never guess, Andrew, so what is the point in me trying?' She asked, slightly irritated.

'But, Mum, you're a detective. You of all people must stand a chance of cracking the innermost workings of your son's mind.' He was smiling broadly now, enjoying this little game, not realising how much he was starting to annoy his mother.

'OK... You have won millions on the lottery, and you are buying me a big house somewhere warm, and I can retire to a life of sunshine and gardening?' she said, hoping Andrew would just shut up and tell her.

'Do you think I would be as calm as this about winning millions on the lottery, Mum? What sort of detective work is that?' he goaded.

'You've cooked me something very special for dinner tonight?'

'Err, no, but I have cooked something,' Andrew said, still smiling.

'Look, Andrew, I am tired; I've had a tough day, and I just want to relax and drink my tea. No more silly games. Either tell me or don't.'

'You're hopeless at this game, Mum; what sort of detective do you think you are? I can see I have no other choice, so I'll just tell you.' Andrew knew it was time to stop.

'Go on then, Andrew, tell me. Hurry up; I'm getting hungry. That food smells good; what is it?'

'It's home-made meatballs in a fresh tomato sauce, with hand-made pasta.' He then stood up and theatrically stretched out his arms, ready to announce his news.

'And Mum, my surprise is that Andrew Smith, chef supreme, has got himself a job!'

'That's fantastic news, Andrew; what is it?'

'I am going to be a chef,' he said proudly, and then carried on with all the details. There was no stopping him, and his excitement was clear for Ali to see. 'Well, not to start with, I will be helping out in the kitchen at first, but I should be doing my own chef shifts as soon as I have found my way around and shown them how good I am.'

Ali sat smiling as her annoyance subsided, and Andrew continued.

'It's in a pub in East Oxford. I can get the bus to it; our bus stops practically outside. I'm only working a few lunchtimes and a couple of evening shifts a week to start with, but they are paying me, and I will still be able to help out at home.'

'I am really pleased for you, Andrew; I hope it works out well, and you already help far more than most young men of your age – I am a very lucky mother.' Ali's reaction was genuine; she was pleased for Andrew and relieved that he seemed to have found a job.

'And it means I will only be leaving you on your own a couple of evenings a week, Mum,' Andrew said in a concerned tone.

'What makes you think I don't want to be on my own? I may want a bit of space!' Ali said, partly teasing Andrew but also partly because maybe she did want some space. 'What makes you think I will be on my own all the time anyway?' she laughed and stood up before Andrew could answer, saving him any embarrassment.

'Can we eat now, Andrew? Let's have some wine to celebrate!'

'Mum, we always have wine, celebrating or not!' he said, and they both laughed.

Ali was exhausted again, but as soon as her head hit the pillow, instead of falling rapidly to sleep, her mind became alive and alert. The images of the day played a disturbing slideshow as a backdrop to her thoughts. *'Collecting rings, why? Why did the killer choose that particular family? Did he know them? Were there any connections? How does he do it without being seen or heard?'* She touched her own ring finger gently. No wedding ring was there anymore. She had stopped wearing it after Andrew's father walked out on them, when she had stopped being a wife and had once again become Ali Smith. Andrew and Patricia were all that mattered to her since her husband left, and neither she nor Andrew nor Patricia had any contact with him since that time. She had not known him, not really, and she had spent years going over that, questioning what happened. In truth, he had never really known her either. It was consigned to history – just something that happened. Andrew and Patricia were her only reminders now, and they never knew what really happened; only Ali knew that, and she wanted it to stay that way. It was her secret, no one else's.

She tried hard to sleep, but the nightmarish images were relentless: the Daltrey family lying in the caravan in pools of their own blood. She questioned herself: Why couldn't she be immune to the horror like Graham Nash appeared to be?

She could faintly hear Andrew playing music downstairs; it was one of her records, Bob Dylan's "Desire." Ali had bought the album long before she even met Andrew's father, before she was even a policewoman. They were happy, carefree times then, despite the harshness of the 1970s three-day weeks and lack of jobs. Things had gone almost full circle. Jobs were scarce again, and money was tight. Andrew had done well to find work, especially doing something he wanted to do. They were happy times for her all those years ago when the Bob Dylan "Desire" album came out, but despite everything that had gone on since those times, all the mistakes she had made, her two children had made it all worthwhile, and she would never want to change that fact. She would never want to change them. The track playing, Ali recognised as being "Isis." In the song, Isis is a woman's name, but for Ali, it always made her think of the river Thames, the Oxford stretch that is also called the Isis, that river that runs through the city, the towns, and the countryside, connecting places together and washing things away. The last verse of the song faded away as she eventually fell asleep.

Isis, oh Isis, you mystical child...

* * *

Meanwhile, downstairs, Andrew was sitting at the kitchen table, staring at his laptop. He was on the internet, and the page he had opened was an eBay screen showing all the current items and bids being sold by a seller going by the name of "The Duke of Earl." That was Andrew's secret, no one else's.

Nihonto (日本刀) is a traditionally made Japanese bladed weapon.

Chapter 25

日本刀

Okubo Yasumane stepped out of the heat of his small workshop in the foothills of Mount Noma and wiped the sweat from his brow with his strong blacksmith's hand. Below, in the far distance, he could see fishing boats scattered on the sparkling South China Sea as birds flew above him. Earlier that day, his wife, Sanae, had filled a small lacquered wooden lunchbox with rice and vegetables, which he now sat down to eat. His two sons continued working, keeping the forge up to temperature and watching the fine metal blade change colours as it heated and cooled. The sword being made was one of many hundreds that, over the years, Okubo, now with the help of his sons, had forged, beaten, sharpened, polished, and adorned. A good blade could take two weeks or more to make, but this one was simpler and would only take three or four days to complete, two days to forge, and two days to polish, decorate, and sharpen. The sticky rice tasted good with the vegetables, and the mountain air felt cool and refreshing compared to the heat inside the workshop. He could hear the anvil ringing slowly and rhythmically with each blow his son made with the hammer.

The completed sword was passed on to its customer, who treasured it throughout his life. It then passed from him to his son. Several times through several generations, Okubo's craftsmanship was admired and kept carefully, with each subsequent owner passing it on to the next. Over the years, it travelled many, many miles, and by the time the Second World War had reached its height and Julius Robert Oppenheimer's theories had led to the development of the first nuclear weapon, the sword was in the hands of a captain in the Japanese army, stationed at a camp outside Tokyo. War produces many unexpected things, and the captain's friendship with one of his English prisoners, also a captain, was one such surprising occurrence. With the end of the war came the release of all POWs from the camp. As they said goodbye to each other, the Japanese captain handed over the sword that Okubo had made to his English friend to show him his great respect for their friendship. The sword travelled with the English captain to England and his home in Bristol. Once again, it was passed from father to son and then to grandson. The period of affluence that the English captain's family had long enjoyed was soon to change, and the grandson became unemployed, impoverished, and forced to sell the only thing he had left of value, the sword. It was purchased at an auction by a grand hotel in Bristol and displayed for many years in a glass case in the foyer. The hotel's' décor wore and aged as time passed, the establishment's reputation slowly fading with it until the eventual and inevitable occurred, the business closed. The sword, along with other artefacts in the hotel, was purchased by a company in the West Country that had a huge warehouse full of weird and wonderful objects: enamelled signs, old picture frames, trunks and boxes, books, stuffed fish, animal heads, and antlers. All destined to adorn walls, ceilings, and floors and satisfy the demands of new 1980s theme pubs.

Okubo's sword sat in a dusty box at the back of the warehouse, forgotten for several years. It would have been better for the world if it had stayed that way. The rise in the popularity of Japanese cuisine in the 1990s saw the sword eventually bought by a new chain of sushi restaurants. It found itself displayed in yet another glass case, this one looking out over tables on the first floor of a branch on the High Street in Oxford. There it rested again for several years until it was stolen during a raucous night of partying to celebrate the new Millennium. Whoever stole the sword was never caught, and Okubo's work was not seen again – that is, until Brian Jones heard a knock on his door one night.

One for sorrow,
Two for joy,
Three for a girl,
Four for a boy,
Five for silver,
Six for gold,
Seven for a secret,
Never to be told,
Eight for a wish,
Nine for a kiss
Ten for a bird
You must not miss.

[A traditional children's nursery rhyme]

Chapter 26

TEN FOR A BIRD

It was a rollover, and Brian Jones had been one of two very lucky winners to successfully claim the British Lottery jackpot, netting the Jones family a cool £21,000,000. Brian had worked as a fitter for a local business specialising in supplying and installing kitchens and bathrooms. It was not a job that he hated, nor was it one that he looked forward to every day. With the new-found wealth, he was able to quit work, and he and his wife, Grace, set about looking for a suitable home for himself and Grace's elderly mother to move into. Brian, who was several years older than Grace, had lost both of his parents some ten years previously. The pair of them wanted a big house, one where they could all have their own space and plenty of room for their daughter, her husband, and their two children, along with their son, his wife, and daughter, whenever they all came to stay. Grace loved gardening, and Brian was a keen fisherman. He always dreamed of owning a small boat that he could take off on for fishing trips. The stretch of the Thames between Pinkhill Lock, upriver to Eynsham, and the village of Lechlade, had been more or less untouched over the centuries. Apart from the agriculture, a few pubs, and a sprinkling of big new houses, little had changed. The countryside was serene and beautiful, the air fresh, and a peaceful silence covered the land. On a summer's day, it was mainly the buzz of insects, the chirping of birds, and the rustling of the breeze through the trees that could be heard. The only other sounds were the occasional distant lawnmower from a neighbour's garden and the engine of a sporadic boat passing by on the river.

It didn't take long for Brian and Grace to fall in love with the house when they first saw it. Six large bedrooms, two large reception rooms, a big dining room, and a grand, wide hallway were just some of the features it boasted. At the back, a long, wide, tree-lined garden, just as Grace had dreamed of, led down to its own river frontage with a small boathouse. They paid the asking price and moved in two months later. The few other neighbours, like Brian and Grace, were mostly from working-class backgrounds. Unlike Brian and Grace, the new neighbours had achieved their wealth through successful acting careers or by starting profitable businesses. What they all had in common was their love of privacy. The river houses all offered that in abundance. There was so much space between each property that you would not have realised there were any neighbours at all. The only access to the house was by a small private road at the front, jointly owned and paid for by all the properties it connected. The private road and the river were the only ways in and out.

It was Grace's mother's ninetieth birthday, the first big occasion to arrive in the six months they had been living in the new home. They wanted this to be really special. All of Brian and Grace's family – their son and daughter, their partners, and all the grandchildren – were coming for the weekend. Grace had spent days planning and preparing a big birthday celebration meal. This night, the whole family was seated at the long table in the big dining room, enjoying a pre-meal drink, all ten of them. Brian and Grace could easily have afforded to get caterers in to cook and serve the food, but this, for the Joneses, was a family occasion in their new family home – no place for outsiders, just family. No matter how much money they now had, Grace could, and still wanted to, cook for her family. The smells of the food were drifting in from the kitchen; glasses chinked, and the children giggled. Brian tapped the side of a wine bottle with a spoon to get everyone's attention. The table became silent, and he stood to deliver a short speech that he had been mentally preparing for a few days.

'First of all, I want to thank you all for coming and to say how very welcome you all are in our new home, and by "our," I mean all of us, as this is your home as well.'

Brian paused and looked affectionately at the table full of smiling faces. His happy family: they deserved this.

'And secondly and most importantly, I want you all to fill and raise your glasses and wish "Mum," to Grace, "grandmother" to some, "great grandmother" to others, and "mother-in-law" to me,' a ripple of laughter crossed the table, 'a very happy ninetieth birthday, and may you have many more of them.' They all raised their glasses, and Brian finished with 'To Olive.' The gathered family repeated the toast, all slightly out of sync, as they clinked their glasses. Olive sat with watery eyes, touched by her loving family, as they waited silently for her to speak.

Olive did not get a chance to reply. Before she could utter a syllable, from the front of the house came a loud knocking on the door – knock, knock, knock. The bell didn't work when they moved in, and as they were not expecting any surprise visits, Brian had not bothered to fix it. Since the comings and goings of delivery men and removal men in the first weeks of them moving in, not a soul had actually knocked on the door.

KNOCK, KNOCK, KNOCK.

Brian looked at Grace, slightly puzzled, then at his mother-in-law and said, 'Hang on a minute, Mum, I'll go and get that. Probably one of the neighbours come to complain about the noise; you know what they are like,' he joked. 'Back in a sec,' he said, getting up and leaving to answer the door.

It was dusk outside, casting a grey-blue tint, making the house and garden look like an old, faded, black-and-white photograph. Brian walked along the wide, carpeted hallway leading from the dining room to the front door. He checked himself in the mirrored coat stand and ran his fingers through his hair. He pulled the door wide open, and for a split second, he tried to take in what he was seeing. He stepped back into the hall in shock – a reflex action – and recoiled, speechless. The man that he had opened the door to was wearing a full-faced balaclava and swung Okubo's sword hard and powerfully fast. The only sound was a dull thud as Brian's severed head fell from his neck and dropped onto the thick hallway carpet, his lifeless body falling slowly and gently next to it. Blood covered the mirror, dripped from the ceiling, and gushed from Brian's neck onto the red carpet, where it blended in and almost disappeared. The swordsman stood over the body, breathing heavily from the exertion he had put into the blow.

'Brian?' Grace said as the dining room door gently began to open. Brian's severed head slowly peered around the opening, still heavily dripping blood onto the floor, and was held by the fist of a masked man wielding a samurai sword. Grace dropped her glass. It landed and smashed on her plate; the red wine spread across the crisp white linen tablecloth. The fear and horror of all those seated at the table were as palpable as the impact of a silent explosion. Before anyone could move, the intruder tossed the head onto the table, where it rolled and came to rest on one cheek, next to a crystal wine decanter. The children screamed, Grace screamed, Grace's daughter screamed, and the son-in-law screamed. Her son and his wife screamed. The only one that did not scream was Olive, who sat as if she were still waiting to speak.

Panic ensued as they tried to run, to escape, to get out of the room, but the swordsman was fast, very fast, and it was soon over. The sword was as sharp as the day it left Okubo Yasumane's workshop at the foothills of Mount Noma a century ago, and it made short work of the Jones family. It had taken less than 90 seconds to end ten lives. One of the children had hidden under one end of the table and nearly made it to the door – nearly, but not quite.

The wooden floor was now slippery with blood. Severed body parts were strewn across the room; the birthday table was red and wet. The killer counted the bodies before pulling off his balaclava and wiping his sweating brow with the back of his murderer's hand. Treading carefully around the carnage, he picked up severed arms and hands, carefully cutting off each finger and thumb before tossing the rest of the limb aside, until he found what he was looking for. After slicing them off, he took two of the fingers and the four gold wedding rings and put them in his pocket. He scooped up the rest of the fingers and piled them on the table next to Brian's head. There were ten bodies and four wedding rings this time. *'Not bad,'* he thought. Standing up straight, he looked slowly around the room and then into the large mirror hanging on one of the walls.

'Didn't we do well!' he said, smiling, and then he left the dining room, left the killing floor, out through the back door, into the garden, and down to the river again. Back to the canoe, his clothes soaked with blood, his body slicked with sweat.

Verde que te quiero verde, verde viento verdes ramas
Cel barco sobre la mar, el caballo en la montaña
verde, que yo te quiero verde, ay sí sí
que yo te quiero verde ay, ay ay , yo te quiero verde.

[FEDERICO GARCIA LORCA – "Romance Sonambulo"]

Chapter 27

SPANISH CHICKEN

'Working at the pub is fantastic, Mum. I love it!'

Ali had just got home early for once, and Andrew was there the moment she walked in, giving her all the details of his day in the kitchen.

'We had 15 covers today. That may not sound like much, but the landlord said it was the most food the pub has done at lunchtime so far this year.'

Ali slung her jacket on the hanger, kicked off her shoes, and threw herself down on the sofa, exhausted. She knew there was no point in interrupting Andrew when his enthusiasm was high; she'd just sit and listen. Besides, she simply didn't have the energy to do otherwise.

'My boss, the landlord, is a really nice guy, and he loves my cooking; so do the customers, apparently. I've only worked for six lunchtime kitchens since I started, and now he wants me to work an evening shift on Tuesdays. He even wants me to prepare the menu for it! It's going to be fantastic. I'll make it the best gastropub in Oxford.'

Andrew disappeared into the kitchen for a moment, and Ali could hear the clattering of pots and pans.

'And, Mum,' he shouted from the kitchen, 'my boss is really into music and has lent me some fantastic CDs to listen to, really eclectic stuff. Have you heard anything by Frank Zappa? Canned Heat? Or Gram Parsons? Mum, you would love Gram Parsons; it's that sort of country stuff but really modern sounding, right up your street…'

Ali could hear Andrew's voice getting louder as he stepped back into the living room, still talking.

'Pattie would love it too, Mum. All of those great bands she put me onto, and now I can do the same for her. She'd get on really well with my boss; you would too, Mum. He isn't just a landlord; he's a really clever guy – into art, literature, and music. Tuesday night at the pub, the night I'll be working, is the poetry and open mic night. My shift is from three in the afternoon, mostly prepping, 'till ten or ten thirty-ish, depending on how busy the kitchen has been and how quickly we can tidy up. The kitchen closes at nine…'

As Andrew continued to talk, Ali was thinking about her daughter, Patricia. She missed Pattie like mad but knew she had her own life to lead, and anyway, Ali herself had left home by the time she was Pattie's age.

'So, that means I should be able to get out into the pub and listen to some of the performers for the last hour or so, at the end of my shift.'

'Well, good for you, Andrew, and I am really pleased you are doing so well. It's about time you got out more; so, well done.' That was the first time she had been able to get a word in since she arrived home from work.

'Thanks, Mum. I couldn't have done it without you.'

Ali was puzzled by this; she couldn't think of anything she had done to help, but she accepted the compliment anyway and smiled.

'You're a good cook, Andrew, and that publican is lucky to have you.' She paused for a moment and continued, 'So, what have we got for dinner tonight, Chef?'

Andrew could not wait to carry on talking about food, and he was soon off again.

'Well, I thought I would try one of the dishes that I will do on Tuesday at the pub: lunchtimes are mainly wraps, sandwiches, ham, eggs, and chips, that sort of stuff, but for the evening shifts I can cook proper meals. So, tonight we are having a Spanish dish. The boss's mum and dad are retired and living in Spain – San Luca, I think he said – so I thought I'd try and impress him with some modern Spanish cuisine.'

'It sounds lovely, Andrew, and I'm starving!' Ali said, hoping it would spur him into making some food instead of just talking about it.

'Do you want to know how I cooked it?' he asked.

Ali smiled and nodded, wanting to just eat it but also knowing full well that Andrew was going to tell her whether she wanted to know or not.

'Well, there's diced chicken marinated in…' Andrew went on to list all the ingredients. He loved listing out ingredients for the food he made; he loved lists. Ali sometimes wondered whether he must have a photographic memory; she could barely remember how to make a pancake mix. Anything with more than three ingredients, and she couldn't be bothered. Thankfully, she didn't need to be bothered; Andrew did all the cooking anyway.

Ali had been through another hard day at work; they were all hard days from here on in, the same as they had been for some weeks since the murders started. It would continue until they caught whoever was going up and down the river, killing families one by one. She didn't discuss any of this with Andrew; he knew she was involved in a big murder case, but he didn't need to know any more than that; he didn't need his head filled with the horrific details that were constantly flying around inside hers. Andrew was happy – really happy. In fact, it was the happiest she had seen him in years. He had found a job that he liked, and the pub had given him a chance, despite his lack of training or experience. He had been lucky, but he deserved it, and that pub really should be pleased to have him.

The murders were in Ali's head; no matter how hard she tried to put them behind her when she was at home, they just would not stay away. They were constantly lurking in the background and thrusting themselves back to the foreground without warning, just like the killer. Spencer seemed to cope with the horrors of this better than she did. He seemed to be able to remain detached and not get emotionally involved. She knew that it was one of the golden rules of being a detective – to remain aloof and impartial – but these murders were different; they were families, children, brothers and sisters, mothers and fathers, husbands, and wives. What if it were her family? All those years of caring, watching children grow and learn, all that family time, all that love gone! Lives were over and ended by someone who thought it was OK to kill and destroy families. Someone who thought it was OK to annihilate them.

The meal Andrew had made left Ali with a warm, satisfied feeling in her stomach, and, after another large glass of the tempranillo, she could feel tiredness setting in. Tomorrow was Friday, and perhaps she would get a few hours to herself this weekend and even have a lie-in. Andrew didn't work at the weekend, at least not yet, so maybe they could spend a bit of real mother-son time together and even go out for lunch somewhere, her treat. It would be her way of saying, 'I may be a police officer, but I am still your mum.' She also felt that, in some ways, she was losing touch with her son. She was worried about what he did with his days, concerned that he seemed not to have any real friends. Perhaps some time spent together in a different environment would be good for them. Maybe Andrew would open up a bit more; maybe she could raise some of the issues she was worrying about; maybe she could be a proper mother. It was a lovely idea, she thought, but the way things were happening around her at the moment, nothing could ever be certain.

Lechlade is the highest point at which the River Thames is navigable. The town is named after the River Leach, which joins the Thames nearby.

Chapter 28

FRIDAY

It had been two, maybe three, days that had passed while the ten dismembered bodies had been lying there undiscovered, according to Graham Nash and his forensics team.

'More likely to be three than two, judging by how much the blood has dried,' said Nash, waving a clipboard around as he informed an ashen-faced DCI Ali Smith and a stern-looking DI Spencer Davis.

'Look at this,' Nash said, holding up a sealed, clear plastic evidence bag. 'The blood at the base of the neck has congealed but is still sticky; it takes three days for that much haemoglobin to set. We will know more when we get a chance to have a closer look at what all these flies have been up to and see how far they have got. That will give us a more accurate time of death.' Nash seemed entirely disconnected from the horror that lay around him; in fact, he was positively jovial, unaware of the smell of death in the room and ignoring the masses of black flies that were swarming around the bodies.

'We found it over on the dinner table, next to that lot.' Nash pointed to the blooded table, where a pile of severed fingers had been stacked up. 'Next to the sticky fingers.'

Spencer and Ali stared at the pyramid of severed fingers and then back at the head in the bag that Graham Nash was showing them – the head of a middle-aged man with his mouth and eyes still wide open. Ali wondered how someone as young-looking as Nash could be so totally unaffected by this; how could he bear to be in the same room as this for so long? Even with a breathing mask on, Ali was desperately trying not to gag from the stench of decaying bodies, while Nash was not even wearing a mask. The temperature outside was well below average for August, but it had still been warm, and three warm days had attracted thousands of flies to the corpses strewn around the room. And then there was that overpowering, sickening smell. Ali wasn't sure what it reminded her of until, all of a sudden, it dawned on her. It was out-of-date meat! The room smelled of sickly sweet, rotting, putrid meat. It was the smell of ten bodies – men, women, children, old, young, and all dead. Ali ran outside to the garden, pulled her mask off, and threw-up into a bush as discreetly as possible. There was a chink of metal, a whiff of lighter fluid, and then the smell of tobacco – the heightened senses again. Ali straightened up and turned around to face Spencer, who was holding out a lit cigarette for her in one hand and placing one between his lips with the other.

'I'm sorry, Spence,' she said, wiping her mouth with the back of her hand and taking the lit cigarette from him. She placed it in her mouth and pulled the nicotine-laden smoke so deeply into her lungs that it made her cough and splutter. Spencer put his arm around her and gave her a hug.

'Hey, nothing to be sorry about,' he said, smiling at her. 'Let's get out of here for a while and give forensics some space to do their bit. Besides, there's not much we can do that would be of any use, not for now anyway. Plus, Nash seems to be in his element in there; let him get on with it.'

In truth, there was a lot they could be doing, but other detectives and officers were proficiently going about their business and taking care of things. Ali knew that there were other things she and Spencer could or should be doing, but she was only too keen to get away, leave the smell, leave the bodies, and leave the flies. She wanted to go somewhere else so she could stop shaking and think more clearly. She wanted to compose herself.

'Cheers, Spence,' she said. She smiled and took another huge pull on the Marlboro.

Spencer drove them both to Lechlade; it was a bit of a distance, but he thought she could do with the fresh air coming through the open passenger's window that he had deliberately opened. Getting away from the room full of dissected bodies would do them both some good. Soon they were sitting at a window table in a small café, drinking coffee.

'The world looks so much better when the sun is out,' Ali said inadvertently to Spencer as she stared out of the window on to the Lechlade street. Mothers pushed small children in prams, children walked and giggled, and elderly people with shopping bags went about their morning's ritual shopping. It was normal life out there. She too had pushed prams, first with Patricia and later with Andrew; she had done that and the shopping – the normal life she once had. She sipped her coffee.

'Well, it's better than all that rain, for a change.' Spencer could hear the triviality of his words bouncing around the café. Ali didn't say anything; she knew Spence was just trying to be normal too.

'Ten more, another ten; when will this stop?' she finally said.

'That totals 22 dead. If he carries on like this, we'll need a calculator to add them up,' Spencer joked, earning him a kick under the table from a smiling Ali.

'Thanks, Spence; you're a good partner,' she said, looking at him with sincerity. Spencer tried to interrupt. He wanted to say it was nothing, but she wouldn't let him. 'Honestly, Spence, I really don't know how I would have survived the last few weeks without you around, and I am sorry I threw up.'

'There are no apologies required, Ali.' Spencer didn't usually use "Ali" to address his senior officer, but this was a human moment between them. 'You're as strong as me at handling all this.'

'Thanks, Spencer.' Then, raising her coffee mug up to Spencer's, she chinked them together and said, 'Cheers!'

Spencer nodded and smiled.

'Do you know what, Spence?' Ali said, pausing to make sure he was listening. 'Last night I was dreaming – well, not really dreaming; I was awake, but you know, I was dreaming about walking in the woods with Andrew this weekend, spending a bit of family time, a bit of real time.' Another mother and pushchair passed the café window as she glanced out.

'I owe him so much, and lately I have been the most distracted mother ever. It can't be very nice for him, can it, me being at work all the time? I'm worried about him, too. I'm not sure what it is or why I am concerned, but there is something not quite right. At least he has found himself a job of sorts now, but I don't know; there is something else, and I was hoping that if I spent some time with him, maybe he would open up a bit and I could find out what it is. And now there's ten more murders! All I wanted was an afternoon together this weekend with my son, walking in all this beautiful countryside, not ten more murders to deal with. Goodbye weekend!'

'Ali, take the weekend off; you need a break, and I'm sure it will do you a lot of good. I have no plans for the weekend, fortunately, so I shall be on the job, and I promise I will keep you updated on all that happens. The Super will understand; we all need a break from this at times, and you can return the favour sometime. How about it?' He put his hand on Ali's arm across the table and gave it a squeeze as if to say, "Come on, this is real."

She looked momentarily at his hand, smiled, and replied, 'I'm not going to say thank you again because I know you will tell me to shut up. Let me think about it; see how the day goes.'

'OK, ma'am, you are the DCI after all; your wish is my command.'

They both laughed.

On the way back to the car, Ali's phone rang; all Spencer heard was a series of 'yes,' 'uh huh," 'OK,' 'I see.' The call ended with her saying to the caller, 'Well done.'

'That was Nash. He is pretty sure the deaths would have occurred on Tuesday night; there is no exact time of death, but that makes it almost four days ago. The wedding rings have been taken from all the female adult victims, including the old lady. Usual

MO, and he thinks a very sharp weapon like a sword was used, possibly a samurai sword,' Ali said, filling Spence in on the call.

'And one disturbing thing he said was, and I quote, 'There are ten bodies, which should total one hundred fingers and thumbs in the Ferrero Rocher pyramid. We counted only ninety-eight.' Two fingers are missing; more trophies perhaps?'

'I'm surprised he didn't start giving you a lecture on samurai warfare.' Spencer quipped; he was not surprised about the missing fingers.

Ali smiled again. 'Well, he did start to, but I timed him out.' She made a "T" with her two hands and added, 'He has done a good job though, what little we do have to go on is thanks to him and his team. I can put up with him showing off a little at times, and he is actually very knowledgeable about a surprising number of different things.'

'And he has a soft spot for you.'

'Has he, Spencer?' she replied with a slight tone of sarcasm in her voice, knowing full well that both she and Spencer knew that to be true.

When the pair arrived back at the house, everyone was there, including the press. Someone had let them know that something big was going on, so there would be no way to keep the lid on this now; the press would soon know about the other killings. Not just the whole of Oxfordshire, but the whole country, would shortly find out that they had a serial family annihilator on the prowl.

Ali and Spencer had parked on the small road at the front of the house, just where all the press photographers and journalists were gathering. Spencer approached the group and asked one of them if he could have a quiet word. The two then stepped away from the throng, and Spencer offered the other man a cigarette.

'Is this a bribe, DI Spencer?' The journalist laughed, accepting a light from Spencer's Zippo.

'Well, you could see it like that, Charlie; our budget for bungs doesn't stretch to much more than that these days.' Spencer smiled, and so did Charlie Watts. Spencer had known Charlie on and off over the years from various cases they had both worked on – one as a policeman and the other as an investigative journalist. Charlie could be ruthless in search of a story, but he always stuck to the facts and always told the truth, a trait that had been forsaken by many of the younger members of the journalistic profession. Even so, Charlie's ways of getting at the truth were not always squeaky clean.

'I want to know how you and your lot found out about this, Charlie, everything you know; this is serious stuff we are dealing with here; lives are at stake, and if there is anything that you know that could help us in any way, you need to tell me.'

Charlie took a long drag on his cigarette, inhaled deeply, and then politely blew the smoke away from Spencer.

'We had a phone call, Spencer, a bit of a strange one. The youngster on the news desk who took it thought the caller might have been using some kind of voice distortion device, or maybe it was just a bad mobile connection. It was about three this morning.' Charlie paused to measure Spencer's response so far.

Spencer filled the gap by asking, 'So you knew it was a mobile used to make the call then?'

Charlie continued, 'We have software at the office that does its best to recognise and record all the calls we get; it was a mobile. We even got the number and traced it.'

Charlie took another pull on his cigarette and looked at Spencer, but before he could say anything, Charlie continued, 'It was a pay-as-you-go SIM card that was purchased years ago; the phone company said there was no way the owner could be traced, but we do know that the call was made from Oxford, St Giles somewhere. Don't ask me why; the network provider gave me that information. I can see what you're thinking.'

'Impersonating a member of the police service is a criminal offence, Charlie, you know that.' Spencer spoke without any indication of how seriously or how lightly he considered the matter. 'So, what did the distorted-voiced caller from St Giles tell you then, Charlie?'

'Everything, Spencer, everything – the murders at Day's Lock, the ones where you told the press you were not looking for any other suspects, and the family in the caravan at Bablock Hythe – they were gassed and bled to death. Oh, and the ten inside the house here, chopped up with a sword, a sharp samurai sword, he told us.'

Spencer looked at Charlie and spoke, 'It was our killer then; no one else would know about those details.'

'Not just me, Inspector; your man made several calls from that number – seven calls to seven different local and national newspapers, to be precise. Look at that lot over there.' Charlie nodded towards the throng of journalists. 'One of them is French, and the one with the leather jacket on, even though it is warm, is from El Pais, Spain, London office, and there is even a Yank in there; more to come too. By tomorrow morning, the whole world will know about this, and the press will be descending on Oxford and the Thames Valley like locusts, DI Spencer; ain't nothing anyone can do to stop it now.'

'You didn't think to let the police know about this then, Charlie?' Spencer asked.

'We would have got around to it, Detective; besides, you already knew it all.'

Charlie dropped the stub of his cigarette into the road and stepped on it before saying, 'Thanks for the fag. I will let you know if I hear of anything interesting.'

'Charlie,' Spencer said just as he was about to walk away and rejoin the rest of the press, 'make sure you do, and I want the details of those calls given to my office ASAP, along with any recordings that were made.'

'Gotcha. Will do,' was Charlie Watts' parting shot as he headed back to the pack.

From what Charlie had said, the caller had made no mention of the fingers or the wedding rings; that part was still "in-house." Spencer went straight to the crime scene tent and commandeered a couple of detectives to interview the rest of the press.

'Find out what had been said to them,' he ordered, 'and make sure you get copies of any recordings they made and any other details, numbers, etc., and don't tell them anything.' With that, he left them to go to work.

Spencer found Ali standing outside the door of the house, and he filled her in on what Charlie had told him.

'He is taunting us, Ali. He wasn't getting any publicity, so he started up his own campaign, and he has given us two fingers, or rather, taken them away.'

'We need to check all the CCTV cameras in St Giles from the time of the call,' Ali said, swinging back into full work mode.

'The calls were made at about 3-3:30 am this morning, ma'am; there shouldn't have been too many people on the streets at that time of night. We may be in luck. I will get a couple of officers on that straight away,' Spencer said, and he started to walk away to make the call, but then he noticed something not quite right with Ali.

'What is it, Ali? Are you OK?' he asked.

'I don't think I can go back into that house, Spencer, not back into that room, not now, not today, I…'

Spencer stopped her mid-sentence.

'Why don't you go and organise the CCTV searches? They are our only chance of a lead at the moment. I'll go back inside the house and deal with forensics and whatever else. It's not a problem, Ali, so please do not pull rank on me,' he smiled, adding, 'and please don't say thank you again.'

Ali smiled, her face showing how thankful she was. She didn't know what to say, so she just blurted out, 'I wasn't going to, Spence, but, thank you.'

'Old it, flash, bang, wallop, what a picture...

It is difficult to know how many cameras are in operation in the UK, but it was estimated in 2011 polls that there were 1.85 million public-facing CCTV cameras in the UK.

Chapter 29

CCTV

Ali was sitting in the Audio-Visual Unit, where they had been busy for the last few hours looking through all the available videos from St Giles taken between two and four that morning. There were surprisingly quite a few people still driving, cycling, and walking about, but none that seemed to be standing around or parked long enough to have made the seven mobile phone calls to the newspapers.

'There are three more cameras we haven't checked yet,' the Audio-Visual Unit's manager said. 'They're not ours; they are owned by the Oxford Internet Institute, part of the University of Oxford. They have three cameras, web cams, mounted on their building in St Giles.'

Ali watched in silence as he loaded a DVD into the viewer.

'From what I remember, one camera is pointing towards the corner with the Randolph Hotel, one on the side of the Ashmolean Museum opposite, and the other looks out over the taxi rank and up St Giles towards the Eagle and Child,' he told her.

Ali knew the Eagle and Child well. She knew it, like many others, as "the Bird and Baby." Not only was it the pub that J. R. Tolkien and the "Inklings" used to drink in, but it was also the place where she had met her ex-husband. More recently, it was somewhere she and Spencer had gone now and again for a quick "unwinder" after work.

The CCTV footage down St Giles contained nothing of interest, nor did the footage from the camera directed at the side of the museum, just late-night revellers and passing cars. There was one more camera to look at, and Ali could then update Spencer and go home for her weekend – the one that seemed to never arrive. At first, there was nothing to see on the third camera: a couple of people getting out of a taxi outside the Randolph and scurrying off to their hotel rooms. Then Ali saw something.

'Wait. Stop there. Can you wind back a little bit, please?' Ali asked.

The images whizzed back in reverse; the couples came out of the Randolph backwards and climbed into the cabs, which reversed down the street and out of camera view.

'Stop right there,' Ali said. She had seen something of interest. Around the side of the hotel, leaning against the wall in the shadows, was what looked like a man – a man talking on a mobile phone, to be more precise. The light was poor, and he could have easily been missed, but there he was. Could it be him – the one they were looking for?

'Can you zoom in on that figure?' Ali asked, pointing at the screen.

The viewer zoomed in, but the figure was in the dark, and there was not much to see. They sat and watched for several minutes. It was long enough for him to have made the seven calls, but the image was poor. The figure slowly put the mobile into his pocket; his calls were obviously over. It looked like he put a cigarette into his mouth, and then a stroke of luck occurred as he held up his match or lighter to light it; for a moment or two, his face was lit up.

'Zoom in on that bit and get me the best picture you can,' Ali said as she reached for her own mobile phone.

'Hi Spence. We may have him on camera. It is in bad light and is a bit blurred, but the audio-visual bods say they can enhance it, and we may be able to make out his face. It won't be ready until the morning, so I have…'

She was interrupted by Spencer.

'Just tell them to make sure it gets sent to me the moment it's ready, and you go home and have that weekend you were telling me about. Everything is under control at the house, and there is nothing new to report, so go home and forget about this for a while.'

'OK, Spencer, err… thanks again. They will send a hard copy to the office and text one to your mobile as soon as it is ready; don't hold out too much hope though, it was very dark.'

The whole case was very dark, and as for "forget about it," how could she do that after what she had seen that morning? How could she get the image of that head in the bag and that heap of fingers to go away – the flies, the blood, the bodies, all of it? But she would try; she owed it to Andrew, and she felt now that she owed it to Spencer as well. A walk in the woods and a meal in a country pub – that is what she promised herself she would do, and that is what she would make sure she did. It was not her fault that some maniac was going around slaughtering families. She shouldn't feel guilty about taking some time off from the case. Besides, a little time away from the "frontline" would refresh her, sharpen her up – it would clear her head and make her more prepared to catch the sick, mad, murdering bastard!

She left the audio-visual unit, bleeped her car open, and climbed in. Looking at herself in the rear-view mirror, she ignored the grey under her eyes and brushed her fringe with her fingers.

'Ali Smith,' she said determinedly while maintaining eye contact with herself in the mirror, 'your weekend starts here!'

Back at the murder house, Spencer was also preparing to leave. There wasn't much he could do there now. Forensics would be at it all night, probably for the next few days or even longer. They would need to get the bodies down to the morgue pretty soon, as they were already becoming a health risk. Spencer had a night in front of the TV planned. He and his wife liked nothing more than armchairs and TV in the evening and watching a good movie. That was his way of relaxing. He never talked about work at home; work was work, and home was home. It was easier to deal with it that way. Tomorrow, Saturday, he would be back at the house, back into the investigation tent, sifting through details, looking for clues. With a bit of luck, the flies would have gone, and hopefully he would have a face to associate the murderer with. If that picture was any good, he would get it circulated in the press to see if anyone noticed the caller in St Giles. Maybe someone saw something; maybe this could be a breakthrough, one they were desperately looking for.

Spencer left the murder house and bleeped his car open and climbed in, but unlike Ali, he didn't run his fingers through his hair; he only looked in his rear-view mirror to see if it was clear behind him so he could reverse. As he drove off, he was already putting the case out of his mind. He knew that he could end up late on his own and that his thoughts would return to the killings, but for now it was time to go home, eat, and watch TV like everyone else did – a bit of normality.

Ali arrived home to find the house empty. She could smell food cooking as soon as she walked through the front door, but there was no sign of Andrew. There were a couple of letters, bills, and a handwritten note on the table next to the front door. She picked it up; it was from Andrew:

'Mum, just in case you are back before me (which I very much doubt), we are out of wine. I know how serious that is, so I have cycled down to the supermarket to get some. Dinner is in the oven, and I will sort it all out when I get home. Don't touch anything!!!
Andy'

He had drawn a little smiley face with a chef's hat next to his name that made Ali smile. *'Serious that we have run out of wine, cheeky bugger!'* she thought. She went upstairs, undressed, and stepped into a long, hot shower. The water felt good as it washed away the dirt of the day, the filth of that house and its flies, and the smell of the bodies. She was starting to relax for the first time in days, maybe weeks. A nice, quiet evening ahead and a long weekend to do whatever she wanted – the walk in the forest, the pub lunch, not much in the scale of things, but it sounded like heaven to Ali. *'Cheers, Spence,'* she thought, *'I owe you one.'*

By the time she had dressed and returned downstairs, Andrew was back; she hadn't even heard him come in.

Soon after the meal, Ali went to bed and was asleep before any demons or nightmarish images could sneak their way into her head. She was out like a light as soon as her head touched the pillow. The best sleep she had experienced for what felt like months. Sweet dreams until the morning light.

Ali's weekend was the tonic she needed, and surprisingly, it went to plan. She called Spencer on Saturday morning, and he updated her and told her to not call him again and get on with her break. However, his update was good. He had got the picture from the Audio-Visual Unit and had arranged for the press to publish it with an appeal to the public for further information. The police presence had been ramped up along the banks in the "kill zone," and all riverside residents had been warned to be on their guard. Many of them had already taken heed and moved away for a while, staying in other properties, going on holiday, and playing safe. Some of those had allowed the police to occupy their riverside properties while they were away and use them as vantage points. The story was now in the news and all over the press; everyone knew, including Andrew. Now he could clearly see why his mum had been so stressed over the last few weeks; he knew that she was working on a murder case but could never have dreamed it was as bad as he now realised. Ali asked Spencer about the wedding rings and the fingers; she was still struggling to understand why and what their significance was. Four wedding rings and two fingers were missing, assumed to have been taken by the killer. There was a trail of blood in the grass leading down to the river at the back of the house, and more blood on the bank; this gave the canoe theory gravitas. In reality, they were no closer to catching the killer than they had been all along. The best break so far was the grainy picture of a man lighting up a cigarette in St Giles; this could be the killer, or it could be just a man lighting up a cigarette. There was not much to go on, really, but it was the best they had for the moment.

Andrew didn't try to talk about any of it with his mother, even after finding out about the extent of the murders in the newspaper. What he did instead was spend the weekend just being with her, being as much a normal family as possible. On Saturday, they went into Oxford, shopped in the covered market, and had a coffee and a pizza slice in the market café, then walked along the High under the dreaming spires. Saturday night they watched a film on TV, an old film, Local Hero, *"the last really successful film that Burt Lancaster made."* Andrew had told Ali. On Sunday, the two of them went for a long walk in the forest near their house. For once, it was dry, and even the sun popped out on occasion. The air smelled good and earthy, and the trees had flourished with all the rain they had received that wet summer. Mother and son wandered and talked, laughed, and joked. Ali spoke a little about Andrew's father, but Andrew just said, 'Mum, we don't need him, so it doesn't matter that he isn't around. Good riddance to him! Pattie feels the same way.'

A wave of guilt came over Ali. Andrew and Patricia only knew half of what had really happened, and she hoped that it would always remain that way. It was her secret that they should never know or find out. A red deer ran across a clearing in the woods; it froze when it realised Ali and Andrew were there. The animal was beautiful, standing still and proud and almost invisible in the dappled sunlight that dropped through the trees. It was magnificent to see a wild beast so close – a small reminder that we humans have not destroyed everything natural.

'Pattie will probably be eating one of those for tea in Oslo,' Andrew joked.

They both laughed aloud, and the startled animal ran off, disappearing into the trees as if it were never there.

Their walk finished at a country pub; it was a real old Oxfordshire country pub, the type that is now, sadly, a dying breed. Hundreds of years old, a thatched roof, worn flagstone floors, and a big open wood-burning fireplace gave the place a rustic smell. It was like a living museum full of antiques. Ali commented on how old and heavy the ornate knives and forks were, and how the cruet set wouldn't look out of place in any antique shop window. They ordered their food at the bar and took their drinks over to a table next to a small window in a three-foot-thick stone wall. While they were waiting, Ali took a chance and ventured on her concerns with Andrew: mainly, how did he manage to buy such expensive food and wine all the time? Where did he get the money from? Andrew told her she was being too suspicious and acting too much like a policewoman. It was simple; he just used the housekeeping money that she gave him each week and his job seeker's allowance, plus he was also a very careful shopper. This was actually very true; he was indeed very careful when he was out shopping, mainly being careful not to get caught! Ali was not convinced: fillet steak, fresh tuna, good wine? She did precious little shopping herself these days, but she still had a good idea of how expensive things were, and the little money she gave him, even with his dole money, could never cover what he was spending. She had at least raised it for now, and Andrew did at last have a job; she could maybe wait and see how things went. Besides, she and Andrew were getting along really well together, which was exactly what she needed. Andrew seemed happy most of the time, and he was not really a problem; he never came home drunk, like many teenagers, and luckily he had never been in any trouble, so really she should be thankful. Maybe she was worrying unduly? What Ali was unaware of was that the main reason he had never been in trouble was because he had been lucky. Andrew would have preferred to use the word "skill" to "luck," but it came down to the same thing: he had just never been caught. To say "never" was not strictly true, but as far as the world at large was concerned, "never" would do, at least for now.

As they put their coats on, ready to leave the pub, Andrew checked to see that no one, including his mother, was looking and quickly slipped the salt and pepper pots into his pocket. Nice!

In Greek mythology, Calliope (beautiful-voiced) was the muse of epic poetry, the daughter of Zeus and Mnemosyne, and is believed to be Homer's muse, the inspiration for the Odyssey and the Iliad. One account says Calliope was the lover of the war god Ares and bore him several sons.

Chapter 30

CALLIOPE

The dry weekend and the sunshine were the only encouragement Tom Hunter needed to take *Wandering Aengus* on a trip upriver. Seven years ago, when he first took ownership of the boat, there would have been far more traffic out on the Thames, but the last few years had seen austerity creeping in at a rate of knots, belts were tightening, and the river was now quieter than Tom could ever remember. Living on a boat was one thing, compared to the essential costs of a land-based home. It may have been cheaper, but the expense of owning and running a boat purely for pleasure was proving to be far too much of an unaffordable luxury for most people, and hiring a narrowboat had never been as pricey. It was an expense that fewer and fewer were prepared for or capable of paying for. It was because of this last fact that Tom was surprised to see so many hire boats moored along the river as he cruised through Christchurch, Oxford, heading towards Abingdon. It also struck him that most of these hire boats seemed to have only one or two people on board. The cost of hiring usually restricts the activity to groups of people or families, rarely individuals.

The open fields that flanked both sides of the river were golden-beige and laden with wheat and corn; some had already been harvested, and huge round bales of straw lay scattered on the remaining striped stubble where the combine had dropped them, waiting to be loaded onto lorries and delivered. Their final destinations were bread making, flour, animal food and bedding for the winter, straw, and hay. The river looked magnificent, with its surface sparkling like crushed diamonds in the glorious English sun. Later that evening, as he neared Abingdon Lock and the sun started to set, the diamonds turned to mercury, silver, and neon-bright. Tom removed his sunglasses so that he could see the natural colours. He knew that stopping *Wandering Aengus* half a mile before the lock in Abingdon would give him privacy, peace, quiet, and solitude. It was always a good place to tie up. The ring of the mallet hitting the mooring pins as he hammered them into the grass-covered ground echoed through the trees along the banks. The engine shut down, and silence took over once again. He carried out his usual checks on the boat, then locked up and slowly wandered up the towpath towards Abingdon to pick up a few things for supper, bread and milk, and a newspaper. Newspapers had become more important to him lately than they ever had.

An hour later, he was sitting in the Anchor with an untouched pint in front of him, transfixed by the article that covered four pages of the Oxford Times he had picked up. The true extent and horror of what was happening along his beloved river were beyond belief. It made him feel physically sick to think that something like that could ever happen, and the police even had him down as a suspect. Neither he nor *Wandering Aengus* had been mentioned; he was at least relieved to see that. He stared at the grainy image of the hooded man lighting a cigarette in St Giles – it could have been anyone; it could even have been Tom. Eventually he folded up the paper and slipped it into the plastic bag with the rest of his shopping – bread, a pint of milk, some eggs – the basic fare of a boater's kitchen. It was early, but there were a few people in the

Anchor already; the first nice weekend for a few weeks had drawn them out. Tom recognised a couple of faces from previous times that he had been in there, but he didn't know any of them to talk to. One of the men in the bar was a boater. Tom had seen him on occasions getting on and off a Dutch barge moored near the bridge, but they had never spoken, and he didn't think the guy recognised him. Maybe it was his years as a policeman that made him take note of people around him, and maybe time had also made him suspicious, like a wise old man, suspicious always. In truth, it was really because Tom Hunter had become even more of a loner than he was when he first arrived in Oxford, and he trusted very few. Most of the time, when he was on his own, he didn't try to spark up conversations with anyone; he just watched the world and its inhabitants pass by. Mostly, people seemed to leave him alone, and mostly he didn't even notice. That was the way he preferred it to be.

Abingdon is only about six miles from Oxford, but the river bends long and wide, taking it on a route covering many more miles and making it feel much further away by boat. For Tom, it felt a long way away from the last murders, even if it was only three locks to Day's, where the killing of another family had started the murderous journey that someone was going on. In light of what he had just been reading in the newspaper, the murders of George, Brenda, and their family at Day's Lock were only the start of far worse things. Tom sipped his pint and noticed his hand was shaking. This was really happening, and the harsh truth was that the detectives investigating the deaths seemed to think he was involved. So far, the police hadn't contacted him regarding the last ten murders, the ones he had just read about in the newspaper, but he felt it was only a matter of time. He knew that even though he had travelled from Oxford to Abingdon, they would still have kept track of him. It wouldn't be surprising if he was being followed right now. With that thought in his head, he took another longer look around the room, studying the faces. For a moment, he stared, eye-to-eye, at a man sitting at the bar, shuffling through a bunch of papers in front of him. Before Tom could change his gaze, the man got up and walked straight over to him.

'Hey, do you mind if I join you?' he asked Tom when he arrived at the table. The American accent was easily detectable, New York-ish but softly spoken. The man sat down with his papers before Tom could answer.

'Hugo, Hugo Lewis.' He offered his hand for Tom to shake. 'I hope you don't mind, but I noticed your boat keys.' Tom's key ring on the table in front of him had a cork ball, slightly bigger than a golf ball, attached. It was a "floating key ring" that supposedly stopped your keys from sinking to the bottom of the river if they were dropped in – not something that Tom had ever tested to see if it really worked, but it was a give-away sign that the owner of such a key ring was a boater.

'I am just a visitor here and don't know the area at all. I am on a narrowboat, a hire boat. Can I get you another drink?'

Tom didn't have time to accept or decline before the American visitor went to the bar, leaving his pile of papers on the table. Tom didn't touch them but could clearly see the printed heading on the notepad on top of the pile. He couldn't make out what the pencil scribble below said, but the header read "New York Times, London."

Hugo returned with the pints.

'Sorry, I didn't get your name?' He said, as he placed a fresh pint in front of Tom.

'Tom,' was Tom's succinct reply, 'and thanks for the beer.'

The American took a sip from his own glass and spoke again.

'Look, Tom, to be straight with you, I'm a journalist.' Hugo gestured to the pile of papers. 'I'm The New York Times, London correspondent. I've been living in London for five years now, and this is my first trip up country to Oxford and my first time ever on a boat. I'm here for the murder story – the family killings.'

Tom was not sure how to take Hugo; he seemed genuine enough, and he didn't seem to be hiding anything; he seemed happy to say who he was and what he did. Despite that, the last thing Tom wanted was his name connecting him to the murders in any newspaper. So far, he had been lucky and avoided that. The source of the story reported in the British papers had come from a phone call made by a man who they thought was the killer; so far, the police had not commented. The only thing released to the press was the grainy CCTV still from St Giles. There was no mention of any suspects in the article that accompanied the picture, and Tom wanted it to stay that way. He definitely didn't want to be named in The New York Times by this journalist, calling himself Hugo Lewis.

Hugo continued, 'Like I said, I am a stranger here, and I have never been on a boat before, but as the river is where it is all happening, the paper decided I should get myself on it. I saw your keys, your key ring with the ball thing, and wondered if you would be able to show me how to "drive," if that is the right word, my boat; the boat hire company only gave me a fifteen-minute instruction trip, and I still don't have a clue what I am supposed to do.' He paused and took a sip of his beer. 'I'd be happy to pay for your time, Tom; well, the paper would be, that is.' Hugo raised his glass, hoping that Tom would chink his pint against it to show his acceptance and seal the deal. Tom raised his glass also, but before he let them make contact, he had a point to make.

'OK, Hugo, but I do have some conditions.'

'Just name them, Tom,' Hugo said, smiling.

'The main one is that I don't want my name in the newspapers, and I don't want you publishing it or speaking with any other journalists about me, understand?'

'Anything you want, Tom, understood. I just want a few boating lessons,' Hugo said still, holding his glass up expectantly.

'OK.' Tom chinked the glasses. 'It's a deal. We can start in the morning, say 9 am?'

'I'll be ready. I'm on Calliope. She's a forty-five-footer, moored on the other side of the river, opposite the pub here; she's a "cruiser stern," they tell me, whatever that means.'

Tom drained his glass and left the pub. The sun had almost set completely when he left the pub, and another big pale moon was hanging low in a sky full of black clouds that gathered on the horizon. It was a surprisingly warm evening; normally in August you could expect warm evenings, but this year summer had hardly happened, and the warmth of that particular evening stood out as a reminder of how the weather should be. As Tom left the street by the bridge and started his walk back down the towpath, the rain began to fall. It fell heavily, with warm rain wetting his hair and running down the nape of his neck, bouncing off the path and the surface of the river. Soon he was completely soaked but feeling alive. It had been a long time since he had been drenched by warm rain, and it felt soothing and sensual. There was something reassuringly natural about rainwater, something cleansing. Back in *Wandering Aengus,* he pulled his wet clothes off and dried himself with a towel, then lay on the bed, listening to the heavy downpour pound the roof of the boat and the crackling of fat droplets as they smacked the surface of the river and became part of it again. The noise lessened as the rain eased, and Tom slipped quietly into a deep sleep – a special sleep that only happens when floating in a boat – the sleep of the river, the sleep of the Isis, the sleep of the Thames.

The Thames is maintained for navigation by powered craft from the estuary as far as Lechlade in Gloucestershire and, for very small craft, to Cricklade. From Teddington Lock to the head of navigation, the navigation authority is the Environment Agency.

Chapter 31

KINGFISHER

By morning, the rain had stopped, and the air smelled even fresher than it normally did. Tom sat at his kitchen breakfast bar, drinking hot coffee. A kingfisher landed on a bush outside the kitchen window and started pecking at a branch with its long, straight, thin beak. Tom didn't take his eyes off the bird; he had only ever seen a kingfisher that close a few times. Before living on the boat, all he had ever seen was the very occasional glimpse of turquoise blue as one flew past down by the river in Brentford, where he had grown up. A flash of electric blue, and then it would disappear. The kingfisher looked in through the window of the boat and saw Tom but didn't seem to mind; they were no threat to each other, just looking and checking each other out. Then, as quickly and silently as it arrived, it was gone, darting off along the river looking for fish for its own breakfast.

The sun was starting to come out, and a thin mist hung on the overgrown riverbank as Tom made his way along the river to find Calliope and Hugo. The American journalist was already on the back deck waiting and shouted his greetings as Tom approached.

'Morning, Tom, climb on board,' Hugo said, making an exaggerated welcome gesture to usher Tom onto the back deck. 'I'll get you a coffee; it's just made.'

'Thanks, that would be good,' Tom said as he climbed on, looking at the controls on Calliope, quickly working out what was what. Hugo shortly emerged from inside the boat with two steaming mugs of coffee.

'I can see the attraction of this,' he said, handing one of the mugs to Tom. 'The water, the boats, the way of life. Do you know I had one of the best nights' sleeps I've had in a long time, in spite of that downpour? The great British summer, eh!'

Tom smiled, saying, 'Yes, it did chuck it down for a while, but there is something nice about being warm and dry inside your boat when it is like that. You should try the winter when the snow is everywhere and it is minus ten outside when the wood burner is smoking away. That is my favourite time on board.'

'Well, it sure makes a change from West Hampstead,' Hugo joked.

'OK, Hugo, while we are drinking these coffees, I will give you some boating basics; they probably told you most of these in your fifteen-minute training session.' Tom had started the lesson. He was there for that reason alone, so why waste any time?

'There are three basic styles of narrowboats. A "cruiser stern," which this is, means it has a deck on the back that you can stand on or even put a table and chairs out on. Then there is a "semi-traditional" that also has a deck at the back but only just big enough to stand on, and the rest is all covered; and the other one is a "traditional" that has no outside deck at the back, and you steer from inside with a hatch on the roof so you can stand up and see ahead.

Hugo listened carefully. Listening and absorbing facts was part of his job; it was something he was used to doing. He was a fast learner.

'Before you go anywhere, always give your stern tube greaser a half turn,' Tom said, lifting the engine hatch and climbing down into the hold. Hugo made a puzzled face. This was strange language to him. Tom looked up from the engine hold, and to put

Hugo's mind at rest, he explained, 'The stern tube is the thing that spins round with your propeller on the end; you have to give it a bit of grease so that it doesn't wear out too quickly, that's all.'

He climbed out and slammed the hatch closed. Then he turned the key in the ignition far enough for it to light up and make a whistling noise and held it there for 20 seconds, explaining to Hugo, 'These are diesel engines; you need to warm the plugs before you fire them up or they are reluctant to start.'

Hugo nodded to show he was listening and understanding all he was told and being shown.

'And make sure it's in neutral before you start. Remember to always start your engine before completely untying the boat. If you untie first and have any problem starting her up, you run the risk of being swept away by the river, so keep yourself a lifeline. The boat's steering only works when the propeller is pushing water past the rudder, and that is only when the engine is running and the boat is in gear. Have you got that?' Tom placed some weight on this point because he knew that safety came above everything else.

'Everything you do on the river, safety must come first, yours and everyone else's. Never rush, and always think ahead. If in doubt, slow right down or stop; the river won't dry up; there's no rush. Remember, Hugo, these narrowboats weigh anything up to thirty tonnes or more, and the river is running fast right now, so handle her with care, Bud.'

Hugo untied the boat from its moorings, leaving a lifeline as he had been taught, slipped the engine into gear, and slowly took off. Tom showed him how to steer.

'Always steer from the middle of the boat, Hugo; that is, wait until the middle of the boat is at the point where you want to turn. If you use the nose as the point to start making your move, she will turn too soon. The middle, Hugo, always use the middle of the boat.'

Hugo listened carefully and watched closely everything that Tom was doing. They cruised up towards Culham Lock, practicing turns and other manoeuvres. He was starting to get the hang of it.

'You're a good teacher, Tom,' he said, smiling as he reversed Calliope to practice another turn. Tom smiled, and as they travelled, he became more relaxed around Hugo and much chattier. He had even started to look as if he was enjoying it. *He was*. Tom was taking to Hugo, starting to like him, and it felt good to have a bit of company for a change.

'This boat was the last one they had left to rent; I guess I was lucky.' Hugo slapped the roof of Calliope as if patting her on the back. 'It looks like all the newspapers and all the gonzos are in town; they all want to be on the river, the epicentre of the murders, the kill zone, the river killings.' Hugo jumped on the flow of conversation and risked asking a question. 'So, what do you know about all this murder stuff, Tom? Heard much on the river about any of it?'

Tom was immediately on his guard.

'I only know what you know, Hugo, probably less, what's in the newspapers, that's all,' he replied.

'Sure, but you must have known something before the papers got hold of the story; it's on your river,' Hugo suggested as he slowed the boat down to turn again.

'It's not my river, Hugo. It's everybody's river, everybody's, and nobody's. No one owns the river or the land it flows through; some just think they do. It was here before them and will be here for a long time after they have gone, and like I said, I only know what was in the papers. I have been through Day's Lock many times and knew the lockkeeper to say hello to, so I knew about those murders, but at the time the police said the son had killed the family and they were not looking for anyone else. That was in the paper too.'

'Day's Lock, isn't that the next one along from here?' Hugo asked.

'No, the next one is Culham, then Clifton; there's about four and a half miles between those two, and then you have another four miles or so until Day's,' Tom informed Hugo.

'I don't suppose we could go there now, could we?' Hugo asked; he still felt happier having someone driving or at least being with him, and he was not sure if he could go all that way on his own.

'I can't do that, Hugo; the lesson can only be for this morning; I have things to do; but you will know how to get there on your own when we have finished,' Tom tried to gauge Hugo's reaction to this. 'I will take you through Culham and back, so you know how to deal with the locks; then you are on your own, Bud.'

Tom hadn't liked the conversation turning to the killings and was keen to get the lesson with Hugo over and done with so he could get back to *Wandering Aengus* and move on. They went through Culham with Tom doing most of the work, then Hugo took over for the return journey. Tom helped him moor up where they had started out and wished him luck.

'Tom, that was fantastic. Thank you so much. How much do I owe you, or should I say the paper owes you?' Hugo asked, reaching into his back pocket for his wallet.

'Nothing, Bud,' Tom replied. 'Have that one on me. Consider it a 'thanks' for the beer you bought me last night.'

'OK, Tom, I'll be around here for a while now, so I am sure I will see you again.' Hugo took a card out of his wallet and handed it to Tom, saying, 'Give me a call sometime. Have another beer together?'

'Yeah, will do, Hugo,' Tom said, taking the card and putting it in his back pocket. 'And you remember what I told you – be careful, be safe.' Even as he spoke, Tom knew he had no intention of seeing or contacting Hugo again. Hugo seemed like a nice enough bloke, even for an "investigative journalist," but Tom didn't want the press around him, the press, or the police.

"Behavioural profiling has never led to the direct apprehension of a serial killer, a murderer, or a spree killer, so it seems to have no real-world value."

[CRAIG JACKSON – Psychologist]

Chapter 32

PROFILE

POLICE PSYCHOLOGICAL PROFILE REPORT

Prepared by Dr Philip Goode - BSc, MPS
Requested by DCI Alison Smith

Some background information that may help you better understand my report:

Serial killers have a common personality profile, and the reasons for their behaviour are usually apparent. There are different types of serial killers, and each one has their own agenda and reason for killing. There are, however, traits that are common among all of them. Often in childhood, the signs can include bedwetting, setting fires, and abusing animals. As the future killer grows older, they develop other signs such as the desire to be alone, poor performance at school, being socially inept, and being unable to hold a job. There are usually family problems that also indicate potential future aggression.

Spencer tossed his head slightly backward and rolled his eyes. *'Could be anyone, most of the people I work with,'* he thought to himself and smiled as he adjusted his position in the swivel chair and carried on reading.

A serial killer: A person who kills many innocent individuals for their own personal satisfaction, and each kills in their own horrendous ways. There are different types of serial killers, which I have outlined below:

The Visionary Serial Killer: Those who usually hear voices instructing them to execute other human beings.

The Missionary Serial Killer: This type of killer often feels as if he or she has a responsibility or a special mission to rid the world of a certain specified group of people.

The Lust Killer: Lust killers are often driven to kill due to sexual motivation.

The Thrill Killer: They take lives because they enjoy the experience of killing.

The Power Seeker Killer: This is a person who enjoys having total control over the fate of their victim.

The Gain Serial Killer: One who kills to gain money or items they believe to be valuable.

Another important fact is that approximately ninety percent of known serial killers are Caucasian males between the ages of 25 and 35 and have high IQs ranging from 105 to 120. They prefer solitude to social environments.

Spencer thought it was time for a break and dropped the report on his desk, stood up, and walked off to the coffee machine. There was no one else in the office, so it was just the one cup he needed to get. Psychological profiling – he didn't think much of it other than that it was mostly a waste of public money. He had a short attention span for reading stuff like this, it was just fifty percent common sense and fifty percent guesswork as far as his opinion went. He preferred to use his skills, experience, training, and seasoned "hunches." Hunches were different from just guesswork, he believed. Hunches were what good detectives had, combined with the confidence to trust them and follow them. These psychologists just got in the way and confused the investigation; they got everyone focused on the wrong things most of the time. He returned to his desk, picked up the report again, and scanned through a couple more pages of "background waffle," only slowing down for the bits he considered to be the point of the report.

...and based on the underlining information I have so far provided, the following assumptions may be made about our killer:

'Our killer,' those two words grated on Spencer. *'He is not your killer, Doctor Phil Goode; he is mine!'* He thought quietly to himself and continued to read.

The killer is most likely to be a white male, late twenties to late thirties. Probably he will be unemployed, maybe self-employed, or get an income from something other than work. He is most likely to be heterosexual, as there is nothing that indicates otherwise. In my professional opinion, I would say he definitely had or is having problems at home with his family. The theft of the rings indicates that his family was probably matriarchal; his mother wore the trousers, so to speak. Judging by his knowledge of the river and the surrounding area and his ability to commit these murders and remain undetected, these factors would suggest he is local.
Of the categories of serial killers I have outlined at the beginning of this report, I think we can rule out the visionary type, as there is nothing he has shown to indicate this, especially in the phone calls to the newspapers. Likewise, there is nothing that displays any sexual activity or interest, so unlikely to be a lust killer. Nothing has been reported as stolen, other than the rings and a couple of fingers, so we can rule out gain killing. The positioning of the bodies and the amount of violence he exerts show they are key to this personality; they show that he is, most definitely, a power seeker. He is probably mixed up with some thrill-killing behaviours, and he is certainly on a mission, which would also tie him into the Missionary Serial Killer type. The killer is annihilating families and is

enjoying every minute of it. One thing that can be said with certainty is that he will kill again and again until someone or something stops him.

Please contact me if I can be of any further assistance.
Dr P. Goode

'Thank you, but "no thank you", Doctor Feel Good,' Spencer said out loud to the empty office, smiling at his play on the psychologist's name. He tossed the report into Ali Smith's inbox on the desk in front of him and opened up the case file on his PC. The blurry picture of the man lighting a cigarette, in the shadows next to the Randolph, stared out at him. Spencer studied it for a minute or two. It could be anyone. The calls received since the picture had been published in the newspapers, on TV, and on the internet were not a great deal of help. Spencer selected just the Oxford calls, of which there were only four claiming to have been in the St Giles area on the night of the calls. Each of them thought they had seen the man in the shadows making the calls, his clothes were dark, and he was wearing a hoody. The heights they gave him varied wildly between five feet six and six feet three. None of this was of much help to Spencer, who was aware that they were not yet even sure if this was the man who made the calls to the press. It could quite easily be anyone. It could be a colleague, the man next door, or the man you passed on the street – it could be anybody. It could even be Tom Hunter.

Spencer logged off, picked up a pen, and scribbled a note for Ali Smith.

'Ali,
Gone to check up on Mr Thomas Hunter to see where he was at the time of these last ones. Call me if you need me. Should be back after lunch.
Spence.'

He stood the note up between the keys on her keyboard, grabbed his jacket, and left. It wasn't difficult to find where *Wandering Aengus* was moored. The Environment Agency had been asked to keep a check on its movements. A quick call to them and Spencer soon knew every lock that the boat had passed through and the times, but even better than that, the Environment Agency patrol boat that "polices" the Oxford stretch of the river had reported that *Wandering Aengus* was moored on the south side of the river between Sandford and Iffley Locks. Spencer left his car in the pub car park next to Sandford Lock, crossed over the footbridge, and started to walk towards Iffley. There was already an autumnal feel in the air, even though it was still August. Spencer turned up his collar. The fresh air, the river, and the scenery were doing wonders for his sense of well-being. It was good to be out of the office and get some exercise, especially as it wasn't raining. The river meandered, and the footpath swept along with it. Grassy verges and clumps of trees and bushes filled both banks. The land was open, and nothing was built, leaving it as peaceful and empty as it had always been. Spencer had read that the Thames Path, the footpath he was on, ran the entire length of the Thames, changing sides where necessary to bypass private property or impassable stretches. What a walk that would be to do in his retirement, he thought, but right now he had a job to do.

A plume of white smoke rising gently from the chimney of *Wandering Aengus* and drifting out over the river was an indication to Spencer that Tom Hunter was home. Spencer questioned if it was "home" or "on board"; he wasn't sure which was correct and debated both, deciding that both were. Either way, "on board" or "at home," Tom most certainly was. The door of the boat opened almost at the same time as Spencer knocked. Tom had felt the movement as Spencer stepped on the back deck; he knew he had a visitor.

'Mr Hunter,' Spencer said, trying his best to look friendly. 'Sorry to bother you again, but would it be possible for me to ask you to help me out again?'

'DI Davis, you always seem to know when I have the kettle boiling, you have better come in.' Tom opened the door fully, and

Spencer climbed down the two steps into *Wandering Aengus*. Once again, he was inside Tom Hunter's private world. The same as the last time, the warmth was the first thing he noticed; with another chilly day outside, it felt welcoming. He followed Tom through to the kitchen area; this time Spencer was paying far more attention to detail. He made a mental note that there was a small hand axe and a saw leaning against the side of the steps; he also noticed how clean and tidy everywhere looked. The kitchen area where they sat was the same as Spencer remembered it. There were already two mugs out waiting to be filled with coffee; Tom must have sensed someone was coming. There was a framed lunar calendar on the wall and a couple of photographs of the river next to what looked like the plans for *Wandering Aengus*. The boat felt homely, in a male way, the way Spencer thought he might have styled it had he ever chosen to live that way. There were not really any feminine touches that he could see. It occurred to him that Mrs Davis would soon have a few vases of flowers and lots of bright cushions added, maybe even that cuckoo clock. On the breakfast table were a few newspapers and an open laptop. On the wall above the table was a cork pinboard. Spencer scanned it and made mental notes: a few photographs, looking as if they were from Tom's Met days, a bill from the Abingdon chandlery for fuel, a take-away menu for an Indian restaurant, and three business cards pinned in a line: one was DCI Ali Smith's, another was Spencer's own, and the third read "Hugo Lewis, New York Times, London."

'So, Mr Hunter, I see you have read the full story in the newspapers now.' Spencer nodded his head to one side towards the newspapers next to the laptop. Perhaps you can better understand why we asked some of our questions when you came into the station?'

Tom handed a mug of coffee to Spencer.

'I can't believe you could think I had anything whatsoever to do with that,' Tom said, also nodding towards the newspapers, mimicking Spencer, or maybe mocking him.

'As you will know from your own policing days, Mr Hunter, in cases like this, where families are the victims, we first focus on the nearest and dearest, then we move out. As we moved out this time, you cropped up. In truth, you are the only one that has cropped up again and again, so you will understand why we have to follow that up. We are keeping all of our avenues of inquiry open at the moment; we haven't just settled for you – not just you, Mr Hunter – but we can't rule anyone or anything out.'

Spencer couldn't help noticing how much more relaxed Tom was in his own environment and how much friendlier he was.

'So, you have suspects then, Inspector, other avenues?' Tom asked.

'I'm afraid I can't reveal any of our investigations to you at this stage, again for reasons you will know and understand, but I think I have already alluded to the answer to that one.'

'What else did you want to ask me then?' Tom asked.

'We need to know where you were five days ago,' Spencer started to ask.

'The time that those ten people the newspaper says were murdered?' Tom asked.

'Yes, when the murders took place. Your movements that night in particular.'

Spencer didn't see Tom Hunter fitting the psychologist's profile he had read earlier, at least not any more than he could see many people he knew fitting it. Tom did live alone, and often remotely, but so do most boaters and many other people. He didn't seem socially inept, in fact the opposite; in different circumstances, Spencer may well have enjoyed Tom's company. The boat showed no signs of any strange behaviour, and from what he knew, Tom's childhood hadn't been an unhappy one; normal family life had prevailed. His parents were both dead, but there had been nothing in his records to indicate that this had caused anything other than the grief most feel when losing parents. On the other hand, his marriage had been problematic, and Tom had been very touchy about it when he was questioned, but then Spencer knew plenty of people who had been divorced and were touchy about it. Ali Smith for one, and he probably could have included at least eighty percent of single men living on boats; the wife gets the house, and the husband gets a boat; it was *"de rigueur."* Somehow Spencer could not quite see Tom as a schizophrenic psychopath, but he was, however, still their only suspect, even if it was only a coincidental connection. Exactly what that connection was would play on Spencer's mind for weeks to come. Was it someone Hunter knew? Did he have any enemies that might be trying to frame him for this? Was there something he had done that had caused this to happen? Did he know more than he was letting on?

'I was on the boat; I'm always on the boat. Five days ago, I was on my way up to Abingdon. That night, I was fast asleep in my bed, alone. I was moored.' Tom stopped to think for a moment. 'Near the Isis pub, as far as I remember. Days of the week become less meaningful and less memorable when you retire, Inspector.'

'Retire,' Spencer again thought that Tom was only retired because of his accident, and other than that, he was nowhere near retirement age – too young to be retired but probably outside the profiler's age range for serial killers. But then, what did that mean? Nothing.

'I don't suppose you have anyone who can verify this, Mr Hunter?' Spencer asked.

'Nope,' Tom said flippantly. 'More coffee, Inspector?' Spencer accepted the offer, and Tom refilled the mugs. 'I have a question for you, Inspector,' Tom said as Spencer blew over the surface of his coffee, 'that question you asked me about owning a canoe: is that what you think the murderer is using to get around? There's nothing in the paper about that.'

Spencer looked at Tom and answered, 'I can't reveal details of our investigations at this time, but with your background, Tom, you don't mind if I call you 'Tom,' I'm sure you can work it out.'

Tom smiled before replying. 'Do you want to know something, something that you probably haven't found in all my work files and personal history that you have all been digging around in?'

Spencer sipped his coffee, knowing full well that Tom wasn't expecting a reply and would tell him anyway.

'Well, Inspector Spencer, you may or may not know that a prerequisite for taking a canoe out on this river, especially if you value your life, is that the one in control of it must be able to swim. And it may come as a surprise to you that, even though I live on a boat and grew up very near the river in Brentford, I have never been able to swim!' Tom sipped his coffee and looked out the riverside window, saying, 'Besides, have you seen how strong that water is running at the moment? We have had the wettest summer for decades, and the Thames is at its strongest right now. Half the locks have been red-boarded, and most never get off their yellow boards.'

Spencer looked puzzled, and Tom explained further: 'Red boards are to advise not to navigate boats because the strong flows make it difficult and dangerous, and the yellow boards mean the stream is either increasing or decreasing; either way, it's probably best not to travel.'

'That is interesting, Mr Hunter; I now know something about the river that I didn't before. I notice that you still travel,' Spencer said.

'Only when the stream is decreasing, Inspector, and besides, I have years of experience on this stretch of the river,' Tom explained, picking up Spencer's empty coffee mug and putting it in the sink with his own.

'Before I go, Mr Hunter, strictly off the record, you may think these murders have nothing to do with you, but I'm not so sure. Somehow, in some way, they seem to be very close to you, whether you know it or not.' Spencer looked Tom in the eye and continued speaking. 'Whoever is carrying out these killings is a very disturbed and dangerous person, and if it isn't you, Mr Hunter, I would be very careful, and don't forget to lock your doors at night.'

As Spencer walked back towards Sandford Lock, he thought about Tom not being able to swim. If that were the case, then he was hardly likely to go paddling up and down the river in complete darkness. Spencer was being careful not to rule anything out, but his feelings told him that Tom Hunter was not a killer; for now, that is all they had. And what Spencer had said to Tom, off the record, was what he really believed. Tom Hunter was, in some way, part of all this. Spencer had no idea how or why, but all his training, experience, and hunches said he was.

Built as part of the early development of James Street (sold off in lots between 1861 and 1864) as three small cottages that were joined together to create this public house as one of many that typified the streets of East Oxford between Cowley Road and Iffley Road.

Chapter 33

THE JAMES STREET TAVERN

Tom sat at a small table in the window at the front of the bar in the James Street Tavern, eating one of the best meals he had tasted in a long time. Jamie wasn't in the bar yet; it was still early, and Tom hadn't called him to let him know he would be coming in. In fact, there were very few people in there. Dave, the guy who sang "Stardust," had popped his head in and said hello to Tom, but he wouldn't be back until about nine. It was open mic night again; Tom enjoyed those evenings and always called in when he was around, partially to catch up with Jamie but mostly because he enjoyed the music and even liked some of the poetry, and now it was looking as if you could get some good food as well. "*Make sure you lock your doors at night,*" the detective inspector had said to him. This was actually quite a scary thought. The newspapers hadn't gone into great detail about the actual killings, but there had certainly been a lot of them, and whoever was responsible, as DI Davis had said, must be a very disturbed and dangerous individual.

Tom, however, couldn't see any way whatsoever that he could be involved in any of this, which he found reassuring. He didn't want to consider anything unknown that meant he could be involved; that really would be scary. Even so, he did make a mental note to double lock his doors at night, for a while anyway.

Tom cleaned his plate with the last of the bread. The meal was delicious, Spanish chicken with paprika-roasted potatoes. He went to the bar to get another pint, taking his empty plate with him. He didn't recognise the young girl serving, but then the staff changed frequently, and he didn't really come in very often. He asked her if Jamie was around, and she said he would be in later.

'Thank you,' he said, picking up his pint, 'that was fantastic food, by the way.'

She smiled and said, 'Cheers, I'll pass it on to the chef. In fact, you can tell him yourself if you like; here he is.' She gestured towards the young man who had just stepped through the door that led into the kitchens behind the bar.

'Andrew, this man,' she paused, looking at Tom as if to ask who he was.

'Tom,' Tom said.

'Tom was complimenting your food.' She finished speaking and was immediately distracted by another customer leaving, Tom, and Andrew standing there.

'Yeah, thanks a lot, Bud. That was really delicious. One of the best meals I have eaten in some time, that's for sure.' Tom picked up his pint, ready to return to his table, when Andrew surprisingly held out his hand, inviting Tom to shake.

'Thanks, Tom,' Andrew said as Tom shook his hand. 'It means a lot to me. I have only just started, and I am really trying to make a good impression.'

'Well, you will have no problems there, Buddy. Jamie has never served anything remotely as good as that meal I just had. I will tell him how good it was when I see him; he is a friend of mine.'

'Thanks again, Tom. If you are still here when I finish my shift, I will get you a beer.' Andrew said, beaming from ear to ear.

'There is a good chance I will be, but you don't need to buy me a beer. I may be drinking with Jamie later, so come and join us when you are finished, and I'll get you one.'

With that, Tom went back to his table.

He sat back in the window and watched the world go by; not much actually went by. It was that strange time between after the end of the working day and before anyone had started to go out for the evening, which made it even more surprising when two pints were suddenly placed in front of him and a New York accent said, 'Ahoy their shipmate, here's one of those beers I owe you; do you mind if I join you?' Tom looked up at Hugo Lewis' big smile.

It wasn't what Tom would have liked; Hugo's arrival was likely to bring the murders to him again, but Tom gestured for him to sit down.

'I'm off duty right now, Tom.' Hugo said, cheerfully. 'You mentioned this place to me, so I thought I would check it out, get a bit of the old local culture, and I thought I might possibly catch up with you. I don't know many people in Oxford, just a few of the other hacks.'

'I'm impressed that you managed to get your boat up to Oxford after just one lesson, especially with the river like it is,' Tom said.

'Yeah, that would be impressive, amigo, but, hell no, I took a cab. The New York Times will pick up the tab; I told you I'm on full expenses. You just nod when you need another drink. Have you eaten?'

'I have just finished eating, Hugo, but I have to say the food here is great. Well, it is tonight if my meal is anything to go on.' Tom passed an A5 sheet of paper with the evening's menu printed on it.

'Hmm,' mumbled Hugo, holding the paper almost at arm's length. Tom realised that Hugo must normally use reading glasses. 'I tell you what, Tom, I'm gonna go with your recommendation. What did you have?'

'Spanish chicken, third one down,' said Tom, now feeling he was stuck with Hugo for the evening, but he had warmed towards him again, and so far he hadn't asked any questions about serial killers, so maybe he really was 'off duty.' Hugo went to the bar, menu in hand. Tom could hear him placing his order.

'May I have the same as my partner over there had, sweetheart? Third one down, I hear it's good.' Hugo pointed at the menu. 'And two more of those wonderful English pints you did for me a short while ago and keep the change.' Tom saw Hugo hand a 20-pound note to the barmaid. *'Americans!'* Tom thought. *'They never get it; we don't tip bar staff in Britain.'*

'I tried to take that old boat of mine out, Tom,' Hugo said between mouthfuls of chicken, 'but that river sure has a kick in it at the moment. It's like whitewater rafting in some places. I figured it was safest to take a cab.'

'You did the right thing, Hugo,' Tom said. 'Even I get into difficulties when the river is like it is at the moment.'

Tom looked over towards the bar again to see if there was any sign of Jamie, but there wasn't. What he did see was Andrew, the young chef, peeping through the door that led to the kitchen. Tom nodded hello to him. Andrew gave a thumbs up in reply and disappeared back behind the door. He had work to do.

'Yeah, well, I will try and take her up to Bablock Hythe one of these days, as soon as that old river starts behaving itself. I'd like to take a riverside view of that trailer site.'

Tom didn't want to talk about Bablock Hythe or any of the other places related to the killings; he just wanted to drink his beer and try to catch up with Jamie. Hugo sensed this, and remembering his "off duty" comment, he quickly changed the subject.

'You are not wrong about this food, amigo. This is the best meal I have had since I left London.' Hugo was enjoying tucking into his food that had arrived while they were talking; he spoke quickly so that he could get another mouthful in. He swallowed, took a large sip of his beer, and carried on talking between mouthfuls.

'All those other hacks, those gonzos on their hire boats, will have no idea what to do, especially with that fierce old river. Boy, am I lucky to have met you, Tom!' Hugo raised his glass and chinked it with Tom's. 'They haven't moved since they moored up.

I guess they are all just floating and waiting, waiting for something to happen. I like to think I am a professional, Tom, a real seasoned, genuine investigative journalist. Like the Canadian Mounties always get their man, I always get my story, and you teaching me how to handle that barge has enabled me to do that with this one. For that, I thank you again, sir.'

'Hugo, if you want to sound like a seasoned, genuine boater, never call it a barge; they are narrowboats, occasionally canal boats, but all real boaters call them narrowboats.' Tom couldn't resist correcting Hugo.

'Thanks for the tip, Tom. I guess you can always look the part, but you can't always be the part, eh?' Hugo smiled, hoping that Tom would understand what he meant.

'When this is all over, Tom, I may come back and spend some leisure time on one of those narrowboats; I like the cosiness of them, their independence. It would be a great place for me to start that book I always promised myself I'd write one day. We will have to keep in touch.' Hugo was moving away from the murders, and Tom felt much happier with this new line of conversation and replied to Hugo.

'I'm sure we will, Hugo. I'm sure we will. It sounds like you have a plan.'

Hugo nodded in agreement, wiping his plate clean with the last of his bread in the same way Tom had.

'Man, that was delicious!' he said. 'Now, let me get us another pair of pints.' Before Tom could say anything, Hugo had grabbed the nearly empty glasses and headed off to the bar.

Tom knew it was definite: he was stuck with Hugo for the rest of the evening. However, Hugo did seem to be sticking to his word and not going on about the murders, the subject that most people in Oxford were talking about.

'I have to turn in a piece for the paper in a couple of days and...' Hugo started to speak, and Tom felt that he was about to stray onto the subject of the killings after all; he was relieved when Hugo continued, 'Apart from all the background stuff that everyone has already reported, I'll just re-vamp that; I'm thinking of doing an angle on the "idyllic life on the river" and how this has shaken it all up.'

Hugo paused and looked at Tom to see if he still had plenty of beer before continuing.

'It is idyllic, Tom; I know you will agree with that. I had no idea about boats or living like this until the paper sent me here. I know this isn't the high point of its "idyllic-ness," but I can see how sweet this way of life must be. You have made one hell of a good choice there, Tom.'

Tom smiled and nodded in agreement, saying, 'I think it was the best ever choice for me. I would go even further than that, Hugo: living on the boat kind of saved my life. I was in a mess when I first arrived in Oxford; my marriage had collapsed, my career had terminated, and I had no idea where I would go or what I was going to do. I had no idea where my life was heading; in fact, I could barely understand what had happened and how I got to be where I was.' Tom paused and looked at Hugo to see if he was taking this in, and he saw that Hugo was indeed listening to every word. He didn't really know why he was telling Hugo all this, but it felt good to tell someone to get it off his chest and, in some ways, reassure himself about what he was doing with his life and why he was doing it. The beers that Hugo kept buying, "courtesy of The New York Times," may have had something to do with Tom talking so freely for once.

'The first night I ever slept on *Wandering Aengus* was when it belonged to Jamie, the landlord of this pub, as it happens. I didn't like it much and had an uncomfortable night's sleep. I did see the potential of it, though, and the attraction.' Tom stopped to take a swig of the latest pint that Hugo had bought for him. 'When the opportunity to buy her came up, I originally saw it as a project, something for me to do until everything had settled down and I had more concrete plans. Building the boat slowly sucked me into a whole way of life that I never knew existed, and it started changing me, even though I wasn't aware of it at the time. I hadn't known people like the ones I was starting to mix with, and, to be honest, it uncovered a big hole in my experience. I soon found that things slow down when you are on a boat, and the world around you slows down with it. The maximum speed allowed on the canals and rivers is four miles an hour, a brisk walking pace, and you adjust to that. People have more time for each other – time to talk, to listen, and to help. Some of those people I admit I would have avoided in my previous life, but getting to know them, as I did, opened my eyes and exposed my prejudices and narrow-mindedness. I was still thinking of *Wandering Aengus* as just a project right up until the first night I slept on her when she was mine. It was one of the coldest winter nights for years, and I could hear the canal cracking around the boat as it froze up. I watch two swans desperately trying to keep a hole free from ice so they didn't get frozen in.' Hugo sat, taking in every word Tom spoke. 'The boat was still full of wood and tools; I hadn't finished working on her, and all I had was a sleeping bag on a futon, but the fire was fitted and burning nicely, keeping everything warm inside. Something happened to me that night. I don't know what it was exactly; it was nothing I can put into words, just a feeling, but everything for me changed that night, and I knew from that moment on that I would be living on *Wandering Aengus*, on the canals and the rivers for as far as I could see. I still see it that way.'

Tom stopped speaking and drained his pint, and Hugo spoke.

'Wow, Tom! That is quite some story. I have only spent a couple of nights afloat, but I am already starting to see what it is like. That is why I want to come back and write about it one day. When you say it "saved your life", what did it do exactly?'

'It showed me where I had gone wrong, Hugo, and it showed me how to put it right.' With that, Tom stood up and took their two pint glasses over to the bar for a refill. Hugo had put up a bit of a fight to try and pay for them, but soon realised that it was a losing battle; nothing Hugo said would stop him. At the bar, Tom asked again if Jamie had shown up, but he hadn't; that is all the girl serving knew. Hugo looked over and saw someone at the end of the bar speaking with Tom. Hugo couldn't hear what was said, but he could see that Tom was not happy about it, whatever it was. Tom returned with two more pints, and they raised their glasses to each other again, beer friends. For Hugo, Tom was his way into life on the river, his guide to that world. For Tom, Hugo was someone who was outside his own small world, someone he could talk to; as long as Hugo didn't start reporting things about Tom Hunter in his newspaper, they would get on fine. Rod McKuen, an American poet, once said "strangers are just friends waiting to happen," and in the case of Hugo and Tom, this seemed to be true, and it was happening.

Most of the customers that frequented the James Street Tavern were friendly, happy souls, a mixture of students, locals, and a few serious but also friendly drinkers. This sociable bunch made David Legg stand out even more than he would have anywhere else. David Legg had been a motorcycle dispatch rider, one of the couriers that were renowned for driving recklessly and considered by many to have the half-life of lemmings. True to form, David Legg managed to crash his old BSA motorcycle in glorious style. He crashed on the field-surrounded Eynsham Road, doing well over the speed limit. He skidded across the road, hit the kerb and, still on his motorcycle, flew through the air over the tall hedge that lined the road, landing in a wet field where he lay out of sight for several hours, passing his time by taking photographs of the bones sticking out of his leg. There was no signal on his phone, and all he could do was lie there until, through shock and lack of blood, he passed out. A cyclist eventually spotted David Legg's contorted body lying next to a bent BSA 500cc motorcycle. From his early school days in East Oxford, David Legg had been called by the nickname "Leggy," which was unfortunate for him as after the crash, the hospital struggle to save the leg was successful, but it would never be the same again; it was now bent and shorter than the other leg, leaving David permanently disabled and only able to walk with the aid of crutches. Leggy was not the nicest of men prior to his accident, but since then he had got far worse – bitter and twisted, you could say – blaming everyone and everything for the problems he now had to live with, the problems that had in fact been purely the result of his own foolish actions. He would never accept it was his fault, blaming the council, the roads agency, the police, the other motorists, the workmen, etc. The list went on. He was a big drinker before the crash and an even bigger one after it. Most nights he would drink heavily in the James Street Tavern, where he was known and tolerated, at least to an extent. He would prop himself up at the end of the bar, telling everyone in earshot over and over again about how he lost the use of his leg and who was to blame. The more he drank, the nastier he became, inevitably getting to the point where he would be thrown out of the pub. Recently, for some reason, he started mouthing off about the murders.

As Tom and Hugo raised their glasses yet again, Leggy, the man Hugo recognised as the one Tom had words with at the bar, approached their table and, without warning, started on Tom.

'You, Hunter! Call yourself disabled. I am disabled; look at me! This is what you call disabled!' Leggy leaned on his crutch and let his short, bent, and damaged leg dangle about two inches off the ground. 'And look at you; nothing wrong with you! Not a fucking thing! It don't stop you from claiming all that disability pension, though, does it? All that police money, all that taxpayers' money. Typical coppers, always looking after each other, covering up for each other, fucking bent as a nine-bob note, the lot of you!'

Tom stared up in disbelief at what he was saying and just how much Leggy seemed to know about him. The disbelief was showing on his face, but before he could say anything, Leggy continued his rant.

'Oh yes, I know all about you, Tom "copper" Hunter. Filth! You think you are special, don't you? You think you are better than the likes of us. Even the police didn't like you, your copper mates! I know all about you and your little cowardly ways. I've got friends from the Rock of Gibraltar – friends who knew you from the old days, Hunter. The days when you would get as drunk as the rest of us and mouth off about your poxy toes, your bitch of a wife, and how big you were with a gun in your hands, in a uniform. None of them liked you up there; Hunter, you didn't fit in, and no one trusted you. I don't like you either, and I trust you even less. It wouldn't surprise me if it wasn't you going around killing all those wankers!'

At that point, two of the bar staff pulled Leggy away and escorted him to the door. Expletives shouted out by Leggy filled the bar as he was steered towards the door, followed by what seemed like a long silence, until Hugo spoke.

'Friend of yours, Tom?' he asked, a little surprised and shocked by the outburst.

Tom didn't get a chance to respond as fists hammered down on the outside of the window next to where they sat and muffled shouts.

'You fucking murdering copper bastard! I'll have you, Hunter; I'll have you fucking crippled. Crippled! I'll show you what crippled is; I will fucking cripple you myself. You are a fucking fake, Hunter, a fucking scrounging lying murderer.' Leggy could still be heard in the distance shouting as the bar staff assisted him along the street and dropped him on the Cowley Road for the police to deal with.

'He drinks in here,' Tom replied after Leggy's shouting had faded away. 'I don't know him really. I don't understand why they put up with him in the pub. I think Jamie feels sorry for him for some strange reason.'

'Well, he seemed to think he knew a lot about you, Tom.' Hugo said.

Even before Hugo said this, Tom was already on his guard. He hadn't told anyone in the James Street Tavern that he had been a policeman. Jamie was the only one who knew that – Jamie and everyone else in the pub now, including Hugo. What else had Tom said about himself on those drunken nights in the Rock of Gibraltar – those nights when he was struggling with all that had gone wrong in his life? Leggy had called him a murderer; did he know something? Had DI Spencer or DCI Smith ever questioned Leggy and told him about their suspicions? Tom felt his stomach tighten, and he clenched his fists under the table, making his knuckles turn white where the bone thinned, stretched the skin, and forced out the blood.

'You OK, Tom?' Hugo asked, sensing Tom's discomfort, 'Can I get you another glass of that fine ale?'

'Yeah, Hugo,' Tom said, snapping out of his thoughts. 'That would be sweet.'

'OK, officer, same again,' Hugo quipped as he headed for the bar, not even catching the look on Tom's face as he said it.

The open mic started as Hugo and Tom downed yet another pint. A few poets read short pieces of their work, and Tom noticed that Hugo was listening intensely. A young guy that Tom hadn't seen there before did an acoustic version of the old Fleetwood Mac song "Man of the World," and the evening wore on with Tom and Hugo getting more and more drunk.

'You know what the Chinese say, Tom, about drinking?' Hugo drunkenly asked an equally drunk Tom Hunter. He didn't wait for Tom to reply before carrying on, 'First the man takes a drink, next the drink takes a drink, then the drink takes the man.'

'I'll drink to that, Hugo,' said Tom, raising his pint as they both laughed and drank, and the guitarist sang a Peter Green song.

'Shall I tell you about my life...

Andrew's shift had finished, and when the singer ended the song, he went over to Tom and Hugo's table. More beer was drunk, and the laughter soon pushed Leggy's outburst into insignificance. Andrew liked these two men; they were drunk, but they were also funny and made him feel welcome. It was rare for him to spend time socialising with anyone, so he was especially enjoying having a beer with Tom and Hugo. The three of them drank, drunkenly talked, and laughed until it was very late. There was still no sign of Jamie when the pub closed, and they spilled out onto the nighttime street, still laughing and talking.

Ol' man river,
Dat ol' man river
He mus'know sumpin'
But don't say nuthin,'
He jes'keeps rollin'
He keeps on rollin' along.

[PAUL ROBESON – "Old Man River"]

Chapter 34

WILD HORSES

When Tom woke up on *Wandering Aengus* the morning after the night with Hugo, his head was throbbing, and his mouth was dry. He didn't remember getting home, walking along the river, back towards the Isis. It must have been very late, as he had no recollection of seeing anyone else. His head hurt, his arm was heavily bruised, and the knuckles on his right hand were grazed where he had most likely fallen over, on the steps by the bridge or in the street; it could have been anywhere. Bits of David "Leggy" Legg's outburst came back to him, and he shivered. The last thing he really remembered, and that was only vaguely, was saying goodnight to Hugo, who got a cab from the James Street Tavern back to Abingdon; at least that is where Tom assumed he had gone. Tom shivered again. The boat felt cold. Outside, there was a thick mist, so thick that the bank was no longer visible. He touched the top of the burner with his grazed hand. The fire had burned out during the night, and the cast-iron fire felt barely tepid.

Normally he would have riddled it and filled it with wood before going to bed, making sure it stayed ticking over until morning, but he had obviously drunk too much to be bothered with that the night before. It now needed a bit of urgent attention if he was to ever get warm again. He climbed out onto the back of the boat to get wood and kindling. The mist was heavy, and there was very little visibility. He climbed onto the roof of the boat and found his head was just above the mist, and a clear blue morning sky glowed above. Standing on the roof, the mist came up to his knees. Trees and the top of the Isis pub were the only things to be seen above the silvery white cotton wool landscape. Tom knew that soon the sun would burn it off, and the rest of the world would still be there underneath. Gathering the wood from his small store on the back of the boat, he stepped back down inside the boat and started work on the fire. Once that was blazing away, the next item on his list was hot tea and breakfast. Just how much about himself had he revealed to Hugo come to his mind? How much would Hugo keep in confidence? Just how much had the beer talked? Whatever it was, it was too late now. He had taken Hugo on trust and followed his instincts. He just hoped they were right this time.

Tom asked himself why he had drunk so much the night before. This was a question he had asked himself many times in the past. During his days and nights at the Rock of Gibraltar, the beer would flow in copious amounts. It seemed that everyone who went there was a heavy drinker. Some nights there were a few problems – the odd argument – but more often than not, they all got along with each other, at least to an extent. Tom still liked to have a drink, but, with the exception of last night, he had reined it in a bit from his Rock of Gibraltar days. Some nights, too many nights at the Rock, he had no memory of; too much had been said on those nights never to be remembered, at least not by Tom. Leggy used to drink in the Rock very occasionally, mainly on account of having an old biker mate who lived near the pub. Leggy would get him to fix things on his old BSA. It wasn't often that he was there, and Tom couldn't remember ever having seen him. He only knew Leggy from the James Street Tavern, and all he knew about him was what Jamie had told him and what Leggy had told everyone, many times. Leggy would start up on anyone that he felt like upsetting, for whatever reason he may have had, and it wasn't the first time that he had picked on Tom. Normally, Leggy didn't get to say too much to Tom before Jamie shut him up. Jamie was the only person Leggy had never attacked. That last night, Jamie hadn't turned up at the pub, which may have been why Leggy got particularly mouthy. Tom knew that it was from the Rock of Gibraltar days that Leggy had found out about him being an ex-copper, but some of the things he had said, Tom had no idea why he would have said them. In the back of his mind, he did know, though. In the back of his mind, he knew there were nights in the Rock of Gibraltar when he had said far too much about himself, even things about himself. What was done was done, and besides, no one would have taken any notice of Leggy; it was just beer talking. He sipped the hot tea and broke the yolk of a fried egg with the corner of a piece of buttered toast.

A couple of miles away, upriver, the mist had almost cleared. Despite the fast-flowing river, a hire boat was making its way downstream, albeit with some difficulty. Robert Johnson had paid good money for him and his family to spend a week on the river, and bad weather, high, fast water, or serial killers wouldn't stop him from getting his money's worth. There was now only a thin mist hanging over the bank at Port Meadow. To one side of the wide river lay the vast open mile-long meadow with its free-roaming horses and cattle, and to the other a tree and bush-lined bank with the odd clearing and small beaches favoured by fishermen. The mist was low, hugging the bank, but visibility was still good. As Robert's boat slowly approached one of the gaps on the bank, he could make out four anglers sitting in a line facing the water in what looked like folding chairs. As Robert's boat got nearer to them, he realised that it was what looked like a family fishing together, which seemed to him unusual inasmuch as, from what he knew most fishermen were loners, he didn't really see it as a family pastime. More than that, most anglers were rude to boaters. It was as if they thought they had more right to fish the river than the boats did to navigate it. He could clearly see it was most definitely a family: mother, father, son, and daughter, he guessed. Out of politeness, he gave them a wave but wasn't surprised when none of them returned it. *'Typical!'* he thought as he carried on past, not bothering to look at them further. It was only the loud splash that he heard that made him turn his head. The man fishing, he presumed the father, was now floating face down in the river, still in his chair and still holding his rod. None of the rest of the family were looking at him; in fact, none of them were moving.

Port Meadow is an ancient area of grazing land, still used for horses and cattle, and has never been ploughed. In return for helping to defend the kingdom against the marauding Danes, the Freemen of Oxford were given 300 acres of pasture next to the River Thames by Alfred the Great, who founded the city in the 10th century. The Freemen's collective right to graze their animals free of charge is recorded in the Domesday Book of 1086 and has been exercised ever since.

Chapter 35

PORT MEADOW

This was not how DCI Ali Smith would have chosen to start a misty Wednesday morning, or any other morning for that matter. Robert Johnson had made the three-nines call at 7.45 am, and Ali had received the message from Command and Control as she was driving towards the station to work. She turned around and rerouted immediately. It was now 8.15 am. Leaving her car at the Perch pub, she walked down towards the river, talking to Spencer on her mobile; he was already on his way. She wasn't surprised to find Graham Nash and a couple of his forensics team already behind the police tape that surrounded the area where the four bodies were. Three of them were sitting in their fold-up chairs, still holding their fishing rods. The fourth body, a white adult male, was laid out on a blue tarpaulin sheet. Nash quickly came over to greet Ali as she ducked under the tape.

'Morning, DCI Smith, we've got four bodies here – another family, I would guess. Those three,' Nash pointed to the three in the chairs, 'are as we found them, and that one on the tarp had to be dragged out of the river before he got washed away or eaten; the crayfish have already started feeding on him.'

'What else can you tell me?' asked Ali.

'Well, they are all dead.' Nash started to smile but quickly wiped it from his face, remembering responses he had got from Ali in the past about his "sense of humour."

'The two adults have had the backs of their heads smashed in with what looks like a single blow – a hammer, at a guess – possibly a lump hammer. All of them have had their throats cut very deeply. I'd say with a sharp blade like a Stanley knife, that sort of thing. No sign of any of the weapons has been found yet, and it is doubtful that any will be. If they have been thrown in the river, we will never find them, not the way it is belting along. Another option is that the murderer could have taken them with him. The victims have all been fixed to their folding chairs in seating positions with cable ties, and the fishing rods have been cable-tied to them as well. I guess that one there,' Nash gestured towards the tarpaulin again, 'must have caught the breeze and blown in the river just as the boat that called it in went by, maybe even hooking the line on the prop. That would have felt like one big fish, if he had been alive to feel it, of course.'

Ali ignored the attempt at humour as she looked over at the grey, dead face of a man approximately forty years old, his clothes wet and the wound on his throat washed clean by the cold river water. She looked back at Nash, waiting for more information, knowing that she wouldn't have to ask. Nash carried on speaking.

'All of the fingers were intact and where you would expect them to be, but there were no rings on the man or the woman. Both the male and the female ring fingers show signs that they wore rings, probably wedding rings.'

'Any of them been ID'd yet?' Ali asked

'Not yet, but there was a red gas bill in the woman's pocket addressed to a Mr K Hartley, a house in Wolvercote. I believe officers are there at the moment speaking with neighbours, but they don't tell me everything, so you will need to speak to one of your boys.' Nash cocked his head to one side as he finished speaking. Ali didn't much like him referring to fellow police officers as "boys," but she let it pass without comment. She was, however, really beginning to find Graham Nash extremely annoying at times, but she tried not to let this show when she spoke.

'Time of death?' she asked.

'Too early to say, but I would guess no more than three or four hours ago, say around 3-4 a.m. The dead of night.' Nash couldn't resist slipping in that last bit. He didn't seem to realise that this had the exact opposite effect on Ali Smith as he hoped it would. He wanted her to see how witty and professionally unaffected he was by what confronted them. Ali just found him callous, thoughtless, and annoying. This was a family, not just "another family," as if they didn't matter.

DI Spencer Davis arrived in time to shut Nash up before he made any more inappropriate statements, and Ali brought him quickly up to speed.

'So,' Spencer said, 'we have the same MO. The same repositioning of the bodies and the same bloody method of killing. Fingers were not removed, but it looks like the rings were. The same man, without a doubt.'

'Only this one, Spence,' Ali added, 'is more public than any of the others. This one was out in the open.'

'Do we know for sure they were killed here?' Spencer asked.

'Well, Nash tells me that, judging by the amount of blood on the ground around them, this is where it happened,' Ali replied.

'They were just a family, Spence, out night fishing together. It got very misty, almost foggy last night, and my guess is they were probably thinking about calling it a day and going home; most of the fishing gear was packed back in bags, except for the rods. That must have been when that monster struck.'

Ali and Spencer made a closer inspection of the scene while forensics bagged and marked everything of interest. There were no indications of a boat being tied up nearby, plus the river was running so fast. Combined with the heavy mist, it would have made it almost impossible to navigate in a canoe in broad daylight, let alone at night.

'Maybe he drove here, Spence, maybe even parked in the pub where my car is right now,' Ali suggested as she looked back in the direction of The Perch.

'Or he could have used Rainbow Bridge at the boatyard down there.' Spencer gestured downstream to where Bossom's boatyard was located. Ali looked at him, wondering how he knew so much about the area, the name of the bridge, and the boatyard.

'From there, he could have gone anywhere across Port Meadow with no one seeing him at all, lost in the darkness, undercover of the night.' He stopped and scanned the vast openness of Port Meadow before continuing.

'When the dog unit gets here, we can ask them to sniff around; in the meantime, I'll get some inquiries started up at The Perch and see what can be found. The pub may have some CCTV; you never know. Our man could be getting careless,' Spencer said, thinking fast. 'He is taking more chances than before and is more likely to make mistakes.'

'Let's hope so, Spencer.' Ali said, 'Let's hope he is careless enough to get caught.' She paused and surprised Spencer by taking a packet of red Marlboros from her pocket and offering him one. 'This has to stop!'

'Yes, let's leave it for our New Year's resolution,' Spencer joked, knowing full well that Ali was not referring to the smoking.

* * *

Back at the station, Spencer pinned the photographs of the latest four victims onto the investigation board and adjusted the total number of deaths to 26. In the centre of the board was a blown-up section of a map showing the river from St John's Lock, Lechlade, through to Goring Lock. There was a circle around Day's Lock with the number "1" and a date written inside it. Six lines had been drawn in felt pen connecting the circle to six photographs: four adults and two children, each child with their eyes still wide open but no longer seeing, their faces white and dead. To the far left of that circle, another was drawn around Bablock Hythe, containing the number "2" and another date. This one had six lines connecting it to photographs of two adults and four children, three small boys and a girl. Not far from that was the number "3" in a circle around an area of the river between Eynsham and Pinkhill Locks. From that, ten lines had been drawn, connecting to ten photographs. Spencer drew a new circle around Port Meadow, wrote the number "4" inside, dated it, and drew lines up to the four photographs he had just added. The full-face shots each had, in addition, a shot of the bodies strapped into the fishing chairs.

'Not a pretty picture, is it?' He said, as he sat down next to Ali and stared at the board with her.

'You are not wrong there, Spencer,' she said almost helplessly, adding, 'Where do we go from here?'

'Well, we could speak to all the usual suspects for starters,' Spencer said.

'Don't you mean the usual "suspect," singular?' Ali asked, already knowing the answer.

'Well, I must admit we have very little to go on. We only have a scant supply of any meaningful evidence – bits and pieces – the river hasn't washed away. And no one ever seems to be around when any of the murders occur.' Spencer walked over to the board as he spoke and put a red "X" where he thought *Wandering Aengus* was moored the night of the last killings. There were several other red crosses scattered along the river, and on the left-hand side of the board was the blurry CCTV photo of the unknown man making a phone call outside the Randolph Hotel; next to that was a photograph of Tom Hunter taken from his Metropolitan Police ID card. Hunter was the only other person pictured on the board who was still alive – the only other suspect they knew. There was a question mark under the CCTV photo and a broken line joining it to the ID picture where Spencer and Ali had considered the two photographs could have been of the same man, Tom Hunter.

'I'll try and find Mr Hunter, ma'am. Let's see what he has to say for himself. I'd rather do it myself; I don't want any uniforms upsetting him any more than he is already; he'd probably not be so helpful if he is wound up too much.' Spencer put his coat on as he spoke to Ali. He knew where to find *Wandering Aengus* already; it was just a case of "would Tom Hunter be on board?"

A short time later, Spencer was standing on the bank, looking at *Wandering Aengus*, contemplating again whether to knock on the roof or step onto the back deck and knock on the door. Lost in that thought, he jumped when he heard a voice from behind him.

'Inspector, back again?'

Spencer spun around to see Tom Hunter with a bag of wood slung over his shoulder and an axe in his hand.

'Ah, Mr Hunter, good afternoon to you. I was hoping to find you at home,' Spencer said, trying not to show his surprise.

'It's strange you always know exactly where to find me, Inspector,' Tom said, feeling relieved that collecting the wood had helped him clear his groggy head.

'Yes, but I never know if you will be in,' Spencer replied, smiling, trying to lighten up the situation, having realised that Tom, like most people, didn't like the idea of being followed.

'You had better come in again, Inspector; I'll see if I can help you.'

On board *Wandering Aengus,* Spencer could see that nothing much had changed: there were a few more newspapers than last time and an open book of British birds on the chair near the fire. Other than that, the boat was as neat and tidy as it had been on the other occasions that he had been on board. Tom filled a kettle and put it on the hob to boil. Without asking, he took out two mugs and popped a teabag into each of them.

'Well then, Inspector.' he said.

'I'm sorry, but I need to ask you where you were again, Mr Hunter,' Spencer said as delicately as he could, trying not to upset Tom in the hope he could get to the truth.

'I told you all that before. Nothing has changed since the last time we spoke,' Tom said, taking a teaspoon from the kitchen drawer.

'But I'm afraid things have changed, Mr Hunter; it's not that occasion that I am interested in at the moment; I need to know where you were last night.' Spencer looked Tom in the eye as he spoke, hoping to see a reaction of some kind. All he saw was general surprise and bafflement.

'What has happened?' Tom asked, sounding slightly alarmed. 'Has there been another killing?'

Spencer knew that Tom would hear about it sooner or later, so he decided to come clean with him.

'Another four; Port Meadow last night, two adults and two children – night fishing.' He looked at Tom again as he spoke and saw shock.

'And you think I killed them as well as all the others, do you, Inspector?' Tom's voice was filled with a mixture of anger and what Spencer thought was despair.

'I just need to know your whereabouts,' Spencer said softly, aware of how Tom must feel, especially if he really was completely innocent, as Spencer was beginning to suspect.

'I was out drinking, Inspector,' Tom gave as an answer.

'Where would that have been?' Spencer asked, looking at Tom's ashen face.

'I spent the whole evening from about five thirty in the James Street Tavern, drinking. I left there; I don't know for sure what time, but it was late.' Tom squeezed the teabags out in the mugs as he spoke. Spencer noticed that the knuckles on Tom's right hand were grazed and swollen but decided not to question this – not yet anyway.

'Were you drinking alone all that time?' Spencer questioned.

'No, I wasn't actually,' Tom replied, realising as he spoke that it was one of the few times when he hadn't been alone recently. 'I was with a friend, Inspector. Hugo.'

'Does he have another name, this Hugo?' asked Spencer.

'Lewis, he is a reporter staying on a boat moored up in Abingdon,' Tom answered.

'Do you happen to know the name of the boat he is on?' Spencer asked.

'Calliope. Moored opposite the Anchor pub, I don't suppose he has moved anywhere since last night, not if he feels as rough as I do.' Tom slid one of the mugs of steaming tea over towards Spencer, who nodded his thanks.

'Bit of a night, was it then, you and Hugo? Where did he go when you left?' Spencer asked, picking up the mug.

'He took a minicab back to Abingdon, I assume, and I walked home to here. And yes, it was quite a boozy evening; they happen sometimes – maybe not to you, Inspector, but to the rest of us they do.'

'Do you mind telling me how you came to graze your knuckles?' Spencer asked. Tom looked at his hands.

'Last night, Inspector, I was very drunk, like I said. I think I did this tripping over on the steps on Donnington Bridge.'

The name Hugo Lewis struck a bell somewhere in Spencer's mind. He knew he had heard it before. Then he remembered that he hadn't heard it; he had seen it. The last time he was on Tom Hunter's boat, that was the name on one of the business cards that Hunter had neatly pinned to his pinboard. 'Hugo Lewis, New York Times, London,' that is what it said. He thanked Tom for the tea and left. Walking back along the towpath, he called Ali Smith to say he wouldn't be back; he was going to Abingdon. Just as he left, Tom's phone rang. He was surprised that it was someone he knew from the James Street Tavern. Tom had arranged to go for a drink with him later in the evening, but he couldn't remember anything about the drunken conversation he must have had. A deal was a deal, so despite not remembering Tom, he agreed to meet up; he was feeling much better now anyway, almost back to normal. The last thing Tom said before putting his phone back in his pocket was, 'OK, Bud, six thirty it is.'

"Home sweet home" is an English idiom implying that one's home is preferable to all other places.

Chapter 36

HOME SWEET HOME

Ali arrived, home shattered. She had spent all morning at Port Meadow trying to piece together the gruesome events of Tuesday night. Having put everything and everyone at the scene into motion, she returned to the station to wade through all the reports that were coming in. She studied the board where Spencer had added the four Port Meadow victims and continued searching for everything they were looking for – anything they might have missed. Nothing new was presenting itself to her when her phone rang – it was Graham Nash. He was back at the lab and had received blood samples from the morgue of each of the four victims found that morning. There were five samples in all, and it was Nash's feedback on the last one that really got Ali's attention. It was the toxicology report on a sample of blood found on the young boy's teeth and in his mouth, a sample that did not match his or any of the other victims. Could this be the first piece of real physical evidence they had of the killer? Was he, as she and Spencer had hoped, making mistakes and slip-ups? The findings were preliminary, but she had been extra nice to Nash on the phone, and he had promised to have his completed report on her desk first thing in the morning. He would probably be working on it until late in the evening, but she had asked not to be contacted until the morning. Tonight, shattered as she was, would be family time – her family, her, and Andrew. Andrew had been working the night of the Port Meadow murders. Ali wanted to catch up with him, see how his job was going, see how he was, and be normal for the evening. As tired as she was, she tried not to show it and greeted Andrew with a hello and big smiles when she arrived home from work.

'You look happy, Mum. Why's that?' Andrew asked, smiling.

'No special reason, just happy to be home and to see you, of course,' she said light-heartedly, 'Anyway, what have you cooked me for tea tonight, Chef?'

'See,' said Andrew, still smiling, 'I knew there was a reason for all the smiles and being nice; you just want to make sure that you get a good supper.' He laughed and carried on talking in the way he did when he was pleased or excited about something; in this case, he was both.

'The customers at the pub have started calling my menu 'Andrew's Marvellous Menu'. I'm going to head it up with that title from now on, what do you think, eh?'

'So, it's going well there, I take it? I am so pleased for you, Andrew, really happy for you, and I didn't for one second doubt that you would find a job.'

Andrew was beaming from ear to ear. Seeing her son's smile made all the darkness of Ali's day fade away. This was more important: the "right here, right now," the living, the breathing, the good, and the warm. Not the dead, the still, and the cold, ugly evil.

They sat down at the table, and Andrew ate as he went through everything he had cooked at the pub, all the ingredients he had used, and all the comments he had received from the customers. Ali tried to listen patiently, and she was only too pleased to hear positive, simple things – things that reassured her that life was really alright. There was happiness waiting to be had everywhere, even in the simplest of things. Andrew refilled Ali's glass from the bottle of red he had opened for the meal. Ali couldn't help wondering how much the expensive-looking bottle of wine had cost and how Andrew could afford to buy it.

After a short silence filled with the last of the food and more wine, he announced, 'Mum, I've got a surprise for you.' Pausing for a moment and looking at his mother to try and gauge her reaction, he continued.

'There is someone I met, one of the customers from the pub I have chatted with a few times, and he is a really alright sort of bloke, and we have become, well, friends, I suppose.' He paused again and could see that Ali was already beginning to wonder where this was going.

'He is quite a bit older than me, more your age, not quite as old as you but closer than he is to my age…'

Ali jumped in, slightly alarmed.

'I hope you aren't trying to pair me off with some 'bloke from the pub' that you have met, Andrew Smith!'

Andrew quickly replied, 'No, Mum, but funnily enough, that's exactly what he said when I told him about you.'

'You told him about me! What have you said?' Ali was now getting concerned. Andrew had once tried to palm his sister Pattie off on one of his mates; it was a complete failure, and it was looking as if he was trying his hand at matchmaking again.

'Nothing much, Mum; I just said that I lived at home with you and that, well, dad left years ago. I'm not trying to pair you off, Mum, honest. Look, he is a nice guy, and I don't think he has many friends, and anyway, you can find out for yourself.'

This last remark almost made Ali choke on the mouthful of wine she had just taken.

'What do you mean "find out for myself"? I hope it's not what I am thinking,' she gasped.

'Look, Mum, it's nothing about pairing you off; I just thought he was an OK bloke, and instead of you and me sitting in every night, when I'm not working, that is, we could go for a beer in the village pub.'

Andrew was still speaking when the bell rang.

'That could be him, Mum; I wasn't sure if he would come or not; it was a bit of a boozy night at the Tavern last night.' Andrew got up to open the door as Ali's mood rapidly changed to one of deep concern.

'Don't tell me you have invited him round here, Andrew?' Ali was no longer hiding her alarm over the situation.

'Mum, don't worry, he's cool, and if you don't want to go to the pub, then I'll go on my own; it's not a problem. I can have friends around, can't I? I do live here as well.'

Andrew left to answer the door, and Ali quickly checked herself in the mirror. She didn't feel comfortable with this at all. After the day she'd had, this she could well do without. Her heart started beating faster as she heard Andrew walking back. Not as fast as it would be once Andrew had introduced his guest.

'Mum, this is Tom. Tom, this is Mum; I mean Ali,' Andrew said as he turned and watched his mother's body freeze and the colour almost instantly drain from her face. He looked at Tom and saw that he also looked shocked and silent. Then suddenly, Ali started shouting.

'Get out! Get out of this house! Get out! Go!' Her voice was like something Andrew had never heard before; she was panicking. 'Andrew, get over here; get away from that man!'

It was only then that Tom spoke. 'Look, I didn't know; I'm sorry; I really am. I'll go right now. I'm sorry, sorry, Andrew.' Tom turned and quickly left.

'What's going on?' said Andrew, now very upset. The front door gently slammed shut.

'Just be quiet, Andrew, and stay here while I make sure he's gone, bolt the doors, and make sure the windows are all locked.' Frantically, she went into the small hallway, quickly slid the bolts on the front door, and looked through the spy hole. She saw Tom Hunter go through the front gate and head off down the moonlit, empty street.

'Mum, what was that all about? Do you know him? Why are you so upset?' Andrew said as soon as she returned.

'Andrew, I have to tell you this. That man, your "friend", is the main suspect, the only suspect we have for…' She stopped herself from mentioning the murders that Andrew already knew, most of the country knew, 'the case I am working on with Spencer. Now do you understand why I panicked?'

'You mean you and your mate Spencer think that Tom is a killer?' Andrew's brain was visibly ticking over. He didn't wait for Ali's answer. 'So, you have evidence that he has done these murders, do you?' He was finding this all too hard to believe.

'He is our suspect, Andrew, our only suspect; we believe him to be linked to all of the crime scenes. I can't say any more than that; you have to understand,' she replied, choosing her words carefully and trying not to inflame the situation any more than it already was.

'Isn't he innocent until proved guilty then, Mum? Because I can't see any way on earth that Tom would kill anyone. He is a nice guy!' Andrew was now sounding as shocked as his mother looked.

'OK, we don't have any firm evidence that he is the culprit, but there is enough circumstantial evidence to connect him with most of the murder scenes, and we have to be very careful. He could be a very dangerous man.'

'I can't believe that, Mum. You always said I was a really good judge of character, and I can't believe that Tom could hurt anyone any more than I could, but then you don't trust me either, do you? You are always suspicious of me as well.'

Ali ignored the last part of what Andrew said, knowing it was true.

'Andrew, whether he is connected, which we think he is, or not, he is still very much part of a murder investigation that I am running, and I can't have anything to do with him. You must understand that, Andrew, you have to.' Ali was calming down, partly so as not to frighten Andrew and partly because what Andrew had said was true. They had no real evidence that Tom Hunter was involved. Circumstantial evidence linked him to the murder scenes, but they were all on the river, and Tom lived on the river, so it could be that maybe it was all coincidental. But if she was wrong, then Andrew's and her lives could be in great danger, and she was not prepared to take any risks with those. She couldn't take that chance. Maybe she was wrong to be worried about Andrew too?

'Andrew,' she said, much calmer and more motherly, the mother that lays the rules down, 'you have to promise me you will not see or speak to that man again, or at least until this case is over, and I can be one hundred percent sure that Tom Hunter is innocent and that you are safe.'

'Sorry, Mum, I can't promise that. He is one of the customers at the pub, and I'm not going to jeopardise my work, but I will be very careful, and I won't invite him around again or see him other than if he turns up to eat at the pub.' Andrew had also calmed down but was standing his ground. Ali wasn't very happy about this situation, to say the least, but she could only do what she could and only say what she had said. Andrew had to make his own decisions.

'Come on, Mum, I didn't mean to spoil the evening. I really did think you would like him. I still do think that, if you ever get to know him.' Andrew spoke calmly, and Ali, of course, knew he hadn't intended to upset her. She also knew that he didn't really know just how much it had upset her and how worried she still was.

'I could do with a drink, Andrew; any more of that wine left?' She said, and tried to smile again.

"Fraid not, Mum, but we do have a nice bottle of port.' He was also trying to repair the evening. 'I bought it to try out a pork recipe I wanted to have a go at, but I then decided it was too good to cook with, and I was keeping it for Christmas. No worries though; there is plenty more where that came from. I'll go and open it up.'

Ali checked the street outside through the window as soon as Andrew left the room. It was silent, dark, and empty. They had both been shaken up by the events of the evening and made big headways into the port. Neither of them mentioned Tom Hunter again that night; they just sat around drinking port after dinner, just the way it is supposed to be.

The combination of the wine and the port had made Ali relaxed; she was even a little drunk, but as soon as her head hit the pillow and her eyes closed, the face of Tom Hunter projected onto her mind, and she was suddenly wide awake and clear-headed. Details, information, images, facts, and hypotheses rushed through her thoughts. The blood on the young boy's teeth – they would need to get Hunter's blood group and see if it matched; it must be in his police records. The other news she had got that afternoon was that Spencer was right and the killer had left via Rainbow Bridge, crossing over the river to the meadow side, the Jericho side. Murphy had led his handler over the bridge and up to the huge lake-like body of water that had flooded a large area of Port Meadow. It was really a massive puddle, caused by all the rain there had been that summer. A small stream ran all along the back of Port Meadow, and it overflowed when it became too full and too fast. Port Meadow is a natural floodplain waiting to collect all the overflow water. The sniffer dog had lost the scent at the water's edge, and, after his handler had walked him all the way around hoping to find it again, Murphy looked up as if to ask, *'What now, boss?'* The killer could have gone in any direction, and there was little to no chance of finding out any more than that. They had reached the end of the trail – the end of the line. An image of the bodies with the fishing rods came into her thoughts, and then one of the boys was struggling and biting, struggling with Tom Hunter. She hadn't noticed any wounds on Hunter's hands, but then he was only in her living room for a few moments, during which time she wasn't really thinking clearly. Maybe Andrew was right, maybe they did have it wrong, and maybe Hunter had nothing to do with any of it after all. She really hoped so, for Andrew's sake. However, if they were right – Spencer's theories and hers – then Andrew had just brought a psychopath into their home. Until the truth came out, Tom Hunter would remain a suspect and be treated like one – someone to be very cautious of; he had to be. She heard footsteps echoing in the silent street below. Immediately she sat upright in bed in a reflex action, the hair on the back of her neck standing on end and her skin goose-pimples. All she saw when she looked out the window was a teenager making his way home through the village. No Tom Hunter, no killers, no mad men, no threats – only the peacefulness of the village, the quietness of the English countryside, the silence of Oxfordshire.

Red Kites are very large birds, but neither particularly strong nor aggressive. Primarily scavengers and opportunists, they are, however, predators.

Chapter 37

A PREDATORY BREED

Tom was back on *Wandering Aengus*. Unexpectedly turning up at Ali Smith's house had shaken everyone up: Ali, Andrew, and, not least of all, Tom. He really hadn't known Andrew much at all and certainly had no idea that his mother was a policewoman, the detective chief inspector who had Tom down as some sort of suspected serial killer. He could still see her face clearly; it was full of shock, full of repulsion, and full of fear. How could he have that effect on someone? He was no monster, no killer; why was this happening? He knew there was no way he could explain or apologise to DCI Smith, and he also knew that it would be wise to keep a distance from Andrew. It felt good to be back at home, back on the boat, and back on the river. He had riddled the burner as soon as he arrived and filled it with a couple of big logs that he had foraged to revitalise the smouldering fire. Night had fallen, and the new wood had first smoked, then burst into bright yellow flames that licked the glass in the door of the burner and illuminated the inside of *Wandering Aengus* with a flickering light that bounced shadows around the walls and ceiling. Once again, the boat was the warm place where he wanted to be most at that moment. No matter what the world threw at him, as soon as he stepped off the bank, off solid land, and the boat moved under his feet, he felt better. It was like leaving the world at large behind and entering a private place where he was, for the most part, in control, even if that was all he could control at that time. On *Wandering Aengus,* it was sanctuary; Tom was literally and metaphorically the captain of his ship. He may not have had control over the events in the world that surrounded *Wandering Aengus,* but on board was his environment. Outside events were spilling over the edge and seeping into his self-contained refuge to remind him that you can't stop the world and get off; it is just not possible, and nothing is that easy. He sat back, looking at the flames through the door of the fire, and thought about what had happened and was happening to him; it was never far from his mind. Again, DI Spencer Davis had paid him a visit, and again, he was a suspect in yet another gruesome set of murders that had occurred not far from him and *Wandering Aengus*. Spencer had said that if Tom was to be believed and he was not the killer, if he was completely innocent, somehow, in some way, he was still connected. Even if he didn't know how, why, what, or who, he was part of it. He was involved. Tom thought through everything over and over, and it occurred to him that DI Davis might be thinking that he knew the killer or that the killer knew him. A friend, acquaintance, a relative, or someone out there was connected to Tom, and that someone was a killer. There were people he had arrested when he was a serving officer in the police, but the worst of all of them wouldn't have been wicked enough to have done something like that – even the ones that could have had a grudge against him. The flames carried on gently licking the glass as he considered everything over and over, and still he couldn't see who, why, or what could be linking the murders to him; there were no reasons or answers as to why any of it should be happening to him. The only common element was the river. The mighty Thames linked many things – many people, many places – through distance and time, through all dimensions. The river threaded through everything and everyone, stringing them together and giving them commonality. That was the way it would always be until the water stopped flowing and the river ran dry.

Tom's laptop beeped as it booted up. He switched on his mobile for the first time that day and tethered it to the USB port so that he could hook up to the internet. For once, the signal was good, and the connection was strong. He googled the Oxford Mail, searching through the back issues until he found what he was looking for.

'FUNERAL FOR THE DAY'S LOCK FAMILY'

The headline jumped out onto the screen with its photograph of the crowd at the funeral. Tom immediately recognised DCI Ali Smith and DI Spencer Davis. DCI Smith was looking much calmer than she had at their encounter earlier that evening at her house. Tom again couldn't believe he could scare and repulse someone as he had Ali Smith. There were many other people in the picture that Tom didn't know or recognise; there were always people that seemed to celebrate the macabre or were attracted by the press and the cameras, a strange breed of celebratory seeker. Right at the back of the picture, behind Jamie, were what could have been a couple of boaters. He scrolled the touchpad on the laptop and zoomed in closer, but the image was very blurry. A few of the faces he thought he remembered from his year of re-fitting *Wandering Aengus*, up near the Rock of Gibraltar pub, but that was years ago, and he couldn't remember any names, just vaguely familiar faces. For a moment, there was one face in particular that he thought jumped out at him, someone he did remember, but then again, it could have been anyone. He sat and stared at the picture, getting nowhere and learning nothing new.

The silence on the boat was broken when his mobile phone rang. He looked at the phone's lit screen, telling him he had an incoming call from Hugo Lewis; this immediately put him on his guard. There was one reason in particular that Tom thought would be the most likely for Hugo to be calling him: DI Davis. Tom picked up the phone, which was still attached to the laptop, accepted the call, and spoke.

'Hugo, what's up?' he asked.

'We need to speak, Tom,' Hugo replied.

'What would that be about then, Hugo?' Tom asked carefully.

'Well, Tom, it's about a little matter of a detective inspector who tracked me down on Calliope yesterday afternoon. I have been trying to call you all day, by the way; don't you ever switch your phone on? This cop wanted to know what I was doing Tuesday night, where I was, and who I was with; any idea why that would be, Tom?' From the way Hugo spoke, Tom could tell he knew full well where the police had got his name and location details from, and it was, he supposed, fairly reasonable that Hugo would want to know why. It was easy for Tom to guess that much, but he had no way of knowing what else DI Davis had told Hugo.

'Sorry about that, Hugo, but I didn't really have any choice but to tell him about you. I had a visit too earlier yesterday, and I got asked the same questions.' Tom stopped there, not wanting to say anything more to Hugo than he already had.

'Why do you suppose they wanted to know where you were, Tom?' Hugo asked. Tom was considering how to answer this question without letting Hugo know that the police had him down as a suspect; that was the last thing he wanted a newspaper reporter to find out. Hugo spoke again.

'It wouldn't have had anything to do with the four dead anglers they found on, what's that place called, oh yeah, Port Meadow, would it, Tom?'

It was obvious that DI Davis was no longer treating all of the investigation work as confidential. Hugo continued.

'I don't want to talk about this on the phone, Tom, not a good idea in my book. I will come over to you in the morning, and we can speak then. Breakfast time, good with you?' For encouragement, Hugo added, 'You owe me one, Tom; after all, you sent the police over to me, and now I want to know why.'

Tom explained to Hugo where to find *Wandering Aengus,* and the call ended, dropping the internet connection in the process. He had seen enough for now and did not bother to reconnect. The picture from the Gibsons' funeral was still frozen on the screen. Somehow, in the warmth of *Wandering Aengus*, none of it seemed real, and none of it seemed to matter. But it was, and it did! Tom climbed out onto the back deck to get a few logs from his log store. It had been a strange, eventful, and disturbing evening, but now he was home. He felt the sharpness in the cold air; the season was changing, and the summer that almost didn't happen was now almost gone for another year. He looked up into the clear, dark night sky and saw a million stars twinkling; the more he looked, the more he saw. The Milky Way smudged across the sky with a billion pinpricks of light. Starlight, travelling its journey to Earth from some place ten thousand light years away, so far away, in another place, another space, another time.

* * *

'I understand your apprehensions about talking to me, Tom.' Hugo looked Tom straight in the eye as he spoke so that Tom could see he was being straight with him, not trying to give any false impressions. He picked up the mug of coffee Tom had made him. Outside, a new day had arrived with brighter skies.

'Reporters, by nature, are a predatory breed. Whenever we speak to anyone, there is always a predatory element involved. I know that, and you know that it's part of the job, Tom.' Hugo carried on looking Tom in the eye as he spoke, trying to gauge his reaction.

'That doesn't mean to say that what I tell you isn't true or is not to be trusted.' Hugo chose his words carefully.

'When I tell you that I will keep your name out of our paper and treat everything between us with confidentiality, I honestly mean it. So please trust me on this, Tom?'

Tom bit into his bacon sandwich and said nothing as Hugo continued.

'You are a suspect, Tom; I know you are, and before you ask, the police didn't tell me that. I am a journalist; it didn't take much; I'm grade "A" Ivy League; I worked it out in less than a New York moment.'

Hugo stopped and took a bite from his own sandwich that Tom had made for him, and chewed it, giving Tom time to take in what he had said before carrying on.

'For the record, Tom, you are not a suspect in my book, and I believe you did go straight home after our session in the pub, well straight as either of us could have done in the state we were in.' Hugo laughed at this, but Tom did not.

'So, what do you want from me, Hugo?' Tom eventually asked.

'Not much, Tom, don't look so worried. I am a man of my word, and I will keep your name out of the paper, but I would like you to do a couple of things to help me out in return.'

Tom was realising that he had very little choice other than to cooperate with Hugo, unless he wanted to see "TOM HUNTER, RIVER KILLER SUSPECT" on the newspaper's headlines.

'What do you want me to do, Hugo?' Tom asked reluctantly.

'First off, you can refill this mug with some more of that great coffee you have made,' Hugo pushed his mug towards Tom, 'and then you can tell me everything you know.'

'Keep my name out of this, and you have got a deal,' Tom said.

'Tom, I'm not blackmailing you; I would keep your name out of the press, whatever you decide. I already made that promise to you, and besides, we are drinking buddies now. But you do kind of owe me one, amigo. And there is one other thing I want you to do, no biggie; I'd like to visit all the murder sites with you, starting with the one from last night at Port Meadow, deal?'

'OK, Hugo, I will do what I can to help,' Tom replied, accepting the offer and all that went with it but still feeling uneasy about what he was entering into. However, in some ways, Tom was actually pleased that Hugo had got involved. It gave him someone to share things with; he would not be so alone in this, and, what's more, Hugo, for one, at least didn't believe him to be a killer, which helped. There was also that thing about keeping your friends close and your enemies even closer. Not that Hugo was an enemy, but potentially all newspapers and reporters were to Tom at that point in time.

'So, how *did* you get home from the pub, Tom? You did go home, didn't you?' Hugo asked and took a swig of his coffee.

'Yes, I did go home, Hugo! I walked; I always walk.' It was Tom's turn to look Hugo straight in the eye now.

'What about you, Hugo? Did you go straight back to Calliope?'

'Touché, Tom!' Hugo laughed. 'I don't know where that cab took me, amigo, but I woke up in my bed with the mother of all headaches.'

'I'm not surprised, Hugo; we did sink a few! My head was throbbing too,' Tom said, remembering. It was only the night before last, but already it felt like days ago, partly because other events had occurred that had taken his mind off it, mainly accidentally meeting DCI Ali Smith. How was he to know that the chef, Andrew, was her son? He would be keeping that little escapade to himself; there was no need for Hugo to know about it, and no way would he find out.

'Your friend with the crutches seemed like a nice sort,' Hugo said sarcastically with a big grin on his face.

'Well, Hugo, shit happens. I really don't understand why Jamie lets him in the pub, and I'm surprised no one has ever thumped the little creep,' Tom said, remembering some of what Leggy had said to him. There seemed no sense in dwelling on it, though, and hopefully Hugo didn't remember too much of the detail. Which, of course, is exactly what he did; Hugo remembered every word.

'So, Tom, why did you become a policeman?' Hugo asked out of the blue. 'Strictly off the record, Tom, it won't end up in the paper; you have my word on that. You don't even have to tell me if you really don't want to; I'm just asking, being friendly.'

Tom considered it for a moment and could see no harm in telling Hugo of his journey into joining the police service, so he decided to tell Hugo the whole saga.

'Well, just because it is you asking, that's the only reason. Because I like you, I am going to tell you the whole story, but I'll stick the kettle on and make some more coffee while I tell you.' He lit the gas and rinsed out the mugs as he started his tale.

'It was a summer's evening; for some reason, I remember that clearly. I was 21 years old, just coming up to 22. My dad worked as a delivery driver for a local factory in Brentford, where we lived. He got me a job as a driver's assistant, which mainly meant lugging white goods, fridge-freezers, washing machines, cookers, and that sort of stuff up and down the stairs of flats and houses all over London. We went to other places as well, like Bristol and Brighton, and I even came to Oxford a few times. They were the best trips – the long-haul ones. We would only do a few drops, which meant less lifting and less humping. Most of the time we were out on the road, and the driver did all the work then; all I had to do was look out the window and watch the world go by. I didn't work much with my dad, which was probably for the better; he was a hard taskmaster, and, well, let's say we didn't always get along if we spent too much time together. I worked mainly with a bloke called Lenny. Lenny was a good laugh; he never took things seriously. He got the job done, but he had no loyalty to the company and didn't really give a shit about anything. We used to stop off at a pub on the way back home, after our last drop, and drink three or four pints. Lenny would then drive back to the yard, way over the limit. I liked working with Lenny, and he certainly introduced me to drinking beer. One morning he came to work, went upstairs to the office, and handed in his notice. He'd had enough and was going off "travelling"; he was fed up with driving lorries and wanted to see some of the world before he got old. Apart from one postcard from Australia some months later, I never heard from Lenny again, but looking back at it now, he had a big influence on me and what I am now, and I don't mean drunk!' Tom laughed, sipped his coffee, and carried on with the story as Hugo sat listening to every word.

'Anyway, that evening, after saying goodbye to Lenny, I finished early. I had arranged to meet my mate Ronnie, an old schoolmate, in the Red Lion, a pub on the high street in Brentford. My dad used to drink in the old pub that was originally on the same site when he was a boy. The old pub was pulled down in the sixties and a new one built; that was the one I drank in. It used to be a music pub when I drank there; lots of big bands started out playing there. It's gone now, pulled down, and a drive-through McDonald's was built on the spot; at least last time I was in that neck of the woods, that is what it was. No one was playing that night, and it was still "early doors," so there was no sign of Ronnie. I had an hour to kill, so I got another pint, not that I really needed one, not after saying goodbye to Lenny – but well, that's what you do, isn't it, when you are that age? I started to kill the time by playing on the fruit machine in the corner of the bar. I didn't usually do that sort of thing – waste of money, really – but it was something to do until Ronnie turned up. After losing a few quid, I still kept trying, the way those machines suck you in, and then suddenly I got three melons in a row. I only needed a fourth, and I would win the jackpot – only about a tenner, but that was a lot back then. Anyway, I was considering what to do, seeing if I had any holds or nudges or whatever, when two blokes sort of surrounded me. I vaguely remembered them from years ago, from school. They were both a good few years older than me. *"Nudge the cunt!"* one of them said, and the other one shoved me in the back, and they both laughed. I reached to pick my beer up off the top of the fruit machine, and he shoved me again. This time it was harder, and I smacked into the front of the machine. The beer splashed all over me and down the glass on the fruity, still with the three melons showing. It didn't smash on the floor because the other bloke caught it. *"Looks like you got two nudges!"* He said, laughing at me. They both smelt of booze and looked as high as kites on everything but roller skates, really menacing and psychotic-looking. I don't mind telling you, I was scared. I was more than scared; I was terrified. I tried to move away, but they just penned me in and started saying things like *"Hunter the cunter,"* and laughing. I could smell their bad breath. I told them I didn't want any trouble, and they could have the machine if they wanted; just let me go away. They didn't want to play the machine, though; I knew that, really. This went on for a while, and I was getting more and more scared. I kept looking around for Ronnie, not that he would have been much use against those two animals. *"Who you looking for, then?"* The one with my empty beer glass said, but before I could answer, he clipped the glass on the side of the fruit machine, smashing the rim off and leaving it with sharp, jagged edges sticking out. He then pushed it under my throat as the other one held me. He said something like, "I think it was time you fucked off, son," and the pair of them started marching me through the pub with the glass still sticking in my neck. I pissed myself, Hugo! I pissed my fucking trousers. I thought they were going to kill me. I saw Ronnie looking on in horror as they pushed me past him; he must have only just arrived. All I could do was look at him, and he just stared back.

'It seemed bright outside compared to the inside of the pub. There was a paved level, like a patio outside the front with five big concrete steps, down to the street. The two of them marched me to the stop of those steps, they were still saying things, but I was too panicked to listen; they probably wouldn't have made sense anyway. I felt the spiked glass prick the skin on my throat, and I could feel blood trickling down the front of my neck. I thought it would soon all be over; I'd be dead. Then he took the glass away, and I felt what seemed like a kick in the base of my spine. I went flying down the steps, grazing my knees and knuckles on the way down and cracking my head on the paving stones at the bottom. It was only the fear and the adrenalin that gave me the strength to get up and run. I could hear them laugh, and I could hear my heart pounding. I didn't look back. I ran straight home and told my dad what had happened, but instead of offering me some support or help, he just said, *"What are you like, letting a couple of blokes run you out of your own pub and doing nothing about it? Be a man, not a baby; get back up there and give them what for!"* He had no understanding of how I felt, and it didn't seem to matter to him what they had done to me. All he was concerned about was that I hadn't manned up to them, and that may have come to reflect on him in some way.'

Tom stopped talking, took a big mouthful of his coffee, and looked at Hugo before carrying on.

'That's when I thought I'm not living in this house any more. I'm not staying in this shitty area and lugging fridges all over the place for a pittance. I'm not putting up with psychos like those two in the pub. It just didn't seem right that they could walk around doing that and nothing ever happened to them; they just got away with it. So that was it for me. The next day, I filled out a university application form, and soon after that, I went to Oxford Poly to study engineering. That was a start for me – my way of getting away from Brentford. It was a way to escape. My dad would have said it was running away. Maybe he would have been right, but then he was one of the things I was running away from. I didn't want to be an engineer, but I had enough qualifications to get on that course; the standard wasn't very high, and you could get government grants in those days. I knew that I had to do something with my life once I finished college, and I think I had almost decided that I would try and join the police service. I knew it would be easier with a college degree. What I really wanted to do was make sure that thugs like those two didn't get away with that sort of thing any more. In short, Hugo, I joined the police because I didn't like bullies; I still don't.'

Hugo looked at Tom to make sure he had finished speaking, then said, 'Wow! That is some story. You had a rough time in old London town there, Tom. So, what was it that made you leave the police service after wanting it so much?'

'I didn't have much of a choice,' Tom replied. 'I got forced to leave because I lost a couple of toes in an accident, but in truth, I would have left anyway sooner or later. I found out that there are bullies in the police as well as out here. Now I deal with them in my own way. I'm wise enough to steer clear of them most of the time.'

'What was the accident?' Hugo asked, but he had asked one question too many, and Tom just finished his coffee and said, 'I don't want to talk about this anymore; let's go and see those places you want to go to.' And with that, they got up, put on their coats, and left the boat.

Half an hour later, Hugo was paying a taxi driver that had dropped him and Tom off in Jericho at the Walton Well car park adjacent to Port Meadow. They pushed the metal kissing gate open and stepped onto the meadow. The vast open space with its huge "lake" stretched out as far as they could see, to Wolvercote in the distance and all the way down to the river. Horses and cows were dotted around the grassland, and flocks of geese gathered along the riverbank. In contrast to the treeless meadow side of the river, the opposite bank, where the latest murders had taken place, was tree and bush-lined. Downstream, the river ran through Bossom's boatyard and under Rainbow Bridge towards Oxford City Centre, and upstream, it curved off to the left through the lock towards Godstow. It was a cold day, but there was a bright, clear sky reflecting and glistening on the waters of the lake and the river, making them shine like mirrors. Hugo had seen a couple of

Victorian landscape paintings of Port Meadow in Oxford's Ashmolean Museum when he had taken some time out to sightsee, and he was surprised to see how little the landscape had changed in the intervening years. He was also amazed to find such a vast open space existed so close to the centre of a city.

They followed a wide rubble path down towards the river, and the line of boats moored along a wooden jetty. It was a mixture of white fibreglass cruiser-style boats, "Gin Palaces," as Tom called them, and a few narrowboats. The two men climbed the steps onto the jetty and followed it past the moored boats to its end, occasionally having to step over mooring ropes. From there, they could already see the police presence in the distance on the far side of the river. Without speaking, they turned and faced each other, both experiencing the same eerie sensation, the closeness of the murder scene making it real. The closeness of death was, in a strange way, bringing things to life. After a few minutes of walking, they were opposite the scene, spotting the police tape tied around stakes fencing the area off. A police van marked "Forensics" could be seen through the bushes, and directly behind the opening to the bank where the family would have been, their bodies had been removed and were resting on stainless steel tables in the city morgue. A square white canvas marquee, the investigation tent, was also clearly visible. Tom and Hugo could see uniformed and plain-clothed officers moving around inside the sectioned-off area. Four murders in one spot would mean the police would be there for days, weeks, or maybe longer. Hugo took a couple of pictures of the scene with his mobile, telling Tom it was for the paper. Tom assumed that Hugo would have to justify his time spent in Oxford, and this would be just the story to do it. It could just be that Hugo had been the first of the journos to hear about this, plus he was now on big-buddy terms with the number one suspect. This could be Hugo's lucky break.

As they continued walking north along the bank towards Godstow Lock, Hugo asked questions about the other murders, and Tom answered him as best he could. He explained about the canoe theory and a few other details he had picked up from DI Spencer. They had been walking for about forty minutes when they reached the end of the meadow and climbed out onto the road. Across the ancient stone bridge was the Trout Inn. The pub had just opened up for the day, and Hugo suggested they pop their heads in for a warm-up and a coffee, maybe a nip of scotch, but in the end they decided to carry on walking. Leaving the road after the bridge, they joined the west bank of the river, heading south, and were now standing immediately in front of the ruins of Godstow Abbey. Hugo asked Tom what the history of it was, and Tom had to confess that he had no idea. Hugo scribbled the name in his notepad and made a mental note to look it up when he got home, thinking it could be useful for his story. Neither of them noticed the plaque on the side, which would have answered their questions.

They had almost reached the police tape when Hugo pointed up in the sky and exclaimed excitedly, 'Look at that, Tom!'

Tom looked up and saw a large brown and fawn bird with a forked tail soaring effortlessly on the thermals, its wings fully extended and the feathers on the tips fanned out, making tiny adjustments to its flight.

'That must be a six-foot wing span, Tom. What is it, a buzzard? A vulture?' Hugo asked.

Tom looked at the bird for a few moments longer as it silently circled the murder scene. Tom knew what this creature was; it was not a vulture, even if it was flying above the murder scene; it wasn't waiting to swoop down and feed on human remains, but probably looking for mice that might be disturbed by all the activity below; or maybe just out of curiosity, looking down on the scene from high above because it could.

'It's a red kite, Hugo,' Tom said, still looking up at the bird; 'they are one of the biggest birds we have in Britain. Birds of prey technically, but despite their size, they're not aggressive or very strong; they are scavengers, maybe catching the odd mouse or worm. Birds of prey, but mainly scavengers. They were really common in Britain at one time, but people believed them to be attacking and killing sheep. and there were even stories of attacks on children, but they were just stories. Even so, as untrue as it all was, all that bad press caused them to be hunted almost to extinction.' Tom stopped looking at the bird and looked at Hugo to see if he was listening; he was.

'A few years ago, there were efforts made to breed the remaining kites, repopulate them, and return them to the wild. Two release sites were chosen, one in Wales and the other on the Chilterns near High Wycombe.' Tom saw Hugo looking slightly puzzled and added, "The Chilterns" are a range of hills, and "High Wycombe" is a large town to the south-east of here.'

'Wow, I'm impressed, Tom; you really know your nature stuff.'

'It's common knowledge in these parts, Hugo. The reintroduction was a success, and there are now hundreds of pairs of birds that have spread from their original sites. You can often see them around Oxford now, especially where trees are found, like along the river.'

The kite during this time had been gliding with ease; now it flapped its huge wings only once and disappeared behind the treetops in silence.

'Impressive creature,' Hugo remarked. 'They sound like they are a bit like you and me, Tom, mistakenly seen by others as being predators and killers, but are just scavengers, like us, just looking for what we can find.'

Hugo looked up at the sky where the bird had been, and still staring at the empty space, he said, 'All that bad press, I know about that stuff. Do you think we will also be hunted into extinction, Tom?'

The first reference to "News Papers" in English was in 1667.

Chapter 38

READ ALL ABOUT IT

Oxford, England: The River Killings
Death Toll reaches Twenty-Six

As the discovery of four more bodies brings the body count up to twenty-six in the Oxford River Murders, the residents of Oxfordshire are asking if there is a family annihilator active along their stretch of the River Thames. The latest killings have intensified the fear felt by local residents, especially those living close to and on the river. The New York Times London correspondent, Hugo Lewis, has been living on a boat on the River Thames in Oxford in close proximity to the murders and reports as follows:
On Tuesday night, the Hartleys - Keith Hartley, his wife Anne, and their two children, John and Susan - a normal family from the small village of Wolvercote, Oxford, close to the River Thames - went

night fishing together. It was to be their last ever family excursion. Early Wednesday morning, Oxford emergency services received a call from the driver of a passing boat reporting the sighting of a fisherman falling into the water. The caller said that three other anglers on the bank at the time, now known to be the mother and two young children of the family, showed no sign of movement when the fall occurred. Officers from Oxford's Thames Valley Police arrived on the scene to find all four of the family dead. Little information about the cause of death or any explanation of the circumstances has been released, but it is widely thought that it was the latest attack by Oxford's serial family annihilator, who has been active on this stretch of the Thames since April. The killer has been dubbed by some as "The River Killer." Knives, swords, and a hammer are known to have been used in all the killings. The latest four victims bring the number of deaths up to a total of twenty-six, and the citizens of Oxfordshire are asking when this will end.

The killings started earlier in the year, with the first coming to the attention of the police over the Easter break when a lockkeeper and five members of his family were killed in the lock cottage at Day's Lock. The lock is a few miles outside the city of Oxford, most famous for its world-renowned university, and is set in a peaceful, isolated area in the heart of Oxfordshire's English countryside. It is one of forty-five locks on the River Thames. The preliminary police investigation initially believed that the murders were committed by the son of the lockkeeper in an act of family annihilation. The body of Ian Gibson, the son of George and Brenda Gibson, was found in the lockkeeper's cottage along with that of his parents, his wife, and their two children. The conclusion drawn at the time was that Ian Gibson had committed the murders of his family members and subsequently took his own life in the same cottage. This theory was soon to be challenged when a second family of six was murdered a few days later at a riverside trailer park in Bablock Hythe, also in the Oxford district. The bodies of that family were found inside a trailer they had rented for a summer vacation. The police department has revealed few details of the circumstances of these killings, but it is believed they were similar to those of the lockkeeper and his family at Day's Lock.

There followed ten further killings at a large riverside house close to the small village of Eynsham, a few miles west along the Thames from Oxford. Three generations of the Daltrey family were hacked to death at what is thought to be the family's great-grandmother's birthday celebration. The family had recently moved to the $2.5 million house after winning an undisclosed amount on the British National Lottery. Again, little has been revealed by the police other than an appeal to the public to help recover a weapon believed to be a samurai sword, which is thought to have been used in the attack. The house and all the other "River Killer" murder scenes still remain fenced off with police tape as investigations continue.

No connection has been found between any of the families other than their proximity to the river at the time of death. No reasons or motives are apparent, and as of yet, there have been no sightings of the killer, and no witnesses have come forward. Some have theorised that the killer gets to and from the murder locations by river using a canoe, which is silent and almost invisible at night. This would require good local knowledge and familiarity with the River Thames, leading to the assumption that the killer is local to the area and must be known by someone. A breakthrough was thought to have been made when a few newspapers received calls from a man considered by the police to be the suspect. The calls were made from a cell phone, and using triangulation techniques, the source of the calls was identified as being St Giles, an uptown area in the city of Oxford that is home to several prestigious university buildings, the Ashmolean Museum, and Oxford's famous five-star hotel, the Macdonald Randolph. CCTV footage taken from cameras situated in the area provided only a grainy still picture of a hooded male figure lighting a cigarette; police believe this to have been the caller. The photograph was published in several newspapers and shown on local television, but little useful information resulted from this.

Summertime in Oxford is usually an idyllic scene of people punting and boating along the river under the gleaming iconic spires, but this year's extremely wet weather, coupled with the series of savage murders, has left the river almost empty. The few occupied boats to be seen are the homes of people living on the river and others that have mainly been rented by journalists, like me, trying to get as close as possible to the events as they unfold. The inhabitants of the area are making sure they are safely locked indoors come nightfall. The banks of the river covering the stretch of killings are now being monitored 24/7 by a small army of police and Environment Agency officials in an effort to prevent further murders. With the likelihood that the victims have been chosen purely at random and not known to the killer, as well as the absence of any signs of progress by the police in making an arrest, concerns are growing rapidly that even this increased police presence remains unable to make the public feel at ease.

Detective Chief Inspector Alison Smith has stated that over 180 police officers have been assigned to the case. DCI Smith has so far addressed two press conferences, accompanied by Detective Inspector Spencer Davis. DCI Smith, in her last address, gave only scant details of the murders, with her and DI Davis refusing to answer many of the questions fired at them by the press. This has led to speculation that the police are nowhere near solving any of the murders, which, it seems, are likely to continue. Even with the appeals to the public and the months of investigation, there is still only one known suspect, the hooded man caught on CCTV, who has not been identified. Visiting each of the murder sites as I have, you can still see the crime scenes fenced off by police tape and the ongoing activities of the police and forensic teams, a sign that this is still a very live and ongoing investigation. Meanwhile, as a result of the torrents of rain, the river has swollen, making it difficult for boats to navigate and giving an almost impossible job to the police divers looking for weapons or any other evidence that may now be on the riverbed. With the forecast of further rain, this situation looks likely to worsen. After twenty-six murders, here in middle England, the summer that never happened is rapidly coming to an end as the weather gets colder and the days shorter, especially on the Oxford stretch of the River Thames, where I, like most others in the area, double check the locks on my doors at night before going to sleep. A dark and fearful atmosphere of uncertainty and disbelief hangs over this quintessentially English county. It is a fear and dread that looks likely to continue until the River Killer is apprehended and is safely behind bars. When that will be, no one knows.

Hugo Lewis, Oxford, England

The article was accompanied by a photograph showing the police tape, several officers, and a temporary investigation marquee on the bank on the opposite side of the river from where the picture was taken. The grainy quality of the photograph, credited to Hugo Lewis, added depth to the cold and damp atmosphere that was the backdrop to the site of the four dead anglers.

Soon after drinking alcohol, your brain processes slow down, and your memory can be impaired. After large quantities of alcohol, the brain can stop recording into the "memory store."

Chapter 39

WHAT HAPPENED TO LEGGY?

What was it that Hugo had said? *"All that bad press, I know about that stuff."* Tom could not help thinking about these words. What was it that Hugo meant by *"I know about that"*? Was it because he was a journalist and therefore would know about good press and bad press? Tom was beginning not to think so; it had been the way Hugo had said it and the way he had followed it up with, *"Do you think we will also be hunted into extinction, Tom?"* It sounded as if Hugo was hinting that he had been, and maybe still was, in a similar situation to Tom's. If so, what could it be? What did Tom really know about Hugo Lewis? Was he not to be trusted after all? Tom fired up his laptop and googled "Hugo Lewis, New York Times." There were pages of entries relating to articles that Hugo Lewis had written for The New York Times mixed in with various other pages containing things by people going by the name of Hugo Lewis. Tom paged through the search output, scanning each line that was displayed, not knowing what he was looking for or what he would find. It was about 20 or so pages into the search list when one almost jumped off the page. It was for a newspaper in New Jersey, the Hackensack Record. The search listing showed a short section of the text, which read,

"Local Hackensack reporter Hugo Lewis was questioned in connection with the disappearance of five women from the Hackensack area over the last..."

Tom clicked on the link, and a page of the Hackensack Record displayed on the screen. The article was from an edition of the Record that was nearly 20 years old. Tom read the full story, almost in disbelief.

"Local Hackensack reporter Hugo Lewis was questioned in connection with the disappearance of five women from the Hackensack area over the last three months. All of the missing are single young women who disappeared without trace, all of whom were thought to be out jogging when last seen. The last sighting of three of the women placed them close to various parts of the Hackensack River, which runs through quiet parkland areas as well as the centre of the city. The Hackensack Police Department raided Mr Lewis's apartment at approximately 7.30 am yesterday morning. According to construction workers that are still completing the building, which currently contains only a few occupied apartments, Mr Lewis was handcuffed and driven away in a Police Department vehicle accompanied by four patrol cars. It was believed that it was the first real breakthrough the police had made in trying to find the person responsible for the

missing women. The disappearances have put fear into all women in Hackensack, as it is widely thought that the victims are unlikely to still be alive. Mr Lewis, who is a reporter for the *Hackensack Advertiser*, a free newspaper, was held in the Hackensack Central Precinct overnight and was released this morning. No charges were believed to have been made, and no police statement or any details have been released.
The *Hackensack Record* (this newspaper) interviewed Mr Lewis on his release, and he told us that he did not really understand why the police had taken him in for questioning. Mr Lewis, as well as many other reporters in the city, had been following the disappearances of the women closely, and he believes that it may have been his proximity to some of the last sightings during his own investigations that drew the attention of the police.'

The article continued on and recapped details of each of the five women that had disappeared, but nothing more was said of Hugo Lewis. Tom searched for the missing women of Hackensack and found that the disappearances had never been solved, and they stopped featuring on the front pages and eventually stopped being reported altogether. There were very few further mentions of Hugo Lewis. Tom couldn't really be 100 percent certain that the Hugo Lewis in the Hackensack stories was even the same man as the one he knew, but the coincidences were compelling. Again, he asked himself how well he really knew Hugo. Who was Hugo Lewis? What it came down to was that he actually knew very little about him. If this man in Hackensack was the same Mr Lewis, then Hugo had certainly kept quiet about it. 'All that bad press, I know about that stuff.' Was Hackensack the reason why he knew about such things?

Doubts about Hugo grew in Tom's mind as his trust in Hugo shrank. Would Hugo keep his word and not report on Tom being the River Killer suspect? He switched off his laptop, locked up *Wandering Aengus,* and headed off towards town to buy a newspaper. As he walked, the greater his suspicions of Hugo became. He would confront him with what he had found and see what he had to say. For an instant, it crossed Tom's mind that maybe, just maybe, Hugo could somehow be involved in the River Killings; after all, he seemed to be around them as much as Tom. Why did the police not have Hugo down as a suspect as well, or did they? What else was Hugo maybe keeping quiet about?

* * *

Tom folded up the newspaper and placed it on the table next to his pint. He was pleased to see that Hugo had kept his word so far and not mentioned *Wandering Aengus* or made any reference to him being a suspect. This was the first time Tom could remember ever buying a copy of The New York Times. It had taken him about an hour to get to the centre and find newsagents that sold foreign newspapers, and it was a long walk back again, so he stopped off at the Head of the River for a sandwich and a beer. Not far from where he sat was the police station where DCI Ali Smith and DI Spencer Davis had interviewed him, where they had pried into his private life, implied unpleasant things, and told him he was a suspected serial killer! Tom sat with his beer and ran through everything that had happened silently in his mind. He had been avoiding the James Street Tavern since the night at Ali Smith's; seeing Andrew just wasn't a good idea. Andrew must now know that his mother suspected Tom of being the River Killer, and Tom didn't know what he could say to Andrew that would make that any better. He'd had no idea that Andrew was Ali's son; he would never have gone to the house if he had known it was Ali's. All Tom knew was that Andrew worked for Jamie as a chef, and he had chatted with him a few times but didn't really know him very well. It was the night that he had been drunk with Hugo in the James Street Tavern that Andrew had spoken with him about coming round for a drink and meeting his mum, the same night Leggy had started up. Tom had been so drunk that he hardly remembered Andrew speaking with him about going to his house or agreeing to it. It was Andrew's call the following day that reminded him, but he still wasn't sure how it all happened. Only a few days had passed since then, but it felt like it could have been weeks. So much had happened; another family had been murdered, and four more dead bodies had been found. Hugo had been busy trying to meet his paper's deadline and write up his article and had not been around. Tom had also wanted a bit of space and had avoided everyone. He had gone from being on his own most of the time to drinking with Hugo and socialising with Andrew. Now he needed a break from everyone; somehow all these new people in his life had more impact on his world than he would have thought possible.

Even if Hugo or Andrew had tried to call, Tom had switched his phone off and would have known nothing about it. Had he switched it on, he would have seen six missed calls from Hugo Lewis, two from Jamie, and three from DI Spencer Davis. The phone stayed silent, and Tom remained blissfully unaware of any of the attempts to contact him. He finished his pint and ordered another. That would be it then – the last pint, no more. He had been trying to cut back on his drinking since that night. Leggy had said something along the lines of 'all those things you used to mouth off about in the Rock.' That had shaken Tom up a bit as it made him remember that there had been so many nights from those times in the Rock of Gibraltar that he didn't remember, so many things he may have said, so many things he could have said. He didn't want to repeat those mistakes, and not remembering chunks of the evening with Hugo was a sharp warning. Again, doubts entered his mind: *'Did Hugo really go straight back to Abingdon?'*

Tom could have taken a bus back to Donnington Bridge, back to the boat, but decided to walk again, only this time he walked back along the river and not down the road. Some distance away, along the towpath, he caught his first sight of *Wandering Aengus*. He began to make out several men standing around on the bank next to the boat, and some were even standing on the back deck. Police! He slowed down, trying to work out what they were doing, and then he saw one of them open the back door and go inside. With that, Tom broke out into a run, and a few moments later, he reached the boat out of breath and already agitated.

'What the hell is going on? What the fuck are you doing on my boat?' He said angrily, as well as trying to get his breath back. None of them answered, and two uniformed officers stopped him from climbing onto the boat.

'Who is in charge here? I want to know what you think you are doing!' Tom almost shouted.

The back door of *Wandering Aengus* opened, and Detective Inspector Spencer Davis climbed out.

'Let him go,' he said to the two officers holding Tom back by his arms. 'I realise this is a bit of a shock to you, Mr Hunter, but we do have a search warrant. I did try to call you so that we could have maybe avoided breaking in, but I couldn't get an answer.'

'What is going on, Inspector?' Tom was still angry, shocked, and surprised, but had regained control of his breathing.

'I am going to have to ask you to come to the station with me, sir. Don't worry about your boat. I have told my men to be very careful not to break anything and to leave things as they find them. We will get a locksmith down here to repair the lock before we leave. You are welcome to see the search warrant if you wish to.'

'Are you arresting me for something, Detective?' Tom asked, still no calmer.

'No, not at the moment, Mr Hunter, but I can arrest you if you would prefer that, or you can just accompany me to the station for a few more questions.'

Tom realised the hopelessness of the situation and agreed to go under his own free will. He wanted to know what was going on. They would need a good reason to be breaking into his home and searching through his private belongings. Spencer went over to the officers on the boat and spoke to them. Tom couldn't hear what was said, but he quickly returned and said to the two officers flanking Tom, 'OK, I'll take over from here.' Then, turning to Tom, he said, 'Would you like to come with me, Mr Hunter? I don't think there is any need for an escort, do you?'

They walked to the back of the Isis pub. The pub is not accessible by road and has to take all of its deliveries by boat or along the towpath. There is a small private road across the fields at the back of the pub – more of a dirt track, really. It leads down from the main road to the pub, but the owners of the land had been reluctant to give the pub landlord permission to use the track. Spencer was a DI investigating a series of murders; that was all the permission he needed to use any route he wanted. Spencer asked Tom to sit in the front passenger's seat as he drove back to St Aldate's. He tried to get out of Spencer what was going on, why they were on his boat, and why the sudden interest in him again, but Spencer just told him to wait until they were in the interview room. The only thing that Spencer was prepared to say was to give some reassurance that *Wandering Aengus* would be OK and that special care had been taken during the search. Tom gave up trying and became silent. He sat and stared through the windscreen, watching the traffic and the people in the streets of Oxford as Spencer drove up Abingdon Road towards the city centre, towards St Aldate's police station.

At the station, Tom was soon seated in the same stark interview room as on his last visit. This time, however, Spencer had provided him with a mug of coffee. Opposite him sat DCI Ali Smith next to DI Spencer. DCI Smith started the interview.

'Mr Hunter, we meet again,' were Ali's opening words; Tom immediately felt more uncomfortable than he already was as he remembered Ali screaming and shouting and young Andrew looking shocked on that evening.

'Thank you for coming, and I must remind you that you have come here of your own free will and are not under arrest or being charged with anything,' Ali said, not looking at Tom as she sifted through a stack of papers in front of her.

'There is no requirement for you to have any legal representation, Mr Hunter, but you do have the right to have some should you wish to do so,' Spencer chipped in, slightly more friendly than Ali. Tom found this performance a bit "good cop, bad cop," but he was familiar with that technique, and other than annoying him slightly, it didn't really bother him. Even though he had been told that he was not being accused or charged with any offence, he wondered if they would turn around at some point and do so anyway; his trust in what people said was no longer as good as it once had been. Regardless of these concerns, Tom didn't ask for any legal representation, believing he had done nothing they could accuse him of that they had not already done.

'Mr Hunter, we already have a statement from you covering the night you were in the James Street Tavern with Hugo Lewis; is there anything you would like to change or add to that statement regarding the events of that night, anything you may have overlooked previously?' Ali asked, sliding a printed sheet of paper in front of Tom with his signature on the bottom.

'No. Nothing,' Tom replied without even bothering to read the short statement in front of him.

'Did you not have a conversation with a Mr David Legg during that evening?' Ali continued.

'I wouldn't call it a conversation,' Tom replied.

'It appears nowhere in your statement, Mr Hunter,' Ali said, looking down at the sheet of paper in front of Tom.

'I didn't think it was relevant to anything; like I said, it was hardly a conversation; it was just Leggy mouthing off. He does that a lot,' Tom replied, feeling slightly puzzled by this line of questioning.

'Would you mind telling us what Mr Legg said to you, sir?' asked Ali, taking off the top of her pen as if ready to write.

'Like I said, he was just mouthing off rubbish; I didn't pay much attention to him; I don't remember what he said,' Tom said as he shifted in his seat uncomfortably.

'Perhaps I can help jog your memory, Mr Hunter. Did Mr Legg not make a reference to you being an ex-police officer?' Ali prompted.

'Yes,' was Tom's short reply.

'And did he say something about your…' Ali paused as she considered the most appropriate word to use, 'your disability?'

'He may have done; I tried not to take too much notice of him at the time,' Tom answered, knowing that he was no longer being as truthful as he was trying to make it sound.

'We understand he also accused you of being a murderer. "You murdered all those families, Hunter," we believe is what he said?' Ali was building her questions one after the other.

'"You murdered all those wankers" is what he actually said.' Tom replied, showing his annoyance.

'So, you do remember, Mr Hunter. Is there anything else that may have come back to you?' Ali asked calmly.

'That is all that happened, Detective Chief Inspector. Leggy came over to the table where I was sitting with Hugo and started ranting. He often does that sort of thing when he is drunk, which is most of the time, he picks on whoever he feels like upsetting at that moment. At some point, not far into his outburst at me, two of the bar staff threw him out, and that was it; that was all that happened,' Tom said; this time he felt better knowing it was an accurate and truthful description of what actually occurred.

'How did it make you feel having this man shouting these things out in front of everyone in the pub?' Ali asked.

'I would have preferred it if he hadn't. He was very annoying, and it was embarrassing, but it didn't last long; as I said, he was very quickly thrown out,' Tom replied.

'Did you not feel angry? Did it make you want to do anything to stop him?' Ali asked.

'Like I said, I was annoyed because he had interrupted a conversation I was having with a friend.' Tom replied.

'That would be Mr Lewis?' Ali asked.

'Yes. Hugo. I didn't have a chance to do anything to stop Leggy, even if I had wanted to. They threw him out of the pub, and that was that.' Tom finished speaking and sat back in his chair. He had no idea why they were asking all these questions. He was wondering if somehow they believed Leggy really did know something about the murders – maybe they believed the things he shouted out that night.

Spencer had been sitting silently as Ali fired the questions at Tom, but now he put down the pencil he had been holding and asked, 'Would you mind telling us again how you came to get the grazes on the knuckles of your right hand?'

Tom immediately covered his right hand with his left, looked at Spencer, and replied.

'As I said in my statement to you the last time we spoke, Detective Inspector, I had quite a bit to drink that night and don't remember exactly, but I think it was probably when I tripped on the steps leading down to the river from Donnington Bridge. I think I must have caught them along the wall as I tried to stop myself from falling,' Tom answered, but he knew that the real truth was that he hadn't remembered much at all about getting home that night. Falling down the steps was just something he thought may have happened; he didn't actually remember doing it. He was beginning to feel really uneasy at this point, and he wanted to know even more about what DCI Smith and DI Davis thought was going on.

'What is this all about? What are you trying to say? Leggy is a nasty drunk who has a go at whoever he feels like, whenever he feels like it. That night he decided, for whatever his reason was, to have a go at me, and if anyone said that something different happened, then they are lying. You should be asking them about it, not me!'

'We have asked them, Mr Hunter,' Spencer said, looking straight at Tom. 'What they told us is that you looked quite upset and angry, and you and your friend Mr Lewis drank heavily for the rest of the evening.'

Tom sat and stared back. He still had no idea what they were getting at. It was Ali Smith who spoke next.

'Yesterday morning, Mr Hunter, a local resident, was out walking his dog near the allotment along the river, not far from Donnington Bridge. Their dog ran into an overgrown part of the ditch that runs along the back of the allotments. I'm sure you know where it is, Mr Hunter.' Ali paused and looked at Tom and then at Spencer before continuing.

'They lost sight of the dog in the undergrowth, and when it didn't come out after being called, the owner climbed down into the ditch to see what had happened. He found the dog sniffing at the body of a man with flies buzzing around his eyes, long dead. He was lying next to a pair of crutches. Much of the face had been eaten away by foxes and other animals, but the body was quickly identified as Mr David Legg, the man you call Leggy.' She looked up to gauge Tom's reaction. He looked shocked.

'Mr Legg's body was undiscovered for several days and the time of death has been dated as that same evening you and Mr Legg were seen arguing in the James Street Tavern...' Ali was forced to stop speaking as Tom interrupted her to say, 'We were not arguing, Inspector, I didn't even speak to him, he was just ranting. I told you that already.'

'Mr Legg had bruising about his body consistent with being punched and kicked. He also had a heavy blow to the side of the head with what we believe could have been one of his own crutches. These injuries are not thought to have killed him, but they would have almost certainly knocked him unconscious. He was left to die in the ditch, Mr Hunter,' Ali said, barely disguising up the disgust in her voice. She stopped for a moment, then continued.

'The allotments where Mr Legg's body was discovered are on a route you may have taken to get back to your boat from the James Street Tavern, so you will now understand our questions, Mr Hunter.'

'Are you accusing me of killing Leggy now as well as all the others you seem to think I have murdered?' Tom asked angrily.

'Did you kill him?' Spencer jumped in and asked.

'No, I did not! He was not a nice person, and he did lay into me that night, but that was Leggy. I never liked him, but I also didn't kill him. I haven't killed anyone!' Tom replied to Spencer but looked straight at Ali Smith as he spoke.

'We are not accusing you of anything, Mr Hunter,' Spencer said calmingly to Tom. 'We are merely trying to piece together what happened that night. Some of our colleagues have already spoken to your friend, Mr Hugo Lewis, and he backs up what you have told us. We have also spoken with the taxi driver that drove him back to Abingdon from the pub that night, so he isn't a suspect either.'

Tom listened with interest to what he was being told about Hugo. When Spencer had finished, Tom asked, almost desperately, 'Am I a suspect, Inspectors?'

Tom was beginning to think that it might have been sensible for him to have had a solicitor present after all, and he did now understand why *Wandering Aengus* had been searched.

'Mr Hunter.' Spencer said, and it was obvious that Spencer had thought carefully about what he was about to say. 'This murder, Mr Legg's murder, we believe, at the moment, to be unrelated to the other murders that are at the centre of our investigations, but as you are…' again Spencer chose his words carefully: 'Part of that investigation, it has been necessary for us to speak to you regarding Mr Legg's death.'

Tom felt confused by this. He now understood that he was still a suspect for the river killings, where there was no evidence against him that he knew of, whereas there seemed to be several things connecting him with Leggy's murder, and he was being told he wasn't a suspect for that. This confusion was soon cleared up when Ali added, 'We do not believe the murder of Mr Legg is related to the other killings we are investigating, but Mr Legg's murder is part of another murder inquiry being handled by a different team from ours. They will, I am sure, want to question you as well at some point, Mr Hunter, so don't disappear.' Ali started to tap the pile of papers together on the desk, indicating that she was finished with her questions. The questioning, for now, was over.

How sweet the moonlight sleeps upon this bank
Here we will sit, and let the sounds of music
Creep in our ears; soft stillness, and the night
Become the touches of sweet harmony.

[WILLIAM SHAKESPEAR – "The Merchant of Venice"]

Chapter 40

TAKE CARE, BEWARE

It was not only the realisation that Leggy was now dead, murdered, or at least left to die in a ditch, and he was suspected of another killing that was eating away at Tom Hunter's thoughts; it was also Hackensack. Was it the same Hugo Lewis that he now knew? If so, what did Hugo know about the missing women in Hackensack? How was he involved? Tom had searched the internet again and again, but he found nothing other than what he already knew about the Hackensack reporter, Hugo Lewis. Tom was spending most of his time alone on *Wandering Aengus,* watching, listening, thinking, and worrying. He was constantly expecting a knock on the door from the police wanting to question him again about Leggy's death and all the other murders they seemed to think he had committed or was at least involved with. DI Spencer Davis had called him and said that nothing of interest to the investigation had been found on Tom's boat, adding that other officers were still interested in his connection with David Legg's death. This had only confirmed Tom's concerns and anxieties. He knew that Spencer and DCI Ali Smith still had him down as a suspect for the river killings, even though Spencer had not said anything about this when he rang. These were not comfortable or happy days for Tom, and the defences around his world had been badly damaged; they'd left him weakened and vulnerable, with nowhere to run, nowhere to hide, and no one to trust.

He paced around in the boat, feeling trapped and helpless, and getting more and more stir-crazy with every step. The Hackensack story was eating away at him, but he still hadn't raised it with Hugo; he wanted to do that face-to-face so he could read Hugo's reactions and see if he was telling the truth. With that burning in his mind and the pressure of the cabin fever, Tom rang Hugo and arranged to meet in the James Street Tavern. Not knowing what Hugo's response would be or what could happen when he confronted him, Tom also called Jamie and let him know when they would be at the pub so that he could join them. Throwing another log in the burner and turning on some music, he went to the back of the boat to look through his clean clothes. He had let himself go over the last few days; neglect was something he didn't usually allow in his life, and he needed to re-group. A shower and a clean shirt would help shake off some of the stress he was feeling. Soon he was standing with his eyes closed, feeling the hot water break on his head and run down his body. The media player on his laptop was set to play random songs, and everything from Oasis to Sly and the Family Stone came floating through the steam of the shower. With the music, the warmth, and the water, the tension in his neck slowly eased, and his spine felt straighter and stronger. The troubles, for a moment or two, washed away.

* * *

It was dark by the time Tom arrived at the James Street Tavern, and Hugo was already sitting at their table in the window. Tom had been thinking about what to say and how to say it since he had got out of the shower. In the end, after exchanging the usual greetings, he asked Hugo straight out.

'Did you ever live in Hackensack, Hugo?'

Hugo physically flinched. He took a few moments before answering, then said, 'Been doing a bit of cyber investigation on me, have you, Tom?' Hugo didn't wait for Tom to answer; he lowered his voice and continued, 'You see now why we have a lot in common, amigo? I know what it is like to be in your situation, to be suspected of something, caught up with things you had nothing to do with – I really do believe you had nothing to do with the River Killings any more than I had to do with those women that disappeared in Hackensack, Tom.' Another customer came to the table and asked if they could take one of the chairs that were not occupied. There were two empty seats at the table, and Tom told the stranger that he could take one, but they were expecting someone else for the other. Jamie had not yet arrived, but Tom was hoping he would turn up soon. Hugo stopped talking until they were alone again, and he lowered his voice and continued speaking as Tom listened carefully.

'It nearly ruined me, Tom; I can tell you that much. I was hounded by the police and distrusted by my fellow workers. My neighbours would scurry into their apartments and lock their doors whenever they saw me. The relatives, husbands, fathers, mothers, and boyfriends started stalking me, spray painting my car and my apartment building with words like "guilty" and "murderer." The newspaper I worked freelance for stopped buying my stories, and in the end, I had to leave town. They never found those women, and even though 20 years have gone by, I still worry that someone will try to get their revenge on me. Revenge for something I didn't do. I thought I could keep it all at arms' length in a city like New York, and I did for many years, but even there I was hunted down and threatened. A boyfriend that never got over the loss of his lover, a husband still grieving for his wife – I don't know who, but stuff happened – scary stuff, Tom. I feared for my life for a while. Luckily for me, The New York Times was a bit more understanding than that Hackensack rag, and when I explained it all to them – the truth, all of it – they gave me a transfer to the London office. I have been safe there. No one followed me out, and no one has threatened or tried to kill me. The story of the Hackensack women never reached Britain, and I didn't exactly go out of my way to publicise it. You can understand that, Tom, can't you? No one knows, and I would really like it to stay that way, for my own safety if nothing else.'

Tom stared at Hugo for what seemed like an eternity. He was not expecting Hugo to be so forthcoming, and now Tom was evaluating everything he had been told. Hugo had certainly appeared to be frank, open, and honest. It not only sounded feasible, but Tom could also relate to it – that situation, that series of events. It also occurred to him for the first time that if the police's suspicions that he was suspected of being the River Killer were to become public, he too might be persecuted, threatened, and run out of town, driven from the river, or even worse. It made more sense now why Hugo had so willingly kept his name from the articles he had written for his newspaper. Hugo obviously knew the dangers of publishing speculations that could drastically impact others' lives, and it did seem that he thought Tom was innocent, and he might even have seen him as a friend.

'Is that the truth, Hugo, or is that just what you want me to believe?' Tom eventually said: Hugo replied instantly; he hadn't needed to think about it.

'It is the truth, the whole truth, and ain't nothing but the truth, so help me god, amigo. It is every bit as true as everything you have told me.'

Things had changed between them; they now shared a commonality, bringing them somehow closer. Tom and Hugo were now sharing and protecting each other's secrets. They looked at each other expressionlessly and chinked their two-pint glasses together as an indication of their agreement and acceptance of the situation.

At that moment, Jamie arrived with three full pints and plonked them on the table.

'What are you two conspirators up to then?' Jamie said jokingly, unaware of the many nerves that his words struck within Tom and Hugo. They looked up and smiled as best they could to make it seem as if nothing had happened.

'We were talking about Leggy, Jamie,' Hugo said as Jamie sat on the chair they had kept for his arrival. 'The police questioned me about him because I was in here the night it happened.'

'Same with me,' Tom quickly added, taking a large sup of his beer to cover up what he thought might be signs of guilt on his face.

'Yeah, they questioned my staff too. They even gave young Andrew, my chef, a grilling, no pun intended.' Jamie said, causing Tom to hide another guilty look behind his pint. Jamie continued, 'I wasn't here that night, but they still questioned me. I know most people hated Leggy, but he had been drinking in here long before I ran the place, and I, well, I tolerated him.'

'He was a real arsehole!' Tom snapped before looking up and adding, 'But no one deserves that to happen to them, not even Leggy.'

'The police told me that he was left in the ditch to die; hit over the head with one of his own crutches, almost "poetic justice," some would say.' Hugo pitched in.

'Well, at least he won't be stinking the end of the bar out and upsetting any more of my customers,' Jamie said, smiling. 'I don't suppose many will go to his funeral. I will probably go and pay my respects; after all, he did spend most of his disability allowance in here.' With that, the three of them smiled uncomfortably and moved the conversation on.

'So,' Jamie asked, 'is anyone going to try some of Andrew's food tonight? He has cooked some delicious-looking dishes.'

The mention of Andrew made Tom feel uncomfortable again, as he wondered if Jamie knew anything about the night he had been at Ali Smith's house. Had Andrew said anything to Jamie? Did Jamie know that Tom was suspected of being the River Killer as well as Leggy's murderer? Or was it still a secret that only Hugo knew?

Tom had drunk just enough beer to make him feel like getting back to the boat and switching off the world for the rest of the night, maybe even for a few more days. He thought of Leggy as he walked, of Hackensack, and of the River Killer. The sliveriest of moons hung in the blackest of skies, pinpricked by a trillion stars, illuminating the world below them with the softest of light. Time was moving on, changing the seasons and turning the air cold as Tom walked along the deserted towpath to *Wandering Aengus*, listening and watching all around with every quiet step he took.

Autumn moonlight
a worm digs silently
into the chestnut

[Matsuo Bashō – "Autumn moonlight"]

Chapter 41

FAREWELL TO HUGO

The nights had started to arrive earlier each evening as September came and went almost unnoticed. The stars of the winter sky were starting to appear as the hands of autumn reached out and took hold. Temperatures dropped and leaves fell from the trees, creating a thick mulch carpet on the floors of the woods and along the towpaths on the riverbanks. Blankets of autumn leaves floated slowly down the river, which, with the unexpected easing of the rain, almost returned to normal. October arrived and brought even sharper, colder weather along with it. On board *Wandering Aengus,* Tom, was rarely without a fire, and plumes of feathery white smoke could nearly always be seen rising from its chimney. In the homes of DCI Ali Smith and DI Spencer Davis, the central heating could be heard firing up and shutting down as it maintained the temperature throughout the rooms. There had been no further murders and no further progress towards catching the River Killer. Even Leggy's death seemed to have faded away. There was still fear and apprehension hanging over Oxford and the surrounding areas, but people had begun to learn to live with this, and life gradually returned to carrying on as usual and as normally as possible. Newspapers still reported on the murders, but the story had gone from the front pages; there was little new news to report. Cold westerly winds blew along the river, bringing in colder, harsher, and once again wetter weather. Seeing this front arrive and knowing the signs from past experience, Tom understood it was time to find a safe place for him and *Wandering Aengus*, a bolt-hole where they could securely moor up and sit out the harshness that the coming months would bring. There was a remote bank on a stretch below Eynsham Lock where he had spent a couple of previous winters, and this was where he moved to again. Tom knew it was rare to see anyone during these cold weather months in that remote spot, and solitude is what he wanted more than anything – for a while at least. Behind the trees that hugged the bank and created *Wandering Aengus*' hiding place, there was an animal path running across a field that led up to the road into Eynsham. It was only a ten-minute walk to a bus stop from there, and Tom could get to Eynsham or Oxford for his supplies, or if he got the "stir-crazy" in him. There was no shortage of firewood to be found along the heavily tree-lined river, and *Wandering Aengus* had a fuel tank full of diesel and a full water tank. Tom Hunter was digging his boot heels in for another hard, wet winter.

Since he had taken Hugo on a tour of the murder sites and cleared the air over the 20-year-old events in Hackensack, they hadn't seen much of each other in the weeks that followed. When they did meet, it was usually Jamie who instigated it. Andrew was still working as a chef at the pub, but Tom and Hugo never saw more than glimpses of him. Andrew would have liked to have met up with them again; he had told Jamie as much, but Tom knew that it wasn't a good idea, not at that time anyway. When Tom was no longer suspected of murder by Andrew's mother, he thought he could maybe speak to him again. Tom also knew that DCI Smith probably had someone watching over him whenever he visited the pub or anywhere else he went, and she probably had people watching over Andrew as well. Tom had initially tried to explain to Andrew why he felt it was best if they kept their distance, and Andrew reluctantly agreed to do so. Hugo, in the meantime, had written a few more articles about the murders for The New York Times, but like most of the other newspapers, The New York Times had also dropped the River Killer story from the front page, and Hugo had been given instructions by Head Office to return to the London office. The Hackensack story had not been discussed again between the two of them, nor had they spoken any more about Leggy or the River Killings. Jamie had raised the subjects once or twice but soon realised that no one wanted to speak about them. They were still prominent in Hugo and Tom's minds, but they tried to keep them there, hidden away in the background, but it was hard to do so. They were constant reminders of how they knew each other and the bond of secrecy that sat uncomfortably between them; the doubts about each other never fully left.

Tom had arranged, at Jamie's request, for them to meet up with Hugo one last time in the Tavern, the Tuesday before Hugo left to go back to London; it was intended to be Hugo's farewell. Whatever doubts Tom and Hugo held about each other, it seemed fitting to have a drink together in recognition of Hugo leaving Oxford and leaving the river. Jamie seemed oblivious to anything going on between Tom and Hugo other than friendship, and after all, he too had spent many evenings with them in the James Street Tavern, so a farewell drink with the landlord seemed appropriate. Hugo had been to a few open mics at the Tavern over the last couple of months and had become one of the regular crowd. Many of the performers had got to know Hugo as well as they did Tom, probably better than Tom, as Hugo was a lot more outgoing and talkative. *"My old man used to say I'd been vaccinated with a gramophone needle,"* Hugo had jokingly told Tom.

Tom remembered how the word "gramophone" had instantly painted a picture of a bygone era, of a New York City without internet, iPods, or MP3s – a New York City where music was probably listened to on longwave on valve radios, not streamed and downloaded – simpler times. Tom always thought you could tell Hugo was a writer by the way he spoke – not that he spoke in an elaborate or wordy way, but just by using everyday language, he could paint images and bring a story to life. He could be very funny at times too, which made him a popular figure in the James

Street Tavern. Hugo didn't just talk; he also listened and observed everything that was said and went on around him, not so it would draw your attention to what he was doing, but that is what he was almost unnoticeably doing all the time.

Even though Oxford, the River Thames, and the world around seemed to have relaxed, Tom continued to take great care when venturing out, especially at night. He would leave carefully placed twigs near the boat, a dry leaf subtly trapped in the locked door, so it would fall if someone or something opened or tried to open it. He was cautious and ever-watchful, both on *Wandering Aengus* and while crossing over the field on the animal path. Since mooring at his quiet, remote spot, nothing had actually happened, but even so, he remained vigilant, checking on every unexpected sound or movement around the boat and taking every precaution. Only twice had he seen another human being down there, a dog walker. They had chatted, and the dog walker seemed friendly enough, but even during that meeting, Tom remained on his guard. DCI Davis had not paid him any more visits and had been true to his word after breaking into and searching for evidence in *Wandering Aengus*. They had found nothing of interest relating to their inquiry, and as Spencer had told Tom, the lock on the door was repaired, and the boat was left as clean and tidy as they had found it. There had been no more questions. Tom was hoping the detectives had come to their senses and given up thinking he was a suspect; however, he also thought from what he knew of the police that "giving up" was unlikely. As well as the murders, he had expected to have heard more of his accidental and awkward visit to DCI Ali Smith's house and more questions about Leggy's death, but surprisingly, the police seemed to be leaving him alone, for a while at least.

Tuesday evening came along, and Tom followed the animal path across the field to the road, ever watchful at every step. Hugo had rung that afternoon and asked Tom to get to the James Street Tavern early so he could treat him to a farewell dinner. It was early evening when Tom left, but darkness had already fallen; outside the boat, the world had slipped quietly into the half-light that comes just before darkness of night. Tom carried a small torch in his pocket but rarely used it; he knew the animal path well, and our eyes quickly adjusted to functioning in the moonlight. There is a "night vision" that gets stronger from living on boats – all those dark nights with no streetlights to guide the way, just moonlight and starlight, twilight, and senses. Torches throw shadows that can be deceiving; they distort things; holes can seem to appear in the path where there are none; or the torchlight beam could fail to pick out an overhanging bramble until it is too late. Using natural light, Tom found it gave a far more accurate and detailed view of the world around him, one he could safely navigate and freely walk. Many times, he had seen wild deer standing on the far side of the field. With a torch, the deer would have seen him, but Tom would not have seen the deer. In the darkness, in the starlight, and in the moonlight, Tom felt invisible and safer, and in many ways he was. Like the wild deer, he preferred the natural light the way he thought it should be.

Arriving at the pub, Tom found Hugo already there, sitting at their usual table by the window. Jamie was sitting next to him, the pair deep in conversation, with a steaming cup of coffee in front of Jamie and a pint of ale in front of Hugo.

'I've talked Jamie into having dinner with us as well, Tom,' Hugo said as Tom arrived at the table.

'And this one really is on me; the paper stopped paying my expenses in Oxford as of last Monday; I'm supposed to be back in London now, but I called in and told them I was taking a few days off first. I want to say goodbye to a few people and a few places before I get back into the crazy world of London Town. Get yourself a drink, Tom. I have a tab running behind the bar. Just ask that pretty young lady who is serving.' Hugo lifted his glass up, and said, 'And good to see my amigo.'

'Yeah, hello, mate,' Jamie chipped in. 'Good to see you too. Hugo has just been telling me how much he will miss living on the boat when he becomes a "landlubber" again in a few days. Like me, eh? Do you remember me telling you about how addictive life on the river was when you first came to see *Wandering Aengus*, Tom? That was long before I sold her to you?'

'Strangely enough, Jamie,' Tom replied, 'I remember it very clearly, and strangely enough, you were absolutely bloody right!'

The three of them laughed, and Tom went to get a beer. Andrew popped his head around the kitchen door, and Tom nodded a hello, which was returned, then Andrew disappeared back into the kitchen.

'Tom, I was just telling Hugo how good his writing is; he captures the feel of life on the river really well for a new kid on the block, don't you think?' Jamie asked Tom when he returned with two beers.

'Well, I taught him everything he knows about boats,' Tom jokingly bragged.

'And I taught you everything *you* know about boats, Tom,' Jamie joked back.

'Look boys, don't fall out over me. I'm grateful for everything you have both done. Jamie, you taught Tom well, and Tom, you were a fantastic teacher. Let's drink to teaching!' Hugo had a broad grin on his face as he raised his glass towards Jamie and Tom.

'It must have been strange for you, Jamie, when you moved off the boat, I mean,' Hugo said. 'I have only been a river rat for a couple of months, and I know I will miss it. You lived on that old *Wandering Aengus* boat for years, so Tom tells me. How did you find it, moving off, back to terra firma?'

Jamie was contemplating his answer even as Hugo spoke and quickly replied.

'Well, you know what, Hugo, I have been so busy with the pub and all the other things I do that I haven't really had time to think about it much, but yes, I do miss it. I particularly miss the river.'

Jamie turned and called over to the barmaid to bring him a pint; it was not often that he drank, but it wouldn't be Hugo's leaving drink without "drink."

'There is a poem,' Jamie said, then paused to sip his beer, 'by Thomas Love Peacock, written in about 1810, if I recall correctly. I can remember a verse or two.' Jamie took another big swig of his beer, cleared his throat, and began to recite "The Genius of The Thames" by T. L. Peacock.

'The woods are roaring in the gale,
That whirls their fading leaves afar;
The crescent moon is cold and pale,
And swiftly sinks the evening star.'

Jamie spoke aloud and recited as if from the heart; Tom and Hugo sat and listened attentively.

'...High on this mossy bank reclined
I listen to the eddying wind,
While Thames impels, with sinuous flow,
His silent rolling stream below;
And darkly waves the giant oak,
That broad, above, its stature rears;
On whose young strength innocuous broke
The storms of unrecorded years.'

They both clapped when Jamie had finished, causing Jamie to break out into a big smile.

'I'm impressed, Jamie; that is some memory you have there, amigo, and that is a beautiful poem; I must look it up.' Hugo scribbled "Peacock" on the corner of a small notepad that lay on the table in front of him, causing Tom to think quietly to himself that journalists are always being journalists and wondering what other notes Hugo would take during the evening.

'Yes,' said Jamie, 'a lovely poem and a very long one. Peacock originally completed it as a short couple of verses but then expanded it into a bit of a lyrical epic.'

Jamie's love for poetry was clear to see. Literature had been the subject he taught as a teacher in schools and the one he studied at university. Tom remembered Jamie once saying that he got a great deal of pleasure teaching the kids that were interested and as passionate as him about the English language, but that was just a handful of them; the rest of the little oiks he said he would have happily strangled.

'OK, guys, let's get some food to this party!' Hugo said enthusiastically when the conversation dried up a little. The three of them sat in the window, drinking, and eating. To any observer looking in, they would have seemed to be the best of friends, sharing the best of pleasure, which was, at that moment, in spite of all their doubts, exactly how it was.

Hugo talked about his flat and his life in London, adding, 'You guys will have to promise me you will come and visit. I have a spare room and a sofa in the living room for one of you. I'll look forward to hearing tales from old Oxford town.'

When the food had been eaten, leaving three clean plates, Hugo asked, 'Jamie, do you remember any more of that poem by that guy…' He looked at his notepad, where he had scribbled the name, 'Peacock?'

Jamie thought for a moment and said, 'Just this bit…

'Ah ! Whither are they flown,
Those days of peace and love,
So sweetly sung by bards of elder time?
When in the startling grove
The battle-blast was blown,
And misery came, and cruelty, and crime,
Far from the desolated hills,
Polluted meads, and blood-stained rills,

Their guardian genii flew;
And through the woodlands, waste and wild,
Where erst perennial summer smiled,
Infuriate passions prowled and wintry whirl-
winds blew.'

Duke of Earl: A title, a status, if you will, given to one who always comes through for you in a clinch – someone who overachieves at anything.
Note: You can also achieve duke status!

[Andrew Smith's notebook]

Chapter 42

THE DUKE OF EARL

The Montblanc Meisterstück Classique ballpoint pen had a bid against it of £167.00, not including the £8.00 postage and packaging. Andrew checked a list in his notepad: it had retailed in Debenhams for £265.00, so the bid wasn't too short of what he expected. Still, there were another two hours of bidding left, and it could go up. The seller's name was "The Duke of Earl," and also listed under that name were a couple of other expensive pens, two sets of tungsten darts, perfume, and, in total, about three pages of other items. One set of the tungsten darts had sold for £18.00, a snip considering they were retailing in the "Sports for All" for £36.00. The money had been transferred online via Pay Pal and into Andrew's account, no problem. He dug the darts out of the locked trunk in the bottom of his bedroom cupboard, slipped them into an addressed bubble-wrap envelope, popped it into his shoulder bag, and added it to his "to-do" list. He would post it in the morning on his way to work, along with any other items that he received payment for that night. He checked his bank balance online and saw he had over £14,000.00 in there – not bad for less than a year of part-time work! It was money for old rope, or "new" rope if it was one of the Duke of Earl's eBay sales, "never used, as sold in the shops." Why didn't more people do it, he wondered?

The next morning, Ali dropped Andrew off in the city centre, and he strolled down to the main post office. He wanted to make sure his envelopes stood the best chance of getting to the buyers, so he always used recorded delivery; after all, you can't trust anyone these days, can you? Three envelopes today netted him a total of £287.00, and it was only Tuesday. Ali had asked him lots of probing questions over the weekend, and he had done well to answer all of them almost truthfully. That is to say, he didn't tell any lies; he just answered where it was possible to be truthful, but not to reveal anything he didn't want to, and avoided answering anything where truth would have equalled a confession. Andrew was a thief, not a liar; at least that was how he saw it. He had become an expert at bending the truth, but he would probably have been the last one to admit that, especially to himself. It was almost as if he could see no wrong in what he was doing; he was just being entrepreneurial. After all, Robin Hood stole from the rich and gave to the poor, and Andrew wasn't rich, so where was the difference?

In the early days, Andrew would plan his moves, meticulously mapping the store layouts and security details. Now, though, filled with those successes, it was too easy to do that and too safe. The buzz didn't quite hit the spot without the elements of risk, danger, and uncertainty. He had moved on to taking a more risky approach, sometimes not even bothering to look at the store for a minute or two before going in and going to work. It was that risk, that chance of being caught, that increased the thrill of getting away with it. Not knowing made his heart race and the adrenalin rush through his body; it was the thrill that drove him on, and that was why he did it. It was no longer the money; he had plenty of that now, and there was plenty more where it came from; it was all about the buzz. Andrew found it compulsive, and he was addicted.

Now that he was working at the James Street Tavern, Andrew would often get dropped off by Ali in town. From there, he would walk back across Magdalen Bridge and up the Cowley Road, a street lined with small independent shops selling a multitude of various goods. This was virgin territory for Andrew – a whole new world of buzzing experiences to be had – and all on his way to work. Hundreds of new goods were begging him to take them, put them in his bag, and take them for The Duke of Earl. Professional Music Technology was the first shop he tried on his new hunting grounds. There, he managed to get three Lee Oscar harmonicas. Andrew didn't know much about music keys or harmonicas, but what he did know was that they fitted into his bag easily and retailed at £30 each. Someone on eBay was bound to make a reasonable offer for them. This was followed by artist's sable hairbrushes, acrylic paints, expensive crayons, and anything else the art shop opposite had that would fit in the bag. He avoided clothes as they were too difficult to sell, and he didn't really have a clue what sort of stuff people were after. The last thing he wanted was to clog up his trunk with big items that wouldn't sell. Tesco's and all the other food shops he avoided and would always pay for anything that related to food, but his buzz and the thrill he felt afterwards never came with paying but only from five-finger discounts! Ker-ching!

Despite doing all the preparations and planning in the early days, he nearly came unstuck on a couple of occasions, and once he was actually stopped. On one occasion, breaking his own code and lying by saying that he had intended to pay for the item, he inadvertently put it in his bag and was really sorry and embarrassed about any mistake he may have accidentally caused. After that, he slipped the subject of shoplifting into a conversation with his mother to try and find out how the law worked with such things. What he learned from Ali did not deter him; far from it, it gave him encouragement. Not only were penalties very low, but most retailers were aware of the seriousness of making a false arrest and would only attempt to apprehend a person if there was absolutely no doubt about their guilt. They must prove that the person being arrested unquestionably intended not to pay for the goods. Ali had complained that it was another example of where the law was powerless and let petty criminals walk all over them, making the police a laughingstock. This was all music to Andrew's ears, and it gave him carte blanche to do exactly what he wanted. Andrew wasn't charged at that time when he was actually stopped, probably because of what he said when questioned; leaving room for doubt as to his real intent. Luckily, he hadn't been stopped since then; he was too good, but if he ever was, he now knew all the right things to say, and nothing would happen. He would just avoid going into that shop for a few years. As Oxford had hundreds of shops, there would always be fresh hunting grounds and new routes to get his kicks on.

The James Street Tavern was closed and the blinds down when Andrew arrived before lunch. Jamie had given him a key for the side door of the pub, which he used and entered. Taking a freshly laundered chef jacket from a pile of clean clothing, he changed and started prepping the lunch menu. The kitchen was peaceful when it was empty, and there were no customers waiting for meals. Sometimes he would have the radio on or play some music, but more often than not, he would leave the silence as it was. He could get into the zone that way – no distractions, just concentration and cooking, that is what made his food stand out. He was so much in the zone that he hadn't even noticed that Jamie had opened up the bar and the first lunchtime customers had arrived. Andrew popped his head through the door and into the bar, and he was surprised to see so many there. No longer was the usual pair of crutches leaning against one end of the bar; no longer was Jamie discreetly chatting with David Legg about things Andrew never heard, and it wasn't his place to ask.

The Environment Agency has patrol boats (named after tributaries of the Thames) and can enforce the limit strictly since river traffic usually has to pass through a lock at some stage. A speed limit of 8 km/h (4.3 kn) applies.

[Hugo Lewis' notebook].

Chapter 43

AFTER THE FLOOD

For a while, things slowly returned to almost normal on the river. There had been no more killings, and the water was running with a calmer current after a few weeks without rain. It had been a while since Hugo returned to London; Tom still heard from him now and again, usually when Hugo called to see if there was anything more on the "River Murders' story." There was not. Soon, a very different story would be filling the front pages of the newspapers. Hurricane Sandy had ripped through the East Coast of the United States, and the front page of Hugo's New York Times, along with four other complete pages, were now filled with tales of death, devastation, and heartache left in its wake. As well as the billions of dollars of destruction and the taking of many lives, Hurricane Sandy had also shaken up the world's weather system. This may have had something to do with Oxford, in early November, seeing three days and three nights of heavy, if not torrential, rain. It was the end of the brief dry spell as the rains covered the south-east of the United Kingdom, falling on the hills and fields of Oxfordshire, ground that was still saturated from the extraordinary wet summer. The sodden earth could no longer soak up the continuous rain, and the water stayed on the surface, making its way to the only places it could, the rivers. Already swollen for the time of year, their water levels had risen even more. Drains overflowed and streets flooded, as well as homes. Cold, dirty water gushed out of drains, manhole covers, and any other holes it could find. Sewers filled to the bursting point, forcing out water and rats. The rivers almost doubled in size and rapidly burst their banks. The flow of the Thames became a lethal current, and boats were washed away, buildings flooded, and trees uprooted. Port Meadow turned into an ocean, with the cattle and horses that remained cramming together on the few high spots that were not covered by the icy water. Remnants of the murder scene where the family of four anglers' future was decided prematurely, when their lives were taken from them, were either washed away or sitting under several feet of water. The police tape had gone, and the investigation tent straggled and torn on the surrounding bushes; the murder scene had gone, washed away; cleansed by the mighty Thames, a river that was taking no prisoners on its furious journey to the sea. It was the same story at the Bablock Hythe murder scene: the water level had reached the bottom of the caravan door and spilled into the floor, where the carpet stained with the blood of the Daltrey family used to be. The carpet had long been removed and placed within the dry confines of the police forensic evidence storage building. Surrounding Bablock Hythe, the land had been swallowed up by the water. At Day's Lock, the water reached the base of the lockkeeper's cottage and spilled in through the bottom of the doors, washing away the remains of dried blood, the chalked outlines of the bodies, and the dusted fingerprints. Only the big house near Eynsham, the home of Brian Jones and his family, escaped the flooding as it was built on higher ground; it remained the only murder scene still intact.

DCI Ali Smith and DI Spencer Davies were still working long and hard hours on the case; for them, it was still very much alive. Their team had been reduced, at first because of the murders coming to a stop and then the flooding, diverting resources to deal with the crisis that ensued. The police "river watch" was no longer possible as the Thames had now been declared an unsafe area. No new clues had been found, and little, if any, progress had been made. Now, with the destruction of most of the crime scenes, it was unlikely that any more would be revealed. As much as they didn't want it to happen, they needed the killer to strike again; it was the only way there would be any hope of catching him.

The "River Killings" story may have dropped from the front pages of the newspapers and from the minds of many, but in Oxford, especially for those close to the Thames, people were still fearful of venturing too far at night, still keeping their doors locked, knowing that the killer was still out there, out with the flooded houses and the scurrying rats – still free, still a threat, still unsolved, still unresolved.

* * *

Tom Hunter had lived through floods on the river before, and he knew only too well what to do. *Wandering Aengus* was now completely surrounded by water. The animal path and the field it crossed were covered by a black, wet lake too deep to walk through safely. He had loosened the ropes on the boat and dropped his rarely-used anchor over on the riverside to prevent it from drifting onto the bank. He had seen many boats in past floods that had become marooned high and dry after the waters had subsided. He knew that these conditions would only last for a week before the river fell back to how it should be at that time of year. All he had to do was sit tight. All he could do was sit tight, safe in the arbour of *Wandering Aengus*, warmed by the Morsø fire filled with wood foraged before the rains hit. There was enough food and water on board to keep him going for a week or so, and a couple of books that Hugo had given him – something to read – to pass the time. He would just wait it out. Tom enjoyed the safety of the solitude he now found himself in. No humans or animals would be able to get near *Wandering Aengus* for a while, either across the land or via the torrential river. There would be no unexpected callers, no visits from the police, and certainly no canoes. His remote winter mooring was now completely inaccessible and isolated by the floods. Only birds, ducks, and fish could navigate this water-locked wilderness near Eynsham. Peace, quiet, and waiting – that's all there was.

* * *

After three days, the rain stopped. Water made its way down from the hills and fields into the streams and rivers, causing chaos. The levels rose higher, rivers burst their banks again, and they flooded even more. Then, as the waters made their way to the sea with a strong, steady flow, the levels slowly dropped, and gradually, things returned to normal. Tom had known this was how it would be. The flood had left behind a muddy landscape and a deluge of insurance claims. A few boats now braved the river, and some of the more seriously inclined walkers ventured out along the muddy towpaths. Two teenagers, for the want of something to do to break the boredom of being cooped up at home during the floods, decided to walk down to the canal near the Rock of Gibraltar pub, then along the bank of the Cherwell to inspect the devastation. Trees had been washed away, and clumps of the bank had been taken with them. The boys were fascinated by how much damage had been caused. The going was tough and muddy, but this was an adventure for them and an escape from their normal monotony. The flood devastation was something happening in a place where nothing ever happened – something of interest to them, something to do. The younger of the two boys saw it first, still tied up, but half was now hanging into the Evenlode. It had been washed from its hiding place by the flood water. The Canadian-style canoe was old, battered, and now covered in mud, but it looked as if it could still float. The boys thought it must have been there for years, lost in the undergrowth, in the bushes; surely no one would miss it if they returned with some mates and carried it back. A little bit of work, fix it up, and it could be a good laugh when the weather cheered up. With difficulty, they made their way around a big chasm left by a chunk of bank that had fallen into the river. Squeezing their way through the prickly gorse, scratching them, and snagging their clothes, they reached the canoe. Lying upright and full of water and mud, it took all their strength to haul it back onto the bank. They both lifted and pushed, and at last, they managed to tip it onto one side. The black mud and water cascaded out, along with the final slushy silt that poured like black lava, and with it was a long, thin, muddy object.

'Look at that, it's a fucking great big, long sword!' the younger of the two excitedly said.

The other teenager felt the colour drain from his face and a tingling of fear go down his neck and through his spine.

'What is it? What's wrong?' The younger one said, no longer excited but suddenly concerned.

'It isn't just a 'big, long fucking sword,' his friend, the older, said. 'It's a big, long fucking Japanese sword, a fucking *samurai sword*!' He put his arm out as he spoke to stop the other boy, who was about to reach down and pick it up. 'Don't touch it! Don't go anywhere near it!'

'Why not? What's going on?' the other asked, now paying much more attention to what his friend was saying.

'The River Killings! You Muppet! The police were looking for a samurai sword. It said so in the newspapers. That rich lot that got killed in that big house, near Eynsham, the police said they had been hacked to death with a sword just like that one.' He pointed at the muddy object lying next to the canoe and looked at his friend, who just said, 'Fucking hell! Let's get the fuck out of here.'

And they did.

The call was passed on to DCI Smith, who immediately organised DI Spencer and some other officers to go with her to speak with the boys and locate the canoe.

'Better give Nash a call,' she said to Spencer, 'we will need some forensics. I shouldn't think there has been much that's not been washed away, but it sounds like we have the boat and the weapon, if that is what they are.'

Ali was sounding calm and collected, but she and Spencer knew that this could be the first real piece of hard evidence they had. The boys took the detectives to the place where they had dragged the canoe out of the water.

Graham Nash and his metal suitcase of forensic tools had joined them.

'It has to be it!' exclaimed Spencer positively when he set eyes on the upturned boat and the mud-covered samurai sword.

Graham Nash looked at the sword and said, 'Easy peasy, Japaneasy!' causing the two unamused faces of the detectives to look at him. Nash became silent.

'Secure the evidence items as much as possible, please, Graham,' Ali said, to the head of forensics. 'And Spencer, put a call in and get a few officers here to carry this canoe out.'

'Will do, ma'am,' Spencer said, taking his mobile phone out and starting to dial.

'...And Spence,' Ali added, 'tell them to bring a flatbed truck and to wear their wellies.'

Spencer smiled at that last remark and put the call in.

Even with all the mud and the rain, Graham Nash and his team were still able to find some forensic evidence on both the sword and the boat, nothing more than low grade – but it was something, and it was blood. Lost and stolen property records were delved into as the team looked for anything related to a canoe or a samurai sword. The maker of the boat and the markings on the sword were also investigated, but the age of both meant even identifying their origin probably wouldn't help much. House-to-house inquiries were immediately started in the area near the Evenlode. This covered mainly the few houses around the Rock of Gibraltar and the handful of boaters living on that part of the canal. The same part of the canal that both Ali and Spencer knew was where Tom Hunter had refitted *Wandering Aengus*. The landlord of the pub was interviewed, as were "Froggy" the moorings warden, Jake Fisher, the boat mechanic, Craig Wolf, who lived near the pub, Graham Jones, the tow bar fitter, who lived in the bungalow next to the pub, and all the boaters. Nothing of any note was discovered, but nearly all of them knew or knew of Tom Hunter.

Boys will be boys!

Chapter 44

DARK PLANS

They finished their questions, and he closed the door. His heart was pounding, and he could feel the clamminess in his palms. The rings under his shirt hung heavy on the chain around his neck and pressed against his chest like a cold lead weight. That fucking sword! He knew he should have got rid of it as he was told to, but no, he thought it was too nice; he'd had too much "fun" with it to just toss it in the river. Besides, no one would ever find it, not in the canoe; it was well hidden. But now someone had found it, and the filth was asking questions. They had come to his house, knocking on his door. He didn't let them in, mind; he just chatted on the doorstep with them, acting all surprised; he didn't know anything about it. Those meddling fucking teenagers! He knew them well and lived just a couple of doors away. He could kill them, but no, this wasn't a time for fresh killing, this was a time to make plans. The time had come to scheme, to plot, to deceive, to cover, to camouflage, and to hide. He should have started this ages ago, but never too late, eh? There was still time, but he needed to act fast before "someone else" found out what he had done and what he hadn't done.

"The time has come, the Walrus said, to talk of many things: of shoes and ships and sealing wax, of cabbages and kings, and why the sea is boiling hot, and whether pigs have wings."[1]

The time had come to act. This was the time. This was the time to stay alive. This was his time. This was a time not to get caught.

---

[1] LEWIS CARROLL , "The Walrus and the Carpenter"

There are 33 bridges across the tidal Thames, from Teddington Lock to the open sea.
Waterloo Bridge is the only Thames bridge damaged by German bombs during the war.

[Hugo Lewis' notebook]

Chapter 45

LONDON'S BURNING

Tom woke up shivering. The boat was freezing. The fire in the burner had gone out for the first time since the cold snap started. He quickly grabbed some warm clothes and set about getting it lit again. It was one of the coldest mornings so far that late autumn, and the Morsø couldn't have chosen a worse time to burn out. Using some screwed-up newspaper, a handful of scavenged twigs for kindling, and a few shards of candle wax, he soon had the fire blazing away again. Keeping the warm clothes on, he made a pot of tea with real tea leaves – he had never been one for teabags. It would take an hour or so for the boat to get back up to a comfortably warm temperature, and the steaming hot cuppa helped. Outside, a light frost had covered the boat and grassy bank. *Wandering Aengus* glistened in the faint morning sun. Footprints of small birds lay criss-crossing trails in the thin white, frosty coating on the boat's roof. The bank was still virgin white – not a print, not a footstep – no one and no "thing" had passed by recently, animal or human. Tom sat down opposite the stove, clutching his mug in both hands and feeling it warm through his fingers. This was it, winter starting again, his seventh on the boat. Life in cities carries on almost untouched by the seasons, inside climate-controlled buildings, subways, tube trains, underground car parks, and the great indoors, where seasons come and go, almost unnoticed and everything remains constant, controlled, and man-made. Not so in the countryside, and especially not so on the river, where small changes impact everything; the wind, the rain, and the temperature all have a noticeable impact on the wildlife, the vegetation, the flow of the river, and all that lives in and on it. Every change has an effect, and every change can be felt, even the small ones. Tom had grown to love these tweaks, movements, and alterations in the seasons, the smells, the colours, the looks, and the sounds. He particularly liked the winter season. In winter, everywhere was much quieter; the cold kept the tourists away, and the hire boats were all moored up until the spring, being serviced and painted. Many of the birds had migrated, and many of the animals had slept. Autumn had dropped the leaves from the trees, leaving more space for the paler but still illuminating winter light to penetrate the riverbank. There was no place he would rather be than inside the warm, comforting embrace of *Wandering Aengus*, looking out during the day over the cold river flowing and at night up at the star-studded sky. The winter night sky was special – very special, something to behold. Clearer skies and the position of planet Earth made winter a stargazer's dream. When snow arrived, it transformed everywhere into a winter wonderland – clean, fresh, bright, and vibrant. Winter was always a time to reflect, a time to plan, a time to look backwards and forwards. Winter was a time to dream.

Tom gazed out of *Wandering Aengus*' windows at the surrounding scenery. It was something he knew he would never get tired of, no matter how long or how often he looked. How could anyone ever get tired of the beauty and power of nature? As expected, within an hour, the boat had warmed up, and some of the warm clothes could come off. Tom had cooked, eaten, cleared up his breakfast, and run the engine to heat up water for a shower. Not having worn a watch for many years and having no clock on board, he switched on his mobile phone to check the time. It was

7.30 am. The shower was hot and warming and steamed up the bathroom and the window. He lathered his hair with shampoo and had started rinsing out the soap when his phone rang. Whoever it was would have to wait; the shower was more important and more appealing. By the time he had finished and towelled himself dry, the fire had really heated the boat up, so much so that a few windows now needed to be opened. His phone was on the kitchen breakfast bar, and there it stayed until he put another kettle on to boil for more tea. Not until he was sitting down by the fire and holding a fresh, hot mug did he turn his attention to the phone. There was the missed call with a symbol letting him know he had a voicemail. He didn't recognise the number, but then again, there wasn't really any number he would recognise; not many people ever called him. Hugo was about the only one who called regularly, and it wasn't his number; that would have shown as Tom had stored it, "Hugo NYC"; besides, since Hugo had returned to his normal life in London, even he rarely called. Tom dialled the number to retrieve his voicemails and was stunned when he heard the first message start. Even after all the years that had gone by, the voice was unmistakable.

'Don't you ever have your phone switched on, Tom? I have tried to call you so many times!' His ex-wife's voice hit him like an unexpected punch.

'I got your number from Simon in Charles Street' *Simon*, that was someone else Tom hadn't heard from in a while.

'I told him it was an emergency, and it is, well, sort of. My flat was broken into, Tom. I came home one night last week, and the front door had been forced open and the place had been ransacked.'

Tom clicked the mobile onto the speaker and placed it on the arm of his chair as he carried on listening.

'I called the police, and at first they didn't seem too interested, as you can expect, but then a day or so later, a couple of detectives came back to talk to me about it. They were interested in the only thing that had been stolen and also very interested in you, Tom.'

Josie's voice came clearly through the speakerphone and filled the inside of *Wandering Aengus*.

'They wanted to know when I last saw you, if you had called me recently, if we were still talking, and they told me to be very careful and gave me a number to call should I be concerned about anything. All they managed to do was scare me half to death, Tom. I can see now why you didn't like the job. Please, can you call me?' She recited her phone number, knowing that Tom would no longer have it, especially as it had been some six years since they last spoke.

'Oh yes, and Tom, the thing that was stolen…' she added before the message ended, '…it was my wedding ring.'

Tom sat staring at the phone in his hand. The last bit had really shaken him up. A wave of fear ran through his body. DI Spencer, when he decided to open up his investigations and be a bit more forthcoming in the hope of flushing out more information, had told Tom about the wedding rings that had been taken from the victims and that it was thought the killer may have been collecting them as trophies or "souvenirs" of his "work." This had to be why they were asking his ex-wife questions about him. Could this really be related? Could the killer have broken into Josie's flat? Was he, Tom Hunter, connected to the murders in some way after all? Was Josie at risk? Was he at risk? A chill went down his back, and he looked out of the window, half expecting to see someone standing out there on the bank, but all he saw were the remains of the light frost, now thawing and rapidly disappearing. Tom played back the message and jotted down the number. It was another 20 minutes before he finally got the courage to call Josie back. "Courage" perhaps isn't the correct word to use, as although there was a tinge of fear involved, it was more a reluctance to open a window on the past and confront all of that time again. He had shut the door on his old life and moved on; he didn't want to look back, go back, or even think back to how things were for him before his life on the river began. But somehow he had brought all this on, and he owed it to Josie, if only for her safety, to call her and try to get to the bottom of what was happening. The River Killings were not only spreading their fingers out along his river, reaching into and touching Tom's world; they were now feeling their way into his past, scratching and opening up old wounds, picking at the past.

'Hello.' Her voice sounded much calmer than it did in the voicemail message that Tom had listened to on his phone. There was such a long pause before he spoke that she repeated the word again, 'Hello?'

'Hi Josie, it's me, Tom. I got your message,' he eventually said.

'Thank God you have called me back, Tom. I was beginning to wonder if you would or not.' There was another long pause; this time it was her working out what to say and how to say it so as not to make the situation any more upsetting than it already was. 'I have been worried sick, Tom. The police asked me so many questions about you, and, well, they made me think I should be afraid of something. It worked. I am!'

'What did they say exactly, Josie?' he asked.

'Well, they asked me if I had seen or heard from you, but I already told you that. Then they asked a lot of questions about the wedding ring. Was it from our wedding? Did you still have yours? Did I still wear it? I told them the truth, Tom; it has been tucked away in a box in a drawer so long I had almost forgotten it was there.'

Tom didn't say so, but the fact was he had no idea where his wedding ring was; it was on the boat somewhere, probably, but he didn't have a clue where. He hadn't thought about it in years.

'Tom,' she continued more cautiously, 'they asked me if I had heard about the murders, those poor families that were killed in Oxford. I told them that of course I had, everyone has, and there were reports in the newspapers and on the TV. Why would they ask me about them in the same sentence as asking me about you, Tom? What is going on?' She was starting to sound very upset.

'I don't know… That is, well, the police have been asking me questions about those murders as well. They seem to think I am linked to them in some way. I don't know why. I have tried and tried to think of ways I could be involved, but I can't see anything that could connect me to them or them to me.' Tom was careful not to say too much, but he felt he owed it to Josie to be honest about what was going on.

'What about the ring, Tom? Why were they so interested in that?' she asked.

Tom couldn't bring himself to tell her the gruesome truth; she was already sounding distressed, and the truth would have frightened her to death.

'I'm not sure, Josie. I don't think we can discuss this over the phone. Can we meet? I'll come to London, of course.'

'OK, Tom, but promise me you will tell me everything, and I don't want to drag up our past; we have moved on from that, I hope. I know you have, and believe me, Tom, I've moved on too.'

'That is just fine with me, Josie. I need to sort a few things out, and I will call you back. When will be a good time to meet?'

'Any evening is good for me. I work during the day. I don't have all the time in the world like some people.'

Even though she said this last sentence with no emotion, Tom could tell it was a dig at him. He thought she saw him as living a life of luxury on his disability allowance. He thought she hated the fact that their marriage ended, or at least ended the way it had with her having to carry on working, supporting herself and Tom, who retired very early. He didn't rise to this dig; he knew that far more serious things were now going on, more serious than she could imagine. He calmly said, 'I'll call you back this evening.' And with that, the telephone conversation came to an end.

He sat motionless for a considerable time. As much as he didn't want that past to open up again, Josie was his ex-wife, a human being still very much alive and kicking. She had never gone away, and whatever he did, whatever anyone did, the past cannot be obliterated; it was always going to be there.

* * *

Tom walked to the bus station; it was quite a walk, but he only had a small bag slung over his shoulder, as he wasn't planning on staying for more than one night. He originally thought he would take the bus to London, meet up with Josie, and then get the next bus back to Oxford, but Hugo had persuaded him to stay the night so they too could catch up. The countryside looked wet and grey as the bus cut along the M40 through the fields of Oxfordshire and onwards to Victoria Coach Station, London. The dankness of the day fitted Tom's mood; he wasn't looking forward to seeing Josie again after all the years that had passed, nor was he looking forward to the conversation he would need to have with her. What would she think? How would she take it with him being a serial killer suspect? It was for that reason that he let Hugo talk him into staying so easily; he felt he might need a drink and a bit of friendly company after his session with Josie. Trying not to think about it too much, he sat at the back of the bus alone, switching between staring aimlessly out of the window and trying to concentrate on reading the newspaper he had picked up. The newspaper eventually won the battle for his attention when he saw the story about the samurai sword being found. He read the article in silence, hoping this find would mean the police were nearer to catching the monster, but to his horror, he saw yet another connection he had with the killings. The sword had been found on the River Cherwell near Enslow. It was where the Cherwell runs alongside the Oxford Canal, even becoming part of it for a stretch. This was where the Rock of Gibraltar sat and where Tom had refitted *Wandering Aengus* seven years ago – more evidence to link him to the murders, albeit circumstantial. He started to feel even more uncomfortable than he had when he first set off on the journey back to London. No doubt other papers were carrying this news, which meant that Josie would probably have read it. She might be making the connections herself.

Darkness fell quickly as the bus neared London. The headlights and taillights of the other vehicles on the motorway stretched out on the road before him like glittering strings of diamonds and rubies. All Tom could see in the window now was his own shadowy reflection. There was still an hour and a half left before his rendezvous with Josie when he stepped off at Victoria Coach Station without paying attention to the other passengers. They, too, scurried off in their separate ways. In the street outside, he hailed a taxi to take him to Embankment station; there was time to take the tube, but he hated it, as he always had. Even growing up in London, he avoided the Underground whenever possible. Tube bombings from the IRA and later from so-called Islamic extremists had done nothing to reassure him that taking the

Underground was a good way to travel. Josie worked on the South Bank, on the other side of the river from Embankment Station, and they had arranged to meet at Gordon's Wine Bar in Villiers Street, just at the back of the station. It was where they used to meet in happier times when they first started going out together. Gordon's hadn't changed throughout all the years Tom had known it. The same old, narrow, rickety stairs lead down to the bar set in the vaults of the ancient building. In a conversation Tom once had with Jamie, Jamie told him that Gordon's bar was the oldest in London and possibly in the world, and that not only Samuel Pepys had lived in the building above, but in the 1890s Rudyard Kipling was a tenant and wrote 'The light that failed' in the parlour that sat above the bar. The bar and its old low vaulted ceiling were dimly lit, mainly by candles, below street level, windowless, and underground, with no telling if it was day or night, wet or dry, warm or cold in the world above. It was like going back in time to a hundred years ago in Gordon's, and to Tom, that is how long ago he felt his marriage had ended.

Not knowing if Josie would prefer red or white wine when she arrived, he ordered himself a beer to get on with while he was waiting and found an empty table at the back of the long subterranean bar room. Gordon's was always busy, but particularly after work, when office workers would flood in for drinks before getting their trains home. Tom had always thought that you must need a drink to face the ordeal of standing in a crushed, smelly tube carriage for an hour or so. The main thing that he noticed as having changed since the time he and Josie used to go to the bar was that now it was no-smoking like every other enclosed public place, and the smell was of wine, food, and the flaky whitewashed walls. He took his time drinking his beer, knowing that if he left the table for a moment, he would lose it, as the bar had filled up and there were groups of people standing around waiting to pounce on any table that became available. He saw Josie long before she saw him, or so he thought. She was wearing a long coat and carrying an umbrella and a bag, and she looked from where Tom was sitting to be older and thinner-faced, but then six years had passed since they had set eyes on each other, and he knew he too had aged considerably in that time also.

'Hello Tom, you haven't changed a bit,' she exclaimed as she arrived at the table.

'Hello Josie, I was wondering if you would recognise me, if we would recognise each other even,' Tom replied, not really knowing what to say even though he had played it out in his mind whilst he had been sitting there nursing his beer.

'I'll get a bottle. What would you like, Josie?' That was the only bit he had rehearsed that he actually got around to saying. He was thankful that he now had the opportunity to be on his own at the bar for a few moments. When he got back with a bottle of dry white, Josie had taken off her coat and tucked her bag and brolly to the side of the small table. She looked thinner in her body as well as her face. Tom thought maybe the stresses of the divorce could have contributed to that, but in truth, it was really that she had started to take better care of herself. She was still a young woman and would one day meet someone, her Mr Right. Unlike Tom, who had given up the idea years ago, he'd had the odd unsuccessful date but had since settled down to a life on his own, no longer looking for anyone else or anything. He wouldn't even have known where to begin with a relationship; consequently, he didn't bother looking for one.

They talked for an hour. Tom explained as best he could how he had inadvertently found himself part of a murder investigation, and not just any old murder investigation but the one that had for a while filled the front pages of newspapers all over Europe and even some in the States. Josie had asked him about the ring and was horrified when he told her what he knew. She also questioned him about the sword: she had read about it in the newspapers, and Tom was right; she did remember that he had refurbished his boat not far from there, and he had lived on it near there for several months. He tried to explain that the Cherwell wasn't navigable with a narrowboat and how he had never even walked along that stretch; very few people ever did. An air of uneasiness crept into their conversation, and Tom felt Josie pulling further away from him the more he told her. Did she not believe him? Was she also now beginning to think he was involved in some way? Did she, for one second, think he could be the killer? Tom wasn't wrong; Josie was starting to feel very uncomfortable and concerned, full of doubts. She was glad they had arranged to meet in such a public place; at least that made her feel safer and slightly more comfortable. Could Tom have broken into her flat and stolen the ring? Why would anyone else do that? Who would want to? How well did she really know him? When they were married, where did he go those nights he didn't come home? Were the police right to have made her feel very concerned? Right now, she was thinking maybe they were right; she wasn't noticeably concerned, but inside, trying not to show it, she was completely frightened and terrified. She didn't know what she would do next but felt very vulnerable and very scared; she was only too pleased when they had finished the wine and left. On her way to the Underground, she constantly checked to see if she was being followed and to see if Tom was following her. Could it be that she never knew him at all?

* * *

Tom stood in the middle of Waterloo Bridge, looking east along the river. The skyline of London, different in many ways from the one he had grown up with, twinkled and beamed. The Shard and many other new skyscrapers reached up into a black, starless night sky. The city was full of life, full of excitement, full of mystery, beautiful, and enticing, pulling people in. It was a different life – a city life. It was a life Tom had said goodbye to many years before, and although he felt the power, charm, allure, and temptation of London, it was no longer the place he wanted to be, not in the slightest. His attention turned to the boats below, which were also brightly lit and sparkling in the river. That is where he wanted to be – on his boat, in his world, in the open countryside, far away from all the madness that now surrounded him. But a far more menacing, sinister madness had now surrounded his world and was reaching out and touching his past as well. Tom Hunter was a very worried man.

'Hey, Tom!' Hugo's voice made Tom snap out of his thoughts. 'Jump in the cab, Buddy; we have some drinking to catch up on; welcome to London, amigo!'

It was like a weight being lifted from Tom's shoulders. Hugo's smiling face and a few beers were just what the doctor ordered right now. He climbed into the back of the black London taxi. Hugo shouted the name of a bar that Tom hadn't heard of to the cabbie, and off they went into the night.

Happy birthday to you
Happy birthday dear Ali

[Written in Ali's card by Andrew]

Chapter 46

HAPPY BIRTHDAY?

'Happy birthday, Mum.' Andrew had a big smile on his face as he handed Ali a handful of envelopes that he had retrieved from the mat inside the front door. He had already placed the neatly wrapped parcel containing a bottle of Chanel No. 5 on the kitchen table and laid a place for breakfast. Ali had only just woken up and was standing at the bottom of the stairs, rubbing her eyes.

'And there is a present for you on the table in the kitchen, along with the best birthday breakfast you have ever had!'

The smell of bacon and toast drifted into the hall, and Ali took the envelopes from Andrew, smiling as she did so. She sat at the kitchen table, where a small glass of freshly squeezed orange juice sat next to an empty plate and two small, gift-wrapped packages. As Andrew got busy with the frying pan, Ali looked at the different coloured envelopes, obviously birthday cards. Two had local Oxford postmarks; one had a Norwegian stamp in the corner, franked with an Oslo postmark; the other was a white envelope with dark brown ink, slightly smudged, with a London postmark, London Victoria. The first one she opened was locally stamped; it read:

"Wishing you a very happy birthday, Ali, and hoping you have a nicer year than the one we have just been through. Best wishes, Spence."

'Just been through,' Ali thought, *'and we are still going through it!'* And they were still going through it in every way; it wasn't over yet, not in the slightest.

She stood the card up on the table and opened the next one, also locally postmarked. That one was from Andrew; she had already guessed correctly. He looked around and smiled at his mother when he saw she was reading his card.

"To the best Mum in the whole world. Wishing you the best birthday ever. Thank you for everything. All my love, Andrew xxx"

The envelope with the Norwegian stamp Ali knew had to be from Patricia in Oslo.

"Wishing you a very happy birthday, Mum. Miss you loads and wish I could be there on your special day. Love you as always. xxx Pattie."

Andrew turned from the cooker, saying,

'Come on, Mum! Hurry up and open that last one; breakfast is ready.'

Ali picked up the last card. She didn't know anyone in London who would send her a birthday card. She looked at the address written with brown, smudged ink but didn't recognise the handwriting. It was very neat and precise. Using her breakfast knife, she carefully slit the top of the envelope open and removed the card from inside. On the front, in big, bright, glitter-covered letters, it had the word "MUM" and a picture of a bunch of flowers. For a moment, Ali thought it was another card from Andrew that he had got a friend to post for him for some reason, maybe as a joke, but then she opened it and read the message:

"Happy Birthday, Ali, I know you aren't my mum, but we have had some fun together this year, haven't we, and I feel very close to you now, very close."

The message was written in the same ink as the address and ended with three crosses for kisses. The last "kiss" was smudged with a splatter of deep red next to it. Ali froze.

'When did this card get delivered, Andrew?' she asked, not disguising the concern in her voice.

'About a half an hour ago, Mum, with the others, the postman delivered them. Why, what's wrong?' He said as he plated up the breakfast.

'I don't know, Andrew, I don't know.' Her voice was shaky as she spoke. 'Give me that roll of plastic bags from the drawer, please, Andrew.' she asked.

Andrew passed her the roll, and she peeled off one of the re-sealable freezer bags and carefully placed the card and envelope inside it. She wasn't sure, but the ink – the ink, she thought – looked like blood.

Ali started putting on her coat as she made a call to Spencer.

'Mum, you aren't going, are you? What about breakfast? And you haven't even opened your presents. What is it?' Andrew asked, with concern.

'I'm really sorry, Andrew. I can't explain at this moment, but I have to go to work right now. I will be back early, I promise. I will tell you all about it when I know some more, and we can celebrate my birthday then if you are in. I am so sorry, Andrew.' Ali spoke as she buttoned up her coat and held her mobile to her ear with her shoulder.

'And Andrew,' she added before leaving, 'please promise me you will be careful. Make sure you know who it is before opening the door to anyone.'

'But Mum, what's up?' He pleaded, now beginning to sound alarmed.

'I don't know at the moment; maybe nothing. I will tell you later, I promise. Just be careful, please?' Ali said as she left the room. The front door closed, and she was outside the house in the sharp morning air, feeling in her pockets for her car keys.

'Spencer, pick up the bloody phone!' she said out loud, but the ringing tone continued unanswered.

Halfway to the station, her phone rang. It was Spencer.

'Morning, ma'am, I was in the shower when you called. What's up?' he said when Ali answered.

'I'm on my way to the station, Spence; I'll speak to you there,' she replied, checking her rear-view mirror not just for traffic but with a concern, almost fear, making sure she wasn't being followed.

'I'm on my way!' Spencer exclaimed, and the phone clicked as the call ended.

Graham Nash had driven over to collect the suspect's birthday card in person. He held up the clear plastic bag that Ali had placed it in and read the envelope. He agreed; at first glance, it looked like blood, but it would need to be forensically examined. Managing not to make any inappropriate remarks or crack any unfunny jokes, he took the bag away, saying he would get back to her within the hour and let her know what they found. Spencer made Ali another coffee; he could see how shaken she was. He tried to reassure her by telling her that it could have been a crank or a hoaxer, but both of them knew it was not. This was the killer bragging and taunting his pursuers – a killer that hadn't killed for a while and was missing the excitement? Did that mean he was getting ready to kill again? Would they have another murdered family on their hands? Why the London Victoria postmark? There had been tails on Tom Hunter, and both Ali and Spencer knew he had been to London, and the visit fit in with the time the card was posted. They knew about Tom's wife's stolen wedding ring, and they knew he had met up with her. They also knew that Hunter, with his police training, would be only too aware that he was being closely watched, so why would he post a card that pointed to him? That was all they knew – everything and very little.

As promised, less than an hour later, Ali received a call from forensics. She put the phone into speaker mode, and both she and Spencer listened carefully as Graham Nash spoke.

'I have the preliminary results of the test carried out on your birthday card, DCI Smith, and some details from the other investigations on the other items of evidence my team has been looking at. You will get a detailed written report, but you did say you wanted to know as soon as we found out anything.' Nash's voice carried with it a certain smugness, and Spencer and Ali could visualise a bragging look on his face.

'Well, firstly, your card. The card itself could have been purchased from any number of supermarkets, corner shops, or card outlets, so we aren't expecting to make much progress with that line of investigation, but…' he paused, then continued, 'the writing on the envelope and inside the card are both in human blood. The blood group doesn't match any of the victims known to us so far; I am assuming there may be others that we don't yet know about. What is interesting, though, is that it is the same group as the samples we took from the blood smeared on the teeth of the boy murdered at Port Meadow. We can't say one hundred percent that the two samples are from the same person until the full DNA results are obtained, but they definitely matched blood groups, which points to it being the same person, possibly the killer?'

'What else have you found out?' Ali asked.

'Well, the blood on the teeth – what we do know for certain now is that it doesn't match that of your main suspect, that Hunter chap – completely different blood group. And that's all I have on the blood samples, but we have made some progress with the samurai sword. Some of the cuts on the bodies found in the house near Eynsham definitely correspond with the cuts that would have been left by the sword. This doesn't conclusively prove it is the actual weapon used, but there were also some very minute traces of dried blood at the hilt of the sword. We are having trouble analysing these as they are only weak samples, but should they prove likely to be from some of the victims at that house, then we will know for sure if it is the weapon. I will let you know when I find out, and that, I'm afraid, is about it for now.'

'Thank you, Graham; I appreciate you getting back to me so promptly,' Ali said politely to Nash, but rolled her eyes up as she spoke so that Spencer could see what she really thought.

'My pleasure.' Nash replied, 'Oh, and happy birthday, Alison.'

Hallucinogens and psychedelics have been in use by people since the dawn of civilization. Shamans of the native tribes of North America used them to contact the spirit world of their ancestors.
LSD is an illegal, mind-altering drug.
Heroin is processed from morphine, a naturally occurring substance extracted from the seed pods of certain varieties of poppy plants. It is both the most abused and the most rapidly acting of the opiates.
Heroin is an illegal, highly addictive drug.

[From a drug fact sheet]

Chapter 47

HEROIN

The last thing Tom remembered was being on the back deck of *Wandering Aengus*, taking his boat keys from his pocket, and putting one of them into the lock. It was at that moment that he was hit from behind with such force that it smashed his face into the metal door and knocked him unconscious. Now he was beginning to come around, but something was wrong – something was very wrong. He was seated in a chair in the kitchen area of *Wandering Aengus,* and he couldn't move his arms; he couldn't, in fact, move at all. All he was able to do was open one eye, and then his vision was blurred. His other eye was stuck closed with congealed blood. His arms were held out straight on either side of him, fastened with plastic cable ties around his wrists at each end of an oak floorboard placed across his back. He had been crucified! His mouth was dry and bloody, his body was hurting, his heart was racing, and his mind was swirling out of control. Slowly, he began to make out the dark shape of someone standing in front of him. As the image cleared, he could see that it was a man. Tom's one eye cleared slightly, and he began to take in more details. The man in front of him was smiling, talking, and smiling, his voice gurgling in Tom's ringing ears. The man's arm was moving quickly; he was holding something; he was tapping the side of it, tapping the side of a hypodermic syringe. Even with Tom's blurred vision and his head all over the place, he started to recognise who the figure was. It was Craig from the Rock of Gibraltar, the oddball. Craig, the one who had helped him when he was refitting the boat, was the one he used to play pool with. Craig Wolf!

Craig Wolf finished tapping the syringe, moved forward, and stuck it into a vein in Tom's outstretched arm. Tom didn't have room to even flinch as another 10 cc of class "A" drugs flushed into his system. He felt the rush as the drug entered his body and careered on its run through his blood system. Craig stepped back and continued talking, leaving the syringe sticking in Tom's arm; it hung down with a trickle of blood, forming a blob at one end and dripping to the floor. This time Tom tried very hard to listen; with everything he had left in him, he tried. He knew now that he was fighting for his life.

'Well, Tommy boy, as I was saying, someone has to take the blame for all those dead people, and it sure as fuck ain't going to be me, no way Jose! Even if I did kill them,' Craig laughed as he spoke – a nervous laugh. He stepped forward again, pulled the needle out, and squirted some of the blood that filled the hypodermic all over the front of Tom's already bloody shirt.

'Force of habit that, mate; *flushing out the works*. Sorry about the mess, old son.' Craig gave Tom a friendly, gentle slap on the cheek and carried on talking. 'I've been a bit worried about you since you saw me on the bench at Day's Lock that morning. I've been watching you since then. I didn't think you recognised me, but at some point you could have worked out who it was, and I couldn't really take that chance. Me and you, Tommy, are similar, you know, we're both orphans. Remember telling me that, eh? We used to have good talks together in the Rock, didn't we? The only difference between us being both orphans is, well, Tommy boy, it's that your parents just died, natural causes you told me, whereas mine, I offed the pair of them myself, killed them both, years before I met you. I was still a teenager – just a kid, really. I snuffed out my dear old Mum and then I finished off my dearest daddy. I sat them around the kitchen table with me – well their wet, limp, bloody bodies, that is – while I had a cup of tea. Then I dragged them out and shoved them into dad's car, took 'em for a drive. Put dad at the wheel and ran it off the road. Not with me in it, you understand, just those two dead cunts. He was full of alcohol; was dear old Daddy. I had forced him to drink a bottle of whisky while I held a knife to Mum's throat. This was before I killed them, of course. He wouldn't have drunk much after, would he! He slurped it all up, scared shitless he was. It was only cheap stuff, mind, one from the supermarket. There was no point in wasting a decent bottle on him; he wouldn't have appreciated it. Then, after he'd drunk it all down like a good boy, I killed Mum anyway; I whacked her over the head with a lump hammer.' Craig let out another one of his nervous laughs.

'Thump! Crack! That was the noise it made. The old man's eyes nearly popped out, as did hers!' Craig made the movement of swinging a hammer down violently and banged his fist on the kitchen worktop.

'Dad started whining and crying, but I'd had enough by then, so I whacked him in the face with the same hammer, right in the gob. I'm not sure if it killed him, but it shut him up. He may have been alive still when I loaded them into the car, but fuck him, he deserved it. They both deserved it!' Craig stopped talking and picked up the syringe, staring at it for several moments as if contemplating using it on himself, but then he put it down again.

'You still with me, Tommy boy? We don't want you going to sleep and missing the end of my story, now do we?' He slapped Tom around the face again, this time harder. Tom tried to speak, but just a mumbled noise left his mouth, and a trickle of blood mixed with saliva made small bubbles and ran from the corner of his lips. His chest gurgled. Craig continued.

'Ah, good. Back with us again, then. Where was I? Oh yeah, I loaded them both into the back of the car at first. Mummy and Daddy, I'm talking about, Tommo. Are you following me? Then I covered them over with the horrible tartan car blanket they used to make me sit on when I was a little boy. I hated that, Tommy; it made my legs itch. It was when I was still in short trousers and all that; you know what it's like. Anyway, I drove to a place near Brighton that I knew. We used to go there a lot when I was little, on *"family outings,"* so I knew where to head for the "Devil's Dyke." What a great fucking name for a place, eh? The Devil and his missus are buried there! When we got there, I dragged Dad out of the back of the car and stuck him in the driver's seat like he was driving, and then put Mum next to him in the passenger's seat. I soaked the car in petrol, then pushed them over into the Devil's Dyke itself. It dropped down proper horribly like. The trouble was the motor didn't go up in flames like I expected, so I had to climb all that fucking way down and sling a match in. It was worth the effort, though. That really is the work of the devil, you know, Tom. They looked good in front of the old, mangled Rover. Well mashed up. You couldn't make out where my lump hammer had been. The motor was all burning nicely by the time I'd climbed back up to the top. I watched it for a bit to make sure it didn't go out, but I thought it best not to hang around too long, so I walked into Brighton. It took me nearly two hours, but I was buzzing. Lucky for me, it wasn't raining either. I could have got soaked, Tommy; worse still, my little fire could have gone out before it had destroyed anything that could have looked like I was involved in any way. I went into that pub when I got there, Brighton, that is, Tom, the one under the arches on the sea front, had a few strong lagers, quite a few, thirsty work all that killing, swinging hammers around, lifting bodies, climbing, and walking, Tommy. After the beers, I got an early evening train back to London and took the Oxford bus from Victoria Coach Station. The Rock was still open when I got back, so I was in time for a few games of pool and a couple more sherbets. Orphaned! Job done, me old mate. Sorted!'

Tom felt the joints in his neck crack as he tried to move his head. The plank was pushing into his nape and the bottom of his skull, making it impossible to move more than an inch or so. The blood felt as if it had been drained from his outstretched arms, and he could no longer feel his fingers. He was full of fear – more than just frightened; he was terrified. On most of the armed response manoeuvres that he'd taken part in, when in the job, he had been frightened. He knew what fear felt like, but this was something else. This was pure terror; he was helpless and in fear of his life, in fear of a long, slow, painful death.

'How you feeling there, Tommy boy?' Craig's voice cut through Tom's fear. 'Got a touch of the old paranoias, have you? That'll be the acid. Oh, I didn't tell you, did I? I shot you up with a little mix of nice golden-brown heroin and a sprinkle of acid, LSD, or Lysergic Acid Diethylamide. D'ya know what I mean? One of my own cocktail recipes. I got the idea from "Surf and Turf" meals in the pub. This is my "Laced and Spaced" mashup. Want some more?' he laughed again, picking up the syringe and waving it in front of Tom's one open eye, the other eye still stuck closed. Tom would have flinched if he could move, but he was not only tied up, but he was also frozen with fear. He made an involuntary gurgling sound that rose from deep in his lungs; it was all he could do.

'No? Maybe later. I like a bit of needlework myself, but not right at this moment; I'm too busy. Work to be done.' Craig put the syringe down on the kitchen breakfast bar; his hands looked white. Tom thought they looked like they were made of plastic. Craig carried on talking.

'It was the next morning when the old bill came knocking on the door to tell me the sad news about Mummy and Daddy. Course, I'd cleaned it all up by then, the mess in the kitchen, and washed all their lovely blood away – not a trace left – cleanest the place had looked in years. Much better than when those two lazy, filthy fuckers were alive. I'll tell you what, it was all I could do to not burst out crying. The old bill were so nice to me. Especially the bird, PC Smith; that's who she was. She sat and held my hand for a bit. Nice soft hands she had, and she smelt nice. Course, you were a copper yourself, Tom, you would have smelled lots of them. They didn't tell me my poor old daddy was drunk until a few days before the funeral; he didn't want to upset me any more than I was.'

The drugs in Tom's body were making him feel sick, and he was fighting hard to regain some kind of control. Craig carried on.

'It served them right, Mum and Dad. It was their fault for having me and making me look like this.' Craig pointed at his own face with both hands and said, 'Do you know how I suffered at school, Tom? They could be so hurtful, those kids at school and so nasty to me just because I looked a bit strange and didn't always act like them. They should never have let my old man and woman breed! They should have shot them two at birth!'

Craig picked up the syringe again. Tom couldn't make out much of what was going on due to his blurred vision from the smack on the head and the even blurrier vision from the heroin and acid now surging through his veins like a narcotic tsunami. Craig was laughing again and holding a flaming lighter under a spoon held in his white plastic hands. Tom watched through one blurred eye as Craig dementedly refilled the syringe with a murky liquid. Fear and paranoia were surging through Tom's body as another shot of drugs rushed around his body. He desperately fought to gain control. His arms were still stretched wide on the oak board across the back of his head. He took a deep breath and could feel his heart pounding. The more control he gained, the more it became slightly clearer to him how hopeless and helpless he was. The calm voice that belonged to the crazy mass-murdering Craig Wolf was also clearer.

'That plank came in handy after all, Tommy, the one around your back with your arms tied on to it, didn't it just? I bet you are pleased you hung on to that for all these years. I remember when we carried all that flooring down the towpath near the Rock of Gibraltar. Do you remember that, Tom? Must have been what, six or seven years ago? Don't time fly when you are having fun? Still, the floor looks good – nice oak floor.' Craig laughed again.

'I loved all that "night work" you know, out there when half the world is in darkness. That's what we've been doing, Tommy Boy, we've been having fun – the chopping, cutting, drugging, killing, and bleeding type of fun. The families – the dead ones – the murdered ones – were all fun; that's what they were – just for fun, just to keep us amused. We didn't even know who they were. Fucking families! Fucking cunts the lot of them.'

Tom noticed that Craig had started speaking in the plural, "we." Was that the royal "we"? Tom couldn't make sense of any of it; was Craig schizophrenic as well as mad? This was too far out there, way beyond the pale. There was no sense to be made, especially in Tom's beaten and drugged head.

'I didn't feel anything for them. I didn't know who they were. Just families breeding children that could end up like me – I was doing them a favour, really, doing their kids a favour. Plus, I got a few more rings for my necklace. It always seemed a bit light with just Mum's on the chain.' Craig had gone back to the singular. He stretched his arm out and waved a gold chain so Tom could see the chain with several gold rings on it.

'I'll be sorry to see these go, these old wedding rings, but needs must, Tom, and it's time to move on; besides, plenty more where they came from!' Craig punctuated that with a burst of sharp, crazy laughter. Crazy laughter it was, for even the drugged-up, beaten-up, and tied-up, Tom Hunter could see that Craig was indeed crazy.

'I'll keep this one though, Tommy; if you don't mind, it was me mum's.' Craig cackled with laughter again and tossed the necklace of rings into the air over Tom's head, somewhere behind. There was no sound of them dropping onto the wooden floor.

Putting every ounce of his strength into trying to lift his head up, Tom managed to straighten his neck slightly. On the kitchen wall he was facing, there was a big mirror he had put there some years ago to make the boat look and feel more spacious; in it, Tom could see the reflection of the side window and the onset of the night. There were no lights switched on in the boat, which was making it even harder to see inside. For a moment, though, he thought he caught sight of something in the mirror – something moving behind him – but the drugs were making everything look as if it were moving. Tom was hallucinating; the acid was doing its work, doing what it did best.

'I like you, Tom; this isn't personal. It's just that someone has to pay for all this, or the police will never stop looking, and there will always be a chance they will find me. Now I can't have that, can I? After all, they've already been around my house, asking questions about that fucking sword. They asked about you as well, Tommy. It's me or you now, which means it's you. You can understand that, Tom, can't you? When the filth gets here, they will find you off your head on class "A" drugs, babbling like a fucking madman. They already have you down as a suspect, and I have planted enough clues on your boat to condemn Mother Teresa! If she were still alive, that is.' More laughter followed that one.

'Of course, it can only be "if" you survive. Some people overdose very easily, and if their hearts can't take it, pop! Then they are dead. Either way, you will be a result for the Old Bill; they will get what they want, a murderer, dead or alive, just like the old westerns, eh, Tom.' Craig started to flick the syringe he had filled up earlier.

'Well, are you ready for this one, one last shot of Craig's old "Laced and Spaced", Tommy Hunter? I'll call the Old Bill when I leave, and they should be with you in about half an hour, I'd guess; they may even be in time to save your life if things don't get nastier on the overdose front.' He moved closer to Tom and pushed the needle into a vein on his arm, staring closely into Tom's one open eye as he slowly pushed the plunger. Almost immediately, Tom felt his blood rush and boil like fizzy lava in his body. His heart felt as if it would explode, and his brain felt as if it had exploded. He felt Craig cutting the cable ties, and his arms fell to his sides. He didn't remember falling off the chair or anything else that happened after that. The unconsciousness of the dead took over his body, and the darkest blackness of emptiness filled his head. He was no longer there. His mind was in a different world, a different place, a different space, a different time. What was left of Tom Hunter's broken body would need to carry on without him if he was to survive; carry on if it could.

The Asian Poppy produces a milky latex fluid or resin found in the unripe seed pod. The plant produces resin, the resin produces opium, and morphine is derived from the opium.

Morphine is, reportedly, the most powerful pain reliever known.

Chapter 48

THE JOHN RADCLIFFE

It wasn't the first time that Tom had woken up in a hospital bed, not knowing what had happened or how he got there. This time, however, instead of his ex-wife Josie sitting at the bedside, it was Detective Chief Inspector Alison Smith and Detective Inspector Spencer Davis. Tom looked around and took in his surroundings. His eyes were sore, his mouth was dry, and his head ached. His whole body ached. Bottles of clear liquid hung next to the bed, with tubes running from them to needles taped into his arm. The sight of the needles made him shudder with the thought of Craig Wolf. Tom was very weak, so weak that the starched hospital bed sheets felt as if they were pinning him down. A nurse adjusted the pillow behind his head and cranked the bed up, enabling him to see more of the room. Unlike when he had shot his toes off and was put in an open ward at Hammersmith Hospital, he could now see that this time he was in a private room with two uniformed police officers standing outside the door. Tom recognised the two detectives in the room with him. It was DCI Smith who spoke first:

'Thomas Hunter, I am arresting you for the murders of George, Brenda, Ian, Fiona, Peter, and Elizabeth Gibson, and on suspicion of 21 other murders of…'

DCI Ali Smith's voice roared, soared, twisted, and faded in Tom's head until all he could see was her lips moving without making a sound. The silence exploded in his head as her mouth continued to move for what seemed like an immeasurable amount of time until, slowly, the sound faded back, and he heard her voice clearly once again.

'Keith Hartley, Anne Hartley, and their two children, John and Susan Hartley, and finally, for now anyway, the murder of…'

He couldn't take in what was being said to him, his head was spinning.

'You have the right to remain silent. Anything you say may be taken down and used as evidence.'

Even if Tom had the energy to speak, the shock of what DCI Ali Smith had said froze him where he lay. His face must have shown the horrors going through his mind when a man in a white coat, whom Tom assumed was a doctor but hadn't previously noticed, stepped forward and spoke sternly.

'I must ask you to stop there, officers. My patient needs time to recover and adjust, and this distress will only prolong that process; so, if I can ask you to leave, please.'

The doctor turned away from the two detectives and spoke to the nurse, who started to check the charts at the foot of the bed as he led the two officers out of the room. Tom lay there, stunned. Eventually, he spoke quietly and croakily to the nurse.

'Water, can I have some water, please?'

The nurse poured a glass from a small water bottle on a bedside cabinet and held it to Tom's lips. He gratefully sipped the liquid and felt it reach every corner of his dry mouth and slide down his even dryer throat. It tasted like the best drink he had ever had. It was his "Ice Cold in Alex" moment. He finished drinking, and the nurse placed the glass back on the glass top of the cabinet.

'Thank you,' Tom said, more clearly than he had spoken before. 'Where am I? How did I get here?'

The nurse looked towards the door with the two policemen outside before she spoke.

'I'm not supposed to talk to you, Mr Hunter, but they brought you in yesterday morning. You are in hospital, the John Radcliffe. You had a lot of physical injuries and were suffering from a drug overdose, heroin, and something else. They are still trying to find out what the other drug was. It was touch and go for a while, but you made it through the night, and it looks as if you will be OK now. You just need to rest.' She took the empty glass from him and placed it upside down over the neck of the bottle.

'What happened just now?' Tom asked. 'What was that all about?'

'They are police officers, Mr Hunter, and they just arrested you for all those murders – that's all I know. I can't say any more; just rest.'

With that, she readjusted the head of Tom's bed and left the room. He closed his eyes, and his mind and body dragged him back into a heavy and restless sleep. It was not an easy sleep for Tom; it was full of dreams, in one of them *Wandering Aengus* was sinking, and he was frantically trying to pump the water out as it flowed in, using his white plastic hands. It was a losing battle, and all he could do was stare helplessly as the mighty Tamesis swallowed up his home and all his worldly goods. Objects from his life started to float downstream towards locks and weirs. Some of them would make it past Teddington, leaving the non-tidal Environment Agency stretch and drifting into the tidal Port of London Authority water, floating by Brentford, where Tom was born, then through Embankment, past the London Eye, and through the great flood barriers in Tilbury, the Thames Delta, past the roots of the Rolling Stones and the real Doctor Feelgood, into the sea, where the tides would take them wherever they chose. Some would sink to the bottom of Davey Jones's locker; others would land on the beaches in Europe, America, or even remote desert islands soaked in tropical sunshine; the light at the end of the tunnel – the end of the journey?

According to the ward clock that Tom could just about make out through the window on the door to his room, the door with the police officers on the other side, it was 5 pm. A different nurse had placed a tray of food next to the bed, and a different doctor was checking his charts. Fragments of Tom's dream were floating around in his head, but it was much clearer. White plastic hands? They were the same as Craig's, the ones that he flicked the syringe with before he stuck it into the vein, the same hands as the doctor's. A glimpse of Craig's distorted face sprang into Tom's mind's eye. He felt his body physically flinch with a combination of fear, revulsion, and pain. It was coming back to him in fragments – the horror he had lived through in those few hours on *Wandering Aengus*. Craig, it was his doing; he had caused this. Craig had put Tom through all that hell. It was Craig who murdered those families. Craig was the killer, not him. Now Craig had put Tom well and truly in the frame. He had been arrested for multiple murders, but he could easily clear his name, and they could arrest Craig, and it would all be over.

'You should try to eat some food, Mr Hunter.' The doctor spoke impassively as he re-hung the chart clipboard on the foot of the bed. 'You need to regain your strength. The police want to speak with you, and I have kept them at bay as long as I could to give you the best chance to recover, but I have done all I can for now. They are very persistent.'

The doctor turned and nodded to someone outside the door, and it opened. Tom now recognised DCI Smith and DI Davis; they looked as tired as he felt. The doctor took a seat in the corner of the room, and the two detectives sat on either side of Tom's bed.

'Mr Hunter, feeling better, are we?' There was more than a little sarcasm in Ali Smith's voice. 'Well, as soon as you are, we will be moving you to the prison hospital. Get used to the idea, Mr Hunter, because you are going to be spending a long time at Her Majesty's pleasure.'

Tom felt his heart beat faster again.

'It's Craig Wolf who you want, not me. Craig Wolf did all those murders; he told me all about it. He knocked me out, drugged me, and held me prisoner. He is the one you should be after before he gets away,' he blurted out.

DCI Spencer spoke next.

'Can you describe this Craig to us, Mr Hunter?'

Tom could describe him alright. His maniacal face was etched into his memory for good.

'He isn't easily mistaken, officers. Longish, dark, greasy, straggly hair, and a squint in one eye. He has a muscle defect in his left cheek that makes him look like he is sneering all the time. He's probably sneering as well.' Tom could feel his hatred for Craig showing in his voice.

'Doesn't sound like there is much love lost between the two of you,' Spencer interjected.

'After what he did to me and what he did to those families, what do you expect me to feel?' Tom asked angrily.

Spencer didn't answer that question, and he prompted Tom to continue with his description.

'He's about five foot ten, and he was wearing a short black leather bomber jacket and jeans.' Tom stopped speaking aloud, but to himself he added, 'and white plastic hands.' He added for Spencer to hear, 'I think he may have been wearing surgical gloves.'

Ali spoke before Spencer could respond.

'That sounds like an exact description of the man we found hacked to death on the front deck of your boat, under the "cratch" cover, I think you call it, Mr Hunter. We also found his blood all over the clothes you were wearing when we found you unconscious with an empty syringe sticking in your arm!'

'His name was Craig as well, Tom; coincidence?' Spencer added.

Tom's head was spinning again. What were they saying? Was he being accused of killing Craig too? Craig was dead. Dead on *Wandering Aengus*? He felt a surge of panic run through him. His predicament started to sink in fully. But Craig did those murders; he had told Tom all about them; he can't be dead. This was all part of Craig's plan to frame Tom for the murders. The police would get to the bottom of it soon enough and see that Tom was innocent. Wouldn't they? Tom felt his heart racing, and his breathing became more and more difficult.

'And, Mr Hunter, there is the little matter of the glass jar we found in your fridge. The one containing two severed fingers – women's fingers. Ring any bells?' Ali emphasised the word "ring."

Tom started to feel vomit filling his mouth and running down his chin. At that point, the doctor stepped in again.

'That's enough now, officers. This man is still my patient for the time being, and he needs rest. I have to ask you to leave.'

The nurse reappeared, cleaned Tom's mouth, and placed a plastic mask over his face.

'It's only oxygen; there's nothing to be worried about,' she said reassuringly, in the same way that she did several times a day to patients on her ward. Tom breathed deeply and felt the clean oxygen fill his lungs. The panic slowly ebbed away, and his heart rate gradually returned to near normal. Again, an almost uncontrollable need to sleep took over his body, and he slid from the waking world into the sanctuary of darkness and the safety but uncertainty of dreams. The untouched tray of food still sat by his bedside as he slipped deeply into the other world.

Fitting out a narrowboat:

Professionals: between 650 and 1050 hours to complete

Skilled amateur: half this time again.

Someone with limited experience: twice as long, around 2100 hours' worth of hard work!

Chapter 49

DECONSTRUCTING AENGUS

After days of questioning, days of struggling to remember, days of trying to make sense of what was happening to him, and days of battling to recover mentally and physically, Tom was sitting in the office of DCI Smith and DI Davis, with Ali Smith telling him that he was free to go. No prints had been found on the inside of *Wandering Aengus* other than Tom's. The syringe that had been hanging from his arm also had no prints, not even his. Tom's account of what Craig had said, what he had inflicted on him, and how throughout all that, Tom thought Craig had been wearing surgical gloves, "plastic hands," now had credence. The residue of powder, the type that surgical gloves are dusted with inside to make putting on and removing them easier, had been identified on Craig Wolf's hands, but no gloves had been recovered. And importantly, the blood splattered over Tom's clothing was not consistent with what forensics would have expected to result from the savage attack on Craig; Graham Nash had said that from the splatter pattern, it looked more as if a cup had been filled with Craig's blood and simply thrown over Tom than the result of a frenzied attack. Ali and Spencer now knew for certain that Tom Hunter was not the killer. They had started to listen and believe him and what Craig had said to Tom when he was being held captive. If Craig had committed, or at least taken part in, the murders, then he had not done so alone. Craig certainly hadn't stabbed himself in the back and ripped the knife up so hard that he had completely severed his liver, kidney, and spleen, and then, not satisfied with that, sliced open his own throat. Craig Wolf was murdered, but not by Tom, who was probably unconscious and left for dead by that point. There were a couple of other things found on the boat, including the knife, which was thought to have been used to kill Craig Wolf, but neither Ali nor Spencer were prepared to elaborate on this or give Tom any details of the other finds.

The impact of exactly what Tom must have been put through at the hands of the demented Craig Wolf, and then of being arrested for multiple murders, was beginning to dawn on Ali and Spencer. They had got this one wrong – completely wrong. Spencer had hinted earlier in the investigations that he wasn't convinced that Tom knew anything about the killings, but then they had both fallen for a poor set-up job that was quickly uncovered, wanting too much to get a result. Valuable time had already been lost.

'I hope you can try to understand why you came under suspicion, Mr Hunter.' Spencer was sharing the blame and trying to find the right words to say sorry to Tom. 'Everything pointed to you. We know now that there was another person, a third person, on your boat when Craig Wolf attacked and drugged you. That other person killed Craig and was likely to have been involved in all the other murders, working together.'

The blurry image of something behind him, reflected in the kitchen mirror when Craig was swinging the necklace in his face, sprang into Tom's mind.

'Do you know anyone who may have wanted to set you up like this, Mr Hunter? You told us you knew Craig Wolf.'

Tom spoke for the first time since sitting down in the office.

'Like I said, I didn't really know Craig very well. I didn't even know his surname was Wolf. He helped me on a few occasions when I was fitting *Wandering Aengus* out, which was years ago. We sometimes had a beer and a game of pool together in the Rock of Gibraltar. I never even knew where he lived; I just knew it was somewhere near there, near the Rock. I can't remember the last time I saw him.'

'We are checking with the landlord of the Rock of Gibraltar to see what he and his customers know about Wolf. We will also be reopening the file on his parents' car crash in Brighton based on what you have told us.' Spencer tried to make this sound reassuring to him. Ali had been sitting silently opposite Tom as Spencer spoke. A fusion of many different thoughts and images had been going through her mind. The damage, sadness, and hurt that had been caused by Wolf and his accomplice were almost beyond belief: the women and children dead, the husbands and wives, the grandfathers and grandmothers – all for what? And Tom Hunter, what had they – her and Spencer – done to him? They'd ruined his life and were in the process of destroying his home; she now had to break that news to him as well.

'Do you have any idea who could have been in league with Craig Wolf, who could have helped him with these killings, anyone who would have wanted Wolf dead?' Spencer asked. Tom just stared at him blankly. Realising that he wasn't about to reply to Spencer's last question, DCI Ali Smith spoke up.

'You are free to go, Mr Hunter, but there is something else you need to know. It will not be possible for you to return to your boat; *Wandering Aengus* is now a murder scene under investigation and is being held in a secure dry dock whilst…' she paused, searching for how best to put it, 'Whilst forensic officers dismantle the interior structures, trying to identify any further evidence that could help us with our ongoing enquiries. I know that may sound harsh to you, but you must remember that there have been so many murders committed by Craig Wolf and whoever else was on your boat that night. I'm sorry, Tom, but it is a very necessary action.'

Tom sat in stunned silence; it didn't even register that she had called him "Tom" for the first time. Years of work he had put into *Wandering Aengus*. It had been the biggest, single most important thing he had ever completed in his life. *Wandering Aengus* was not just his home; it contained all he owned in the world. Now the police, people he used to work for and was once one of, were undoing all of that in a fraction of the time it had taken to create it, probably causing irreparable damage in the process. *Wandering Aengus* was being deconstructed, dismantled, dissected, and destroyed.

Ali was still talking, but Tom was missing most of what she said and only hearing it clearly again when Spencer started to speak. 'We realise this has all been a big shock to you, Mr Hunter, and counselling is available should you feel you need it. I would recommend that you give this some serious consideration.'

Tom looked up at Spencer and gave him a quick reply.

'I have, and I don't need it!' There was controlled anger in Tom's voice. 'That is my home you are tearing apart; it is where I live! It's the only thing I have left.'

Spencer tried to console him. 'There will be compensation for the damage done and any work that will be required.' Spencer paused and looked at Ali. Tom sensed there was a "but" coming, and he was right. 'Unfortunately, we aren't able to say how long this will take to come through, and as your boat is a murder scene and maybe linked to others, it could be many years before we are able to release it. It all depends on how quickly we apprehend the guilty culprits. Being an ex-police officer, Mr Hunter, you will understand these things, I'm sure, and being an ex-police officer, Tom, we would like you to help us as much as you can to achieve that. You are our only living connection with these killings; the only link we have.'

Spencer wasn't wrong; Tom was indeed in shock. The shock of all he had been through and now the numbing shock of hearing about his world, his boat, his home, and his life being torn apart. Ali could see the pain inside him; she felt for him. Her opinion of

Tom had changed since she realised he wasn't a psychotic killer, and she could now see him as a man who had built a new life for himself from the ruins of a career that had deserted him and a failed marriage. She could relate to part of that, but at least she still had her home and her life; she and Spencer had taken both of those and more away from Tom Hunter. What did he have left? Tom was right when he said they had destroyed everything. Ali, Spencer, the police, Craig Wolf, and whoever else was involved – between them, they had left Tom crushed. Ali knew it was the same as with the effects of all serious crimes; they reach out and touch, mark, and harm all those around them, but for her part, her misjudgement of the broken man sitting opposite her made her feel full of guilt. The mothering instincts in her became stronger than her police training, and she felt not only guilty but responsible for the hapless place that Tom was now trapped in. Tom Hunter was a good-looking man, about eight or so years younger than Ali, but sitting opposite her with his head down, he looked haggard and twenty years older. She thought of what it would be like for her to lose everything – her home, her job, Andrew, and Patricia. She couldn't even begin to imagine the torment Tom had been through.

'Tom,' she said softly, 'I want you to know that you are not on your own, you haven't been deserted. We will offer you every bit of help we can, I promise you.'

Tom looked up and saw Ali Smith as a human being for the first time – a softer person, a woman – not the DCI Smith that had questioned him aggressively and relentlessly for days. He could see she really was concerned about him, and in a small way, it helped. He held her gaze as she looked at him; she made no attempt to look away.

Not everything that can be counted counts, and not everything that counts can be counted.

[ALBERT EINSTEIN]

Chapter 50

FOREVER CHANGES

When Tom was held captive and drugged, Craig Wolf said to him, 'I have planted enough clues on your boat to condemn Mother Teresa,' and he was as good as his word. Tom would probably never want to move back onto *Wandering Aengus* if the full details were ever revealed of what the police search team investigators found as they took apart *Wandering Aengus*. Descriptions of some of their findings were passed on to Tom, but only some; details of other things were kept from him and marked as "CONFIDENTIAL." The file described several items that had been sent to Graham Nash's team for a forensic investigation. It also detailed an area along the skirting board at the front of the boat, near where Tom's bed had been before it was dismantled – a secret compartment had been discovered. A piece of the skirting board that looked attached was actually just wedged in, and underneath it sat a small, narrow wooden box. Inside the box, along with a few old door keys, the search team had found a necklace – a necklace full of wedding rings. Each of the rings was identified as belonging to one or other of the murder victims, except for three of them, two of which were not traced and one of which would later be identified by Tom Hunter. It was Josie's wedding ring that had been stolen from her flat in London.

Tom used what was left of his remaining willpower to struggle on. Slowly mending, gradually getting physically and mentally stronger. He was no longer in the hospital but was still receiving treatment as an outpatient. Having been told that it could be years before *Wandering Aengus* was released and that even then she would need rebuilding, he was homeless again. Tom was back to square one; this time, however, his starting point was less than zero. There would be financial compensation given to him for all he had been subjected to and for the loss of *Wandering Aengus,* but no one seemed to know how long that would take or how much it would be. Nothing could ever really compensate him; his losses were beyond that. Simon and Jacky had visited Tom in the John Radcliffe once the police had allowed them access, and now he was back with them again, back in his old room on Charles Street. Hugo had also visited him in the hospital. The New York Times had sent Hugo back to Oxford to catch up on the story that was now breaking; this time, however, he was staying in the Randolph Hotel. He would have come to Oxford anyway to see Tom; Hugo was genuinely shaken when he went to visit Tom in his sickbed and had insisted that he come to stay with him in London when he was feeling up to it. This was a genuine act of friendship, and not just so he could get an exclusive story; at least it seemed that way. For now, however, Tom had taken up Simon and Jacky's offer; somehow it felt more comfortable to him, more familiar, and he wasn't ready to go back to London yet; he didn't know if he ever would be. Simon and Jacky were very patient, considerate, and understanding towards him; not that anyone would ever really understand what Tom had been put through. He hadn't seen much of them over the last few years, so it was what he thought was a special kindness, born out of a lifelong friendship that had opened its doors to him once again. No fuss was made, and they gave him all the space he needed.

Tom couldn't forget the thought of Josie's wedding ring being found on his boat, along with those of the victims of the river killer. He kept thinking of how frightened she had seemed when she left him at Gordon's Wine Bar by Embankment Station that night. She had every right to be scared, every reason to be terrified, and every reason not to trust him. For the first time since their divorce, he wanted to speak to her, wanted to know that she was OK, and wanted to say sorry for everything. Something told him that she, on the other hand, would not have wanted to hear from him; his apologies would mean nothing to her. So, he chose not to contact her; he just wrestled the thought in his head along with everything else that had happened. Still, he didn't understand most of it, and maybe he would never know why it had happened to him or what had driven those involved to do the horrific things that had been done. He had never actually seen any of the murder victims' bodies and had no image of them, unlike Ali and Spencer, who would have the dead faces etched into their memories forever. The most vivid images Tom had were those of Craig Wolf's twitching and twisted, demented face and Josie's gold wedding ring. The diamond set in the clasp of the ring was small; it had been all he could afford at the time, but then it didn't matter; then they were in love; that was all that mattered back there in what now was a different country for Tom, a different world, another life. How did Josie's wedding ring get into the secret compartment on the boat, mixed with all the other rings from the victims? Thinking about it was exhausting him; he was using the last of his strength, struggling to think of answers. - *The rings*? Josie's wedding ring? Tom used the secret compartment to keep his spare keys safe; he would have put other items of value in there, but he didn't really have any. He did have things he valued, but they had no real value other than to him; no thief would have been interested in them, so he never bothered to hide them. Josie's wedding ring had been found in the boat, but Tom's own had not turned up in the police search. There were still a couple of small boxes full of his bits and pieces in Simon's shed. They had been there for so many years that Tom couldn't remember most of the things in them; his wedding ring could be in one, for all he knew. He was back in Charles Street and would have time to look through each of them. There was part of him that wanted to just get rid of those old boxes without checking their contents. Boxes full of what – memories, the past?

It was a distant past he wanted to leave behind, as well as the most recent part of his life; memories of that last period would, however, stay with him forever.

* * *

Alone in his room in Charles Street, Tom's eyes filled with water; warm, salty tears ran down his face as he sat with the first of the boxes in front of him. He carefully removed the lid and revealed a stack of papers: the very top sheet was a neatly handwritten copy of the W. B. Yeats poem his boat had been named after, "The Song of *Wandering Aengus*." Tom silently and slowly started reading the poem for the first time, feeling every word; a teardrop splashed on the page, smudging the red ink that had been used to underline the last verse:

'Though I am old with wandering
Through hollow lands and hilly lands,
I will find out where she has gone,
And kiss her lips and take her hands;
And walk among long dappled grass,
And pluck till time and times are done
The silver apples of the moon,
The golden apples of the sun.'

Again, the questions ran through his head: Why had it happened? How was he connected? Who could have done such things? The more he thought, the less he had answers. The rings? Craig Wolf? The dead families? Where did he fit in with those things? Then, from nowhere, it occurred to him – the connection wasn't him. There was one single thing that joined them all together, and it had been staring him in the face all the time – *Wandering Aengus*! The boat threaded through all the places – the people, the murders, Tom just happened to be living on her. Craig Wolf had been a killer; then he was killed by someone else. Tom had a second realisation; he was astonished why he hadn't thought of it before, maybe because it seemed so unbelievable, but now it seemed blatantly obvious – the secret compartment where the wedding rings had been found. Tom had never told anyone about it, including Craig. There was only one other person alive who knew of its existence. Tom's hands were shaking as he held the sheet of paper and stared at the poem in shock as it hit him as to exactly who that person was.

The phone ringing in the hall shook him out of his state of disbelief, and he slowly got up to answer it. He was about to be both proved right and shocked again when he eventually picked up the receiver.

'Hello, Tom,' the voice on the other end of the phone said brightly and cheerfully.

'I'm sorry about all this happening to you, but it was unavoidable; collateral damage, you could say. No hard feelings, I hope, "twas nothing personal."'

Tom's mouth went dry as he listened in silence to the voice he knew only too well. His body was shaking, and his legs no longer had the strength to support him. With the phone still against his ear, his back slid down the wall until he was seated on the floor, still shaking and still silently listening.

'Craig, he was a good worker, ah, but you knew that from when he helped you with refitting *Wandering Aengus*. For a while there, when Craig and I were working on our "nightshifts," out after dark bits, we were like brothers. Not just ordinary brothers; no, we were blood brothers. I was on there, my old boat – your boat, I should say, of course – when Craig was telling you all about his mother and father, when he had you tied up and pumped full of those nasty drugs. Yes, Tom, I was standing behind you. I'm sorry Craig was a bit rough with you, but I knew he was about to be killed, so I thought it only right to let him have his last little bit of fun. He served me well, and we had some enjoyable experiences together, but it was time for him to go. As much as I liked him, he was really a horrible little person. I'm sure you would agree. He had got careless, you see, as if phoning the newspapers wasn't stupid enough; he insisted on defying me again by keeping the sword. It was only a matter of time after that before the police would be after Craig, and he would have led them to me. He did make those pathetic attempts to frame you for all that had been done; I knew it wouldn't help him, but even so, I assisted with his pointless deceptions, purely for my own ends. I knew the police would find out fairly quickly that you were not responsible for Craig's death or any of the others, but with him setting you up the way he tried to, it gave me some time – time to get my finances together and leave the country. I had it all planned from the beginning, just in case Craig became "unreliable." I always thought he would eventually be that type. I didn't really need much time to make my departure, just a few days; you were the bit of distraction that would give me the space to do it. I was out of the country before the police even knew you hadn't killed poor old Craig Wolf. I had to walk out of the James Street Tavern, of course. It was a pity; I enjoyed that for a while, but there will be other bars and pubs and other ventures I can take on. It is a big world out there, Tom, much bigger than that little world on the river, on the boat.'

Tom sat listening in shock. Eventually, he uttered the only words he could bring himself to say on the phone. 'Why, why did you do all that?'

Jamie's reply was quick and short.

'Why not?' And with that, he carried on talking. 'It's all about the journey, Tom; that's what I have always said. We each have our own journeys, my friend; theirs was theirs, yours is yours, and this one, and well, "this one" is mine. I'm sure you'll get to understand it as time goes on; we aren't so different, you and me, Tom. Now, where was I? Oh yes, I was about to say that I'm glad you didn't die. I would have missed our conversations, which is why I called the police and told them where you were. After all, what would have happened to *Wandering Aengus* if you were not around to take care of her? I loved that boat so much. I had so many good times with her during the years I lived on her. You wouldn't believe what went on inside that boat, you really wouldn't; I don't think many people would. I have to say, I am very happy that she is in your safe hands now. You will look after her, won't you? And remember, Tom, "I will find out where she has gone" because she really is my "silver apple of the moon" and my "golden apple of the sun."'

The phone clicked as Jamie replaced the receiver, and Tom sat back against the wall, trance-like, listening to the dialling tone.

Most of the things that make up a "traditional" English Christmas were actually invented (or imported into England from other countries) in the 19th century. That includes Christmas trees, Christmas cards, Christmas crackers, paper decorations, and Father Christmas with his white beard and red costume.

Chapter 51

IT'S CHRISTMAS!

Ali sat at home in front of a log fire that was burning patterns into the soot at the mouth of the chimney, making orange sparkling outlines of images that moved, twinkled, and faded away. She had watched these as a small girl in the fire at her parents' home. It reminded her of the Christmases she had spent growing up – happy, uncomplicated times. On her lap rested a thick manila folder stamped "CONFIDENTIAL" in bold letters. Ali had received the forensic reports on the findings in Tom Hunter's boat just as she was leaving work and had taken them home with her; Christmas didn't mean she didn't have a job to do. She poured herself a glass of wine before starting to read Graham Nash's report. Under *Wandering Aengus*' oak floorboards laid by Tom Hunter, there had been another floor, the original marine-ply boards that had once been painted blue. The forensic search team had found several human finger bones lying in the hull of the boat underneath that second layer of flooring. The original floor that had been laid by the previous owner was mostly untouched by

Tom Hunter's later work. The DNA from some of the bones had found a match on the national DNA database for a teenage girl who had gone missing some eight years earlier. The girl was never found, and she was still filed under missing persons, with the last sighting of her being alongside the Kennet and Avon Canal, near Hungerford. "The previous owner." A shiver ran down Ali's back as she realised what this meant. Immediately, she thought of Andrew, who was still out, having a Christmas drink with people from work. Before she had time to even begin to panic, her landline rang.

'Ali, it's me.' Spencer had stayed on at work, going through the reports.

'I already know, Spencer; I have read the reports and worked it out. Andrew! He is out drinking with people from that pub! The Christmas bash, he said. Spencer, he may be with him, with that monster!' There was alarm in Ali's voice; now she was panicking. Spencer quickly interrupted.

'Don't worry; Ali, we have someone on that. Andrew is OK. He is drinking with two of the girls that work behind the bar, and they are all safe and sound in All Bar One that pub on the High. We have a car outside that is keeping a very careful watch on them. Andrew doesn't know anything about this yet. I'll leave it for you to tell him when he gets home.'

'Thanks, Spencer; what else do you know?'

'We are in the process of searching the James Street Tavern. Our man had long gone when we arrived there. I have an all-points alert out on him, and all the airports and ferry ports have a photo of him, but I fear we may be too late. He may have slipped onto the Eurail or a ferry and could be anywhere now. Interpol has been informed, and we are in the process of issuing warnings telling members of the public not to approach him. I don't have to tell you what this one is capable of.' There was a short pause while Spencer considered just how much to say to Ali; she was obviously shaken, and he didn't want to upset her any more, but it was burning away at him, so he said it anyway.

'That freak sold his boat to Tom Hunter with the bones of a girl he had killed still under the floor. You would have thought he would have considered that risky.'

'Maybe he liked the risk, Spencer?' Ali said, still looking for a reason.

'Or is it that he has been doing this for years, and maybe, Ali, he just forgot about them, lost track, just another unknown victim to satisfy his need for whatever it is he needs? I know what he needs now, alright! And we will get him!'

'Let's hope we do, Spencer, and thanks again for looking out for Andrew.' Her head was still full of what Spencer had just said, but she couldn't think of any more horrors at that moment; knowing Andrew was safe was all she cared about.

'Are you OK, Ali? I have a car near your house as well, just as a precaution, but I'm sure you don't have anything to worry about, he'll be as far away from here as he can get by now, but they are there if you need them.'

Ali's mobile bleeped a "message received" tone, causing her to look over to where it sat on the coffee table. Reassured that Andrew was safe, the message could wait; she carried on speaking with Spencer.

'I'm fine, thanks, Spence. I'm a bit shocked and surprised and still taking it all in, but I'm OK now that I know you have taken care of Andrew.'

'I'll call you if there is any news, and, Ali, you can call me any time. Don't worry about your son; we will make sure he gets home safely. I will see you at work tomorrow, and we'll catch up then. There's nothing we can do now, so let's hope that he gets spotted and caught pronto; unfortunately, though, I think we may have lost him for now. He's a smart cookie, but we will get him. Take care, Ali; see you tomorrow.' She placed the phone back in its cradle and stared at her mobile.

* * *

Sitting by the fire with the lights of the real Christmas tree Andrew had insisted on getting, twinkling through a series of patterns, the room filled with the smell of fresh pine and the burning logs, the manila folder still resting on her lap, Ali tried to take in all she now knew, finding it almost too hard to believe. She glanced over at her mobile again. It was probably a message from Andrew, checking up on her and seeing if she was OK at home on her own. But Andrew was busy with other things at that moment, and making calls home to Mum wasn't one of them. She placed the folder on the floor next to the armchair, stood up, and stepped over to the coffee table. She was surprised to find herself shaking. Picking up the mobile, she pressed the "1" button to access her messages; surprisingly, there was enough signal for once. She put the phone to her ear. "You have one new message… new message from… number withheld…"

'Hello, Detective Chief Inspector Alison Smith. It's surprising how easy it is to get hold of someone's telephone number these days, isn't it? It's me, by the way, James Pescador. I'm happy for you to call me Jamie; may I call you Alison? I think Alison is better than Detective Chief Inspector; after all, it does feel like we have got to know each other over the months, albeit from a distance. Some of your colleagues spoke to me as well, but that was months ago. Very polite they were, hmm. I hope you liked the little card I sent you for your birthday. Birthdays should be celebrated, lovely family occasions.'

The voice was calm, clear, soft, and engaging. She could hear classical music faintly playing in the background: Bach. If she hadn't known what the owner of that voice had done – the evil that it disguised – she might have even found it seductive. But Ali did know who it belonged to; she had everyone connected with the case etched in her mind; she had gone over every statement and every link over and over again many times during the last six months. Far from sounding seductive, the voice filled her with revulsion, sickening, stomach-churning disgust, and fear. The hairs on the back of her neck felt like needles digging into her skin. With the phone held to her ear, she automatically locked the front door and looked through the window as Jamie's message continued to play back.

'It seems a long time ago since Day's Lock, that little 'family affair'; doesn't time fly when you are having fun, Alison? Don't tell me you didn't enjoy it as well. It must have been much better than your usual, boring workload of cops and robbers. You were so close at times, yet so far, and you never really knew. What is it they say? 'Close but no cigar'? Ah, but it's Marlboros you like, isn't it? Cigarettes, not cigars; that's what you and Detective Inspector Davis enjoy puffing on. You see, I know a lot about you, Alison. Oh, and please say hello to that lovely son of yours for me, Andrew, such a fine cook. It makes my mouth water just thinking about it. He is a little tea-leaf, though, isn't he, Alison? He stole from me, from my kitchen, all the time – that boy can't keep his hands off anything. But then we all have our dark sides, do we not? Ask Tom Hunter about his sometime; maybe you should ask him again about Leggy. And you, Alison, what is your dark side? What is it you don't want anyone else to know about, and what would you do to protect it? Hmm…'

There was a pause where all Ali could hear was Jamie breathing deeply, then he sparked into life again.

'Still, it has all been fun though, hasn't it, and not without its moments of humour, like the big house. That was a bit messy; we were all "fingers and thumbs" with that one. Don't tell me you didn't enjoy it, Alison. There is nothing like the cut and thrust of the chase, is there? And Tom, with his dark sides as well, what a lovely chap he really is; he wouldn't harm a fly, *would* he? You should maybe see more of him, Alison. I think you two would get along well together, especially as he isn't one of your suspects any more. I will miss our little games though: you, Spencer, Craig, and me, but you never know, never say never; we could do it all again sometime – well, not poor old Craig, of course. You must say hello to the nice detective inspector for me as well, Alison. Old Spencer enjoyed it all as much as us, I'm sure.

'You know I would have loved to talk to you in person, Alison, but unfortunately that may have to wait. I won't have another chance to contact you again for a while, so this will have to do. I have to be careful after all, I'm sure you can understand.'

Ali felt her mouth drying up, and the effects of the wine she had drunk were now completely negated by what she was hearing. The next part of the message left her frozen with a feeling of pure, intense, first-degree terror, a terror like she had never known – one that sank deep into her every bone.

'The winter has arrived here in Oslo, Alison; it's getting colder every day, minus fifteen degrees at night, freezing! Luckily, I packed some nice, warm sweaters for my short stay. I'll be wearing one tonight. I'm going out to dinner with a lovely young woman that I met – not purely by accident, if the truth be known. Ah, but what is the truth? We are going to a first-class restaurant; it's one that she chose especially for me. After all, she was so pleased to meet someone who knows her mother and her brother so well. I hope the food is as good as she says. I haven't had a decent meal for days. What with being on the run and everything, I could eat a whole elk! I won't be staying in Oslo for very long, Ali, for obvious reasons, so I don't suppose you will catch up with me here. Besides, it is very expensive in Norway. Anyway, it was lovely talking to you. May I wish you and Andrew a very happy family Christmas? I must dash now; I wouldn't want to keep Patricia waiting. I'll pass on your regards. For now, I'm afraid it's bye-bye, DCI. I'm sure we will be in touch again; you never know, I may even give you a ring sometime.'

THE END

Chapter 52

EPILOGUE

Tom Hunter moved back to London, where he stayed with Hugo and spent his time designing the interior of the Dutch barge he hoped to buy when his compensation money came through.

Hugo Lewis, with a lot of help from Tom, was praised for the series of articles he published around the aftermath of the River Killings and the continuing hunt for the killer. He hasn't returned to Oxford to start writing his book.

Josie never saw or contacted Tom again and moved to a different part of London; she never felt safe in her old flat after the break-in.

Andrew Smith lost his job at the James Street Tavern when it closed down and is still struggling to find another while keeping himself busy in other ways. Some say crime doesn't pay, but the Duke of Earl would argue otherwise.

Patricia Smith is still living in Oslo but remains under constant police surveillance for her own protection.

DCI Ali Smith continues to hunt for Jamie, liaising with Interpol every time a sighting is reported. The rest of her time, she is back to "cops and robbers."

DI Spencer Davis continues working with Ali Smith; the series of killings has built a strong bond between the two of them, similar to those that survive plane crashes. He still has the cuckoo clock.

Murphy, the sniffer dog, carries on sniffing things out at crime scenes and continues to eat anything put in front of him. He seems to be oblivious to all that has happened, which is maybe the best way.

Graham Nash wrote several papers that were published in the Journal of Forensic Criminology and continues to have a crush on DCI Smith.

Simon and Jacky still live in Charles Street. They only went to visit Tom once in London; the city wasn't really for them.

The James Street Tavern became an investigation scene and was closed. It still remains boarded up to this day. The poets and musicians moved their open mic night to another public house in East Oxford.

Wandering Aengus remains in bits and pieces in a police warehouse, where forensic teams continue to review findings relating to not only the river killings but other murders that occurred many years before.

The mighty River Thames is still flowing, rising, and falling, pushing, and pulling, washing, and cleaning, the same as it ever was.

Jamie, well, where he is and what he is up to is what everyone would like to know. What can be said for certain is that he is still out there somewhere doing something – just "what" is anyone's guess.

bill.dring.author@outlook.com

Printed in Great Britain
by Amazon

6189523d-ad1b-4fd6-8a41-28f5dbeea66fR02